TEXAS COWBOYS

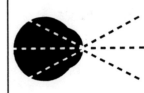

This Large Print Book carries the
Seal of Approval of N.A.V.H.

TEXAS COWBOYS

TIM MCGUIRE

WHEELER PUBLISHING
A part of Gale, Cengage Learning

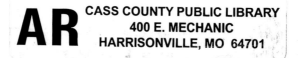

GALE
CENGAGE Learning™

Detroit • New York • San Francisco • New Haven, Conn • Waterville, Maine • London

GALE
CENGAGE Learning

Copyright © 2009 by Tim McGuire.
Wheeler Publishing, a part of Gale, Cengage Learning.

Wheeler Publishing Large Print Western.
The text of this Large Print edition is unabridged.
Other aspects of the book may vary from the original edition.
Set in 16 pt. Plantin.
Printed on permanent paper.

LIBRARY OF CONGRESS CATALOGING-IN-PUBLICATION DATA

McGuire, Tim.
    Texas cowboys / by Tim McGuire. — Large print ed.
     p. cm.
    ISBN-13: 978-1-4104-2370-2 (softcover : alk. paper)
    ISBN-10: 1-4104-2370-0 (softcover : alk. paper)
    1. Texas—Fiction. 2. Large type books. I. Title.
PS3563.C36836T45 2010
813'.6—dc22   2009043683

Published in 2010 by arrangement with The Berkley Publishing Group,
a member of Penguin Group (USA) Inc.

Printed in the United States of America
1 2 3 4 5 6 7 14 13 12 11 10

To Joy

You have been my world for more than 25 years.
Here's to a new beginning.

ACKNOWLEDGMENTS

Whenever a writer begins a new project, one seeks the best information available. I am no exception. Actually, part of the fun is researching the facts that base the story. As I started thinking of this novel more than five years ago, I began a search for the known, but not the well-known information about Abilene, Kansas, in 1871. What I found pushed me even more to pursue this story.

During my search, I read the writing of George L. Cushman's *Abilene, First of the Kansas Cow Towns* along with Stewart P. Verckler's *Cowtown-Abilene* and Henry B. Jameson's *Early Days in Abilene, Kansas — Where It All Started* in which the Charles Gross encounter with Hickok and Jesse James is based. I learned the facts of the town and that era, but there was still more to know.

John Wesley Hardin's autobiography

served great use to understand the man. And *John Wesley Hardin: Dark Angel Of Texas* by Leon Metz is excellent at cutting through Hardin's delusions and setting the record straight with factual evidence.

Also, I'd like to cite the works of Joseph G. Rosa, James Reasoner, and the collection of vignettes found here and there during my research.

1

May 1871

Wes Hardin had a taste for turkey. He rode through the prairie scrub looking for the same marks in the dirt he'd seen the day before. Low clouds blanketed the sky above and to the west, but were broken to the east. The orange of the dawn haze made it hard to search for tracks in the dry dust. The early May chill twitching his muscles disturbed his focus, yet he was determined.

Four hours in the saddle had ended an hour ago, but he couldn't get to sleep. Remnants of the trail from Texas were still on his lips, and his mouth watered for the meal of a juicy roasted bird. Though breakfast was already on the fire, the anticipation of rotten bacon on a hardtack cracker didn't compare. Just the idea of a bird pulled him from his bedroll with more power than a team of mules, and in little more than pants, boots, and suspenders, sent him into the

9

dark. Impulse was the rule of all his actions.

At first he'd thought it a good notion to join the drovers headed north so as to avoid the law's search, but the expected adventurous journey had turned into a monotonous repetition of sunrises and sunsets while he'd ended up nearly mounted the whole time. Just before camp, he'd seen something to capture his concentration. Among the few distractions from chasing strays had been the tracks of a hefty gobbler. With little else to cause his mind to wander, his appetite took control of all his concentration. The urge wouldn't leave him.

He turned his head to the side. The spittle splattered the dirt inches away from some peculiar scratches. Intrigued, Wes dismounted and bent to have a closer look. Soon, he spotted another, and a small distance away found one more. The unique three-clawed gait of a tom turkey brought a smile.

Enthused at the thought of eating a roasted bird, he came to a straight stance to quickly draw his Colt. His mood was giddy at the mere suggestion of the tender flavor, but hooves pounding the plain turned his attention behind him. He swung the barrel in line with the noise, changing the aim from between the thick bushes to the next gap in the greenery in order to shoot whoever approached.

"Wes? That you?"

The familiar voice had him ease the barrel to his side. "Hush, Manning. I think I found me breakfast." The next moments brought the aching stretch of leather and the sight of his cousin emerging from among the tall brush.

"What are you doing out here?" Manning asked. "The herd is nearly two miles or more north. We'll catch hell if we're found this far away. This ain't Texas no more. Is Indian Territory it is. We're likely —"

"Hush, I said." If there was anything Wes hated, it was fretting when food was not yet on the plate. "Ain't worried about no Indians. I'm worried about eating another plate of slop ain't fit for the hogs at home." Wes turned his attention forward to where the tracks led. "I seen me the markings of a fat turkey on the prowl of hens. He's going to be mighty surprised when he sees me coming with this." He angled his head back at Manning. "And I don't need you helping him spot me. So, get low and keep them spurs quiet. If I lose this bird, I ain't going to be in no mood to be around." It took a mere glance to insure the point was understood.

"I can't see a damn thing," said Manning.

Each word uttered irritated Wes. "Well, then, stay back so you don't trample on these tracks. Head back to the other side of this brush. He may come out from the tall grass." He gave his shorter cousin a last glare and turned his attention toward the bushes. The tangle of blossoming branches snarling amongst the greening weeds provided more cover for his quarry to hide. Carefully, he took one step at a time so as to not spook the bird into flight, making for a more difficult shot. Despite the brags he'd spread in Texas, to kill a bird on the wing in only the light of the dawn was a task he'd just as soon not deal with.

With the Smith and Wesson .44 in his right hand, he pushed the growth from his path with his left and proceeded through the small thicket. Small clouds drifting in front of the emerging sun teased his vision. Not sure if shadow or object was before him, he readied the hammer for a quick shot.

As he was about to take another step, a rustle from just beyond his approach froze him still. If he was to make a clean kill, he'd have to react fast. Wes inhaled as silently as possible and without any further noise in front of him, decided the time was right to spring upon his prey.

He launched through the brush, which abruptly merged with open plain. Motion turned him to the right. A man knelt ten feet from him. An Indian. A fat lump of feathers lay on the prairie with an arrow stuck in its side.

Wes was sure what he saw. He aimed the revolver at arm's length and fired a single shot. The bullet cracked into the Indian's skull, sending him into a lump on the prairie next to the feathers. The echo rippled through the still morning air. Sunlight illuminated the land.

Loud snaps of twigs turned the pistol back to the thicket. Manning emerged from the brush. "Damn you, cousin," said Wes. "You're going to have me shoot you yet this morning."

Manning eased his own pistol back in the holster. "What happened?"

Wes motioned at the Indian. "The son of a bitch meant to kill me with his bow." They went to the body. Manning pushed the shoulder over to lay it on its back. A bullet hole in the forehead continued to ooze blood. Wes knelt next to the turkey. "This is going to make a fine breakfast."

2

June 1871

Jody Barnes kept the sorrel at a trot just enough to quicken the approach but not send Les Turnbow over the cantle. Jody felt her firm clasp of hands around his waist as they rode over the green rolling hills toward Abilene.

The sunny June afternoon would soon provide a clear view of the city at a distance, and he knew she was anxious to catch the first sight of her hometown in nearly two years. Each crest of a hill only teased their anticipation upon sighting even more hills to cross.

"Can you see it yet?" she asked.

Her constant eager inquiries were met by his same answer. "No." Although he had been to the railhead twice before, he wished to get there as quick as she did just to quiet her questions. He didn't dare suggest resting and watering the sorrel for fear of thinking of more reasons why they weren't in Abilene already. His own hunger was a factor as well.

The long trip from Colorado had been one deprived of any luxuries. Food and water had to be scavenged to survive for the next day. Almost all they ate was taken from the land. What few supplies they could afford at the start of the journey had been exhausted weeks ago. However, the desire to reach the friendly salvation they both knew awaited kept them spirited enough to continue. More than once along the trail, he'd reminded himself that he'd promised to bring her home. He owed it to her. Now, they were just within hours of realizing the fruits of their sacrifice.

"If we stayed along the creek, we'd be there now."

Her remark was less sharp, or so he took it that way. No need to spark another fight. Not now. They were too close. "Suppose you could be right. But this way, the ground seemed easier to cross." His reasoning was a meek defense and didn't make much sense. However, she didn't pursue the weakness.

Another hill crossed led to the next. The mild warmth of the day helped them maintain their strength. It was a small blessing after so many harsh times that had stolen away his dreams on the way to Denver from San Antonio. The loss was not only his. Jody closed his eyes to clear his head of the hardships his ambition had brought him and others. Despite his best intentions, overlooking the risks, now, nearly a year later, seemed foolhardy. The meager stake he'd started with heading along the newly mapped Goodnight-Loving Trail had dwindled to almost nothing. Only fulfilling his word had made him cross the plains rather than head south to Texas. He took stock in remaining honorable. He'd given his word. A word backed by his name. His family's name. Reassured by that thought, he opened his eyes as they crested one more hill.

The view showed a group of wooden structures clumped together. "There it be," he said with relief.

Les leaned out from behind his back to take a look. She didn't say what she thought, nor did she show a joyous reaction. Instead, he could see from over his shoulder just a single tear streaming down her cheek. The promise had been kept. He reached behind him and quickly felt her hand in his. It had been a long trip. It was time to end it.

To rest the sorrel, he kept it at a walk for

the remaining mile. Not only did it allow comfort for the horse, but the view could be savored as the buildings grew larger with their approach. The vision of Abilene in the back of his mind didn't match the one before his eyes. As they neared Mud Creek from the west, the number of structures since he last was here appeared to have increased more than tenfold.

"You remember it this way?" His question went unanswered as they crossed through the wide but shallow stream. Once on the other side, they came upon the railroad tracks bordering downtown on the north. The stretch of steel went past a distant structure resembling a depot with a wide angled roof over the platform. Jody didn't remember such a building. It was apparent that in two years the Kansas Pacific had come to think enough of Abilene to protect their customers from the sun, wind, and rain as they waited for the next train. Les pointed to the street on the right where the Novelty Theater stood on the corner, and Jody turned the horse.

The many men on the boardwalks crowded them so that a number were pushed into the streets, which blocked the sorrel's path. So many drovers, some with their chaps still laced on, were either crossing the streets or standing in the center of them that Jody had to guide the sorrel as if in a forest. The glee on most of the faces put him in a festive mood. He had reason to celebrate as well.

To the left stood his most vivid memory of Abilene. With its wide double glass doors and broad awning, The Alamo Saloon was the biggest, longest, and fanciest establishment in town. Most of his pay had gone through those doors, and what little he'd had left had gone out the back to the women in the cribs. From the commotion of the drovers, he sensed that business was good.

Across the street was the Pearl Saloon. Its tall sign was easily seen over the rooftops. It, too, was known for catering to the need of the trail hands for stout drink and rambunctious relief.

Seeing a minor gap among the crowd, he nudged the horse ahead, but the gap soon closed and the horse collided with another drover.

"Control your animal," the man barked in a slurred voice. "You damn fool."

The tone turned Jody's mood. He leaned forward to return the insult to the younger man for straying in the street, but Les's clasp on him grew firmer. "Jody. Don't."

Her voice was enough to guide his eyes to the short-barreled pistol stuck in the trail hand's belt. An armed and threatening drunk was too risky. Les poked at his shoulder and pointed to a sign nailed to a post.

SURRENDER ALL FIREARMS WHILE IN TOWN
BY ORDER OF THE MARSHAL.
VIOLATORS WILL BE JAILED.

Jody sat back in the saddle. He didn't need trouble. They'd come too far to be killed.

He continued to guide the sorrel through the throng of drovers while crossing Texas Street. He sensed Les bobbing her head to the side, trying to get a good view, while he strained to remember the landmarks of the town, which now seemed out of place.

The crowd, mostly hands fresh from the Chisholm, walked about in a carefree manner, from one side of the street to the other, to sample what they yet hadn't sampled. Jody saw one hand talking to a youthful street walker with her ankles and neck showing in bright daylight. The two no doubt dickered over the price of her time and the location of her service.

At the corner stood the Old Fruit. It appeared almost unchanged, but just to the right of it stood another saloon he didn't remember. The sign above depicted a bull. With the path clear for the sorrel to walk, Jody couldn't exactly see the entire image as they moved away, but the proportions of the animal appeared odd. He made another note to visit that place as well. The horse was forced to veer by the compacted mass in the street. A sign posted on the side of a building indicated this was Cedar Street.

"It's gone," she said.

"What?"

"The sheriff's office. It's not there."

Jody peered to the side, spotting the Elkhorn Saloon where Les pointed. He hadn't recalled the sheriff's office. His last time in Abilene he'd been more concerned about staying out of that place. As he tried to take in all the sights of Abilene and put them in their proper place in his memory, he heard Les's faint command. "Stop."

He reined the sorrel in. Les slid from the saddle with the help of his arm. In a slow walk, she stepped onto the boardwalk in front of a small two-story house. Les stopped at the front step. Jody recognized that this was why she'd returned. He dismounted and tethered the sorrel to a small tree. He came to her side and looked at her.

The fright was written on her face. As re-assurance, he put his hand on her back. After a few seconds, Les let out a breath and approached the house. Maybe a minute passed before she removed the short-crowned hat and rapped on the door. It didn't take near as long to open.

An older woman with a touch of gray on the sides of her short hair answered. At first puzzled by the two of them standing at her door, she took another second and then dropped her jaw.

"Les?!"

"Hello, Miss Maggie," replied Les in a choked voice. A few moments needed to pass before the two embraced. Jody felt content to stand by and watch the reunion. Once the women finished their hug, he saw the older woman glance at him. "This is Jody Barnes, Miss Maggie." Les looked to him and paused. "He is a very good friend of mine. From Texas."

The older woman's grin shrank slightly. "You're from Texas?"

Jody removed his hat and nodded. "Yes, ma'am. Not far from San Antone."

The woman accepted the answer with remorse, but her mood brightened slightly and she invited both of them inside. Jody observed the polished furniture in the small den. A single flight of stairs led to the second floor. A rug lined the center of each step. The two women spoke while walking, with him following, through the foyer and into a sitting room. The invitation to sit on a small couch didn't come too soon. However, the older woman eyed Jody oddly when he sat next to Les.

He hadn't thought much about it as he looked at the girl, still dressed in duds to befit a man. The clothes were needed to deal with the elements, but since he and she appeared cut from the same cloth in their appearance, it must have been a disappointment to the older lady.

In that instant, he recalled meeting the young girl almost two years before not far from this very spot. It turned out to be a ploy for her to be taken to Texas for a chance to recover hidden Confederate gold. Instead of gold, they found worthless scrip, but to make the trip, Les played the part of a young man. She had Jody fooled for weeks. Maybe that was when he first held feelings for her, despite his anger at being duped.

Les tried to explain her reasons for leaving in the middle of the night to follow her dream of riches to the woman who took the place of a real mother, but the older lady teared up at the story. "I'm just so sorry," Les finished.

The woman wiped her eyes. "The town's changed since you've been gone. I was so panicked fretting where you were that my troubles worsened. The day after you left, Mud Creek spilled over its banks from a storm north of here and flooded the whole town. Two feet of water above the streets. It took a day before it receded, but my floors were packed with mud. There was no one to help for they had to tend to their own houses and businesses. I had to face it all alone."

Les put her hand on the woman's. "Oh, Miss Maggie, it must've been bad. I'm sorry for that, too." Les looked at Jody for an instant. "It must have surely been bad. But it appears all the hurt from that has passed. We saw all the new places. It's like Abilene grew double since then."

"Oh," the woman said, wiping her nose. "It's more than just the buildings. The whole town's been taken over by their kind. Texas cowboys. More than ever. Everywhere you turn, they're leaning on a post, filling the boardwalk, blocking the streets. They gather here like locusts." Jody dipped his head at this. It was hard not to take the remark personally. He sensed Les looking at him.

"Not everyone from Texas is like that." Les touched Jody's knee. "I can say it because I know it." She looked at the older woman. "I been there for nearly a year and I met a bunch of fine people there. Hard-working people just like you taught me there was all over. And this man is one of them."

The woman looked long at the both of them. "A year? You've been gone for almost two."

The statement came as a surprise, but the explanation had been planned. Jody knew the truth had to be told. "We didn't come directly from Texas, ma'am. We didn't come in with this drive today." He took a deep breath, darting an eye at Les for strength. "Truth is, we came from the west. Colorado. You see, we saw some stock took sick more than a year ago. My pa and me thought it best to drive them out of Texas soon as we could."

He paused for a breath, again glancing at Les, but he needed to get it all out, in part for the woman, in part for the girl he had feelings for, and lastly for himself.

"Talk was, there was a new trail just open-ing up. Going west, through the high plains into New Mexico, straight to Denver. Miners there were paying good money for beef. So, we gathered our herd and others and set out. Nothing much went right from then on. Ran into rustlers in west Texas. Got through that, and your girl here was as brave as any man could brag. But once we got past there, the weather turned bad. Grazing grass was hard to find. Then, when most had said winter would break for us come late spring — well, it didn't." He gulped to get it all out. "Snows kept falling and so did the stock. Often a dozen at a time. Truth is, we got to Denver with less than seventy head. As scrawny as they was, they didn't bring five dollars. Weren't much to share. Since it was my plan, I gave my share to the others." He looked at the girl. "Les said she wanted to come home. So, I brung her."

Despite the confession, there was no pity in the woman's voice. "I know you think it kind of you to do so, Mr. Barnes. But to take this young girl on a cow drive couldn't have been a sound idea."

"Miss Maggie, it was me. I wouldn't be left behind. I wanted to go. The same as I wanted to go to Texas," said Les.

"To go to Texas?" The woman's voice quivered. "To be with those people, instead of with me, who brought you here from the East so you could have a life . . ." Sobs

25

stopped the words for an instant. "After what they've done to our little town."

"But, Miss Maggie, they've been here ever since you brought me here."

"Not like now," was the abrupt reply. "Not like now." The older woman teared up again and excused herself to a back room. Jody sensed it was time for him to leave. He rose and Les followed him to the door.

"I've not seen her this way," said Les. "I always remembered her telling me to keep a smile on my face no matter what." She looked into his eyes. "Don't take offense at what she said about Texas. She's never thought much of the men passing through town. I'll tell her you're not one of them."

Jody nodded. "Can't expect the woman to take a shine to me right off after being alone so long. It's likely she believes I was the one that took you away."

"I'll tell her the whole story," Les said with a smile. "Be back before six. I'll expect you for supper. And Jody . . ." She stole a peek down the hall, then stood on her toes to place a peck on his lips. "Be on time. Stay out of trouble."

3

Jody turned and stepped off the porch. A moment's pause to reflect on the long journey to Abilene was all he could afford himself. Empty pockets pushed him to mount the sorrel and steer back through town.

In a place full of trail hands, finding a job stood as a tall order. Habit headed him toward the stock pens. In times past, he'd seen others fill the feed troughs and rake the dung to get ready for the next herd. The work was hard, but no different than the chores he'd performed all his life.

The path to the pens took him back to Texas Street. Again, he had to thread his way through the constant traffic of mostly men crossing to get to the next saloon, no doubt in hopes of someone's drunken generosity, buying drinks for those who'd used up their three months' pay. Jody grinned, remembering when he foolishly did the same.

At an intersection, the traffic stopped the sorrel. Curiosity turned his head to catch a glimpse of the sign he'd seen before. He turned the horse left and went to get a better look. As he approached, the name and figure painted on the false front became clear. BULL'S HEAD stretched the width of the board and SALOON was centered at the bottom. In the middle was a profile silhouette of a longhorn with the pizzle erect with nearly the same length and girth as the horns. The implication was clear if not eye-catching. Its success was apparent from a glimpse at the crowd inside.

He couldn't help but chuckle, but curtailed his humor upon sighting a mother and her young son moving past the place. She held the boy's face close to her waist to keep him from seeing the sign. Jody felt embarrassed just at being noticed looking at the sign. About to head toward the pens, he saw a small placard in one of the windows. HELP WANTED.

It could have been the job he needed, but a second thought stopped him from dismounting to find out. He didn't know much about the establishment, and now with Les to think about, it likely wasn't a good idea to take a job in a saloon. Working with cows better fit his nature. Convinced of the decision, he turned the sorrel down Texas Street and headed for the far side of town.

Leslie Turnbow climbed the stairs of the home she'd left two springs before. It was the only one she remembered despite having only lived there for less than five of her eighteen years. The scent of the wooden house, the feel and sounds of the steps beneath her feet, the closeness of the narrow hall brought back both good and bad memories.

She turned at the first door on the right. Placing a palm on the knob, she pushed the door open and saw the room that had been her sanctuary not so long ago. Only two small paces brought her to the center. The comfort of the walls surrounded her. She had missed them.

This was where she came to giggle and dream, and to cry. She sat on the made bed. There was little doubt Miss Maggie had kept it intact as a small shrine hopeful for a return soon after her silent departure two years ago. Les took off the muddy boots and let her toes absorb the coolness of the varnished floor.

As relief and regret filled her senses, she allowed the hardened veneer she'd learned to show on the frontier to crumble. She had made it at last. She didn't mind her chin quivering. The tear on her face was an earned reward.

So many times in the past she had yearned to leave these confines. Since arriving at the simple wood-plank depot several years ago, a passenger on the orphan train west from the forest of buildings and streets called New York City, she had hoped to satisfy the urge to find a final place to keep her heart, to erase the bitter remembrance of living in a single room with others she never knew, had nothing in common with, except for having no living mother or father, no one known as family, nowhere to belong.

Les lay back on the mattress. The ceiling was as she recalled. Every crack in the plaster was a reminder of her dreams, leading her like lines on a map to another place. It was how she put her mind to rest, always seeking a better home, without the constant chores or what seemed at the time the unfair bindings of labor, dress, and manners expected of young women.

This room was where her thoughts pushed her to never let go of those possibilities. This was her world, the garden of her ideas, and the fortress guarding her inner sanctum.

Only now could she realize how foolish

were the dreams of youth. After two years away, only now could she realize that what lay beyond the horizon wasn't green and lush with happiness. Instead, there lay the uncertainty and insecurity of the untraveled. The harshness of cold, heat, and hunger was a daily occurrence. No matter what direction she gazed in, no rainbows guiding the way to prosperity awaited. She only knew this because she had ambled in those directions and found only the same or worse conditions.

Despite her welcome by Jody's family, she'd never felt wanted or accepted. Perhaps those emotions came from her never-ceasing desire to secure a safe haven, something she never found. Texas held out the larger-than-life promise of the best in life, but only for those who came from there. Now, she knew why. It wasn't home to her. It wasn't little Abilene.

However, now she was home. And she'd brought back the best thing she'd ever discovered about Texas in the form of a tall, broad-shouldered man who showed he cared deeply about her. Les smiled. Staring at those same cracks leading her to other places beyond, she wondered if maybe this was the place meant to keep her heart all along.

■ ■ ■ ■

Jody found it easier to lead his horse on foot through the streets than attempt to ride. Walking always seemed to give him time to think. The sun heating his face as he strode west down Texas Street didn't help his attitude. He tried to clean the anger from his mind, but the disappointment at the stock pens wouldn't leave him. Despite spending two hours to find the foreman, luck hadn't favored him.

In fact, he should have known better. The chore of keeping the pens was left to a few of the drovers themselves, and they were paid extra to tend to the herd until it was loaded for market. Still, the foreman's rebuke didn't sit well with him.

Just a glance at his surroundings showed that money was much needed to stay in this town. Ten paces would bring a man to three separate saloon doors. It was the kind of boom that was built by gold and silver. The place had an appetite for dawn, noon, and dusk and every minute in between.

Pride wasn't about to let him depend on the grace of Les and her kin for his keep. Yet the challenge to find a job appeared a steep one. With drovers aplenty spreading their pay about the saloons and brothels within hours of receiving it, most of the establishments meant to catch those loose coins were firmly in place. As the notion entered his head, the figure of that painted bull caught his eye. He didn't linger long on it, but rather sought the sign still hanging in the window looking for help.

At first, he peered about to see if any respectable folk could be watching, but with the day a third from done, only the rowdies seeking whiskey, then women stood on the boardwalks. Jody took a deep breath.

The decision to enter wouldn't have been as hard before. He himself would have been counted among the many looking only for excitement after three miserable months over grass and stone on the Chisholm Trail. But he never counted himself as a servant. It was easy to think of the reasons why he didn't want to ask, but that the sign would lure another to take his place was only a matter of time. He left his pride when he tethered the sorrel to the hitch post. Another deep breath was needed to step onto the boardwalk and, before he could talk his way out of the decision, stride through the doors of the Bull's Head Saloon.

A dozen tables were easily spotted, most with cards strewn over the tops and with eager trail hands trying their luck against an experienced gambler at each table. In the corner, most of the crowd stood in line for their turn to try and buck the tiger at the faro table. The long bar took up the west wall. Feeling eyes size him up as another mark, he walked to the bar and inquired about the sign in the window. The bartender didn't at first seem interested in helping, but when Jody stood firm at the bar with no intent on moving or spending coin, the robust man went around the bar and sought a dapper fellow behind the faro table. A nod to an assistant to continue the deal allowed the man to leave off scalping the marks and come to the bar.

A man of average height, he had light-colored hair. A thick mustache made up for what was lacking on the scalp. He extended his hand with a warm smile. Jody had to take the hand whether he trusted his sincerity or not.

"Ben Thompson, proprietor."

A nod and equally firm grip was needed to make a plea. "Jody Barnes, Mr. Thompson. I come to see about the job in the window."

A peculiar look came over Thompson as he sized up the taller man in front of him. "Wasn't really looking for a man of your

stature, Mr. Barnes. What we need is someone to clean the glasses and sweep the
floors. Might not be work of your suit."

Jody kept his eyes locked onto Thompson.
He'd come this far and there was no point
in letting what remained of his esteem stand
in the way. His mind was made up. "I'm
from Texas, Mr. Thompson. But I didn't
come in with the last herd. I lost mine in
Colorado near a year past." He paused to
swallow not only his spit but a little more of
himself. "I need some money, Mr. Thompson. I'll take what you got."

"Only pays ten cents a day."

The salary wasn't a white man's wage.
However, before he knew what choices he'd
be offered tomorrow, he decided to take
what was there now. "Good enough for me."

Thompson again offered his hand.
"Done." He grinned. "I'm from Austin. I'd
like to help a Texan when I can."

Jody grinned and it felt good. "I'm
obliged. Start now if you like."

Thompson shook his head. "In the morning. Let's say seven." He looked around at
the crowd in the place. "You'll have plenty
to sweep out of here by then." He looked
back at Jody. "Get some rest. You got a place
to stay?" He nodded his head to the second
floor. The invitation appeared genuine and

very gracious. The idea of a warm woman to shed more than a year's urges was tempting. Two years ago, he wouldn't have hesitated, but although he had desire, a presence in the back of his head had him decline.

"I've got a place, but I thank you for the invite." He squeezed the grip a bit firmer. "I'll do you a good job, Mr. Thompson. And I'll be here before seven to start the job."

The firmness of Jody's grip was met with equal firmness. "Call me Ben."

4

He threw water on his hair from the first clean trough he found. With the light from the dipping sun firmly in his face, he raked the locks from his eyes and slicked them back the best he could. An overdue haircut would be at the top of the list once he had four bits to spare. There was nothing to be done about the dusty clothes. He mounted and made his way down Cedar Street. He stopped in front of the boardinghouse and gave thought to snatching some flowers from a neighbor's garden, but thought better of it when he realized the theft would be easily recognized. So, with little else to bring but himself, Jody went to the porch, removed his hat, and rapped on the door.

Five seconds didn't pass before it opened and Les stood to greet him. His heart skipped a beat to see her no longer in the trail duds of a man. She wore a gray dress with tiny white spots, buttoned from the waist to the collar. Her cheeks were free from the grime of the long journey, and as he stood there, he wondered to himself if he'd ever seen her hazel eyes so clearly. He took a step, then restrained himself from attempting an embrace.

Les glanced at the empty hall, then gave him a peck on the cheek. He sensed it was all she could show. It was all he would get in this house and he had to be content. They went to the den. He saw the table laid out with white linen and plates ready for the meal. The older woman brought a pot of browned dumplings with bits of fresh pork scattered about. Jody paid respects to the woman and her cooking. Les smiled, proud at his gentlemanly show, and the three sat to enjoy the meal. The food was very tasty. Jody stayed silent while eating, which appeared appreciated by the woman.

With only scraps left on the plate, Jody felt some promising news was needed. "I got a job today."

Les looked surprised, as did the woman, but Maggie's approval wasn't the one he sought. "Where?"

Instantly, Jody thought the truth might not be welcome. "Well, it's not the best, but I'm going to work the stock pens."

Les rose and took the empty plates while

Maggie sat with a confused expression. "I didn't think they hired men for that."

"I had to talk him into it," Jody answered, hoping to stop further questions.

Les sounded supportive while she cleaned the plates. "I think it's great news."

The older woman still sat almost in a stupor. "It is good news. I'm happy for you," she said in a monotone. "At least it's not in one of those saloons."

The remark churned those dumplings in his stomach.

"I'm sorry to be so forward," she continued after a pause. "It's just that everything about this town changed when those cowboys showed up, and it's gotten worse each year."

Les returned to the table. "I know you never liked them here. But they did bring the railroad. And that brought you the chest of drawers you liked so much."

The woman peered at Les. "I would give it back if it would return Abilene to us. And Joseph McCoy brought the railroad here, not those cattlemen. In fact, he's the one to blame if any one person should shoulder it." The bitterness in her voice stopped Jody from entering the conversation. He glanced at Les, and she showed no inclination to speak either. However, like a dam leaking water, the ill words spilling from the woman's mouth came with greater volume.

"I came here not long after the Hersheys made it a stage stop. You remember, Les. I've told you."

"Many times," Les replied.

Maggie at last let a small smirk crease her lip. "But I haven't told *him*." She looked at Jody. "Just a few mud huts at first was all there was. And we were happy with that. There wasn't much, but we knew we'd get by. I came from Missouri and we were used to hard work. And there was plenty to do." She giggled at the recollection. Soon, her mood changed. "Then Joseph McCoy came here talking up the notion Abilene could be a stop for Texas cattle. To ship east and north and all other places where people would pay good money for them. At the time, I didn't see what he was talking about, but then they came. Hundreds of them, then as many as a thousand or more. The men that brought them here stayed for a few days, and it didn't take long until those looking to charge for liquor were in business."

"I remember," Les said in a solemn voice. "You said they were a curse." She cast an eye at Jody. "And no cowboys would set foot

40

in your house." Jody cocked his head to the side.

The woman continued her story, staring straight at the wall. "Every summer day seemed worse than the one before. It got to where decent folk couldn't even walk the street. These men from Texas shouting their vulgarities, looking for money to pay for more whiskey." She darted her eyes at Jody. "Or women. And those showed up, too. It feels like as many whores came as cattle."

The word surprised Les. "Miss Maggie!"

"It's what they are." She stopped and cleared her throat with a sip of water. "There were a few well-mannered business gentlemen that came by for a room, but the Drover's Cottage kept building on, and now they all stay there."

"I saw when we came in. It's much bigger than when I remember it," Les said.

"It and every place here now. Every time I'm out, it seems every alley has a new hotel on it. The hammering of nails never stops even all through the night. And more whiskey and debauchery gets sold. If it's not the hammering, it's the gunshots waking me all through the night."

"Sheriff Tibbits doesn't put a stop to it?" asked Les.

The woman huffed. "Norville Tibbits left

41

a long time ago, as well as any law Dickinson County thought of providing, soon after those cowboys tore down the jail when a colored cook was locked up. They built one from stone to take its place." She paused in thought. "No, it was Tom Smith that did the best. Oh, he was a strapping man, taller than six feet, and he knew how to put a stop to all the rowdiness. He enforced the law of the town council against the shooting by taking all the guns away. And he made it stick, too. They made him town marshal and he made his rounds on a regular basis, keeping the peace, and when one of those cowboys would get out of hand, he'd punch him to the floor and chase him from town. He didn't need a gun."

Jody sat confused by the her story. "Beg pardon, ma'am, but what happened to him?"

The woman answered plainly. "He was murdered." She stopped a moment. "But not by the cowboys. They wouldn't dare. No, it was two vagrants he chased out from town. James McDonald was the county deputy that should have gone after them, but he asked Tom Smith to help. The story in the *Chronicle* said the vagrants rustled cattle, and Tom Smith was made a U.S. marshal then and had to go after them because McDonald was too scared. When Tom Smith got to their cabin, they ambushed him." The woman paused to exhale a long breath. "The account said they cut his head off with an ax. When the posse caught those two, they should have hung them that moment out of respect for Tom Smith, but it was said he would have wanted them to stand trial, and they did, and they went to state prison. But this town will never see the likes of Tom Smith again. That was a man." She paused to sip water. "Had the biggest funeral for him in the town's history."

Curiosity forced the question from Jody. "So, who do they have now?"

The woman curled her lip. "Some famous frontiersman named Hickok. They say he goes by the name of Wild Bill. But from what I see, all he does is sit and play cards while the deputies he hired and charges the town for make the street rounds. I have seen nothing to resemble what a lawman Tom Smith was. But he did keep the ordinance about the guns."

"What good that does," remarked Les. "We saw one of the drovers tucking a pistol in his belt. Plain to see."

"That is the way Hickok plays it," the woman said with a nod. "He enforces the law when it suits his needs. I have read that he is no friend to the Texans. I've heard they hate him and he hates them. There is going to be a fight. I wished they'd take their fight somewhere else." The woman closed her eyes and took a deep breath.

"It's been a long day," said Les. "You should get your rest, Miss Maggie."

"I've got to straighten the house."

"I'll do it for you," Les told her. With more encouragement, Les eased the woman's resistance and led her to the bedroom door under the stairs. After a few long minutes, Les returned to the den. Jody thought about stealing another kiss, needing one badly after all the bad words said about Texas. Instead, Les took him upstairs. He held a deep breath creeping up the steps in boots, not wanting to disturb the older woman and unsure of what the girl had planned. She brought him to the first room on the right.

"I wanted you to see this," she said, standing in the center of the room. Jody didn't know what awaited him. "This is what I've thought about all the while in Texas that I wanted to show you. It's special to me. It's my very own." As he stood there, Jody didn't know what she meant.

"And just what is it that you're going to

show me?" he asked in a mild voice.

She hesitated, as he'd expected, not knowing how each of them might react. Finally, she spoke and opened her arms. "My very own room."

He didn't understand at first, then stopped thinking like a man and admired what the girl seemed so proud of. "Oh, I see," he responded to the small walled square in which the cotlike bed took up more than half the space. "It is pretty." He offered the compliment as a gesture. "This is what you come back for?"

"It is," Les said, still with some excitement in her tone. As the girl sat on the bed, explaining her pride at having something belonging only to her, Jody was attracted to the laced-curtain window.

"But I am worried about her."

The words caught his attention as he parted the curtain with a finger. "How's that?"

"I haven't seen her so spiritless. She always was talking about the good in things. Now, she's a crone, I hate to say. While you were gone, she was saying how bad things were."

As Les continued, Jody peeked through the glass. He spotted a solitary figure with a broad-brimmed hat with a flared curl and an open coat silhouetted in the darkness strolling in the middle of the busy street. A pronounced mustache could be made out, along with the glint from a pair of pistol handles holstered in the belt.

"All she talks about is how the town has worsened. I've never seen her like this." There was a pause while Jody eyed the man walking the street in front of the house. "I know she hasn't much money. She said the many hotels and the Drover's Cottage have stolen all her boarders. Even the fine ones with manners."

When the figure walked beyond his view, Jody turned to Les. "Now that you have work," she said, rising from the bed, "I'll find a job. I'll help her pay the taxes on the house." Les came to stand in front of him, and put her head on his chest and wrapped her arms around his waist. "Thank you for bringing me back, Jody."

He stood, at first reluctant to put his arms around her for fear of being discovered in her room. But her warmth calmed his fears. He wrapped his arms around her back. The sensation of the girl's body touching him forced another deep breath and more re-pression of his male nature. "I always keep my word. You know that."

She lifted her head and looked up at him

with a fond gaze. They left her room and silently slipped down the steps. Jody opened the door and stepped onto the porch. Les peeked toward the loud activity at the corner intersection. "And where are you going tonight?"

He put on his hat and cocked his head. "Don't have money for a room at the Cottage." He teased her with a glance down the street. "Nor a bed in any other place, I guess." He delighted in her curled brow. "But I still have a saddle and soogan. I'll ride out where I won't get stepped on by a hoof or boot. Just someplace under the stars where I can get some rest."

5

July 1871

The crowd kept coming in. Each time Jody looked up, more drovers came through the swinging doors with smiles on their faces and money spilling from their pockets fresh from the pay office. While most sat, a sizable number stood where there was space, each looking for their turn up the stairs.

More empty glasses meant more work. It wasn't the chores that got his goat as much as the stares that seemed to wonder why a white man would be doing those chores. He took the glasses and dipped them in the filthy soap bucket to wipe them as clean as possible in as little time as possible. He knew thirsty trail hands wouldn't wait long before leaving for another saloon or causing trouble. Suddenly, loud voices came from the center of the bar among the tangle of shoulders, hats, and smoke.

"He's a damn Yankee. He only picks out

Southerners to kill, especially Texans. Someone ought to kill him."

The crowd muffled their voices at the shout. When a few men parted, allowing for a clear view, Jody saw the source of the proclamation was his boss, Ben Thompson. Keeping to his duties, Jody kept an ear on the conversation that had captured the attention of all around.

"He wants us out of this town, and I say it's him or us. This town wouldn't be a town if not for the cattle we bring here. Just a dusty way stop for the stage. Now, with all these license fees charged for supplying to the needs of our own, it's like we were criminals. I say, the only criminals in Abilene are wearing badges."

There were some votes of agreement among the mob. The bartender handed Jody a broom. He took it and walked from behind the bar.

"I am not doing anybody's fighting right now except my own, but I know how to stick to a friend," said a young drover leaning against the bar near the door with a broad white hat and dark wool coat. His face was reddened by the sun, like the faces of many like him, but the eyes had a peculiar shape, either from too much drink or his ingrained nature. "If Bill needs killing, why don't you kill him yourself?"

The dare hovered in the air in dead silence. Ben Thompson drew on his lit cigar while in the middle of the room with all watching him. A smile creased his face. "I would rather get someone else to do it."

Despite the chuckles from the crowd, the drover at the bar didn't appear amused. "You have the wrong man for the job." He swigged the remaining whiskey from his glass. "I haven't met him, but I'll try my luck."

A brief silence followed. "As long as you're trying your luck, why not give a try while you're here," said Thompson. The drover slammed his glass on the bar as he proceeded to the gaming tables. He placed a bet on the faro board while a man Jody had come to know as Phil Coe took the wager. Once the draw wasn't in his favor, the drover and others tried their luck at ten pin, all the while buying more whiskey and spouting their tributes to Texas.

"If not for Texas, this nation of ours would still belong to the British." As Jody tried to distinguish the source of that last brag, another quickly followed from near him. "Texas should never have joined back with the Union. I say she should have remained on her own as a republic, do as she damn well desires, and to hell with the rest of the carpetbaggers that malign her." Cheers erupted. More shouts followed. "All good men are from Texas. Hurrah to the Yellow Rose."

Jody bit his tongue at the words. The legendary woman all Texans knew as the Yellow Rose was a freed slave that had coupled with Santa Anna the night before Sam Houston routed Santa Anna's Mexican army at San Jacinto. However, to talk sense to the drunken crowd during a celebration might cost him the job.

"How dare these sodbusters claim rights over us Texans. We should burn them out. Let them really know who it is that rules," said a loud voice near the bar. The crowd cheered. The rant continued, coming now from a man in fine clothes unlike the men dressed fresh from the Chisholm. "Let's annex this place as Texas and take all that is here, along with the lands bestowed to the savages to the south, so the greater good of the descendants of Sam Houston and David Crockett shall be served, to promote the independence and sovereignty of all white men among those of the nigger-nurturing Northerners." Louder cheers erupted in a toast, and then glasses were quickly refilled by the bar in exchange for coins.

Jody swiped at the boards with force. It wasn't the first time he'd heard similar talk, but his upbringing didn't allow him to agree with the sentiment brought along by those from the plantation states. His blood boiled as he recalled the words of Les's foster mother. This was the manner, she thought, of all Texans. His tongue pierced his good sense. "You ain't doing Texas no favors."

Despite his low tone, his speech was heard by those around him, which quickly squelched the gabbing by those farther away. Several seconds went by as his words hung in the air, until one man challenged him.

"What's that you say, wash boy?"

Despite pushing a broom, Jody couldn't back off for the sake of ten cents a day. "I said, you ain't doing Texas no favors. This town thinks of us as a disease. One they have to bear for half the year for the sake of the cattle and money you bring. I think it proper we men from Texas abide by their hospitality." He had more to say, but felt a chill despite the summer's heat beaming into the room. A glance at the dismay on Ben Thompson's face showed him he'd be looking for another job.

"Bold talk from a kid with a broom. You say 'we.' You from Texas?" asked a drover.

"Bexar County," Jody proudly proclaimed. "Born and raised. And all this talk about burning people out only makes for trouble among the people that live here."

"To hell with them," shouted a voice from the back.

Jody repeated his sentiments, which no one seemed to share in the room. "I am like you. Been here two years ago and thought much the same, that this town was for us to get what we wanted after a summer's drive. Whiskey. A warm whore in the sack." He took a deep breath, hoping what he said would be heard. "But this town don't belong to us. Maybe there's folks that really do live here. That bring up families. Just want to get on with their lives and not fret over bullets crashing through their walls."

"You're from Texas?" asked the red-faced drover with the broad white hat. His face passed between smile and scowl easily without hint of which was an act. "Don't sound it. What it does sound like to me is you ain't been in Texas in a long time. Might not be from there at all." Temper fringed each word. Jody never backed down from a fight. Despite this drover's build, Jody would tangle with him if it had to be. The next second, he saw the pair of pistols on the drover's hip belt. With only a broom, it was a fool's play to spark a fight.

"I've been gone. Left south Texas more than a year ago."

"For what? To come here and sweep floors?" Guffaws showered the room for the moment. Now Jody had to watch his temper.

"Took a herd up the Goodnight-Loving headed for Denver. The snows wiped us out."

"So?" Ben Thompson demanded. "You came here to take up for these fine people of Kansas? Get out of my place."

Jody put the broom against the bar and unstrung his apron while he took a step for the door. That drover stepped in his way. "I don't think you're from Texas. That makes you a liar."

"I got no cause to settle with you, mister. I done been fired, so let me be." As Jody tried to step around the drover, a shove against his chest forced him backward to stumble over the broom.

Lying on the floor, he looked up at the drover, whose eyes widened as he spoke with a devilish smile. "When I'm done talking, that's when you leave. I called you a liar. That mean anything to you? It should. Would mean something to a man from Texas." He cleared his coat away from the

54

pistol on his right hip.

"Don't kill him, Wes," came from the side.

"Mister," Jody said firmly. "I ain't heeled. Be murder to shoot me, on my back, for all to see."

The drover drew his pistol. "It can be." He cocked the hammer and aimed the barrel directly at Jody's eyes.

"You ought not play with those guns, son," came from the door. Standing with two others was a tall man with long hair to his shoulders and a thick drooping mustache, dressed in a wool frock coat and a broad-brimmed hat with a flared curl. A pair of pistols reversed into the hip holsters sat at the ready and a badge clearly displayed his authority. "Someone's likely to be hurt."

The drover's smile returned and he spun his pistol around his finger twice and caught the butt in his palm ready to fire. "We was just having some fun in here, sir. I was showing my friends some tricks."

The lawman didn't react to the play, instead shifting only his eyes to the faro table. "What did I tell you about that sign, Phil?"

"Concerns you so bad, why don't you paint it yourself?" shouted Coe.

"If it come to that. I don't think it will,

though." The lawman came closer into the room while others scattered out the door. The polished black boots sent thuds through the wooden boards. A red sash wrapped his waist and the white shirt was made from fine fabric. "So what's going on here?"

"What do you want in here, Hickok?" asked Thompson. "You're not welcome."

"No, But I'm still the law in here as I am across the street. Got wind there was some trouble. I thought I might be able to keep matters at a peaceable level."

"Ain't going to be no trouble in here, Marshal," said the drover. "I was just show-ing my friends some tricks and this fellow here was so amazed, it put him to the floor."

The lawman looked at Jody. "That the way it was?"

Jody sat up, still wary as the drover held his gun firmly in hand. "I guess that's the way it was."

The lawman eyed the drover and then Jody. "You lying to me? I hate liars."

"That's what I told him, Marshal," said the drover. "He's a lying dog. Tell you any story crosses his mind."

The lawman only glanced at the drover. "Secure that weapon before someone does get hurt." He then looked at Jody. "Looks to me like you're a troublemaker. I can't have troublemakers in my town."

"It was him," Jody said rising to his feet. "Him that started trouble. I was leaving here and —"

"There you go changing your story," the lawman said, then turned and waved to another man wearing a badge. "Mike, take this liar to jail. Let him have time to find a story he can stick to." The deputy walked directly to Jody and grabbed his arm. With more commotion about to start if he resisted, Jody went with the deputy, but his pride was hurt and he had to make it known.

"Wasn't me, Marshal. I wasn't the one waving a gun around, pointing it at my head." Once he was marched out of the Bull's Head Saloon, Jody turned his ire at the deputy. "You got no call to jail me. I wasn't the one with the gun in my hand. I thought there was a law about carrying weapons in this town." They crossed the street and went directly to the first structure. Jody felt the eyes of all the passing townspeople, and heard polite applause as he and the deputy entered, no doubt in support of his arrest.

Still with a clamp on his arm, the deputy pushed him into a cell while Jody continued his plea of innocence. When the deputy slammed the door and turned the key in the lock, the short stocky man stared straight into Jody's eyes.

"Just hush your mouth. Was Bill that done you a favor in taking you out of there." He pointed through the window at the Bull's Head. "That's John Wesley Hardin in there, the worst killer of men ever given birth."

6

James Butler Hickok stood surrounded as
Daniel was in the lion's den, facing the most
dangerous mankiller known from that spot
to the Rio Grande. To challenge with a test
of a pistol draw might settle the trouble or
worsen it. He hadn't enough lead to go
around the room. Yet this kid had shown no
disrespect and displayed considerable good
spirit. The papers against him weren't an
Abilene dilemma. Hickok looked the kid in
the eye. "What say we go for a walk?"

The kid closed his mouth but kept the
smile, then bobbed his head. "Yessir, Marshal. Anything you like." He slipped the
pistol in his holster and straightened his
wide-brimmed pale hat. He went to the
door and Hickok followed. Before they left,
the kid looked to the side at the ten pin
game. Hickok found his eyes wander that
way and as they walked through the portal,
he saw Phil Coe resuming the deal at the

faro table. "See to that sign, Phil."

Once outside and out from under the awning, Hickok walked shoulder to shoulder with the kid in silence, unsure of what to say so as not to spark a fight. Hardin's reputation of a quick temper with an equally quick draw put Hickok in a wary frame of mind. It would have been easier to have collected the kid in the dead of night, when he was sleeping, with a posse of deputies, but somehow Hickok sensed that maybe the kid and he were kindred spirits. With the kid facing forward, the two men hadn't gotten ten feet from the door when a wail of excitement came from the Bull's Head.

"Set up. All down but nine."

Hardin turned his shoulders. Hickok's instinct put his hands on the twin Navy Colt .51 revolvers to draw them, hammers thumb-cocked and triggers pulled. In an instant, he recognized the kid had only turned in reaction to the shout. Embarrassed by his own jittery reaction, he felt something had to be said to justify the abrupt confrontation. "What are you doing with those pistols on?"

The reply came in a calm voice. "I'm just taking in the town."

Now with his iron drawn, he wasn't about to let this kid have a chance at his back.

"Take those pistols off. I arrest you."

A moment passed with Hardin's face in befuddlement. He slowly removed the pistols from their scabbards, palming the weapons butt-first. He took a step closer. Hickok noticed the concerned townsfolk scattering behind Hardin. In that instant, the kid rolled the pistols forward, spinning them with fingers in the trigger guards and cocking them in a fluid motion. Both barrels prodded Hickok's chin.

"Now, you take off your pistols, you long-haired son of a bitch, thinking you're going to shoot a young boy in the back."

Hickok was caught for the first time needing to talk his way out of a fight for his life. He tried a friendly tone. "Little Arkansas, you've been wrongly informed."

The commotion in the streets brought bigger crowds of gawkers. "This is my fight and I'll kill the first man that fires a gun," Hardin called to the crowd. Hickok's concern for the safety of the citizens wasn't primary in his mind. He continued his tactic of compliments.

"You are the gamest and quickest boy I ever saw." He peeked at the four pistols now held at point-blank range by the two men. "Let us compromise this matter and I'll be your friend." He slowly bobbed his head to the side toward the Apple Jack Saloon. "Let us go in here and take a drink as I want to talk to you and give you some advice."

An uneasy trust burgeoned in a few seconds. Hardin's eyes darted to the saloon and just as quickly, the flame in those pupils vanished. He smiled and eased the hammers to rest. Hickok was appreciative of the good fortune, and gave thanks by responding in kind. With all four weapons carefully holstered, the two men walked into the saloon, where all eyes watched them stroll through the bar and into a back room. While Hardin placed both his pistols on the table, Hickok signaled the bartender. In a short time, a bottle of wine was placed on the table between them along with a couple of glasses. Hickok assumed the duty of host, screwing the cork and popping it from the bottle.

"We will have us a time. After we finish this bottle of fruit and maybe another," he said as he filled both glasses, "we'll go whoring." Hickok picked up his glass to toast the sentiment. Hardin took a brief moment before answering the gesture with a clink of glasses.

Les recognized the dogwood painted on the door. Just like with Miss Maggie, she needed a moment and a deep breath or two before daring to approach. Many times when she lived in Abilene, she needed advice she was unable to get from her foster mother, and this was where she came. Although, normally, she entered through a back window, she wasn't sure if she would be as welcome now. As she stood in front of the door, she knew not to bother to knock. She entered.

Some girls milled about in the front room casting eyes at her as she entered, thinking she was new. Les averted her gaze and instead looked toward the room in the rear to the left. With the door slightly ajar, she angled her head to the side to see Lady Shenandoah. "Hello," she said with some caution.

The lady looked up from her table. Her auburn hair was down and over her shoulders. The look of puzzlement and surprise made her stand. She wore no coat and her bodice wasn't fully buttoned. Les concentrated on the eyes, which were the brown tone she remembered. Feeling encouraged, she entered the room, but the look of dismay on the lady showed she was less than glad to see her.

"Les? Is that you?" A nod was the answer, and they came to hold hands. "Look at you. You're grown. And into a real woman now."

The greeting didn't have all the tone of glee Les expected. "I remember you leaving for Texas. Why are you here?"

Les recalled the night she entered through the window and asked the lady for help to get to Texas. It was this woman's help that got her disguised as a young cowboy and allowed to her meet Jody. "I've come back. Come back home."

The comment was met with the same lack of enthusiasm. "Not much of what you left here. It was two years ago, right?" Les agreed, and the woman went back to her table. "You should have stayed in Texas. Why are you at my door?"

Still apprehensive, Les took a deep breath and came out with it. "I'm staying with Miss Maggie and, well, her boarding business has suffered with all the new hotels here. Especially the Drover's Cottage. I was needing to help her with her needs." Not sure how to say what needed to be said, Les blurted out her purpose. "I'm needing a job."

The lady's lips came to a tight straight line. She looked at Les from the shoes to the hair. "As puny as your cunny is, these big Texans will send a crack through you like a rail spike in a two-by-four." Stunned by the blunt assertion, Les was at a loss for words, but more came from the lady. "You even been poked by a man yet? Most of the women here lost it days after they first spotted the rag. Some by their own kin. You sure you want to try this line?"

Les shook her head, trying to get a sentence to form. "No," she said with some disdain. "I didn't come here" — she paused to peer behind herself, then faced the lady again — "to sell myself." She let her head dip.

"That's what the women here do, Les. It's the only job I got."

Les lifted her head. "I thought I might help take care of the place. Do some sweeping, maybe some washing."

The lady sat at her table. "They take care of their own rooms and linens. It's part of their appeal. The cleaner they are, the more they get spent on them."

Les grasped for ideas. "Maybe some of them don't like doing it. Maybe they aren't in a mood to do their cleaning."

The lady looked at her, still with a stern face. "This ain't no charity. I run a business and it's got to pay. Competition has gotten a heap stronger since the days you were here last, and every fifty cents spent makes a difference." The lady paused. "If you think you can get money from the women for some of the chores, I have no disagreement. But it will come out of their cut. Not mine."

Les couldn't help but agree. She nodded and stood still. After a moment, the lady relented in her stern resolve and took Les by the hand and into the center of the parlor.

"This is Les. She's hiring out her skills as a cleanup girl. I told her if any of you want to pay her to help with your business, you can strike a deal. But it won't come out of the house money." The lady gave Les a hint of smile. "I've got ledgers to attend to." The lady headed for the back room on the left. Les remained standing among her prospective employers.

Three women more the age of girls sat on a long couch. Two of them had smudges of rouge and white powder still on their faces. All three appeared without interest in taking up Les's offer. Their blouses and skirts hadn't been laundered in some time by the looks of wrinkles and creases in the wrong spots. Still, none of them showed much indication that Les was in the room. Something needed to be said.

"Hello," she stammered. "My name is Les." She tried to think of the benefits of her service, but she was as nervous as a schoolgirl in front of her class. "I am a hard worker." The announcement was met with snickers.

"So are we, honey. We're hard workers, too. All the time we're here." The reply set off cackles from all three.

Then, the woman in the center responded, "I have a penny to empty my piss pot." Louder cackles followed.

Les felt the rush in her face, but she'd been through worse and not shed tears. She stood her ground. "Two is my rate for that service." Her defiance raised eyebrows, but did not stop the giggles.

"Well, then, see to it," said the woman in the center. "I'll pay upon satisfaction." The laughter increased, then stopped when the front door opened.

A tall man with a thick drooping mustache removed his fancy hat upon entry. Another man of equal height but younger age, in newly store-bought duds, followed close behind. The mustached man nodded to the women on the couch. They quickly stood and attempted to brush the wrinkles from their skirts. It wasn't until Les noticed the badge on the lapel that she realized why this man commanded such respectful attention. The other had no badge.

"Afternoon, ladies," said the mustached man, while the other one took off his hat. "I have come to show my young friend here the finer parts of the town."

"You've come to the right place, Marshal Hickok." Les turned to the last room on the left to see the lady of the house standing in her doorway. The door next to hers opened. Les expected to see Arlene emerge, a young blond girl she knew from two years ago. Instead, a raven-haired temptress leaned against the threshold. Her brown eyes were outlined with black to match the locks draping her tight-collared blouse down to the bosom. There were no wrinkles in her skirt nor in her youthful face, which Les thought couldn't be more than a year older than her own.

"Where you been, Bill?" asked the temptress.

The marshal showed his delight at the question with a smile. "Away too long, my dear." He walked toward her, pausing only a moment to speak to Lady Shenandoah. "I promised my friend a treat. Please see to his full complement of choices." The lady appeared pleased with the business from the reputable man. The marshal then walked into the room with the temptress leading the way. The door shut.

The lady came to the center of the parlor. She gracefully pointed to the woman in the center and the one to the left. "This is

Carolina, and this Kentucky Sarah."

The young man looked to the one on the right. "And her?"

"This is Virginia," replied the lady. "But it's her time."

"Nothing's wrong with my mouth," Virginia said by way of offer.

The young man grinned, then eyed Les. The lady noticed his wandering eye. "She's a cleanup girl. Don't mind her." The tone, though dismissive, was welcomed by Les. The young man resumed his inspection of the three, then shrugged.

"I'll take them all."

The lady raised her brow to the three. "You heard what he said." The three marched in order to the room near the front door with the young man behind. As the door slowly swung shut, Carolina unbuttoned her collar, while Virginia sat in a chair and unbuckled the young man's belt. The creak of the door hinge ceased with the snap of the latch.

7

Les swept the floor to the broom bristles' frazzle. She'd already pounded the rug against the porch rail. With each stroke, she swung and swiped harder in an attempt to keep out of the rhythm of the grunts and groans echoing through the walls for the last half hour. While sweeping the couch for the third time, she heard a door open. Marshal Hickok came out of the doorway without his tie or hat on, but with new wrinkles in his fancy shirt. The lady quickly met him at the doorway. Despite speaking in whispers, Hickok's low nasal tone could be heard.

"He still in there?" The lady nodded and whispered something to the lawman that caused him to look surprised. "Send for me once he's done or wakes up." More whispers followed, and Hickok sent a glance at Les. "Young lady, please come here. I wish to employ your services." Les went to him.

Only when she stood directly in front of him did she realize why such legend might follow this fancy-dressed man. He handed her a silver dollar. "Please assist Jesse and these other girls my guest has been enjoying the company of, will you?"

Words escaped her, so she nodded. Hickok started for the door. About to turn the knob, he looked at the lady and spoke clearly and calmly. "First sign of trouble, you come get me."

Shenandoah nodded and the marshal left with a tip of his hat. The lady looked to Les. "You heard him. See if Jesse could use you. He just paid you for the next week." She went back into her room, leaving Les as the sole occupant of the parlor. Fearful another customer might arrive and mistake her for a harlot for hire, she knocked on the door to the right.

The door opened and the satin-robed woman at first appeared confused by Les. "Marshal Hickok paid me to help you . . ."

"Help me with what?"

An answer needed to be supplied. "With whatever needed helping." The confused look continued, but Jesse opened the door wider and Les entered. Feeling a need to begin, Les first cleared her throat while the raven-haired woman picked up the thick wool blanket from the sizable bed. "My name is Les. I'm here to assist you as told by Marshal Hickok." The woman peered back at her. "See, I once lived here and knew Lady Shenandoah," she said, then paused in thought. "But not in that way. She was more of someone . . ." Les trailed off while trying to explain. The raven-haired woman finished the thought.

"Someone to tell you why things about you were changing? That it?"

That was it exactly. Les nodded. "Yes, ma'am."

The woman stood straight and looked Les in the eye. "I ain't a ma'am." She extended a hand. "My name is Jesse. Jesse Hazel is how I'm known."

Les accepted the handshake as a kind gesture. "Les Turnbow."

"How old a gal are you, Les?" she asked while folding the blanket.

"Eighteen, or thereabouts."

"Thereabouts?" Jesse inquired. "You don't know?"

The long story of her orphaned beginnings had to be shortened. "Should be the first of March. So I was told."

Jesse snickered. "You got me there. I won't be eighteen until this September. It's good to have someone of similar age, Les. Most of these gals are two to three years older with envy in their hearts over me. I don't intend to do this for as long as they." She picked the blanket from the bed, revealing a patch of burlap at the foot. She noticed the confusion Les showed, surprised over the rough material in such a soft place. "Spurs," Jesse said.

A shriek pulled Les from the room to look across the parlor. The tall woman called Carolina came from the room near the front door wearing an unbuttoned bodice and nothing else. The view of the hairy spot turned Les away in an instant.

"Sounds like Bill was right," said Jesse without even a pause in making her bed.

The door to the room on the left opened and the lady came out and took one look at the frantic Carolina, then at Les. "Go get him. Now."

Les ran to the front door, but couldn't resist peeking inside the open room. Kentucky Sarah yanked the skirt up to her waist. "Bastard," she said. A man's guffaw followed. Les turned the knob and ran from the porch.

She sprinted, using all her youth, her arms aching from holding her hem above her ankles to maintain stride. Once at Main, she crossed the alleys and boardwalks, dodging elbows and shoulders, until she crossed Cedar and ran along Texas Street.

Once she saw the barred windows, she grabbed the latch and with her momentum crashed through the door. Marshal Hickok sat at a small desk next to another table where another man with a badge sat. Both men appeared shocked at her entry. Les huffed in air to speak. "Marshal, the lady needs you."

Hickok rose from the chair, buttoned his coat, and put on his fancy hat. "Stay here," he said in a commanding voice. Les took it to mean her, but the other man wearing the badge nodded his head. The marshal left the room without another word, leaving Les to stand in front of the deputy in awkward silence. He, too, appeared to be feeling odd, and so he spoke.

"So, what is your name, miss?"

"Les Turnbow is my name. I live with —"

"LES!"

The shout came from the rear of the room down a small hall with a door that wasn't yet shut. She knew the voice. "Jody?"

She went toward the voice, past the deputy, and peeked through the door opening. She caught barely a glimpse of him before she rushed into the hall. Jody stood behind the bars. "What are you doing here?" she asked in a panic. A thousand thoughts ran through her head, the worst of which was how she'd explain this to Miss Maggie. "You can't be in jail." She felt her own voice crack and her eyes moisten.

"They brought me here against my will. I had done nothing to deserve this."

"Now hold on," said the deputy. Les looked at him. Now he was not so friendly. "He was arrested for disturbing the peace and —"

"That's not true, Les. It wasn't me. It was another fellow." Jody shouted at the deputy, "Look, Mike. You're making her cry."

The deputy put his hand on her shoulder and looked her in the eye. There was a softness surrounding his face and his touch was gentlemanly and kind. His manner seemed friendly, but it didn't explain why Jody was in his jail. "The boy is here for his own good."

"Boy?" Jody challenged loudly.

Mike, the deputy, looked at him and nodded with confidence. "Son, wait until you're shaving on a daily basis and have aches in places one morning you never had before. Enjoy your young years while you got them. To me, you're a youngster. A boy. But I mean no disrespect." He looked at Les. "I would be calling this one a young girl ten years from now and hope she thought it a compliment." He grinned at his own comment, but the matter of Jody behind bars still stood.

"When are you letting him out? By six o'clock?"

The deputy turned to head back to the table in front. "That is the decision of Marshal Hickok to make. So, until then, no matter how long it takes, I would get used to him here and we'll try to make it easy on him."

The deputy left the hall. Les looked at Jody. "What did you do?"

"I swear I didn't do nothing," he said with the most sincere eyes. A single gulp later: "I was trying to mind my own business. But I just couldn't stand the talk."

"Talk?" The meaning escaped her. "What talk?"

Jody scowled. "The talk coming from Texans. It was the same your ma complained of. All their loud claims of being the best and claiming Texas should annex Kansas so they can do what they want. It just made my blood boil. It turned me mad that I was from the same state. One of them damn near killed me. Then Hickok came into the saloon."

The last part she heard the clearest.

"What saloon?"

Jody took a deep breath. He had something he didn't want to say, and took several moments avoiding her eyes. "The Bull's Head. I took a job there."

It didn't make sense. "No. You're working the stock pens."

"No," he replied shaking his head. "I storied that to you and your ma 'cause I didn't want to make her mad. When she said what she did about 'cowboys,' I didn't want her think me one." He looked Les straight in the face. "I really wanted her to like me. I wanted" — he paused — "I wanted her to like me for you. But it was the only job I could find by the end of the day, and I didn't want to go back in that house without a job."

Les pursed her lips from the bottom to the top. This man she brought from Texas was anything but the same as the "cowboys" so dreaded by Maggie. The same need to confess came over her, but an instant later, she was convinced this was not the time and place for such. "I'm going to get you out of here, Jody Barnes," she said, approaching the bars. "I don't know how yet, but I'm going to see to it."

She nudged against the steel rods as close as she could in order to taste his lips once more. After she lingered as long as she dared without the deputy returning, she stepped back from the bars. "I'm going to get you out of there, Jody." Emotion boiled up into her throat, but she didn't want to let him see her cry, nor anyone else. She went through the front office as quick as her feet could take her. Once outside, she went farther from the door and wept.

Exactly what could she do? She had a single silver dollar, and nothing else. Of course, she knew people in the town, but none willing to help get a Texan out of jail. There had to be another solution. She kept walking on the boardwalk trying to think of an advantage she could use. As she wandered, she came upon the telegraph office.

Thoughts filled her head. One man could help, and he might be only a wire away. There were so many ways this might go wrong. He might refuse, even if she could get the telegram to him. However, she had to try something.

When she went into the office, she grabbed the pencil and began writing. The clerk looked up at her from his desk, peeking beneath his visor. She wrote what she wanted sent and handed it to him. When he read it, he shook his head.

"Denver? It's a long ways. Has to pass

through five connecting stations." He pursed his lips at her. "It will cost a dollar."

Les, without a second thought, slapped the silver piece down on the counter. "Send it."

8

John Wesley Hardin rose from the bed and slipped on his pants. Vigorous play and satisfaction from the three whores calmed his nerves and set him in a giddy mood. It filled him and he cut wind again, which moments before had emptied the room. He left the room to find a tempting bare target, and his present delight overwhelmed his country manner, so he swatted it. The tall whore yelped like a wounded pup, then put her hands to her rump, and he let out a laugh.

"Ain't included in the service," said the red-haired boss lady. "You've had your fun. The marshal's money's played out. If you still need someone to hit, you can try the ones in the cribs in town."

The admonishment displeased him, but he wasn't going to get mean over it. He eyed the black-haired one at the far side of the parlor. "What about her? What's she rent for?"

"I'm not for the likes of you," was her cocky answer. "Bill doesn't like any of his friends going where he's been."

With two strict tongues wagging at him, the good-hearted nature of the visit lessened. He wasn't about to stay in a house where the whores gave orders. "I'll be taking my leave of you ladies," he said, picking up his gunbelt and hat and opening the front door. "I enjoyed the time here. At least the beginning." He presented his hat to them as a gentleman, then left the house. As he donned the belt and hat, a hack cab approached the place. It stopped, and out stepped Hickok with a surprised face.

"Everything all right?"

Hardin nodded and turned to glance at the front door. "Yeah, it was good. I'm beholding to you for the treat." He felt compelled to speak his mind. "There are some feisty women in there that like to talk back."

Hickok grinned. "Don't you ever like peppers in your eggs?"

The thought had them both laugh. The lawman waved him into the hack and they headed to town. "Little Arkansas, what are your plans while you're here?"

The question didn't have a definite answer and it bothered Hardin to say that. "As I said, I'm planning on taking in the town." The jostle from the dirt path sent the two to bumping shoulders. Hardin thought the action more than accidental and an intimidation ploy. He didn't take kindly to it, but thought not to provoke a disagreement with his host and new friend. "I must say, Marshal, this is the gamest town I've ever been in. I never seen as many sporting men" — he paused — "and sporting women in one place at one time. I'm truly impressed and appreciative of the hospitality." The hack turned south on Cedar.

"That it is. We have a place here where a man can relax the burden on his mind." Hickok paused. The hack came to the crossing of Cedar and First. Hardin knocked on the roof. He didn't want a further sermon, but Hickok patted his shoulder as the cab came to a stop. "Don't forget what we talked about, Little Arkansas," said the marshal as he darted his eyes to the guns resting in the belt. "We're a peaceful community. I'm sworn to keep it that way."

"I ain't done nothing," said Hardin, exiting the cab.

Hickok leaned across the seat. "I know that. Let's keep it like that."

Hardin paused only a moment, neither taking exception nor nodding agreement.

He closed the door and the cab went on its way. As he stepped on the boardwalk, it bothered him that the old man had warned him like he was a child that might take a licking for misbehaving. He wasn't no kid, and he would never take a licking from Hickok even if he deserved it. The idea crossed his mind that maybe he should have taken the head off the famous gunman when he had the chance. It was a plain case of self-defense, and no jury could say different. The more he thought about the next time, given the chance to make another choice, the more he realized that he wasn't in Texas. No kin here except for those he brought with him, and too few to fight all who would want to hang him.

He entered the Elkhorn to forget his troubles, and the cheers brought on by success at the games of chance took away his worries. A winning streak at faro encouraged him to keep wagering, and after four sour results, he took away seventy-five dollars with the last turn of the card. He whooped at the luck and newfound money in his pocket, and felt compelled to buy all at the table a shot of rye to celebrate. A tap at his shoulder turned him, his hand instinctively palming the pistol butt on his right hip, but the sight eased his grip.

"Paine?!" The surprise found him at the same time he received his bounty. The single-armed drover stood with an amiable smile. "Good to see a familiar face," said Hardin.

"I thought I recognized that cry. Had to come say howdy."

Hardin presented his winnings as a trophy. "Hell, yes. Did you see what I won? Ain't every day a man gets enough money to spend a few more days here. This will pay for a month of high living. What's been your luck?"

Paine shrugged. "Can't say the same. Been drinking my pay and gathering the gumption to buy" — he hesitated, shaking his head side to side — "to have a woman before I go back to Texas."

Hardin understood. The loss of an arm meant the absence of more than the limb. They'd shared a few plates of beans by a fire during the drive and he'd found the shy man lacking the same outward pride most men from Texas naturally possessed. He winked at his friend.

"Don't you worry. I know of a place with good women. Not the old cows in the alley neither. Had some of that just this afternoon and am building an appetite for some more dip in the honey. But, you know, spouting your manhood takes something from you when you're done. Let us continue with some spirits and see if we can improve our luck." He winked again and placed another bet on a presumed lucky number on the pretty green table.

Faro was a guessing game. The dealer drew the cards from a small cage. After the first was discarded, the next two decided whether there were any winners or losers at the table. And so on after that with every two cards drawn. Many said it was a contest where the dealer knew the answer before the bet. However, from what he'd seen, there was no sleight of hand in view, and the occasional win made the game intriguing to the simplest of minds. Hardin knew all of this, but couldn't resist his chance to buck the tiger.

After a few minutes passed, his seventy-five-dollar stake dwindled to a mere fifteen. The disappointment and his lack of confidence in the game turned him in a new direction. He nudged Paine and after finishing his glass of rye, he left the Elkhorn to pursue a different interest.

"One thing you got to remember about this town," he said with a slight but noticeable slur. "You got to know when to leave." He walked down the boardwalk looking for

85

his next opportunity. Before he saw a saloon, he saw the image of a steer drawn on a swinging shingle in front of a restaurant. The smell of burning beef swayed his plans. "I'm hungry. How 'bout you?"

The two of them walked into the restaurant and seated themselves at the first vacant table. A gal walked up to them with hair dangling in her tired face. Hardin ordered two of the best steaks they could cook and a bottle of the wine he'd developed admiration for from his previous encounter with Hickok. The bottle arrived before the meat. Hardin became a gracious host, pouring a generous share of the bottle into Paine's glass. When he filled his own, they imbibed the fruity liquor with abandon. Before the meat arrived, the bottle was empty and replaced with a full one. They both traded stories of those they had known on the trail and what had occurred since. The steaks tasted like butter. The day had starved Hardin for beef. It reminded him of home and the closer it brought him, the better he felt.

"Those Texans are ruining this town. Their smell alone carries the same as those stinky longhorns they push up here."

The remarks crept into Hardin's ears. He eyed the source, a portly man at the bar with a pistol tucked in his belt. The fellow was older and had a greedy appearance as one who was accustomed to insulting others for the sake of gain. A second glance at Paine showed the shy man's panic. Hardin winked again as more slurs came from the bar.

"The stench is powerful. Can't help from watering the eyes with every southern breeze."

The line had been drawn. Hardin nodded politely at Paine and excused himself to find the nearest privy. He headed for the door, then turned on his toes to come upon the back of the offender with suddenness.

"I'm a Texan."

The two men gauged each other in an instant. The matter had only one settlement. The portly man reached for his weapon and so did Hardin. They drew at each other with mirrored speed. The portly man fired wild while retreating, the spin on the lead whizzing past Hardin's ear. The return was aimed at least in the right direction, but the motion of the target put Paine in line of fire.

The bullet exploded into Paine's good arm. Blood spewed into the air. Cries of agony resonated in the room, but the distraction could cost Hardin his life, so he drifted to the center of the room while the portly man dodged behind the wounded Paine for cover. The man the portly one had conversed with fled the room faster than a ghost, leaving only Hardin, Paine, and the portly offender along with the tired waitress, whose screaming was loud enough to pierce all ears in the county.

Smoke clouded the room. Hardin pulled back the hammer waiting for a clear shot. The portly man crouched while aiming his weapon at Hardin from behind the wailing Paine. The passing seconds of anxiety forced a shouted threat.

"You son of a bitch. Show yourself from behind my friend, you cowardly bastard!"

The shout was enough to flush the portly man to try to make a run to the door. Hardin retreated, waving his pistol in attempt to aim straight while stepping backward. With a crouched target, and sensing the man's escape was only moments away, he aimed above the head of the slumped waitress and at the portly man's head. Another second and this fight would have no decision. He squeezed the trigger.

Gun smoke filled his eyes. An instant later, he saw the result. The portly man's head jerked to the side. Blood popped along the cheek. Another scream came from the waitress while the portly man spilled out the door.

Hardin stood, inhaling calmly. It was done. The moans from Paine and the hacking high-pitched bawl from the waitress hit him like a smash to the chin. There wouldn't be any way he could talk himself out of this. Despite regret for wounding his friend, escape was foremost in his mind.

He went to the door and hopped over the portly body prone on the boardwalk. Footsteps turned his attention to the left. Reflex brought the pistol to a straight aim. A star reflecting the twilight kept him from pulling the trigger. "Hands up!"

The lawman complied. It wasn't Hickok or he'd be dead. Hardin ran across the street toward greater darkness. Surely, there would be a horse to acquire.

9

Ransom Bonaparte cash made the decision, while looking through the grimy glass window of Room 212 of the unfinished Union Hotel overlooking the muddy streets of Denver, Colorado, that he needed a shave.

The reflection showed a scruffy man. He ran his hand over his bristled cheeks, wondering if it had been a single day or just a matter of hours since his last shave. It was a curse from his ancestors to have to clear his face of whiskers so often. Usually, in the center of a civilized society, the needs of proper grooming weren't the challenging task he was faced with at present. The confines of the new yet rickety structure, where one dodged the constant drips from the melting snow through the roof, didn't allow for the luxury of toiletries, nor a basin nor a water pitcher. The thought forced a look at his latest contribution to the cuspidor in the corner.

Denver was another in his increasing list of poor choices, often made in the haste of pursuing a promising fortune. Barely surviving for the past six months on the few risks these miners were willing to take had become tiring. He forced himself to the realization that miners mine. They didn't have the luxury of time, nor the money spilling from their pockets, to take a chance on the turn of a card. After struggling to survive after the disaster of a cattle drive through the high plains, he'd been certain his luck would change. However, fate remained a cruel puppeteer. The prosperity gained in this region was based on hard work and long-term investment, neither of which his character had ever been comfortable with. Good opportunity could only be found during the evening hours, when a few would frequent his game. Their wages dwindled and so did his.

He needed a new location. Somewhere his skills would flourish. If only he had the means to seek such a place. His billfold rivaled the desert in its lack of bounty. A plan had to be hatched, and at present he had no ideas.

"What are you doing?" The inquiry came from the other occupant of the room. The former Mrs. Harold Barkham, known more widely as Hattie McCown, singer of tunes and folk dancer, sat up in the bed without modesty due to the lack of nightshirt.

"Gauging the future, my dear," he answered after only a glance in her direction. She hesitated before replying, perhaps due to the early hour or from the previous night's experience with him and a bottle of cognac.

"So why the hat and shirt and no pants?"

A peek below reminded him of his lack of pants. "I was awakened by nature. The hat seemed necessary to stand in front of the window. Besides, my dear, you weren't concerned by this appearance last night."

Loud knocking shook in the room. "Rance, I got to talk to you."

He looked at the door. "Penelope? Is that you?"

"I got a wire from Les. Jody's in jail in Abilene."

"Come in," he answered without thinking of propriety.

The tall girl rushed in with her blond braids, blue blouse, and brown skirt. She took only an instant to view him in his natural form, then eyed the red-haired singer who recoiled under the cover of the sheets. Her face in a panic, Penelope then looked back at him. "It says to come quick. She needs you."

"Who is this?" Hattie complained.

Before Rance could think of introductions, Penelope provided them. "It ain't like I never seen what you're hiding, sister." Penelope's focus shifted to him. "Or what he's got."

Some vestige of normalcy was needed. "Yes, however, there should be some accordance with custom," he announced while slipping on his trousers. "What does it say?"

"Only that," said Penelope. She handed him the telegram while he buttoned up the front. "I heard the courier asking for you. I reckoned you were up here."

"You reckoned!?" repeated Hattie in a proud voice.

Penelope looked at her plain face. "You ain't the first unmarked female he's bedded." He felt Penelope's attention upon him while he reviewed the telegram. "I just reckoned if there was a woman of any prominence hadn't been around the town yet, I'd find him with her."

Hattie's jaw dropped. "You what!?"

"Talk is as thick as the mud around town, sister. Even though they ain't seeing what I'm seeing, they reckoned as much."

He folded the paper, then smiled at Hattie.

"This isn't as it seems, dear." He went to his belongings on the floor while looking at the tall blonde. "This was sent two days ago."

"I know," Penelope answered. "That's why when I read it I had to find you."

He cracked a grin. "Reading my mail? Now I am embarrassed." He reached down to the floor planks and picked up his protection. Bolted into a spring-loaded slide was a .41-caliber over-and-under derringer. He looked at the woman in bed. "It's not as if I wasn't sincere when I said I wanted to spend some time with you." He paused while shifting his view. "We'll have to figure out somehow to get there," he said to Penelope, then strapped the metal contraption to his right forearm.

"I already went to Union Station. The next train east leaves at nine-oh-seven. Abilene is the fourth stop. Takes three days."

He removed his watch from the vest pocket. It was 8:36. Again, he smiled at her. "I've always admired your" — he paused, distracted by her sizable bust, before continuing — "practicality in times of crisis."

Once the contraption was in place, he tested its operation by pulling the ring trigger, which released the spring, jutting the pocket pistol into his palm. He cocked the hammer just for practice, then eased the hammer to rest and reset the spring. He gave a last look at Hattie. "Time's up. You were delightful."

He grabbed his coat and waved Penelope into the hall. They hurried to the staircase. "How are we going to pay for the tickets?" she asked.

He shooed her down the steps, answering as they descended. "An anonymous donation." It took Penelope until the middle landing to figure out the comment.

"You took the money from her?"

He shrugged. "Well, at least I don't believe she knows it. Yet. Maybe we'll call it an involuntary loan." They came through the small lobby with quick steps and out the front door with the same pace. He put on his coat and straightened his lapel. A shriek came from above.

"Thief!"

He turned to see Hattie hanging out the open window of Room 212 with only the wrapped bedsheet as a cover beneath bare shoulders. She pointed at the two of them.

"She knows it now," Penelope said.

He picked up the pace. "What time did you say the train was leaving?"

Penelope raised her skirt hem to keep up with him. "Nine-oh-seven."

■ ■ ■ ■

The Cottonwood River was a welcome sight
for Wes Hardin. The summer heat had taken
a toll on him and the horse he'd stolen. He
slipped off the saddle and dipped his hat
into the flow, dumping the water over his
head. The relief didn't come a moment too
soon. It had taken him riding two nights
and a day to get to this spot. Always looking
behind, he'd feared for the first time that
he'd be tracked down for his actions and
shown little mercy.

In the past, he had avoided capture and
retribution with his knowledge of the land
and the many friends and kin who protected
him. However, he wasn't in his own pond,
and sensed that a man like Wild Bill might
take personal offense at Hardin killing
someone in his town. It was that doubt as
to his ability to stay free that pushed him
south.

Refreshed by the cool water, he wiped the
drops from his eyes and peered into the
bright distance. The image of four riders
and a dual-teamed canvas chuck wagon
came into focus. Their approach brought
his hand to the pistol butts. An instant's
thought of flight on the horse faded away as

a poor choice. The animal was winded from the long and constant ride from Abilene. He stood and took a deep breath. If it was meant to be, then he'd take as many as he could with him. The next seconds eased his fears with the recognition of Jim Rogers.

When they pulled in reins across from the stream, he shot them a friendly smile, still not convinced that their presence was coincidental. Despite the slow-moving wagon, there were too few men to drive any cattle, of which there were none in sight. "Howdy, Jim. Good to see a friend like you out here."

"Same here, Wes," Rogers answered, looking about in all directions. "You heading back to Texas alone?"

A shrug came in reflex. "Just got restless. Thought I'd mosey back, see what came along that might be of interest." Curiosity had him concentrate on the wagon and its hidden contents. If this were some posse, at least two shooters could spring from it.

Rogers grinned. "Restless is your nature, Wes." The grin faded to a sobering stare right into Hardin's eyes. Unsure of the cause of the change in mood, Hardin slowly slipped his right hand to his hip, prepared for a quick shot at Rogers, friend or not, if there came any sign their intentions were aimed at doing him harm. After a few seconds, Rogers spoke. "Billy Cohron's dead."

The news came as a shock and a minor relief of tension. Despite the sorrowful news, Hardin gained confidence that these men weren't there after him. "How'd it happen?"

"Murdered by a Mexican," replied another rider Hardin didn't recognize. The relief turned to spite at the idea of an inferior taking the life of a white man. A glance at Rogers confirmed the truth with a nod.

"One called Juan Bideno," Rogers said. "Shot Billy in the back during a quarrel over orders Billy had gave. We're here to see him get buried proper. Seen any Mex riding fast?"

Hardin merely shook his head. However, despite the chance to leave these men and set off on his own without further disturbance, his inner pride as a Texan began to boil. "You have Billy now?"

Rogers again nodded. "We're taking him to Abilene for burial. Too far to take him home."

Without considering all consequences, Hardin went to the horse and mounted. "I want to see him." He smacked the rump to cross through the water. He slid off the saddle and went to the back of the wagon. The driver loosened the ties on the canvas, revealing a white cloth–wrapped body. Although all five men surrounded him, Hardin showed them his back and went into the wagon on his knees. He yanked the cloth from the head and saw the bloody damage to the spine below the shoulders.

"Couldn't do much about the wound," Rogers said. "We gave him whiskey as much as we could to take away what pain it could, but he still moaned for a day before it took him."

The sight, along with the news of Billy's Cohron's last day on Earth, seized at Hardin's gut. Billy was a good man. An honest man known by all as one to be trusted. It was no surprise he'd been chosen to boss a herd. Whatever the cause of the disagreement, he wasn't a man to be shot. Not shot in the back. And not shot in the back by a dirty greaser.

"Where the man done this foul and treacherous act go?"

"Can't say," replied Rogers. "Reckoned he'll head south and hide out in the Nations. He may get to Texas or maybe even Mexico. Can't never tell about their breed."

The idea of returning to Abilene wasn't wise. Although he was a moral man who desired to show the proper respect, the prospect of Wild Bill's men seizing him for trial remained. He would have to extend his condolences in another way. "Don't take all of you to get him to Abilene. Why don't they take him there?" Hardin said, pointing at the men he didn't know or trust, then looking at Jim Rogers. "You and me go looking for this Juan Bideno."

10

J.B. Hickok leaned against the awning support of the Novelty Theater. The bright afternoon helped his view of the activity on the street. Despite nearly being noon, it was still early before a game at The Alamo would start. So, he contented himself with the sight of the people traversing the boardwalks to perform the duties of daily life. It was a good day, so far. It was quiet.

Upon taking this job, he'd thought that what had plagued him in Hays City would be easier to deal with here due to his experience, but Abilene proved different. This town was bigger, had more outsiders with the aim of taking it over, and certainly had more venues of vice in which to spawn the type of trouble his reputation was meant to put down. Had he known from the beginning back in April that there were so many competing problems vying for his attention, he might have turned it down. However, he wouldn't have known how to come up with a steady wage if he had.

His thoughts must have foreshadowed the approach of the man who appeared on the boardwalk. He was shorter, with a thick mustache and a dress coat and tie, and came at a leisurely pace. Hickok expected the visit to be anything but pleasant. "Afternoon to you, Mayor."

Mayor McCoy nodded at the greeting. "Marshal, enjoying this fine sunny day?"

Hickok shrugged. "I am. Also never hurts to have one as a peace officer be noticed about the town. Lets folks know that we are doing as we're paid for."

"I agree. Especially with the talk that's going around about these Texans and their behavior toward our women."

That certainly wasn't a chance comment to pass the day. "I expect most of them are still sleeping off last night's liquor. I'll be looking for them in another hour or two." He paused, contemplating whether to pursue the implied accusation. "What have they done to our women?"

"Well," McCoy replied scoffingly, "they're calling out to them from across the street."

The answer seemed easy. "Those likely aren't Abilene women, Your Honor. Most of those gals are from parts all around and it is their business to be called to."

The statement was received poorly. "I wasn't referring to those women, Marshal Hickok. No, these are the people that live here. This is their home, not some shanty meant to be moved to a better spot in the alley. I'm talking about respectable women. Ones with husbands and children. It's been said that they have been accosted by these Texans in a state of drunkenness seeking a kiss, or even . . . Well, you understand what is sought."

Hickok did, and so he nodded. "I do. And there's no putting up with it, even if it is good-natured or a mistake made in the dark."

"Respectable women in Abilene aren't outside after dark."

The mayor's correction was worthy. Just as in dealing with army officers, often what was needed was a quick admission that there was a problem and a definite promise to solve it. While answering, Hickok pondered where he could replace this steady wage he was drawing. "You're right, Your Honor. I'll see to it stopping." Hickok lurched away from the post on his way to a shadier and more peaceful spot, but discovered he wasn't dismissed yet.

"Still see that bull up there," McCoy said.

The reference stung Hickok slightly. It had been a town embarrassment since before he arrived. It had been a constant point of discussion each time they met. "I know that, Mayor."

"Every day I hear more complaints about it. The school is not a couple hundred feet from it and the children have to walk right in front of it to and from."

It was the same ramble heard many times before. "Aware of that, Mayor. I've been looking into it." Hickok didn't want to hear it anymore, and decided to speak plain on how he saw the matter. "But, you see, I ain't hankering to start a fight which likely will turn into an event where people lose their lives over it. Thompson and Coe see it as their right to put what they want on their property. They know the council has ordinances against it, but they prefer to be stubborn to make a point. If we make it the issue you're speaking about, the hard feelings will fester and they'll have cause to do something else you'll approve of even less." He took a breath and tried to calm his own nerves. "Don't get it wrong. I have no appreciation for Thompson and Coe nor the other Texans. But unless you're prepared to send a call to the army, if the council keeps pushing the license fees higher and restricting their trade with ordinances, they'll be pushed to defend their interests, and that often means bullets flying, which won't give your citizens any more peace."

The mayor's face showed no appreciation for Hickok's speech. "So your position is to allow for all this lawlessness? To ignore the ordinances laid down by law-abiding people? To let these Texans rule the town and do as they wish? To let the street walkers peddle their pole chutes in broad daylight as decent folks make their way to Sunday sermon?"

Hickok had heard enough. "With all due respect, Mayor McCoy, I'm doing the job you hired me to do. To keep the peace. To keep tempers from flaring." He held his tongue long enough to ease his mind. "Let these boys have their fun and leave town after they spread all their pay for three months about your town's businesses, which thrive on their patronage. They're just kids. So they drink cheap green whiskey, get cheated at card games, and relieve their male nature upon women of low virtue willing to sell it to them. As long as they don't get riled enough to draw iron and spray lead about the town, we can weather this season and tuck in for the winter with an extra layer of money."

The appeal for sense didn't make a dent on the face of the mayor, who no doubt had heard opposing perspectives on how to deal with the problems facing Abilene. Hickok could see another volley of protests coming from the mayor, but was spared hearing them by the arrival of another man of more education and greater faith than the stocky, salty, opportunistic McCoy.

"Councilman Henry, good to see you, sir," Hickok said in greeting, stifling McCoy's anticipated retort. He extended his hand, which was accepted. The tall, distinguished, goateed gentleman dressed in coat and tie and derby came nearer. Henry acknowledged his political rival with a biting salutation. "Joseph, I am surprised to see you out on such a fine day."

McCoy smirked. "Yes, the marshal and I were just speaking about the very same thing."

Henry squinted at the sky. "Fortunate weather we're having lately. Perhaps we're past the spring floods. It will make for a good growing season."

The reference confused Hickok. "Are you speaking about the prairie grass for the cattle to graze?"

A slight snicker met the question. "No, no, Marshal Hickok. That will grow no matter the conditions as it has for hundreds of years. I was speaking about the crops grown by the farmers. It should make for a good season for them."

"Nesters," as they were called, were another concern for the town, and whether he liked it or not, a concern for Hickok. He cringed slightly, but had to pursue the matter. It was better to be asking questions than thinking up answers. "I heard them folks were getting in the way of the herds. Building fences, plowing fields to plant crops, forcing the drives out of their way."

The tall man appeared amused. It was no secret T.C. Henry was no advocate of the cattle trade. It was McCoy who had originally lured the cattlemen to drive their longhorns to Abilene despite having lost all his holdings in the volatile beef market. However, Henry didn't mind handling the money the drives brought, selling hay to the drovers while their stock waited in the pens. Still, as a former mayor and current councilman, he was a man who planned ahead.

"In the long term, farmers are a better solution for Abilene, Marshal. There have been instances where property has been damaged, and we should be concerned it goes no further. We need to encourage settlement. Men who 'toil in the soil' are far less a threat to the community."

Hickok couldn't help state the real reason for such an attitude. "It don't hurt to own thousands of acres of land to sell to these nesters when they come to plant roots here, does it, Councilman Henry?"

An unashamed shake of the head was the response. "I can't say it hurts, Marshal. We all here are in the habit of bettering ourselves. That was the dream of those of us who came here long before you did. And that was the foundation of this town. It was the Hersheys, myself, the mayor here, and others who made it possible for new people to prosper and earn a living." He paused, casting a squinted eye at Hickok. "Such as yourself." There was no reason to argue the issue further. Hickok reminded himself about keeping tempers from flaring, but Henry wanted to press another matter. "I heard of some recent antics between you and one of the Texans. In the street for all to see, pistols drawn, endangering the population. Is that true?"

"I heard the same thing," McCoy chimed in.

Hickok took a breath and nodded. "It wasn't the affair you might think. I quelled an argument in the Bull's Head and arrested one of the troublemakers, who is still in jail since he can't pay the fine. As far as gunplay, well, it was just that. No shots were exchanged. Just a friendly show of skills. Nothing more." He hoped the matter would be dismissed. He was wrong.

"The talk about this Hardin fellow is troubling. I heard he is wanted in Texas on charges of cold-blooded murder," Henry calmly stated. "I understand another man lost his life the other night due to reckless gunplay. It's rumored to have been this man Hardin who did the killing."

Again, Hickok responded first with a nod. "Likely is so. But the deputy didn't get a good look at the killer in the dark. Some said it was an argument that led to a killing in self-defense. Reckoned he left town since we haven't seen Hardin the last few days. But he is a man of violence. He did brag about town that he beefed an Indian while crossing the Nations. As for charges of murder from Texas, all I know is he hasn't broken any laws in Abilene yet and I plan to keep it that way. I have deputies watching for him and his cousins. If they stir up trouble, we're prepared to run them from town." Fearing further inquisition, Hickok seized on the first reason to come to mind to part company. "If you gentlemen don't mind, I promised J.B. Case to arbitrate a complaint from a customer who claimed to be sold a wild mustang instead of a tame mare. Good day to you both."

He left the two businessmen standing alone, no doubt conspiring as to his own future as senior peace officer. Neither of the men were to be trusted.

11

By the time Hickok got to the jail, he was fuming. He opened the door and slammed it shut. "Damn politicians. Should put them all at the end of the rope." He marched to his desk and saw Mike Williams stand at attention. To put the deputy at ease, he continued his rant at the people not in the room. "McCoy, Henry, they don't know what's good for this town." He removed the twin fifty-ones and put them on the desk so he could sit in some comfort. He pondered a moment as to why he sat in that exact chair.

When he took the job, the title of town marshal appealed to him because of its steady pay. His luck at poker hadn't been consistent. To parade about with a badge didn't seem so difficult. Running the rowdies out of town, leaving the ones with sense to drink, whore, and enjoy themselves, appeared a simple task at first. However, the prominent citizens of the council were pushing him into a corner. Now they expected him to enforce laws curtailing the acts that brought money to the very streets they all walked upon. He sensed what was coming. Soon, the very practices he enjoyed would be jeopardized by restrictive ordinances, which put him at odds against the sort he favored company. These were the very times when he considered returning to life as a wandering celebrity. But that life didn't pay well. So, despite its agitation, the need for pay on a regular basis won out over the job's disadvantages.

"They egging on you, are they?" asked Mike.

Hickok looked his longtime friend in the eye, knowing his intent would be understood. "The sons of bitches think this is a town of churchgoers, and want it that way during the summer season. Can't have it both ways. If it was nothing but churchgoers, we'd not have a job." The very statement alerted him to how he needed to enforce laws among the lawless just to keep his position. If he were to make the town into the law-abiding community sought by the council, it would a be place he himself would not want to stay. "Sons of bitches." During his lament, he caught the image of someone in the jail hall. He looked at Mike. "Who is that?" he asked in a softer voice.

"Oh," Mike answered with some reluctance. "That's the prisoner's sweetheart. She's been here most every day since we put him in, bringing him food and the like."

Hickok concentrated on the figure. "She looks familiar."

"I think she's working for the Virginia lady. Not as a dove, but I believe she may be a cleanup girl."

The statement got him to thinking. This girl's knowledge of what he was doing at the parlor house might be a problem for him. "Keep her away from me," said Hickok.

"I'll do what I can. But she is feeding him, which ain't costing us nothing. Could be a help. Unless we let him out."

Hickok shook his head. "I can't say when Hardin will be back, and I have a notion should he stray into town with that one loose, we'll find the body in an alley. I'd as soon keep him here until I know Little Arkansas is back in Texas."

"Like I said," Mike told him, "I'll do what I can."

The office door sprang open and in walked Deputies Tom Carson and James Mac-Donald. Hickok decided to relay the mayor's complaint to the two deputies. "Where you been? Sampling the local liquor?"

Carson looked at Mike for an explanation of the marshal's mood. Mike shrugged. Carson responded, "We've been walking the town. Like you said, making our presence felt."

"Well, it isn't enough of one according to the mayor. He sees all the vice strolling about the town and comes to believe that we ain't doing the job we're hired to do. I brought you men in to keep the place civil. He says the street walkers are getting too close to the school. Making for complaints by the church folk." He snorted an angry huff. "So, I leave it to you to make sure that no whores are straying too close to the school, or the church, or any other place of respect where they're not wanted." He eyed all of them. "Or I'll find me other men who can get this job done."

He knew the threat was stern, but also precise. If he were to keep his steady pay, then he would make sacrifices, whether personal or professional. Tom Carson was a favorable selection. His heritage as Kit Carson's nephew deserved respect, as his uncle was a legendary figure in Hickok's esteem. James MacDonald was held in no such esteem. A crony of the local establishment, he was hardly Hickok's choice for a deputy. It was common knowledge he had been a cowardly bystander when the heroic former marshal Tom Smith met his demise. Had MacDonald lent more support during the apprehension of the two drifters, Tom Smith would still be alive and holding the job of marshal to this day. However, due to MacDonald's contacts with certain powerful people, hiring the former county deputy had been a requirement for Hickok to get the job.

"You take care of me, and I'll take care of you," Hickok told the deputies.

The inferred warning was meant to reinforce the need to show a greater compliance with the laws of the town. Without anything to add, he shooed them away with a wave of his hand. The two deputies went to the door and opened it with confused faces.

Voices and a slow methodical drumbeat echoed from the street outside. "What is that?" asked Hickok.

"The funeral," Carson replied. "A drover named Billy Cohron. The talk is he was murdered by a Mexican gone crazy on the trail. Other talk says this Mexican swore to take back Texas for Mexico and kill all the whites living there."

"Aw, that's just talk," Mike replied. "That can't be true. That's just the Texans trying to make more of it than just a killing."

"Can't say you're wrong," Carson said. "But the streets are full of mourners from here to the Drover's Cottage."

Hickok huffed. He got up from the chair and went to the door. In front of him, he viewed mostly drovers, but there were also others with derbies and dress coats walking five to six abreast through the street. "I heard there was a crowd. Didn't think it would be this many." He stepped out from the doorway and onto the planks. The cortege stretched the length of Texas Street all the way to Buckeye Street, and probably beyond the stockyards if he could see that far. "Looks like Eicholz did a good job with the undertaking."

"Appears every Texan in town is marching," MacDonald remarked.

The body was laid out in a glass-sided hearse that appeared freshly painted and was polished and perhaps on its maiden duty of carting the dead. More wagons and carriages followed along with riders, some in lined ranks befitting any fallen cavalry officer. The showing was both impressive and surprising for a relatively unknown victim of a crime committed well away from

116

the city limits. Having seen enough, Hickok returned to his chair.

"And it means trouble." Carson looked at Hickok and continued speaking. "Some have said Wes Hardin is chasing after the killer." Hickok turned his head in puzzlement. Carson's nod assured him that the statement wasn't misunderstood. "I heard Colonel Wheeler asked him personally to hunt down the shooter. A Mexican named Bideno. Either dead or alive."

The rumor brought more disappointment. "I think we can count on which way that will turn out." Nevertheless, the present had Hickok's attention. "As long as he doesn't come back to town, I'll not worry." The moment, the situation, the date all slammed into mind. "One hell of an Independence Day." Carson and MacDonald chuckled and walked out the door. The talk had muddled Hickok's thoughts and brought frustration. If there was to be plotting involved in the next few hours, it might as well be for money. He rose from his chair and reversed the pistols into their holsters. "I'm going to The Alamo." While he was making for the door, the girl in the hall again caught his attention. He whispered to Mike, "Be sure she knows nothing about me." Mike, whom he'd known as a soldier

117

while he scouted for the army, had an apprehensive expression, a sign he wanted to say something. "What does she know?" Hickok asked.

Mike shrugged. "Can't say she's said anything about you." The inflection left the question open. Hickok rolled his wrist to encourage Mike to tell the complete story. "I have heard her tell the prisoner about some man named Cash," added Mike. "Supposed to be a gunman. Shot a man in Fort Worth, but I didn't hear it all from the start. Might be here in the next couple of days."

Another problem. "Find out what you can. Try to make it look like you weren't listening." If there was a drink needed, it was never more than now, with all the conspiracies from the town council, plus the Texans in town who hated him, the nuisance of Little Arkansas Hardin, and now another unknown gunhand coming to town to reckon with. He went out the door and sought the solution to his problems with a stiff drink and a calming game of cards.

The thud of a door shutting echoed into the hall. Les craned her neck to see farther into the front office to be sure the marshal was gone. She looked back at Jody. "I think he left."

"Good," said Jody. "It's quieter without him here." She returned to stand in front of the bars. He began to speak, but hesitated, a sign he didn't want to ask but had to. "Any word from Rance?"

Les shook her head. "I went by the telegraph office before I came here. There was nothing." Jody shaking his head was a sign of losing hope, a condition she couldn't let stand. "Don't worry. I know he's coming. He'll think of some way of getting you out of here."

He smiled back at her. "I know you're hoping that. But you and I know he's never been a reliable sort. If he's not too drunk to get the wire, then he may be run out of Denver, or even dead himself. He ain't one to keep friends."

She knew it to be true. The both of them had been promised money in numbers so high they weren't sure they could count that high, only to be disappointed by the gambler. However, she didn't want Jody to lose heart. "Don't think that way." Les wanted to recite all the positive adages taught her by Miss Maggie, but thought better of it since her foster mother's own attitude had turned so sour. It would be left to *her* to carry the burden of a brighter outlook.

A quick glance outside to gauge the sun's angle told her it was near two o'clock and time for her to return to work. She stretched on her toes to give Jody the best peck on the lips she could. "I'll be back tonight with supper." Before she got out of the hall, Jody called to her.

"Did you remember?"

She nodded. "I got it from the saddlebag. I have it in my room." Once she had assured him of that, she went into the office. The deputy sat at the desk and grinned at her. He opened the lower drawer and gave her his empty plate.

"That was a tasty dinner," said Mike the jailer.

12

Wes Hardin rode the stolen horse hard with vengeance on his mind. Jim Rogers kept the same pace alongside. They feared the Mexican named Bideno had already made it to the Indian Nations, where he could easily become lost among the tribes and wilderness. Wes kicked the horse in frustration that so much time had been lost.

They crested a hill and saw dust in the distance. Usually, the brown haze hanging so low to the ground meant cattle were trampling the Chisholm Trail dirt once more. They steered for the dust, and rode at least a half hour before finally sighting the point men. Hardin inquired from the drovers if they'd seen any Mexicans heading to the south in a hurry. When no one had, he told them why he was searching. The names involved in the incident sparked information. Billy Cohron's brother was with the drive. Hardin chose to tell him the tale directly.

When John Cohron was summoned to the front, Hardin removed his hat.

"You Billy Cohron's brother?" he asked of the kid, not much younger than he.

"I am," John answered with a grin. "What's he done? Got throwed in jail?"

"Wish it was that simple," Hardin said, glancing at Jim Rogers, unsure of how the news should be told. He grunted to clear his throat, and decided if he was the one who had to hear that kin had been killed, he'd want to hear it as quick as possible. "He's dead. Shot in the back by a Mexican named Bideno some ways north of here."

The blunt statement sent first shock, then sorrow to the teenager's face. John's breath quickened and he looked at the ground, his voice cracking. "Where is he now?"

"Body's been taken to Abilene for proper burial. Don't worry. He'll get the best funeral can be bought."

John looked up with moist eyes. "How 'bout the murdering son of a bitch who killed him?"

The pain of the kid resonated in Hardin's tone. "Plan to hunt him down. Bring him in to hang if he surrenders. If he puts up a fight, then we'll shoot him down like the

122

varmint he's showed to be." He angled his head toward the sun. "Hard to know how far he's got. But he'll be harder to find across the Arkansas. Jim and I have been on his trail since I got the news." He sensed the kid needed some reassurance. "Don't fret. We'll find him. There's a lot of cattlemen had deep regard for Billy. They'll pay a high reward to catch him. That kind of money makes people talk. I know we'll find him."

John straightened in the saddle. "I'm coming with you and don't try telling me I ain't."

"Me, too," said another of the drovers. "Name's Hugh Anderson and Billy Cohron was my friend."

"Be glad to have the both of you. Let's us hunt in different spots." Hardin again looked to the sun. "We won't have much time to supply. Ask your cookie for some grub for the ride. I think we can make Wichita near sundown."

Les ran up the path. Sweat dripped from her brow from the heat and exertion. She made it to the porch and tried to slip in unnoticed. She'd only collected seventy cents from the girls, not counting the silver dollar from the marshal, and couldn't afford to lose this job. Trying to calm her heavy breathing, she opened the door and quickly shut it so the blast of heated air wouldn't be felt. On hearing the lady's loud voice, she feared she'd been caught, but an instant later, she realized what was being screamed wasn't about her.

"Without the chance I gave you, you'd still be in one of the cribs!"

Les went to the center of the small parlor house. The lady Shenandoah stood at Jesse Hazel's door. Les moved around in order to see inside the room. Jesse wore a walking dress of light blue. She closed a case that lay on the bed. Shenandoah continued. "You were nothing but a homeless tramp when I found you. And now you're walking out on me?"

Jesse took the matching chip hat and pinned it into her hair with the aid of a mirror as she spoke. "It isn't about what you done for me. It's what I can do for myself. And if it means I don't have to take as many turns and will eventually have my own house, then I got to do it."

"You're not going to get that place. You don't have the money and I know what you got."

Jesse faced Shenandoah, picked up her case and parasol, and left the room. "Bill gave me a hundred dollars to get me started."

"That miserable bastard," shrieked the lady. Jesse kept walking for the door. "You leave here and I'm not taking you back. I don't care if you're bleeding and need a doctor."

Jesse took a glimpse at Les, then continued on her way. "Good luck, honey. It was nice knowing you." She took the knob in hand. "If you need a job, let me know. This place has seen its last days." She laughed, then opened the door and left, shutting it with a slam.

Les felt like she'd been through a twister. Cautiously, she crept toward the lady. "What was that all about?"

"She's going to work for Mattie Silks, the blond tart that likes to brag how she's never been on her back. Amateur. Common street slut. She told Jesse she'd make her a partner and Jesse will take over someday so she can move on to Denver." The lady shook with anger, heaving breaths as Les had only moments before. After a few seconds, she looked at Les. "I'll have another girl in here tonight. I'll take one of the street walkers and make a prime parlor woman out of her in one day." She eyed Les again from head to toe. "You've seen the job. You don't want to make five times the money?"

The offer shook Les to the core. The thought of selling herself was an idea she would never consider. However, she couldn't insult the profession. "I can't be no good at that. Like you said, my bunny is too small for these Texans."

Shenandoah chuckled and caught her breath. Sensing shame, Les kept silent, but knew what was on the lady's mind. "You're a good one, Les. So help me. You've seen the work. And if you ever think about working for someone else" — she paused, her brow eased back, but her chin remained firm and locked — "I'll cut your little heart out."

Wes held the .44 with an outstretched arm. He pointed the barrel at the few clouds and pulled the trigger. They were close. He looked at the flat horizon in anticipation of the next hour. He looked at Hugh Anderson. "You sure?"

Hugh nodded. "Was told by those knowing Billy's horse. They said it's there hitched in front of the saloon."

The information was the best they could get. To see for themselves might spook Bideno into flight. Patience, not a trait Hardin relied on easily, had to be observed.

They waited for the others to respond to the gunshot signal. The hour seemed ten times as long. The idea that the murderous Mexican was less than a mile away had Hardin chomping at the bit. Why would Bideno still be in Kansas when he could have gone into the Nations and mixed with people with darker skin? It didn't make sense.

More thought fueled Hardin's rage. What if Bideno thought nothing of shooting Billy Cohron in the back? Just another incident among men on the trail? It wouldn't have been the first time. Wes himself had beefed another before harsh words were spoken. That did happen, but he was a white man. One white killing another was sometimes needed, but Mexicans, or darkies, or even savages had no right to killing a white man. If that were tolerated, they be thinking of themselves as equals. That right was only reserved for folks of pale skin. God chose it that way.

Jim Rogers and John Cohron rode up with their mounts in a lather. They slid off saddles and pulled their iron. "Found him?" asked Jim.

Hardin nodded. "Down in a settlement they're calling Summer City." He explained how Billy's horse was spotted outside a ramshackle structure presented as a saloon, mostly to capture a few coins off thirsty passersby. Hardin thought to rush the place, but the others convinced him to circle about to prevent an escape. Even though vengeance flowed, he sensed a bit of fear in the others. Perhaps they hadn't been at muzzle point with foes. The reputation of Bideno as a crazed killer also made the others push for caution. Hardin reluctantly agreed.

They all mounted and rode toward the rickety settlement, deciding to tell folks they were on a cattle drive and enjoying a few hours away from the dusty trail. With that story in mind, they entered the main street. Hardin led the way with the others flanking his side. He did his best not to send fear into the few people straying from shelter in the sweltering heat. The temperature did little to cool his mind. Once he sighted the horse vouched for as Billy Cohron's, Hardin's anticipation swelled inside his head, chest, and hands.

They all dismounted near the makeshift saloon, filling the air with giddy talk to mask their intent. Unsure if Bideno was indeed in the saloon instead of perhaps in a privy, Wes decided on their approach. "Y'all circle about the back and be watching," he said, motioning to Jim and John. He turned his attention to Hugh. "We'll go inside." He

128

took a step on the poorly nailed boards in front and proceeded without hesitation.

When he went through the open doorway, he peered into the darkness, ready to draw and fire at the first glimpse of a Mexican. Never having seen Bideno, he only knew that the man wore a wide sombrero, and there were none in the room. The fear of wasting time pushed him to leave and search the rest of the settlement. About to leave, he saw another closed door and turned to the presumed proprietor. "We're looking for a friend. A Mexican herder. You seen him?"

The man merely pointed at the closed door. "Yes."

In an instant, Hardin drew his .44. Hugh quickly did so also. All of the hate penned up inside flowed through Hardin's veins. The long rides during night and day, heat and cold, taking them farther south around and past Wichita, changing horses without allowing rest for themselves, eating cold bites of food when they took time to only slurp water so to not lose any more time — all that drove Wes to the door. He paused for a second to cock the pistol and check that Hugh was ready, too. He turned the latch, while the few others in the structure fled out the front.

Wes pushed the door open. A Mexican stood behind a table, a pistol aimed right at Hardin. Wes couldn't raise his .44 fast enough to fire first. Reflex raised his left open palm.

"I am after you to surrender," he blurted out in panic. "I do not wish to hurt you, and you will not be hurt while you are in my hands."

Bideno shook, but he didn't pull the trigger. Wes inhaled, still waiting for an opportunity. Motion to his right from Hugh drew the Mexican's eyes to the side. Wes reacted. In that instant, he raised the .44 and pointed. His finger, already wrapped around the trigger, never wavered. The shot ripped the air and sent smoke about the small room. Blood splattered from Bideno's forehead. The Mexican collapsed behind the table onto the floor.

Hugh shouldered his way into the doorway.

"He went for his gun," said Wes. "Had no choice." Silence reigned in the room as Hugh entered to view the body and be sure of the death. Hardin went only a single step farther, confident his aim had been lethal.

Footsteps boomed through the planks. John was first inside the small room. Sensing the need to avenge a brother's death,

Wes looked at the young man just as John cocked his revolver to send more lead into the body. "No," said Wes. The slug in the head had done what six more would only copy. Multiple bullet holes would only serve to confuse the outcome. He'd rather it be known he was the sole killer of the bandit. Instead, Wes picked up the sombrero from the table and gave it to John as a trophy.

With a wave of his hand, Wes signaled for them to leave. He wasn't sure he was among friends outside. The proprietor crouched behind the bar. "Take what you want," he said in a cracked voice. The invitation was too good to pass up. Wes grabbed a full bottle of fine liquor and went to the front door. Gawkers surrounded the doorway. With the others behind him, Wes felt compelled to state the facts to clear everyone's mind.

"We come to bring a murdering horse thief to justice. He chose to meet his Maker quicker than we intended." The statement appeared to be taken without anyone objecting to their acting as the law. With some approval of the killing muttered from the crowd, Wes gained confidence there would be no reprisal against him and his friends. He drew out a double eagle coin and flipped it into the air to land in the dust. "That should pay for the burial and any cleaning that needs to be done."

Nothing more needed to be said. Wes went to his horse, with Jim and Hugh expressing relief and satisfaction at the conclusion of the manhunt. Once he was mounted, Wes saw John leading Billy's horse from the hitch in front of saloon. "I ain't leaving it to be drawing no burial cart," John said. Wes thought it a good idea. He steered his horse out of town and they rode north.

They kept a steady pace, passing the bottle to each other with care so as not to waste a drop on the parched ground. Despite heading in a direction that might lead him to harm, Wes Hardin held no apprehension. He had fulfilled the wishes and demands of prominent men of high stature. He should be held in high regard for the tracking and killing of Bideno, and felt his previous indiscretions wouldn't be held against him. A few more swigs from the bottle reinforced his confidence in that notion.

Night fell, but they kept going with a specific destination in mind. Long after sundown, they came upon Newton, a town they all knew well.

They slowed their tired horses enough to gauge their location in the dark, and Jim shouted. "That's Tuttle's place over there."

They followed him until the dim light from lanterns guided them to the saloon and brothel that were under one roof.

They slid off their saddles and staggered near. Young John couldn't resist expressing his happiness at the day's events, and began firing through the windows. The blasts raised a scurry of activity inside. Wes joined in the fun, and sent a few stray shots through the wooden walls.

Jim and Hugh charged inside, Wes followed, picking up a lantern to be able to see any trouble in the darkness. An angry Perry Tuttle came from a back room. "What the hell are you doing here? Trying to get somebody killed?"

Wes, with alcohol fueling his words and temper, responded while placing his palm on the butt of the .44. "We just killed a murderer. We risked harm to ourselves so to make the prairie a safer place for folks like you. We're due a reward and we're taking it."

A feminine shout drew his attention to the left. Wes held out the lantern in time to view Hugh, having shed his pants to the boot tops, hiking a whore's night drape beyond her hips. Wes smiled and chuckled. It was good to see these men finally enjoy the rewards of their success. Similar shrieks and angered words came from other rooms where no doubt the same activity was taking place. Tuttle's loud complaints penetrated Wes's impending stupor.

"You have no right. You have to pay for these women."

Wes, in an impulse, drew and pointed the .44 straight at Tuttle. "We'll take what we want. And we'll leave when we want. And you will leave here and not pester us while we take our holiday with your whiskey and women."

The threat of a loaded revolver at his nose sent Tuttle running for the front door. Satisfied he wouldn't be interrupted anymore, Wes took the hand of a red-haired whore who stood with her back to the corner. Since all the rooms seemed taken, he towed her outside. He didn't have time for words or negotiations, and so he took a grip of her hair and smashed his lips onto hers. The warm texture of female lips, whether willing or not, sent blood pumping through all his parts. Without pause or regret, he yanked her head back and laid her down on the dust.

13

The locomotive slowly crept to a stop. Not much could be seen through the car window. With joints aching from the long, cold, then overly warm ride in the cramped confines, he took a few steps, then had a good stretch. After he'd exited the car and descended the landing steps, Rance Cash took his first full look at Abilene.

He remarked aloud, "So this is it. The famous Kansas cattle town."

"Smells like it."

He glanced over his shoulder at Penelope. "Think of it as the aroma of success, my dear."

"Been smelling that near all my life," she said. "Just cows dumping their waste, only not all in the same spot. Nothing successful about it. It's their nature."

Convinced his metaphor was lost on her, he decided to pursue the purpose of their mission. "Did Leslie mention where we could find her?" They proceeded under the broad depot awning to escape the beaming sun.

"No. She only said to come quick."

With little information, he decided to head into the heart of the town. They came around the depot to view the wooden skyline. "Wasn't she always mentioning a mother who ran a boardinghouse?" he asked. Penelope didn't answer.

Ignoring the signs of commerce advertising dry goods and clothing, he concentrated on the large sign on the roof of one building: THE PEARL. His mouth nearly watered.

A black carriage came rolling toward them, and he instantly remembered the remaining assets of his most recent larceny from Hattie McCown. He took the wallet from his coat and called to the driver of the hack. "Going to town." The driver didn't respond. Then Rance raised a single bill, which was enough to bring the carriage to a halt. Penelope stepped into the cab without hesitation while he talked to the driver. "Looking for a boardinghouse run by a woman and perhaps a young girl."

The driver shrugged. "Could be anyplace here." Recognizing the game, Rance drew another bill from the wallet and showed it to the driver, who suddenly became more specific. "There is a place on Cedar Street."

"Good. Let's start there." Rance climbed into the cab. The carriage began the trek through town. It rumbled on the wooden crossing over the rails, tossing Rance and Penelope from side to side. Once they had recovered to sit straight, the view of Abilene began to appear, and the two of them admired it from either side of the cab.

A theater sat on the corner of an intersection that the driver drove through. Then the cab slowed. Rance poked his head out the side to see dozens of men walking back and forth across the street. Recognizing the garb of trail hands, he looked at them as if they were walking pouches of money.

Once the driver moved through the pedestrians with profane shouts, the cab continued down the street. The Pearl Saloon came up on the right. It was a large establishment with broad doors. Laughter boomed from inside.

"Look at that," Penelope said, almost gasping. Rance looked out the left window as the cab passed by the front of another saloon. He couldn't see the name, but the two huge glass doors showed the prominence of the place. The boardwalk in front was filled to capacity with men wearing dusty hats and dusty clothes. Rance knew from his brief days in Texas that this was the look of hands fresh from the trail and likely newly paid. Time was a-wasting.

Once they passed by the long building, more saloons came into view, the smaller ones too numerous to keep track of, until the cab crossed another intersecting street. Now dozens of gambling houses appeared, with even more men walking the street, some with provocatively dressed prostitutes no doubt looking for a more discreet location to do business.

Rance watched as similar transactions occurred in broad daylight, and remarked to himself that such a town, where sin was so prevalent, was a gambler's dream. The cab stopped.

Rance got out, and the driver pointed to a small, modest two-story house. "This is the place."

Penelope left the cab and brushed off her clothes. The driver was about the shake the reins, but Rance had a final question. "That street back there — what's its name?"

The driver grinned. "Texas Street." He shook the reins and sped off in pursuit of another fare. Rance looked at Penelope with a bit of apprehension. The lean days in Denver and the long train trip had left them in less-than-stylish attire. Despite her modest brown skirt and blue blouse with white specks, she didn't appear too feminine because of her men's riding boots and floppy hat. A peek at himself revealed a wrinkled black coat to match the wrinkled black trousers. Still, despite all that, he knew he would be able to put his charm once again to work. He went up the steps and knocked on the door.

An older woman with gray strands streaming from the side of her hair answered. Rance immediately removed his hat and signaled Penelope to do the same. "Pardon us, dear lady. We're looking for a friend of ours."

"Rance!" The shout came from behind them. They turned to spot Les running along the street, her now reddish hair pinned in a bun. A yellow blouse and blue shirt matched the beaming smile on her face. She ran up the walk and gave him a firm hug. "I wasn't sure you got my wire." She took only a brief second, then went to Penelope. The two gals hadn't been close at first, but now appeared like long-lost sisters from their smiles and embraces.

"It was me that got the wire," said Penelope. "I knew where to find Rance and when we read it, we came as quick as we could."

The older lady stood dumbfounded until

Les made introductions. "Miss Maggie, these are the friends I told you about."

The woman didn't seem pleased. "Like the last one?"

Rance sensed the woman's displeasure, possibly from the predicament Jody was in now. "Dear lady," he said in his most respectful tone. "Please do not judge us by our appearance. We've come all the way from Denver and have not had time to freshen ourselves." He bobbed his head around her. "My, what a quaint abode. Charming in its furnishings. I can see why people of culture would seek it out instead of the brackish places we passed by."

The remarks seemed to make a dent in the woman's attitude. She opened the door wider and they all proceeded inside. With more glowing compliments, the old woman seemed to warm to their presence. As they stood in the drawing room, footsteps on the stairs drew everyone's attention. A tall slim woman of stylish dress descended the steps, her dark hair pinned beneath a broad-brimmed hat with lace. Rance dipped his head in respect. She didn't appear impressed.

"I'll be out for some air," she said, and before Rance could run to open the door, she proceeded to it on her own and left the house.

"She's a city woman from up north," said Miss Maggie to Les. "She's kind of standoffish, but she paid for the room for a week in advance this morning."

"And, if I may ask, what is the woman's name?"

Miss Maggie hesitated. "I don't often share information about my guests. Mr. . . ."

"Pardon me, dear lady. My name is Ransom B. Cash, and my companion here is —"

"Penelope Pleasant, ma'am," Penelope said, then shot Rance a look that said she could tend to her own affairs. Miss Maggie acknowledged her new houseguests with a polite but cold grin. She then looked at Rance.

"Her name is Beatrice LaFontaine. She says she's staying here to meet her husband. The two of them are going to California. That's all I know and need to know, Mr. Cash. I suggest you keep away from her."

At first, he didn't understand. Then the comment slammed into his consciousness. "Of course. I am a gentleman of the South."

Les and Penelope bit their tongues.

Miss Maggie looked toward her kitchen, then at Les. "I made soup for dinner. I have enough for your friends if they'd like some."

"How very gracious of you, ma'am. I accept on behalf of the two of us." Rance shot Penelope a look. "It would be a privilege to enjoy your cooking, I'm sure."

They all went to the table and sat, with Rance and Penelope side by side and Les across from them. The landlady doled out the soup, which, with its vegetables and broth, tasted better than fine cuts of meat. Les told the story of Jody's plight. A name Les mentioned stopped Rance as he was raising his spoon to his lips.

"Ben Thompson?" he asked.

Les looked at him with wide eyes. "Yes. You know him?"

Rance took a deep breath. "Only by reputation. He was a New Orleans ruffian near the riverfront and along the wharf. Stabbed a man to death. The story went that he was defending a woman's honor, but the rumor that the stabbing was over money owed holds more truth. I did hear he left for Texas soon after. I can't say I'm surprised a man of his ilk would end up in a place like this." He looked at the older woman. "Please, I meant no offense about your town, ma'am." He looked at Les. "Tell me more about this lawman."

"His name is J.B. Hickok, but they all call

142

him Wild Bill. I'm not sure why. He put Jody in jail over a fight with another fellow from Texas, but Jody said they didn't even fight and he wasn't the one trying to start one. The marshal didn't care and put him in jail anyway. Now, they say they don't know when they'll let him out. I heard this other fellow is a mean cuss." She looked at Miss Maggie. "Sorry." Les continued. "A man who has killed many other men, according to the deputy. They make it sound like they're protecting Jody, but I think they keep him there because he's from Texas."

"But they let you see Jody anytime you like?" Rance asked.

Les glanced at Miss Maggie. "Well, me and the deputy made friends in a way. When I bring Jody his meals, I bring along another plate for him, too. He's not as mean as the marshal. He's told me stories about him and the marshal from years ago. I think he doesn't mind me around so much."

"And where is this marshal when you're bribing his deputy with food?"

"Mostly playing cards at The Alamo."

Her answer startled Rance. "Alamo?"

"It's a saloon. The biggest in town. He plays most all day and has his deputies report to him there."

Rance shook his head. "Another Alamo

Saloon. I thought we left that in Texas."

"They think this is Texas," said Les in an ominous voice. "They think it is just as if we were in San Antonio. Jody said some of them were making threats to take Abilene over. He said they said it was on the old maps as part of Texas and that the federal government stole it."

Rance sat amused as he finished the soup and wiped his mouth with the napkin. "I wouldn't worry about that. Texans, as we know, think very highly of themselves and their state. Probably empty words brought about by drink." He rose from the chair. "Dear lady," he said, holding his hat out to Miss Maggie. "The soup was delicious. Thank you ever so much for your kindness." He took out his wallet. "I'd like to pay for a room for Miss Pleasant. Perhaps with a pitcher and basin where she can freshen herself."

"I ain't staying here," Penelope complained.

"Yes, you are," he replied in a firm voice.

"I'm going with you. To get Jody out."

Rance smiled as he laid the currency on the table. "I'm going to find the barber in this town." He rubbed the whiskers on his cheek and jaw. "I'm afraid I must look frightful." He looked at Les. "Don't worry.

144

If the man enjoys a game of cards, I'll learn his weaknesses. I'll have Jody out in a day." He dipped his head in respect to the landlady, then went to the door.

"Rance, wait," Les said. She ran up the stairs, while he waited, puzzled, at the door, until she returned. She handed him an object wrapped in a thin white towel. He flipped the edge and saw the Walker Colt revolver that tied so much of their history together. "Smith's. I'd know it in a pitch black room."

"I saw you weren't carrying one of your own. I got it from Jody's saddlebags before they had a chance to take it away." As Rance tested the balance of the .44-caliber handgun, Les continued. "There's a law against them, but if you look like the type needing to carry one, they don't bother you."

Rance winked at her. "I know just how to play it." Again he turned for the door, and when he had the knob in hand, Les stopped him again.

"One more thing," she said.

He turned around slightly, annoyed at her interruption. When he looked into her hazel eyes, he thought of all the times they'd shared on the way to Texas, their time in Texas, and the tragic path leaving it. He didn't have the heart to be mad at her. This little girl, near eighteen by now, had come to be more of a little sister to him despite the fact that he was ten years her senior and they were each from such different backgrounds. "What is it?" he asked.

"Keep the mustache."

He appreciated her advice and felt flattered at her attention. "Has a certain appeal, doesn't it? More sophistication perhaps?"

Les shook her head. "I can't say that. But it does make you look older and especially mean."

14

Rance stepped from the barbershop and felt his smooth cheeks and chin. Then he touched the trimmed mustache. He had never fancied one, but now it seemed appropriate. At least he thought so, for other reasons besides those mentioned by Les. A trimmed mustache was rumored to be attractive to women. An asset he might require being new in town.

The afternoon was wearing on. He needed to establish himself, and headed to the glass-door palace known as The Alamo Saloon. He strolled along the boardwalk to make the turn up Texas Street. The locals all continued their frivolity with abandon. From the look of the new cheap clothes, he figured those he passed on his way were new to town.

He himself had already visited a quality merchant by the name of Karatofsky. He'd bought a new coat of light brown wool and a derby to match. He'd talked himself out of the distinctive walking stick. There was too much to carry as it was. The merchant also had a used holster and a belt traded some months before. Rance made him a deal, and now was able to sport the .44 under his coat comfortably.

Arriving at the open glass doors, he took the customary deep breath he took whenever he was about to venture into dangerous territory. The next few minutes might not be the best he'd experienced to date, and might rival the worst, but they hadn't yet happened.

Through the doors he stepped. Violins played. The surprise halted him a few feet past the doorway. He viewed his image in an enormous mirror that lined the entire eastern wall across the building. An instant's observation told him the floor in front of him was filled with all sorts of games of chance. Mostly cards were played, but as he swung his head from one side to the other, he saw dice, roulette, faro, billiards, and even darts. Long wands harnessed to the ceiling spun with broad wound fans to create a mild but detectable breeze.

Perhaps most of all, he noticed civilized behavior, as if the patrons knew any rowdiness would be dealt with by expulsion. Once you were in this place, it seemed that being bounced would be the same as excommunication.

Inhaling the cooled air awakened him to the task he'd been summoned for. It took but a second to spot his mark. He hadn't had much description, but he saw the long curls of the man. Seated at the south table with his back to the wall and with a clear view of the door and all surroundings, the droopy-mustached gentleman was playing with two others. To approach might seem a threat, or at least rude for a newcomer to the town. Instead, Rance seated himself in a game with two freshly adorned cattle drivers.

Since his stake from Hattie McCown had grown thinner, he played the marks with small talk and compliments while taking advantage of their sloppy, amateurish play. During the game, he slipped a glance to the right, and coincidentally his mark did also. Their eyes met for an instant, but it was enough for each to acknowledge the other. The second passed, and each resumed their play with their opponents at their tables.

Despite the fact that he'd taken nearly fifty dollars from the two adolescents, they left in a pleasant manner. They'd learned not to risk hard-earned wages betting against a master card turner.

Two more joined the game, and Rance prepared for an afternoon of reaping rewards. A tall man with mustache, badge, and sidearm came to the table. He eyed Rance. "The marshal wants to talk to you."

Interpreting it as a summons without appeal, Rance excused himself from the game with the novices and went to the far south wall. While coming near, he observed the long curls that ended at the shoulders, the finely knotted necktie, the white silk shirt, the pronounced beak-shaped nose, and those blue eyes. An open chair was pulled from the table as the marshal invited him to sit. The other players quickly vacated the table. Rance took another breath and took the seat. No sooner did he settle himself than the questions began.

"Your name Cash?" the marshal inquired while looking at the cards.

There was no harm in confirming the name. "Proudly so."

While shuffling, the marshal angled his view at him. "I don't know what your game is, but by the next train, you'll be heading away from Abilene in whichever direction it's going." He finished the shuffle and slapped the deck on the table. "Or you'll be dead."

Rance exhaled and let his nature as a sportsman respond. "Hardly the welcome I expected. I understood my sort was welcome among the mass."

The marshal returned to staring at the cards. "Let me be clear. I don't know you and don't have a mind to change that. I do know we have an ordinance against carrying firearms in town of which you are in violation."

Rance turned to look at the rest of the patrons. It was then he appreciated the view of the broad mirror across the room, which provided reverse perspective on all occupants including himself. "I see no less than a dozen such offenders who aren't subjected to the same ordinance." He paused to eye the man. "Marshal."

"Not talking to them," came the stern reply. "You make plain your intentions, or you'll be routed from here fast. Believe me, Mr. Cash. I'm not inclined to bother with you."

Rance grinned confidently, more reflex than calculated ploy. "Believe me, Marshal. I am a man of peaceful intent."

Those blue eyes darted to Rance's buttoned coat. "If you're so peaceful, why you sporting that hogleg?"

The reply seemed natural. Rance glanced

at the deputy hovering over him, then at the pistol strapped to the hip. "I suppose the same as you." The response wasn't accepted well.

"I am a peace officer, Mr. Cash. My job is to enforce the law by any means necessary," he said with a curt tone. "These men carry their property to use on the trail. If I sense one of these cowboys may be about to use their property with reckless regard, then I take it from them and put them in jail. The ones in here don't show such regard. However, I am getting that sense about you."

Again, Rance eyed the deputy, who no doubt yearned for the chance to draw and commence considerable harm. Instead, Rance settled in the chair. He cast an eye at the deck on the table. He pointed his finger. "Let us come to an agreement, Marshal. I gauge you as a man used to risk. We both have something we wish to resolve. I think you know what that is, since you know my name." The blue-eyed stare didn't waiver, so Rance continued. "You have a friend of mine incarcerated in your jail —"

"He broke the law. Disturbed the peace. Owes a fine of fifty dollars."

"Fifty dollars?" The amount appeared ironic. "Well, since you have him locked up, he can't earn the money to pay the fine. So,

I propose another solution."

The cold frown pierced Rance's heart. He took another gulp and stayed with the play. "We'll cut the deck to see which of us gets his way. High card takes all. Release of the prisoner if I win. Fine paid if you do."

Hickok smirked. "It ain't the fine money I'm wanting."

Rance shrugged. "So be it," he said, allowing his gambling nature to get the better of him. "I lose, I surrender my weapon while in town." The offer didn't dent the steely resolve. The ante would have to be raised. "And I leave town peaceably?"

Again Hickok smirked. "I can have that without any risk."

Once more, Rance eyed the deputy, then turned to the marshal. He looked confidently right into those blue eyes, knowing there was the nature of a gambler lying not far from the steely surface. Rance returned the smirk. "Where's the sport in that?"

The dare was met with an ever so slight acceptance in the fluttering eyelids. Hickok picked up the deck. "There'll be no cutting of cards." He shuffled with precision. Unsure, Rance sat, not knowing if he'd misread the signs and would be hauled to the train depot by the collar. One second later, his hand was slid to him with each alternate card dealt by the marshal. "Draw poker. Winner takes all."

Pleased his ploy had worked, Rance wiped his cards from the table and viewed the hand. Five and six hearts, a club ace, a diamond three, and a spade seven. The wind escaped his lungs. A moment to observe Hickok's manner showed neither glee nor disappointment. A long-held tactic, the act of gab in hopes of diverting an opponent's attention, had known some success. Usually in games where the mark had a losing streak. However, with one hand to decide all, it didn't seem enough time to subtly affect the marshal's mind-set. He'd have to play this one straight.

"There's something you should know," said Hickok, looking only at the cards.

"And what might that be?" replied Rance while rearranging his cards in proper order. He noticed the marshal didn't do the same.

"Your friend, the one in jail. The one with the sweetheart that's there more than I am," he said with a nasal pitch. "He's there for his own good." Hickok paused, looking away from his hand for only a second to meet Rance's. "Cards?"

Now Rance sensed his ploy being used against him. Curiosity was a nuisance not easily dismissed, yet a more important subject demanded attention. How could one be in jail for his own good? Discard the non-suited cards along with Jody? He shook his head. He had to forget about Jody and concentrate on the play. Once he decided that, he withdrew the hearts together and placed them facedown. "Two." Instantly, he silently chided himself for giving up the only suited pair.

Hickok tossed three cards. "There's a man on the loose that will shoot your friend on sight. Dealer takes three."

Rance stopped his retrieval of the cards in mid-reach. After showing obvious concern, he resumed reaching and picked up the cards. The spade ace and club eight. "Exactly where is this man who intends on murdering my friend?"

Hickok drew three cards from the deck and squinted. After a moment, he slipped two in their desired order. "He's out on the prairie. Word has it, he's acting as the law and is looking to kill a Mexican accused of murdering a Texas trail boss."

Rance felt the marshal was about to call. With little in his hand, he needed a few more cards; however, with the stakes already set, he couldn't raise the pot. So, without reason, he ran his luck as far as it would take him. "I'll take three. Why don't you catch this killer since he's not a lawman and intends to kill another man?"

Hickok raised his eyebrows. "The changing of cards has passed."

Rance put on a surprised face. "I'm accustomed to more than one."

"I ain't."

The house rules had been set. He would need to change them. He reached inside his coat to the flinch of the deputy's right hand. Hickok raised his palm to ease the deputy's fear. Rance resumed his reach inside his coat and removed his wallet. "Since your jurisdiction doesn't include the seizing of my assets," he said while removing fresh greenbacks he'd won from the drovers, "we'll make it interesting and play for the fine." Hickok appeared irritated. Rance needed to goad the marshal more. "Are you game?"

Hickok sat stoic for several seconds, then took three cards from the deck. Rance placed fifty dollars in greenbacks in the center of the table. With confidence he could play this out, he again decided hastily and pulled the spade seven along with the diamond three. He'd just given away another suited card, and looked with some apprehension, only to find the heart ace and eight diamonds. He arranged his hand and thought to discover more of what he was really playing for. "You didn't answer my question."

Hickok studied the cards. Rance thought for a moment to repeat the original question, but his instinct to maintain silence proved correct. Hickok remembered the question.

"That's another matter outside my jurisdiction. They could be in the Indian Nations by now. Even if not, I can't say I'm going to risk any of my men to try to save a Mexican, guilty or not." Hickok fanned out his cards in his palm. "Let me ask you something, Cash. What's this kid in jail to you? You don't strike me as a man from Texas."

The inquiry was interesting more from a standpoint of why the marshal cared to know. A chill went through Rance's spine from feeling he was being played. He again looked at the hand and lost confidence in its victory. "Why do you say that?"

"I sense a bit more refinement. More a Southern man than one from Texas."

"Texas is not a Southern state?" Rance asked, peeking at Hickok, then his cards, hoping he'd guessed right.

"Texas," Hickok spoke, drawing the word out, "is an outlaw state." Rance sat embarrassed. At one time he'd held the same opinion. Hickok continued in a matter-of-fact voice. "Hell, it's how it started, ain't it? Mexico giving away cheap land only brings the murderers, beggars, and thieves. Once they were there, they took more than they were given and finally kicked the Mexicans out, claiming independence. Most of the heroic Texans were land swindlers and other criminals looking for safe haven from their own states." He paused. "With that ancestry, the same gets bred, only worse. But I am a Union man and agreeable to President Grant's call to 'let us have peace.' " Hickok curled a brow at Rance. "I call." He put his hand on the table. "Straight flush."

Rance looked at the hand and noticed an error. Then another. The third notice almost had him guffaw. "Marshal Hickok, it's always been my understanding of the game that a straight flush is a hand of five cards all in the same suit." The statement had Hickok look at the cards. Rance continued. "Instead of all diamonds or hearts, you have both. And at last count a seven does not follow a five nor does ten." Hickok squinted at his five cards lying on the table. "Marshal, you have three, four, five, seven, ten. The three and seven, those are hearts not diamonds."

Hickok looked at the window. "The light has never been good in this corner." He then sneered at Rance. "And I suppose you got better."

With the marshal's words about Texas still on his mind, Rance laid his cards down. "Full house. Aces over eights."

Hickok looked at the cards. His sneer became a snarl. "A man could get killed holding that hand." He paused as Rance gathered the deck. Hickok added, "Especially if he does it more than once."

Contemplating whether the warning was a threat or just friendly advice, Rance stacked the cards. A loud voice tore away his attention.

"Hello, J.B."

The greeting came from a tall youth appearing near twenty years old, wearing suspenders and a plain cotton shirt, which bulged at the brawny shoulders and arms. The dungarees also appeared soiled, and they and the weathered cap appeared to be from army service. He offered his hand. Hickok looked with surprise but little enjoyment at the reunion. "What the hell are you doing here?" he said, accepting the handshake.

" 'Spect more than that after two years." The young man took a chair by Hickok, placing the whiskey bottle he held on the table. The deputy eyed the man closely until he was waved away by the marshal. "Look at you. A lawman. Fancy duds, wearing a badge. Never thought I'd see the day."

Hickok looked at the deck of cards. "What brought you here?"

"Came into town with the supply train. Been hunting buff for the railroad and the army." The young man took a healthy swig from the bottle, then raised it. "Good money in it."

Hickok angled a view at him. "So you came into town to spend your wages."

The young man's face soured a bit. "Lost most of it trying to make it into more."

Hickok snickered and pointed at Rance. "To his kind?"

Feeling slighted by the remark, Rance was compelled to improve his image. He offered his hand across the table. "The name's Cash. Friends call me Rance. Pleasure to meet you."

The gesture was returned with a surly expression from the young man, who didn't accept Rance's hand. Instead, he returned his attention to Hickok. "Spent the last of what I had on this," he said while again raising the bottle.

"Where's that partner of yours?" asked Hickok.

The young man shrugged. "He went off mining in the mountains. Said he was too old to do young'ns' work. Haven't seen him in more than half a year." They both paused. Then Hickok took the bottle and filled his shot glass. He eyed the young man and raised the glass in toast.

"The only colored I hold respect for." They both downed liquor, with the young man taking more than a gulp. He swiped his mouth with his stained sleeve. Hickok once more eyed his young friend. "How long you staying?"

The man shook his head. "Maybe a day. Two at most. I got to get north to kill more buff. The army wants them all killed off to keep them off the tracks." The young man paused. "And I think they wouldn't mind starving out the Cheyenne."

Hickok nodded, a reaction either in agreement with the policy or acknowledging the strategy. "So, no doubt you're here at my table seeking a loan for a room or meal."

The young man hesitated before shaking his head. "No. I can get those easy enough. What I have" — he stopped to shoot a glance at Rance, then back at Hickok — "is the need."

The marshal chuckled. "I can understand. Been a long time out on the prairie, I guess." Hickok dug a finger in his vest pocket, then slapped two dollars on the table. "Quarter mile north of the tracks, you'll find the row. The one I recommend has a dogwood on the door. You can use my name."

"Beholding to you, J.B." With the coins in hand, the young man rose from the table without his bottle in haste to satisfy his business. As he took a step, the marshal stopped him while looking at the deck. "Clay. Once you're done slapping stones, I have a job for you."

Although puzzled, the young man nodded, then went to the open doorway.

Rance watched him leave The Alamo, then looked at Hickok. "Old friend of yours? Not much on manners, is he?"

The marshal looked at Rance, the sharp edge drawn about his face faded to a softer, more reflective pattern. "Took a liking to that kid about five years ago when he was a trooper. We rode together for a summer some years after, me and him and a colored." He nodded. "He is a mite impulsive. Tends not to make good first impressions." Rance thought Hickok and his friend were cut from the same cloth in that respect.

162

"But when you get to know him awhile, he is a good friend to have around. He'll fight with you in a room full of enemies . . . share his last ration of bread," Hickok said. "Strong as a bull, and sometimes thinks like one. Will do what you tell him. Harbors no fear for the unknown. And he is by far the best man to throw a knife I've ever seen. If you're in a fight, he's a good one to have along."

15

The wide path through the weeds was well worn. It was a helpful guide to his stumbling steps. A gentle grade had to be overcome; not an easy feat while sensing the effects of the oncoming stupor. This had happened many times before when he drank corn liquor. It sent him marching in short but certain steps at a faster than casual march.

The sun was nearly overhead. Without a cloud in the sky, its light bleached the ground, irritating his blurred vision. A small ache began to pound inside his forehead. What he needed was an afternoon nap, but first he wanted to catch some tail. It had been nearly a full season since he'd had a woman. The whiskey in his blood had sent the spike down his pants. He needed relief. He needed to be a man.

The path led to the first house on the right. With Hickok's instructions in mind, he squinted at the shaded door. A large flower with four sizable white petals and a green center was painted upon it. He stepped onto the porch and rapped on the wood.

A short lass, more girl than woman, opened the door. Clay didn't wait to be invited inside. The door shook with his kick. Her eyes widened as he spied her demure figure and work dress. "I come to do business."

The girl paused, eyes darting to the silent interior. "All the girls are asleep. We don't open for business until two o'clock."

The answer didn't satisfy the pulse between his legs. "I can't wait that long." Despite the fact that she was a female, nothing about her inspired any spark of lust in him. Too tired to seek other brothels down the way, he inhaled deeply to squelch the manly urge. "Go wake one of them up. A white one." He kept his eye on the girl. "A big pair of tits would be better." The order did nothing to change the girl's mood. Her eyes kept darting about as if ghosts were in the room. The longer she stalled for a reply, the bigger his urge bulged. In less than a minute, he'd consider her, willing or no, just to fulfill his need. A second thought took the idea from his head. He didn't know why.

"I'll hump him." The voice came from the main room. A taller pale-complected gal of slight frame, with long raven black hair beyond her shoulders, stood in a thin white sleeping gown. Her nose was near as big as her chest, which projected the cloth in a round feminine form, nipples pushing out the fabric. Like a steam engine with valves open, Clay strutted at her, each step building to a head. He took her by the hand, but she pulled him to the left and into a room where she shut the door. "Two dollars a poke. A suck is two bits more."

He shook his head and dug into his pocket, pulling out the two dollars. "I just want tail." He handed her the coins and watched while she inspected the genuine minting. Satisfied, she placed the coins on a bureau, turned her back to him, and hiked her gown above her hips. Leaning forward, she placed a hand on the wall for balance and widened her stance. Like a call to duty, he unbuttoned his pants and slid them down his thighs. Without pause, he pushed his stiff into her. The warmth was better than any buttered biscuit or blanket could ever offer. Natural instinct took over. Her initial groan sounded pained, but her voice didn't show it.

"You got a big one." A moment passed

while he thrust. "Are you with the drive that came in yesterday?"

The words slowed the concentration on the pleasure. "If I wanted a talk, I'd gone to the barber."

"Sorry," she responded.

His anger pushed him faster and deeper. She exhaled in short huffs keeping cadence with his motion, the last a mite quicker than the one before. Wood creaked beneath him and in front of her. Despite a lack of concern for her pain, the sound added to the tingle and set him at an even faster pace. He took a grip of her long hair like a rein with his left hand, wrapped his right arm around her waist, and stared at her bare rump. Male nature took control over his motion. The final relief buckled his knees and sent sparks, then an ease, throughout his body, even down to his toes.

After a deep breath, he slid out and took a step back. He pulled up his pants as she straightened and let her gown fall loose. While he threaded buttons, a pinch of remorse came over him as he regretted the harsh tone he'd taken with her neighborly inquiry. Despite her looks, she'd serviced his business as a woman should, and didn't deserve to be left with only what he'd spent. But he had no extra coins for a tip. A friendly reply might suffice.

"I come to see a friend that runs this town."

"Mayor McCoy?" she asked while pouring water into a basin.

"No. J.B. Hickok."

She turned with surprise. "Marshal Hickok? You're a friend of his?"

Clay nodded. "Rode with him a few years back. Was him that steered me here. I'll let him know it was a good turn. Might send some private business your way. What's your name?"

She soaked a rag in the basin. A small grin came across her lips. "They call me Sarah the Jew, due to the fact the other is from Kentucky and has blue eyes."

He didn't understand the entire meaning, but felt compelled to ask the obvious question. "And where you from?"

She lifted her gown slightly and took the rag to wipe the region beneath it, all the while staring at the wall. "My parents came from Rouen in France to Canada forty years ago." She faced him without a polite smile. "I come from everywhere in between."

Her response didn't interest him as much as her actions. "You got the crab?"

The smile returned. It was one an elder would present to an innocent child. "I am one of the few girls that clean to keep from getting it."

The simple answer satisfied him. He didn't want to know any more. He shook his drawers to settle his privates, then went to the door. "I'll tell the men you're a good whore. Get some gold coming your way." She continued to rub her parts, and he didn't want to watch. He left the room and went outside. Once on the porch, he stopped to take a deep breath and let the calm wash the boil out of his blood. To the left, that puny girl swept off the planks. She peered into his eyes with fear and disdain. He didn't have time to worry about what she thought. He needed a nap.

16

Penelope Patricia pleasant sat on the sitting room couch trying to be civil. Having been abandoned by Rance and Les in the boardinghouse, she tried to bide her time and wait for one of them to return and share some news. Never one with much patience, she could look to the floor or ceiling only so many times. When the woman owner of the house came from the kitchen, Penelope took a long breath. It'd been many years since she found herself awake indoors for this long.

"I made some corn muffins," the woman said.

Penelope forced a smile on her face. "Oh, no, thank you, ma'am. I ain't very hungry." Her worst fear was realized in the following seconds. The woman sat in a chair wanting to make conversation. Penelope searched for something to say. Something nice. "Fine house you have here." The woman eyed her posture, and Penelope adjusted her back upright, then remembered to push her knees together.

"Thank you," replied the woman. "It needs some fixing up yet after the flood two years ago. But this is my home." The woman cleared her throat. "Les tells me you're from Texas, too."

"Yes'um. My pa has a spread in Bexar County."

So," the woman started slowly, "you know the man Les brought with her?"

The question brought an idea to mind. "Jody Barnes? Yes'um, I grew up very near where his folks have a spread." Even though she'd not been timid about finding her own way, she hadn't given thought to finding Jody herself.

"What kind of man is he?"

The plain inquiry swirled around in her mind. "Jody?" She had to align her thoughts. "Jody is a right good man. He respects his ma and pa, he's not one to drink too much, keeps his money hid," she stated, then trailed off in panic. Penelope was not easy with proper manners, and feared blurting out some of Jody's more manly traits. Then, the most certain one appeared in her mind. "He loves Les. I know it. I saw the two of them give each other the eye."

The words didn't appear to comfort the older woman. "I suppose. I still can't forgive her for leaving me here alone."

Penelope nodded. "She told me about that." She paused. "I guess there's a time in every gal's life when you got to know what else there is besides what you seen already." Her clumsy comment served to bring a confused expression to the woman's face.

After a few moments, the woman grinned at Penelope. "Tell me about you."

It was something she never could talk about. There were too many dark times in her life. Most of those she blocked from her memory, but the worst one she couldn't erase from her mind. She took a breath, then tried to stay polite and offered an easy reply. "Just a gal from Texas. That's all." Fearing more details would be asked for, Penelope rose from the couch. "If you don't mind, ma'am, I think I'm going to see if I can find Jody." Before the woman responded, Penelope walked to the door. "Don't you worry about me. Been in a few cow towns. I can find my way." She opened the door and left with only a quick parting word. "Thank you for the offer of the biscuits." She closed the door behind her and quickly got to the street. She took her first deep breath in more than three minutes. Her hands shook. The idea of telling someone about herself gave her the shakes worse than any growl from a coyote.

The hour Rance spent across the table from Hickok, the fellow gambler, appeared to be going well. Brief exchanges of experiences playing cards lightened the previous heavy mood. With some small reservations, Rance thought the two could be friends. Then, Hickok changed the subject.

"So, tell me about the events in Fort Worth."

Rance paused for a single second, knowing full well what was inferred. Two years ago, his only experience in the Texas trail town was marred when he engaged in gunplay with a gentleman assassin named Colton Schuyler. Rance was following new acquaintances, including Les and Jody, to Texas when they stopped to rest. It was in the White Elephant Saloon that Rance again met up with the gunman Schuyler, who'd been commissioned to kill Rance for indignities against railroad tycoon Harlan Schaefer. Rance remembered the situation with Schaefer differently than the stories would have it, yet it made him Schuyler's target. Only a fortunate misfire from a prized but unreliable pepperbox saved

Rance's life and ended Schuyler's.

"I don't know what you mean."

Hickok smirked. "I think you do."

If he was to continue this uneasy alliance with the marshal, Rance sensed he had to abandon acting coy. "Your informants must be working day and night." The compliment got a nod from Hickok. "Yes, the likely story you heard is true. But it was a clear case of self-defense. There were no charges filed."

"I heard there was no one there authorized to file them," Hickok remarked. "I knew Colton Schuyler." The statement disturbed Rance. Perhaps, he'd been drawn into some vendetta to be settled by the top lawman in Abilene. Hickok continued. "I met him in Cincinnati while on the river. Was a pleasant fellow to me. Knew his card play well."

"That was his spiderweb. I nearly fell into it myself."

The marshal's face still held the same smirk. "I hold no grudge. What happens between two men no kin to me, outside my purview, I cannot take issue with."

Rance sat relieved and inhaled. "I appreciate your understanding."

"But," Hickok injected, "that does not extend inside the city limits." He pointed at the Walker Colt inside Rance's coat. "I shouldn't allow you about with that weapon.

But I could make an exception."

The offer was too intriguing not to ask. "What conditions do you propose?"

The marshal paused to clear his throat and lean closer to Rance's ear. "First would be your oath to uphold and support allegiance to the law and order of this town." The demand didn't alarm Rance, and so he nodded. "Next, you frequent the Bull's Head and act as yourself without divulging our conversation. You see, I know Thompson is actively recruiting assassins to do me in. Phil Coe is nothing more than a fat braggart without sand in his drawers, but Thompson is a man I'd as soon not let out of my sight. Do you understand my meaning?"

Rance knew the reputation of Thompson, and had to concur with Hickok's assessment. "I believe I do. As long as I can go anyplace in the town, and that my friend is eventually released from your jail."

"I have no quarrel with that."

As soon as Hickok answered, the deputy once again approached the table. Concern was etched across his face. "Some more are charging the town." The marshal exhaled in a huff through that crooked nose. He rose from the table and grabbed his hat.

"You'll have to excuse me. Seems more of

these Texas cowboys appear intent to put their stamp on Abilene by driving cattle through the streets. We'll continue this another time." Hickok put on his broad curved-brim hat and went toward the door, resecuring both pistols in his belt. The deputy followed.

Rance left the table as well. The mood of the place wasn't conducive to starting another poker game. As he exited through the open doorway, he saw Hickok had stopped in the street to meet with the friend Rance had met at the table earlier. Thinking nothing of it, Rance walked toward the intersection of Cedar and Texas Streets until he saw Penelope standing alone under an awning.

"Taking in the sights?" he asked in jest as he approached. However, she never looked at him, instead keeping her focus on the street. Rance followed her line of view to see Hickok and his friend.

"Who's he?" Penelope asked with a little awe.

"That is Marshal Hickok. Wild Bill, he is known as. I just got through talking to him. I believe I struck an accord with him about Jody. But I'll have to —"

"No," she said with a firmer tone. "Who is that other man?"

Rance had never heard this girl ever sound so interested in any male. He sensed a certain captivation, not only from her voice, but from her motionless stance. "That's one of Hickok's friends. The only name I know is Clay." Again, Rance looked into her thoughtful eyes, which never turned to him. Once more, he took a long look at the tall, muscular brute standing in front of Hickok. "Beware of him, my dear. I think he may not be of kind demeanor. All I know is he is or was with the army, and stumbled into town in order to borrow enough to frequent one of the local brothels. I doubt he's a gentleman."

As Hickok and Clay parted, each heading in a different direction, Penelope finally looked at Rance. "I ain't one neither."

He watched as she strolled aimlessly down the boardwalks from one establishment to another, without doubt going in the same direction as the buffalo hunter. Rance knew by the obvious look in her eye that she'd been smitten by looks alone. However, he hadn't the time to chaperone her. He'd been assigned a task as a spy for the greater good of the town. It would allow him to visit another of the numerous gambling houses in order to gather information, and perhaps fill his pockets.

■ ■ ■ ■

Penelope kept the stranger in view as he walked with an occasional stagger. She wasn't sure what it was about him, but she'd not recalled seeing such a big piece of man all in the same skin. His shoulders were wide, his arms as big as thighs, he was smooth at the waist, and the back end of his trousers was hard to ignore.

More than once during her walk, she tried reminding herself she'd seen plenty of attractive men with a heap more promise shown in their clothes and jewelry who'd made a play for her. Every time she had refused, sometimes giving them a hefty shove. She wondered, if not that kind of man, what kind did she seek? Relying on the intuition she'd always been told belonged inside a woman's soul, that one day she'd know and couldn't refuse interest, she found herself now, at least a half mile into a town she knew nothing about, crisscrossing streets and passing unfamiliar people in pursuit of a chance to see up close the man she could not get out of her mind.

He made his way to a hardware store. The bright sunlight shone full on his broad back. With him stopped outside the store, she gathered the gumption to cross the street and attempted to get closer. Dodging the wild riders put her on the other side sooner than she'd planned and not so subtly. All on the boardwalk noticed her arrival.

He talked to a clerk in an apron. She pretended an interest in the barrel of potatoes while watching him. He cringed and blew out a long breath almost like he was pained from an injury. The clerk went into the store. She took a step nearer looking for a bandage or maybe a sling. Instead, she focused on his rugged face. But he glanced up at her approach, and she renewed her interest in the potatoes. He took a pouch from his pocket and began rolling a smoke. Not sure what to do next, she once more had to remind herself she'd never been a scared little girl in her life, and although her stomach fluttered like never before, she got close enough to him to start a conversation just as the clerk brought two buckets of whitewash.

"Got another smoke for a friend?" she asked. He darted his eyes at her for an instant. She persisted to get him to talk. "Got some painting to do?"

He glared at her. His features appeared strained. The face was reddened as most men's, but his sky blue eyes captured her attention despite their glassy look. "Who are you?" he mumbled. At first, she wanted to retreat from the snarled reply. However, she'd come this far. Her next thought was that he was somehow touched in the head. It would be such a waste of male attractiveness if he was an imbecile.

Since he'd asked, she decided to introduce herself, and held out her hand in a masculine manner. "Penelope Pleasant. Pleased to meet you."

He looked at her hand with a queer eye. He then stared at her from head to toe. "You a woman?"

She retracted the hand. His inquiry touched a nerve. Her true nature burst through. "Ever seen a man with tits like mine?"

Usually when she spoke bluntly at someone, they shied from any reply and left her alone. She didn't want that, not just now, and feared he would shoo her away. Instead, he looked at the clerk, then at her, and snickered at her vulgar remark and brought his attention to her bust. "You do have a healthy pair at that." The clerk quickly took the money and scurried back into the store.

Penelope didn't know what she wanted to do next. In the past, if a man insulted her, she didn't hesitate to throw a fist at his jaw, but in this case, she accepted what she deserved. After a reflective breath, she looked at him as if to apologize, but she couldn't bring herself to speak the words. "So, you never did answer me."

Again, he responded with a pained expression. "No, I didn't." He bent to lift the buckets. "Usually don't give it out to women looking to put sticks in their mouths." Penelope ignored the inference. At least he spoke to her.

"Need any help?" she asked before she thought. That he would ask a gal to lift a heavy weight wasn't likely. However, he released the handles and stood up straight. For several moments, he gauged her with a raised brow, like someone would judge a horse. As he circled about, he stopped at the potato barrel. Appearing in a thoughtful mood, he picked up a large one and bit into it.

"Who are you again?" he asked while chomping the spud.

She didn't care for being stared at like a horse. "Said my name once," she replied with spite.

He nodded and spoke with pale bits of potato spilling from his lips. "Penelope." He kept nodding as he eyed her again with a sly grin. Then his jaw firmed. "Well, Penel-

181

ope, I can tote my own loads without the help of a girl, no matter how tall and healthy she stands, now matter how pretty the face, or blond the hair, or" — he again looked at her front — "how big the tits. Don't know why you think you should know what I'm painting, but it's no concern of yours. And if it were, I'd be sure to mention —"

Loud voices and cheers came from behind him. A drover with a bottle in hand came first, followed by a procession of folks surrounding one man. The drover came near to Penelope and extended his hand in an attempt to grab at her hip. She swatted it away and thought to throw a fist as she was used to, but Clay shoved the drover to the ground.

The drunk scowled at Clay. "Be watching, mister. I'm a friend of Wes Hardin," he said, pointing at the man in the center of the mass. "He's a hero and don't take to his friends being roughed."

Clay only gave a single eye to the man pointed out as Hardin. "Don't give a damn who he is." Clay motioned at Penelope. "That's a woman and you ain't going to grope at her in front of me." The angered voices drew attention from the crowd. The one referred to as Hardin looked at Clay. Hardin was a tall man, but Penelope figured

Clay was even taller. The next few seconds would determine if there was going to be a scrap, but the two men glared at the other like angry dogs. After a second. Hardin helped his friend off the dirt, then looked at Penelope. He tipped his hat.

"Sorry for Hugh here, miss. Didn't mean to offend your man."

"I ain't her man," Clay quickly proclaimed. A sting went through Penelope at the loud response. "I just don't take to the roughing of women." Clay asserted his view directly to Hardin.

Hardin released Hugh and took a step closer. Clay flung the spud to the side. Again, these two dogs had to test each other. It was clear to see that Hardin carried a pair of pistols in a single hip holster, but Clay didn't back away. After the two men stood nose to nose, it was Hardin who grinned.

"Let's not fight, friend. I'm in a happy mood and want to keep it that way."

Another voice came from the crowd. "Wes here just killed the Mexican bandit that murdered Billy Cohron. We're all heading to the Bull's Head to celebrate."

"Come with us," Hardin invited. "I'll buy you a drink."

Clay didn't smile. "Already had my fill for

the day."

In an instant, Penelope realized why he appeared so dazed. Hardin nodded acceptance of the answer and again tipped his hat at her. She watched the procession keep marching its way toward Texas Street. When she turned around, Clay had a bucket in each hand. She had to say something, but gratitude didn't slide easily from her tongue. She darted her eyes to the buckets, and Clay noticed.

"No," he sternly spoke. "You can't help." She looked into his blue eyes. "And I ain't your man."

His firm statement washed all gratitude from her mind. "Never said you was. And I can take care of myself."

The remark again brought a scoffing smile from him. "Oh, I bet you can. So, why don't you take care back to your home or wherever it is you stay and keep clear of me and what I'm doing." He stepped around her and walked in the opposite direction from where the procession was going. In a short time, he turned a corner and was gone from sight.

17

Through the maze of heads and shoulders on the boardwalks, Rance turned west at the corner of Cedar and Texas and continued until he saw the bars of a stone building. Recognizing it as the jail, he gave instant thought to visiting the prisoner, but didn't since he knew he wouldn't be welcomed. Jody and he never seemed to be close and he didn't want to worsen the situation. Instead, he looked across the street at the Bull's Head Saloon. Struck by its sign, he strayed into the shadows projected by the dipping sun and stared at the image of a bovine with an enormously protruding phallus. The statement made was undeniable. No wonder these Texans thought this town belonged to them, with such a brazen display.

Nevertheless, he continued undeterred, and entered the saloon to find a raucous celebration. Cheers and shouts came from the dozens crowded around the bar and gaming tables. The place was one quarter the size of The Alamo Saloon and had not near the same class of clientele. Rance slipped his way through the crowd, and sought a quiet corner to conduct his business and perhaps gather information. His previous visits to the Pearl and the Elkhorn proved unsuccessful in gaining intelligence on what to expect and how to get a private conversation with Ben Thompson. However, with the premises jammed with drunken drovers, he had to squeeze into a spot at the bar. The stench of spilled whiskey and alcohol breath permeated the entire interior. Had he not agreed to do this job for Hickok, he would have sought more pleasant surroundings.

The drunken drover whose shoulder pushed at his soon took flight like a bird, and the next patron shoved his way in. This young man didn't appear to be a drover, and looked like a teenager, though dressed for the same business as Rance. Since the opportunity to move about was limited, Rance took the opportunity to strike up an acquaintance and offered his hand. "Rance Cash."

The gesture was met with courtesy. "Luke Short."

"Tell me, Luke," said Rance in an above-normal voice to be heard. "How does one work a game in here?"

Luke shook his head. "You can't. Ben and Phil don't allow no cardsharping going on unless it's by their men. Even the girls in back work for them direct. They don't trust nobody. They figure it's their place and they should keep all the money made here." He looked about. "They're not hurting for business."

It made sense to Rance. The operation appeared bursting with business. Luke's insight intrigued Rance. "How do you know all this?"

"I been here since last summer. I came up from Texas to get what I could. Haven't done too bad, but not what I thought."

His matter-of-fact speech encouraged Rance to inquire, "Do you know Ben Thompson?"

Luke nodded. "I met him. Good fellow. Loyal to Texans as you can see." As Luke angled his shoulders to further his point, Rance caught sight of the pistol in a hip holster.

"Have need to use that here?" he asked.

Luke stared him straight in the eye. "Haven't we all?"

The terse reply meant there was no more

need to ask about his past involvement with violence. Even Rance never took pride in his own gun exploits, and he knew when to take the hint. However, this Texan seemed not like the others. Even though he might have killed in the past, he didn't strike Rance as someone to be feared. An immediate change of subject was needed, though. "You're from Texas? Have you ever been to the White Elephant Saloon in Fort Worth?"

Luke shook his head. "Where?"

"Fort Worth. White Elephant. You'd like it there."

Luke continued to shake his head. "Have no plans on returning to Texas."

Once more, Rance felt he'd stumbled on a subject that needed to be dropped. Perhaps for the same reason that Luke didn't want to talk about the weapon he carried. However, Rance didn't want to waste any more time and pay any more exploitative prices for watered-down green whiskey. Yet the clamor among the crowd had his attention. "What's the occasion in here?"

Luke leaned closer, and Rance repeated the question. Then Luke answered with a loud voice. "Wes Hardin killed Juan Bideno."

The names were lost on Rance. "Who killed who?"

"Wes Hardin," Luke said again. "A real tough hombre, as we say down in Texas. Probably killed three dozen men and ain't much older than me. Good to be around if he likes you. Not so much if he don't."

Rance nodded. "Understood. Which one is he?"

Luke pointed to a young man with a broad white hat and cheap dress coat over dirty trousers. A dumbfounded expression was on his face, usually meaning that young Wes had had a good share of liquor this day. Under the coat, the ever-present pistols were easily seen. Rance wondered why Hickok bothered to have a law about firearms when most of the population carried them. Having easily spotted Hardin, Rance was next curious about the man he'd come to see. "Where's Ben Thompson?"

With an angled thumb, Luke pointed at the man at the end of the bar. In a fine tailored frock coat, white shirt, and string tie, Ben Thompson stood smoking a cigar. Thinly haired on top, he wore a thick mustache of the same fair color as his hair. His attention was focused on the celebration and all the money his place was soaking up.

"I'd like to meet him," Rance said, hoping Luke would introduce them.

Instead, Luke shook his head. "Not much chance of that happening. Not tonight. But you can try."

Rance thought better of it and took the advice. The distraction of the crowd proved too much to overcome. Instead, Rance stayed at the bar and observed the operation. The poker tables collected a steady take, along with the faro dealer. It did present a challenge to break into a single game, but he stood content to watch. To watch and learn.

Hickok stood with shotgun firmly in both hands. Flanked on each side by Tom Carson and James McDonald, he watched as the few drovers stirred their longhorns to a trot. Knowing they would be too much to stop at the city limits, he instead chose to meet them on the range a mile southwest of town. When they neared, he presented the twin barrels at the two point riders who rode ahead of the herd.

"Just who the hell are you?" asked one of the young kids with irritation.

"The name is J.B. Hickok. I'm the town marshal of Abilene. And I hereby order you to stop these cattle and herd them in this prairie until they can be orderly loaded into the pens."

The kid scoffed. "I never heard of no J.B. Hickok, and frankly don't give a damn what you say. We're driving to Abilene and have been since the first of April, and we're going to go where we want and put our steers where we want."

As the two kids laughed, Hickok pointed the barrels at them. "I arrest you for contempt of the law. Tom, take them in."

The kid with the disrespectful mouth reached for the pistol in his belt. Hickok cocked the hammers of the shotgun. "Hold on, sonny. You don't want to make a bigger mistake."

"To hell with you, Mr. Marshal. I was told Abilene was a free town. We could do what we wanted."

"Not no more. Hasn't been that way for two years and not going to be again."

"So," the kid said, releasing the gun from his belt and holding his hands high. "What are you to do, Marshal Hickok? Shoot me?"

Hickok didn't want any blood on his hands, and it would be quite an undertaking to arrest thirty drovers. Even if he could, it would require the three of them to round the drovers up, and then he didn't have space for them all. Instead, he appealed to their need to complete their hard work. He drew a matchstick from his coat and put it under his thumb. "Do as I as order and I'll allow you and your friends to enjoy yourselves in town. Otherwise, I light this prairie grass afire and you can gather your herd from here to Nebraska."

The threat did what was intended. The kid waved to the others to slow the cattle to a walk. "We'll bed here for the night," he shouted. He then turned his attention back to Hickok. "If that's all right with you?"

Hickok nodded, satisfied the confrontation had avoided bloodshed. "Seems reasonable to me. Surrender your weapons to the establishments and you'll have no trouble from the law." A train whistle drew the attention of all. Usually, the cars from the west came in empty in order to load cattle unencumbered with other cargo. Yet these cars, running on the distant tracks, were filled with animals and equipment clearly visible on the flatcars. "What the devil is that?" he wondered aloud.

"Circus," McDonald plainly stated.

"What?" Hickok asked confused.

"It's a circus, J.B. They were here the year before. They set up just outside of town. They do tricks, bring some strange critters, and put on a show."

"How come I don't know about this?"

McDonald shrugged. "I guess they come

when they want."

The two kid drovers laughed. "I guess not all feel a need to square matters with you, Mr. Marshal."

The smart remark sent Hickok back to his horse to learn more about this circus. "I'll see you in Abilene, sonny. And it better not be with that iron in your belt."

Rance entered the boardinghouse, removing his hat and creeping in like a child past curfew. However, his presence became noticed by all as they sat at the dinner table. Amends had to be made. "Forgive me, dear lady," he said, addressing the landlady at the end of the table. Slowly, he entered the main room. "I apologize for my tardiness." Les and Penelope sat across from each other and appeared unimpressed with his sincerity. The other boarder, the woman from the north, sat next to Les. She was dressed in a darker blouse than she had worn out that morning, and the matching ear bobs were eye-catching.

Les rose from the table. "You can have my seat. I'm taking Jody some supper." The statement brought Penelope out of her chair.

"I'll go with you. Been meaning to see him."

"I thought you were going to see him this afternoon," said the landlady. Rance saw the puzzled faces on all the women, especially Penelope, who was stuck for an answer. He couldn't resist.

"She must have been looking for that person she thought she knew, isn't that it, Penelope?"

The tall blond girl immediately nodded at the provided alibi. "That's a fact."

He wasn't going to let her off so easy. "And did you find that person?"

Again, all eyes were on Penelope, even those of Les, who returned to the room with a cloth-covered basket. "I did," Penelope said. "But it turned out not to be the person I thought." She looked Rance in the eye. He cocked his head and arched a brow.

"I thought that might be the case." With the rest of the room confused at the private conversation, Les resumed her walk to the door. Penelope followed.

"Mr. Cash, are you going with them? I don't think two women should be out after dark. Not in Abilene. Not anymore." The landlady's question became more of an order. Both the girls looked at him. Then Penelope looked at the landlady.

"Don't fret, ma'am. I been around plenty of trail hands after dark." Penelope's statement seemed inappropriate. Again, Rance felt a need to explain.

"She means, dear lady, that she has been in the company of men at work as she was," he said. But he didn't feel right about how he'd ended, and so he tried to add something. "At their business." Now Penelope took exception to the inference. Once more he tried. "Doing her duties with them." A look of horror came over the faces of the landlady and the other woman boarder. He needed one word, maybe two, to stop the damage to all reputations involved. "Herding cattle." The tension eased and all of them, including Rance, took in a long breath.

"Like I said," Penelope added, "we really don't need his help. We'll be fine."

"Don't you also want to see your friend, Mr. Cash?" asked the woman boarder. He noticed the band on her left ring finger.

"Mrs. LaFontaine?" he began. She nodded. "I believe Jody would much prefer to see them before he sees me. I don't wish to spoil the mood." He turned to the two girls at the door. "But you should take care. There is quite a celebration going on at the Bull's Head."

"Wouldn't be the first time," said Les as she opened the door. Then the two of them were gone.

With the room silent for several seconds, the landlady spoke. "You're welcome to a plate, Mr. Cash."

He smiled. "Very gracious of you. However, I don't seem to have much of an appetite at the moment. Perhaps I could join you two lovely ladies in conversation." He sat in Penelope's chair across from the attractive brunette. "I understand you come from the north, Mrs. LaFontaine?"

She put down her napkin. "Yes. From Chicago actually."

"Chicago," he repeated with respect. "I've not enjoyed a stay there. But I've heard it is very large. Many industries, I've heard, are there. Am I right?" he asked in order to learn more about her. She did not seem eager to share information.

"Yes, you could say. It is a port of entry for much of the commerce in the center part of the nation." She looked him in the eye. "What business are you in, Mr. Cash?"

He offered a smug grin. "I'm a sportsman, ma'am." His anticipation of interest didn't reflect on her face.

"Then you're a gambler."

Her tone held more accusation than intrigue. "Yes, it is true I am in the profession of games of chance," he said defensively. "But I prefer to distinguish myself from the rabble that infests the saloons."

"How so?" Her question caught him off guard. Most women usually accepted his statement. However, most women usually were fascinated with his manner and charm, unlike this woman. "I'm a gentleman, Mrs. LaFontaine. I allow my skill at the game to give me an advantage, not sleight of hand."

The landlady took her plate and the brunette's. With the table clear, the dark-haired beauty clasped her hands and placed her elbows on the table, normally the posture of one who wished to learn more about him and would in short time be in a prone position. But he wasn't getting his hopes too high.

"You're a gentleman from where, Mr. Cash?"

"New Orleans originally. However, I've been traveling through the West for several years now. Colorado as of late."

"And how do you know Mrs. Turnbow's daughter?"

The line of questions seemed more suited to a lawyer. "I accompanied her and Jody and another man to Texas two years ago. When I happened upon Les, I feared she needed my help, and so I went along." It was not exactly the truth, and he hoped the subject would be dropped. He was wrong.

"How chivalrous. I can only assume she felt safe under your protection." He smiled and bobbed his head in modesty until she continued. "I'll have to ask her when I see her again." Now, the brunette had the smug grin as his faded. Sensing it was his turn to inquire of her past, the woman proved too clever to allow him the opportunity. She looked at the landlady. "Thank you for the meal, Mrs. Turnbow. It was very good." She looked at both of them as she stood. "If you don't mind, I think I'll retire to my room. I have some correspondence to catch up on."

Rance stood in respect. "Good evening, Mrs. LaFontaine. Perhaps we'll continue our conversation tomorrow."

She glanced at him as she went to the stairs. "Perhaps, Mr. Cash. But I doubt it."

Disturbed at not being informed about the arrival of the circus, Hickok rode to the spot north of the tracks where man and beast were debarking and the tents were being assembled. He went from one of the odd-looking workers to another in search of the boss of the outfit. Since only a few spoke English, he mostly followed pointed fingers until he saw an already standing tent. He knocked on a support pole. A short woman with hair pulled in a bun moved the flap and came outside.

"Can I help you?" she asked.

Struck dumb for an instant, Hickok finally remembered his manners and removed his hat. "Evening, ma'am. I'm looking for whoever is in charge around here."

"Why that would be me, sir." She extended her hand. "Agnes Lake Thatcher."

It took him a moment before he gently accepted her handshake. "J.B. Hickok, ma'am. Marshal of Abilene." Despite the darkness, he noticed her gazing at him, although she had to be more than a few years older than he was. He wasn't comfortable with it, and all the fluster he'd arrived with had vanished from his mind.

"How can I help you, Mr. Hickok? If it's tickets to the performances, I'd be privileged to provide you with however many you need — complimentary, of course."

It took another moment before he could answer. "Kind of you, ma'am. But —"

"Please, call me Agnes, Marshal."

This woman's eyes glistened. Not finding much to complain about, he decided to make her acquaintance even though she wasn't the type of woman he normally sought. "I will if you insist," he said. She nodded, which made him continue. "I

199

wasn't expecting a circus in town, and thought I'd be neighborly and come and meet you folks. I must warn you, there are some characters who frequent Abilene this time of year who aren't always well behaved."

She smiled. "Oh, I am aware of the wild sort that these towns attract. It's that type of audience we do best with. The ones who have toiled so hard, as miners, loggers, and even cattle drivers, who seek more forms of entertainment" — she paused, her eyes dipping away for a moment — "than those some see as sinful."

"There are those by the dozen here," he replied with a nod.

"Hickok," she said aloud. "I've heard that name. Tell me where I know it from."

"I guess a name travels faster in some parts than the man who carries it."

An expression of discovery came over her face and she shook her finger at him. "I know now. I have heard the name Hickok used to describe the legendary frontiersman Wild Bill Hickok. Might you be the same?"

He was humbled by the flattery. "That is a moniker I am known by also."

"Of course," she said. "I've heard the name used in circles that include Buffalo Bill. I understand he is a friend of yours."

The association with Bill Cody wasn't one Hickok usually bragged about. Cody was a showman before he ever set foot on a stage. One who sought the glamour of attention, he had started a traveling exhibition of Western life and trick shooting, and had invited Hickok, who he only knew through General Custer in their scouting days, to join him. However, the flashy Cody, who needed no one other than himself to promote himself, wasn't the sort of person Hickok usually called a friend. Still, this woman thought well of him, and Hickok didn't want to disappoint her.

"I know him."

"Then I stand in the company of greatness. Please, let me show you about. I know the troupe would appreciate meeting such a legend as Wild Bill Hickok."

He didn't want to offend her and when he held up his hand to decline, he saw a spotted cat nearby on his left. Instinct had him palm a fifty-one, but when he saw a man walking next to the animal with a leash, he eased his grip. "Never seen a leopard before. And not walked like a dog."

She giggled. "Please forgive me, Bill. But that isn't a leopard. It's a cheetah. From the African plain. The fastest animal on earth."

He looked at the thin-boned cat as it

passed and shook his head, then arched a brow at her. "Faster than a horse?"

"Twice as fast," she replied. "Some English folk who have traveled there attest that a cheetah can outrun the fleetest of antelope. That is how it kills. Pure speed."

He found common ground in the statement. "Same can be said for those carrying firearms, Agnes." He looked at her and smiled. "And Bill is not my real name. I was named James. James Butler. Bill is just the name the dime novels remembered."

She smiled. "Well, James, I hope you will come by the show tomorrow night. I would like to see you in the audience."

"I will consider it. I must say my duties as chief peace officer will come first." He nodded to her before putting on his hat. "I bid you a good evening." He turned away and headed back to the hack, not knowing for sure exactly why he'd come initially. However, if ever he could judge women, he knew this one had the eyes for him.

Les led the way on the boardwalk. Penelope found herself bumping shoulders with cowpokes who gave her peculiar looks when she didn't shy away from their leers. Despite the delays, they arrived at the jail. As Les grabbed the doorknob, Penelope found her eyes wandering, and saw the sign above the Bull's Head. She laughed.

"Look at the peg on that one," she said aloud. The comment wasn't welcome to Les.

"Try not to run your filthy mouth in here." The shamed response wasn't offending. Penelope looked at Les and nodded in agreement. They entered the jail.

The dim light didn't stop Les. She proceeded to stop at the desk and look down the jail hall. Penelope leaned around to have a look also. The cell door was wide open, and she saw the armed deputy and Jody playing checkers. The sight of her friend had Penelope walk to the cell. The deputy didn't appear alarmed.

"Jody," she said in greeting. The two friends embraced each other. He felt a bit thin, but looked in good health. "Good to see you."

"How is it you're here?" he asked, puzzled but with his ever-present smile.

"We came, me and Rance, as soon as I got the wire from Les. I couldn't let a friend stay in jail." As soon as she said it, she looked at the deputy, a short stocky fellow with a well-worn hat. He didn't seem to take offense. Instead, he left the two friends alone. Another moment went by, and Les came to the cell door with the basket. Penelope felt like an intruder.

"I brought some fresh pie," said Les. She looked at Jody, who didn't seem pleased.

"Rance is here?" he asked.

The two girls looked at each other, and then Les faced Jody. "He is," she whispered. "And he is here to help. I think he's already met Wild Bill and he's got him talking about letting you go."

"I know it for a fact, Jody," said Penelope. "I saw the two of them come from a saloon. A tall fellow with woman hair in curls, kind of dainty, but with two pistols and a wavy hat."

Jody nodded. "That is him." He eyed both of them with a melancholy face. "I don't want to be beholding to Rance Cash."

Les took his hand. "If it means getting out of here? Wouldn't it be worth it? Rance isn't the kind to hold it over you. He feels a debt. For all you've done for him in Texas."

"That was paid at the trading post." Jody's reminder was about Rance risking his life to free Les in west Texas from rustlers holding her hostage. "We were even after that. Now, I'll owe him."

"Then I'll make it a matter for me," Penelope said. "If it means getting you out of jail, then I'll tell him it was a favor on my behalf." Her voice sounded loud. However, the notion of staying in jail so Jody wouldn't owe Rance didn't make sense to her. Since she'd spoken so loud, she felt a need to leave, and strayed into the office while the two sweethearts held hands.

Once there, she saw the deputy eating the same meal she'd eaten at the boarding-house. "Evening," he said.

"Evening," she replied in the manner of a cowhand. "See you must eat good while you got my friend locked up in here."

He didn't look shamed by the remark. "Matter of fact, I do. Nothing like home-cooked vittles. Ain't nothing compares." She watched him shovel the food in with delight.

"Ain't your wife make the same? Or you more a loner for them that bend at the hem?" She knew her tone was crude, but also understood. He didn't show resentment. Instead, he shook his head.

"My missus is in Kansas City. I'm not that kind of man, miss." He kept eating, savoring every bite. Penelope felt out of place for her rude remarks, but couldn't see herself apologizing. Instead, she found fault in him.

"Then why aren't you with her?"

As the deputy chewed, he spoke. "J.B. found me when I needed a job. Said he needed help here dealing with the cowhands from Texas. I needed the steady pay. So, I

205

came quick before he thought of somebody else." He took another scoop, but continued talking. "Me and him go back to the army days. I knew when he wired for me, he expected a job done and I'm the one to do it." He moved his tongue about his mouth and smacked his lips. "But I miss my wife. I'm going to see her this fall when the season is over."

Penelope looked around. "Why ain't he here? This where he works?"

The deputy chewed, but Les replied as she entered. " 'Cause he's playing cards at The Alamo Saloon. That's where you'll find Wild Bill Hickok. Folks around here don't think much of him."

"Now hold on," said the deputy, finally swallowing. "The marshal is doing his business. Can't find out what's going on out there from in here." He looked directly at Les. "You ought not slur him. He's doing what needs be done to keep this town peaceful and doing business. Not an easy job."

She stood there with slight remorse building on her face. "Then I apologize, Mike. Not for speaking ill about him, but for doing so as one of your friends. I know you don't have to let me in here, and I'm obliged to you. I'll pick up the plates in the morning." She turned to Penelope. "Got to get back to my job."

For the first time, Penelope saw the strain on her younger friend's face. Although they didn't get along when they first met, Penelope had bonded with the only girl she knew who didn't snub her.

With the deputy eating, she went to the cell. Jody was eating his supper, too. "You look like you need to eat ten more helpings."

"When I get out of here, I plan on doing just that," he said without much glee. She thought the open cell door odd, but it was a sign of trust between him and the deputy, so she walked into the cell as he sat on the bunk. He forced an embarrassed smile. "Don't take no pride having you find me in here."

She understood his meaning. "See no shame in it. Les told me the story. Think I saw that fellow this afternoon. Claimed he killed a Mex who killed a trail boss."

Jody nodded. "Heard the same." He looked her in the eye. "You need to keep clear of him. He's more loco than a bull with the itch. His temper boils faster than a pot over the fire."

"I can take care of myself," she said, in part to calm his fears and also to reassure herself that she was self-reliant. As she stood, she sensed he was in no mood for visitors. She really didn't know if she should stay, so she chose to step out of the cell. "Going to be heading back now."

He lifted his head from the plate. With a casual nod, he bade her good-bye. Penelope walked from the hall and went through the office. The deputy's polite parting words weren't enough to interrupt her steps. She went from the jail office out onto the board-walk. Despite the hour, the street was filled with drovers full of whiskey. A thought to join the jubilation left her mind quickly. She wanted to hide, to be left alone in her solitude. In a strange town, with friends she'd come to know as much as she'd ever allowed, she still found herself without any-one.

18

Benjamin Thompson walked toward the front door to his Bull's Head Saloon. Usually, all the drunks had been thrown out during the night by the barkeeps, but he had to step over two in the dark interior. With the sun shining on the street, he felt the need to open for business. When he got to the front door, a crowd had already gathered in front of his place, but they stood in the street and looked upward. Laughter with some loud guffaws drew him from the saloon.

Wanting to inquire as to the source of their delight pulled him further into the street, but most of them were too struck with hilarity to reply. It took five more steps for him to be at an angle to look at his own roof and sign.

A fresh coat of white paint now covered the bull's pizzle.

He stood dumbstruck. A voice called out.

"Might nice heifer you got there, Ben."

Breath left his lungs. His hands shook. Blood rushed to his face. He'd been made a fool for the entertainment of the mob. He turned around to face them. "Who did this?" His shout squelched the laughter. "So help me, I'll cut off the pecker of the man that did this and nail it up there in replacement." His fiery threat thinned the crowd, but with the day beginning, to his embarrassment, more arrived on the boardwalks. He retreated inside and stumbled over one of the drunks on the floor. A boot to the ribs awoke the kid drover in pain. "Get out of my place." He went to the back room and threw open Phil Coe's door. "Get your ass out here. That woman-looking marshal painted over our sign."

Rance Cash wanted to make an early start. The opportunity to work the saloons before the locals invaded the premises could not be ignored. As he made his way toward Texas Street, he couldn't help but notice the commotion. Once at the corner, he followed the flock of interested townsfolk to the spectacle. Above the heralded Bull's Head stood the defiled image of the bull. Rance grinned. Someone, namely Hickok, had been behind such a move. With all in the street and boardwalk surrounding the saloon pointing and making private comments, Rance thought, although it was risky, that perhaps he could use the event to his advantage.

He crossed the street, threading his way through the crowd, and went to the front door of the saloon. A peek inside showed few, if any, patrons. He knew the proprietors would be in no mood to engage in friendly wagering, but if anyone was going to voice an opinion against the presiding authority, now would be a good time to hear it.

He entered the Bull's Head. With a card table open, he sat as if opening up a place of business. The one barkeep gruffly called to him.

"We ain't taking any games today."

"Then you should have locked the door. I plan to stay. If there's a complaint, send out the owners." The defiance hung in the air. He took an old deck of cards from his coat and began the shuffle. With some intrigued eyes cast his way, he began a game of solitaire, knowing his challenge would be addressed. As anticipated, the thinly haired owner came from the back and marched to his table.

"Leave here, mister. I don't want anyone in my place I didn't invite myself."

Rance slowly eyed the man. "And who might you be?"

"Ben Thompson. I run the place. And you no doubt know why I'm in no mood to banter. Now, leave."

"Pity," replied Rance. "And I was so looking forward to enjoying your company. We may have a mutual interest."

Thompson cocked his head to the side like a dog. "Like what?"

Caught with the question, he needed to embellish the bluff. "How we men from New Orleans are to deal with the prejudicial practices of the current constabulary toward our business dealings." The dim-witted would have asked him to repeat the statement in a more common vernacular. When a chair was pulled and sat in, he knew he had guessed correctly that his mark was someone with similar sophistication.

"Who are you?" asked Thompson.

He extended his hand. "Ransom Cash. Friends call me Rance."

The handshake was cautiously accepted. "Ben Thompson. Why are you in my place?"

The play had to be complete. "I've found that the laws in this town aren't to the advantage of those in our profession. I've learned that you are one of the more vocal opponents of the unfair statutes." Although

212

he'd tried to sound like a sympathetic confederate, the doubting grimace on Thompson's face meant Rance had a long way to go before earning the man's confidence.

"Who is telling you this?"

The true source of information would spook the prey. So, he knew of only one other name to drop. "A fellow gambler and Texan, Luke Short."

The grimace didn't fade. "Never heard of him."

If the front was closed, try the rear. "Well, trust me, he is an admirer of yours. And with his and others' input, I've come to the conclusion that you and I might strike a deal."

Several seconds passed before Thompson, no doubt judging whether to throw Rance into the street himself or listen to the offer, came to a decision. He turned his shoulder and signaled for one of his barkeeps to bring a bottle. "What sort of deal do you have in mind?"

"I've come to gain Hickok's trust. We came to know one another with a game or two and he is such a poor player, I gauged him a man of simple thinking."

Thompson poured the two glasses full and shook his head in puzzlement. "What does all that mean?"

"I think he is a man who can be manipulated. Steered in a direction we want."

"We?"

With a sip of whiskey on his lips, Rance nodded. "We're both Southerners. We share the same heritage. We want the same thing, which is to prosper in these times of limited duration. Hickok, he is a man for the Union, and doesn't understand the hardship we faced and our need to rebuild our status." Though he was unsure exactly what point Rance was making, the effect on Thompson's face nevertheless showed that he was fully engaged.

"So, what are you wanting from me?"

His confidence high, Rance spoke without caution. "Allow me a table of my own to ply my trade here, and I'll also frequent The Alamo, which, as you know, is where Wild Bill can be found. When I'm there, I'll influence him to our way of thinking."

After a few moments, a single huff came from Thompson. "Hickok is a puppet, Mr. Cash."

"Call me Rance."

"I'll call you what I want," Thompson responded tersely. "The marshal gets his orders from the town council, and he carries them out like the trained dog he is

214

because he's paid well to do so. He has the same attitude toward the gambling houses and the brothels. I know this. I just don't like him."

The statement ended too abruptly, so the question had to asked. "Why is that?"

A moment passed before the reply. "Because he thinks he is better than us. That we are some sheep who can be scared into doing as he wills. I can't stand the man. Especially now. You've seen what he's done to my place of business, and he expects to get away with it because he is the law and sports those pistols. Had he asked as a man to remove the sign, I might have given it thought. But he came in here demanding we take it down, like some schoolmaster speaking to lowly pupils. I don't take orders well, Mr. Cash. I've been through too much in my life to be ordered around by the likes of Wild Bill Hickok, who himself is nothing more than a slothful cheat and whoremaster of exaggerated repute."

Thompson rose from his chair. Rance wanted to continue, but saw the rage building in the saloon owner's face. "I hope I haven't offended. If so, I apologize."

Thompson merely shook his head. "I have other business to attend to. Matters that need to be seen to." Before Thompson could leave the table, Rance held up his shot glass.

"Well, then. 'To the Rising Sun.' "

Thompson paused. Without changing his the stern face, he also picked up his glass and saluted the toast. They both threw the liquor down their throats. Thompson slapped the glass on the table. Rance held out a glimmer of hope that he'd sold the man as to his true intent. The acceptance of the toast might have made a connection, however frail.

With prospects dim for the time being, Rance left the saloon and went to the corner. Although, at such an early hour, he doubted much business could be transacted, he had little else to pass the time. As he got to the corner, he caught sight of Penelope strolling along the fences of Cedar Street. He wanted to warn her to beware of trouble, and so he met her before she arrived at Texas Street.

"What are you doing here?" he asked.

"Can't take being penned up in that house. Especially with those other two, talking all social. It's like sitting in at a Sunday sermon. So, I'm taking in the air. Why?"

He glanced over his shoulder at the crowd, still growing, then faced her. "I would steer clear of the west end of the street. It seems that someone painted over the sign of the

Bull's Head and it has put all around in a foul frame of mind. So much so, it wouldn't surprise me if there were gunplay."

A look of sheer delight overcame her features. "White paint?"

"Yes," he answered, wondering why that mattered. "Something special about that?"

She grinned smugly. "Not really," she replied in a coy manner. He knew better, but an attempt to discover what was truly was on this girl's mind would require even more effort than with the average female. He decided to continue with his plans, but gave her a reminder.

"Avoid the area, Penelope. As I say, tempers are flaring and someone will be hurt by the end of the day. Mark my words." She gave him an instant's glare, as she usually did when advised contrary to her desire. His conscience satisfied that he'd done what he could, he went north along Cedar.

Traffic on the street increased the closer he came to the tracks, but he sought no train. Instead, his walk ended at The Alamo Saloon. The glass doors never closed. The patrons mostly dressed in coats and ties instead of the drover's clothing seen in every other spot in town. Play was sparse, but the day was young. He'd make his day's wages in little time.

He glanced at the vacant corner table by the south wall. All in the place knew for whom it was reserved. He sought a table nearer the door in order to attract the anxious, patient in the expectation that the man he wanted to talk with would arrive soon.

19

With the early start of the day, Hickok rode the hack onto Texas Street. It was slowed by the crowd of people milling about in the center of the street and under each awning. He debarked several yards away and went through the back of the throng, casually casting an eye at the center of attention. He didn't smile outright, but internally, he chuckled. He got to the front door of the jail with little notice. It was the way he wanted it.

Mike Williams stood at the door looking in the same direction as all the others. Hickok showed no emotion, but Mike thought the obvious needed to be said. "You seen what's been done to the sign?"

"They were warned," replied Hickok in a low voice. He went to the desk he seldom occupied, and looked about at the papers scattered in all directions. He never was one to write, and it took too much effort to read all of them, especially indoors. He was not about to take all those papers out in the sunlight.

"You should have seen Ben Thompson," Mike continued. "He was shaking worse than a wet dog, threatening to hack off the privates of whoever did it."

The announcement wasn't unexpected, and could have real consequences. Yet, to comment could expose the culprit, which he didn't want to do. Instead, he changed the subject. "What's all this mess?"

"Oh, the mayor came by late last evening. He said he needed to see you."

A meeting with McCoy held little promise of good news. "What about?"

Mike shook his head. "He didn't say. Just that he needed to talk to you."

Hickok snorted disappointment. "What now? Somebody trample a fence on Mulberry?" he remarked. "I got a few matters to attend to today. If he comes back, tell him I'll try to fit him in during the course of the day." Hickok came near Mike. "Don't tell him where I am." As he started for the door, Mike grunted, an act usually meant to ask a question or bring up a matter that wasn't easily spoken. Hickok knew the signal in their relationship. Mike Williams had always been a man obedient not only to

J.B. Hickok, but also to the legend of Wild Bill.

Hickok stopped and faced about. "What is it?"

Mike scratched the back of his neck and took a step closer. "The, ah, girl came by last night."

Hickok cast an eye at the Texan locked in the jail. "The chambermaid?"

Mike nodded. "She's been asking about the kid. He's too proud and just moans about being locked up without cause."

"Cause?" Hickok asked. "Did you tell him 'cause we're trying to keep him from getting killed?" Mike shied away from the firm tone.

"I did take up your side of it," Mike said, trying to stem any anger. Hickok took a step closer to the hall. He could see the kid still on the bunk. He had no real reason to keep the kid there, nor any real desire to keep him alive. However, he was certain that the kid's future while Hardin was around was poor at best. He shook his head. "Not just yet. Little Arkansas is back in town." The decision made, he went to the door to address that very fact.

With the Bull's Head still simmering, Hickok went east on Texas Street on a search, and also to make an appearance for the citizens. He didn't care much for the act, he had deputies for that, but an occasional appearance reminded everyone he was still the chief peace officer. A glance at the shadows from the buildings gauged the time as still before noon. It was too early for whoring, but not drinking. He himself didn't mind spirits before midday, and so he proceeded to follow the activity along the notorious thoroughfare.

He heard laughter at one of the newer places and peeked inside. Without spotting his quarry, he went only a few steps to the next one, with the same result. Three more had to be passed until a familiar voice crept into his ear. He knew he'd found the man sought. A deep breath was taken before he entered across the open threshold. There, sitting at a table, he recognized, even in the darkened room, Wes Hardin. Surrounded by friends, the young Texan appeared to be retelling with enjoyment his exploits of a few days before. Now, standing there with all eyes to see, Hickok thought about attempting to run the kid from town, but the task would be difficult since Hardin was now the hero lapping up the hospitality of the grateful population. Word had spread that Hardin intended on putting up a fight if arrested.

Instead, Hickok chose to gradually approach the table with his palms close to the pistols. He didn't want to send lead flying, especially with so many innocents about inside and out. "You remember our talk in the Apple Jack?" They each knew the other understood the reference.

"You cannot hurrah me," Hardin answered in a matter-of-fact tone. "I don't wish to hurrah you." Hardin's eyes wandered to the side and ceiling. "But I have come to stay. Regardless of you."

The statement had been made plain. To challenge the kid, even in the name of the law, would be a conflict with high cost and puny gain. Hickok thought the better of it. Since neither man had been shamed publicly, perhaps another compromise was in order. "Well, you can stay and wear your guns." A notion came instantly to him. One that saved face and would plant a seed in the kid's mind. "But those other fellows must pull theirs off."

The strategy was a risky one, but if he set Hardin on a pedestal with greater privileges than the others, likely the kid would accept and respect the privilege by enforcing it himself. As Hardin kept silent, pondering the demand, Hickok reinforced the idea.

"You're in no danger here." To assure the

223

kid of that, a compliment was in order. "I congratulate you on getting your Mexican. Invite your friends. We'll open a bottle of wine." Hickok went to another table, one where his back was to the wall and he could clearly see the door. Hardin soon joined him, as did the companions.

Hickok treated with two bottles of wine, which were quickly consumed during talk of the past and giddy observations from each man on subjects ranging from theft of another's property to copulating with married women. Laughter and good times reigned over the room, an improved result over gun smoke and lead. After more than an hour and eight dollars spent, Hickok felt secure he'd made an impression on the mankiller kid.

Maybe Hardin would grow homesick and leave for Texas soon. At least for now, the amount of alcohol imbibed assured these rowdies would soon need a nap and be rendered harmless for the afternoon. That in mind, Hickok excused himself from the table citing professional duties yet to be performed.

In all, it was a good day so far. He'd addressed two needs and accomplished both. A game of cards sounded inviting, yet the cloud of a meeting with Joseph McCoy hung over his thoughts. In times before, he never could concentrate with such an unfulfilled task burdening his mind. He decided to get it over with, but before putting himself through the confrontation, he needed a drink. There was only one place where he felt at ease. The short walk did his mind good, and he entered the open glass doors at about noon.

He paid little attention to the room and headed straight for the corner table at the south wall. He removed his hat and signaled for a bottle of rye. Piano playing soothed his thoughts. A deck of cards awaited his arrival. He took them and began his shuffle. In a short time, he had a visitor. That gambler friend of the kid in jail.

"May I join you, Marshal?"

He didn't mind company as long as they didn't block his view of the door. "Pull out a chair." Once seated, the gambler signaled for his own bottle, but there was no need to clutter the table. Hickok poured himself a drink, then pointed for another glass. "Help yourself. I needn't drink it all."

"Much appreciated, Marshal." Without a word said, Hickok dealt a hand to himself and the gambler. Conversation ensued. "Interesting events over at the Bull's Head this morning," said the gambler.

Hickok kept his eye on his hand. "Wasn't like they didn't know it was due. Maybe that pair might not think this town is their personal den." He discarded an eight.

The gambler threw out a nine. "Had an interesting chat with our friend that runs that place."

The statement stopped Hickok for a moment. "How's that?"

"He wasn't in a pleasant mood. However, per our arrangement, I identified myself as someone sympathetic to his cause."

The message sounded too muddled. "I've got a number of matters on my mind. Speak it plain."

The gambler paused only briefly. "I told him I could influence you if he let me have a private table."

Despite being eager for the answer, Hickok eyed the cards. "And . . . ?"

"Well," said the gambler, "I didn't actually get one. Instead, he thought you needed no influencing."

"He said that?"

"More to the point, he said he plain didn't like you."

Hickok grinned. "No news in that. Known that since I got here. So far, you ain't told me nothing worth you staying in this game. And I don't mean with these cards."

The play continued in silence for several seconds. "He made several threats."

Hickok looked at the gambler. "Again, something I already knew. Call." He placed down two pair. The gambler surrendered only a single.

"He made them more against the perpetrator of the act. The one contracted to do the deed. I wouldn't be amazed if he conspires among those loyal to him to avenge the insult in a less public manner."

Although it was no surprise, Hickok expected he would be targeted for revenge. It was the second time it'd been mentioned. "That so. Well, whoever that may be better watch his back. Nothing I can do about it." The facade of ignorance was veil-thin and he knew it. The next deal only frustrated him further with a tangle of low non-suited cards. As he mulled over his play, a figure approaching caught his eye, and instantly the cards were no longer his biggest concern. He slid his right hand down to his belt and thumbed the hammer.

"I beg your pardon," said a short, slim man in a bowler hat and wool dress coat. "Am I in the presence of the famed gunman Wild Bill Hickok?" The voice held a cut he'd heard before, one that came from over in England.

The thumb eased off the hammer. "Depends who's asking," he replied.

"Permit me. My name is Archibald Thorne. *London Gazette.* Sent here to the states to report on the wild happenings of the American wilderness. It is an honor to make your acquaintance. Might I join you gentlemen?"

Hickok nodded at an open chair. "Bring your ante."

The fellow took a chair. "I must say, I'm not much of a player of cards. However, it would be a memorable experience, so I'll give it a go." The dude looked at the gambler and offered a handshake. "Archibald Thorne, London, England."

The gambler responded in kind. "Ransom Cash, New Orleans and parts west. Pleased to meet you."

Hickok dealt a new hand. While he was doing so, the dude reporter kept talking.

"I read your interview with Henry Morgan Stanley a few years ago. I say, I enjoyed it greatly. So much to learn about you and your exploits."

The reference was recalled. Two or more years had passed since he'd talked to another reporter with the same accent. With the same curiosity, Hickok had found himself explaining and defending reasons behind gunplay whether with hostiles, outlaws, or just others with opposite intentions, and also the need for self-defense, distinguishing himself from those killers. He'd liked that fellow who'd had the same glowing flattery, which had furthered Hickok's reputation and gotten him a few dollars along the way. "Where's that fellow now?" asked Hickok, analyzing the hand he'd dealt.

"Stanley?" The dude hacked a laugh. "At this point, unknown. The last I was aware, he'd gone off straightaway to darkest Africa in search of another eccentric, one Dr. David Livingstone, exploring for the source of the Nile. I doubt we'll ever hear from either of them again."

"That's quite an undertaking," said Cash.

"Indeed," replied the dude. "The hazards of that continent are extreme. I know it's said of here in America, but there, there are no such places as here in Abilene. Wouldn't you say, Marshal Hickok?"

The question irritated his concentration, already distracted from the advance of the day and the meeting that awaited. "Can't say. Never been to that place. But I can tell you Nebraska and Wyoming ain't a place to be without a firearm handy." He threw in two dollars. The others raised a third.

"I can only imagine," said the dude.

"However, here in Abilene, it is a virtual oasis to the endless prairie. I can see why so many Texans come here." His eyes wandered. "So many vices to entertain oneself. Liquor and quim enough to fulfill every young man's fantasies. I would imagine it is the first time for some to see the unclothed anatomy of a woman." Hickok followed his glance at the walls. All about, paintings of nude women lounging prone adorned the interior.

"Yes," Cash said. "But hardly authentic copies, if you know what I mean."

"Oh, quite right," replied the dude. "That is not an original Goya." He pointed to another painting over the bar. "I recognize that as Venus of Urbino, but the reproduction is very sloppy."

"Not exactly what I was referring to," Cash remarked.

The talk so distracted Hickok that the game no longer held any appeal. To scatter these two and get new players wouldn't heal his mind. He folded his hand and picked up his hat. "I leave you two to your commentary. I have city business to attend to." He went toward the open doors.

20

Tom Carson enjoyed the benefits of being a law officer in Abilene. He stood wrapped in a sensation as of warm butter melting around his tongue from a soft hot roll fresh from the oven. Savoring the experience, he closed his eyes and thought of the best of times past when he had felt the same.

As a single man, seldom did he get the same attention heaped upon him, although there were occasions when he partook of the advantages of married men, some even lavished on him by their wives. It was oh, so good.

A tingle sent his nerves twitching with a bit of spice. Just as with any fine meal, he treated himself to his heart's content, until he was done. He heaved a breath or two, then took the hair of the young Mex street walker and pulled her to her feet. He spoke and buttoned his front at the same time.

"I know you don't know the words exactly

right, but you'll understand my meaning," he said, staring into her soft brown eyes. She didn't open her mouth, but he knew it got through to her head by her frightened eyes.

"You'll owe me another if I find you anywhere near that church. You *comprende?* It ain't for your kind. It's for your betters."

She nodded quickly. He released her hair and swatted her rump. She ran down the alley between the saloons. He buckled his belt and went back to the street, satisfied he'd done his duty in enforcing the law.

Hickok watched the homes of the east side of town pass by as he rode the hack to Joseph McCoy's home. As he traveled, the raucous nature of the cow town slowly subsided into the decidedly more tranquil residences of the locals. Small white fences and modest wood dwellings appeared to replace the saloons more and more, and were likely due to the prosperity brought by all the dollars spread by the Texans on their sins.

It was a conflicting setting. Most of the citizens hated the cattle business and all the violence and debauchery it brought. Yet, if not for the stockyards, likely as not, the train would never have paused or even whistled as it passed by this town named after a Bible verse meaning "city on the plains." There would be limited mail service. Few if any supplies would be shipped here if there was no one to buy them. The services of doctors, dentists, cobblers, or barbers would never have come this far if not for the convergence of people brought by this rail terminus. And there was only one man to thank or blame, Joseph G. McCoy.

From what Hickok had discovered during his three months here, if anyone had reason to curse the cattle business, it was the current mayor.

As the marshal rode by fancy houses, some two, even three stories, he eventually came upon a large structure. At one time, McCoy's private residence was the largest in Abilene. The house still stood, but McCoy no longer owned it. The previous years had seen the fortune amassed to construct not only the house, but the stock pens and the ornate Drover's Cottage, dwindle to a pittance due to hard luck in buying and selling longhorn cattle.

A few more turns brought the hack to the very simple, modest home McCoy now could afford. Hickok got out of the hack and went to the front door. A rap on the wood took a few moments before it was answered. Without servants to keep the place, the short stocky McCoy himself opened the door and let the marshal in.

"You wanted to see me?"

"Well, I needed to talk to you about the matter I left on your desk." They both went to the single den of the house.

"What matter was that?" Hickok said, removing his hat. McCoy swept documents off two chairs to allow them both to sit.

"Didn't you read them? The new ordinances?"

Embarrassed to admit his increasingly poor eyesight made it hard for him to read, Hickok shook his head. "That desk collects so many papers, they all look the same. Can you just tell me about them?"

McCoy showed his disdain with a shake of his head. "Marshal Hickok, when we gave you the job, we expected there to be law and order in the streets. As you know, when Marshal Smith held the position, there weren't the troubles that we have today."

Since he'd accepted the position, Hickok had heard about nothing other than the legendary Tom Smith, and his gut boiled with every recital. "Tom Smith is dead, Mayor. We've settled that matter. What can I do for you?"

McCoy paused. "Please, don't be short

with me, Marshal. I have great matters on my mind." He picked up the documents he'd laid on the floor. "I am in the midst of litigation with the Kansas-Pacific and expect a decision any day as to whether I will recover my losses." He looked at the floor. "I don't know if I can ever get back what was once mine, but at least I can get back what those people are taking from me."

Confused, Hickok looked away and shrugged. "Sorry, Mayor. It's just that sometimes I don't always get your meaning."

McCoy lifted his head and stared him in the eye. "My meaning? My meaning is that I don't have time to listen and be constantly complained to by the citizens of Abilene. The regulations set forth are not being enforced."

Hickok stemmed his temper at the rebuke. "Beg to differ with you, sir. But I've told all the deputies to keep the street walkers clear of the school and church. With the summer, all the schoolkids are with their families, but I've told all the saloon owners to watch out for them if they see any and not expose their business in front of the children. I think we're doing our job."

McCoy pursed his lips. "Well, it's not enough. And now the council has decided to do something about it. I left on your desk a new ordinance for you to post. It requires all the bawdy houses to relocate southeast of town in a special section in one week. All the street walkers will need to be rounded up and thrown in with the rest of them."

Hickok sat stunned. Many a time, he had heard the fine folks of Abilene complain about the merchants of fornication, but to now want them removed from their own property? He was the messenger and enforcer of the law, and he once more hated the position and asked himself why he was there. Another question arose in his mind. "I expect they are still to pay the same amount for their license fees? The fees that pay for all the expenses of this town?"

McCoy nodded. "That they are. They have no choice in the matter. If they don't like it, they can pack their bags and leave on the next train." McCoy paused and shook his head slightly. "I wish they would. Ever since they've arrived, I've had nothing but scorn toward my investments here and by those who espouse the outlawing of the cattle business altogether." Hickok sensed McCoy's exhaustion, and pitied the man for all the grief leveled on him. For only a brief moment, the mayor appeared genuine in his position.

"I like you, Hickok. I admire the matter-of-fact way you handle things. When I vouched for your hire, I knew I was getting a man used to handling trouble. But matters have changed. There are more settlers here than there were just a few months ago. And they are plowing the land. T.C. Henry, a man I have many disagreements with, has great holdings in the growing of wheat. But wheat takes years to produce, and doesn't have the quick turn of profit as does beef. I still believe there is a great deal to be earned with the transport of cattle to Eastern markets. But the worse the reputation of Abilene becomes, the less I am able to convince investers to support me." He paused only a moment. "I'm asking for your help."

Hickok sat and pondered. This man he sat across from was the one who'd gotten him the job. A job with steady pay. They'd had many arguments, including a time when the high license fees on all the saloons, gambling parlors, dance halls, and brothels had even Hickok on the side of the sellers of sin. Hickok had even raided a game of whist in this very house as a unlicensed game of chance. Now, he saw it as his duty to carry out the will of the town council mainly to square himself with McCoy.

"I'll do as you ask," he said, rising from the chair. "But it ain't going to be easy. A week ain't much time."

"I didn't expect it to be easy. That's why I hired you." Hickok turned for the door and let himself out. He went to the walk. The hack driver had waited all this time. He paid the driver for the ride and time spent, and decided to make his way back to the center of town afoot. He needed the time to think.

Rance entered through the front door of the boardinghouse. This time, he was on time for the six o'clock supper. Greeting all at the table and paying respects to the ladies, with a special courtesy toward Mrs. LaFontaine, he took a chair at the table as the food arrived.

"It looks absolutely delicious. How do you do it, dear lady?" The compliment was sincere. Having cautiously consumed some of the restaurant fare around the town, he found a home-cooked meal a genuine pleasure. He looked at Penelope. "And how did you spend the day?" He was curious to know why she took such an interest in the Bull's Head sign.

She showed no reaction to the question. "Not doing much. I did see some pretty flowers some folks had in front of their houses." Rance sensed the comment was a lie. The last thing this girl would favor would be someone else's flowers. However, he noticed her cast an eye at the landlady, who no doubt would approve of such polite banter.

Les got up from the table, to her foster mother's displeasure. "You leaving again?"

"Got to get Jody his meal, then get back to work."

The landlady wasn't satisfied. "Don't they know at the Drover's Cottage that you have to have some time with your family, too? You've been here almost a month and I haven't seen more than a few hours of you."

Rance himself was confused as well. The girl appeared worked to a frazzle. "Perhaps I should speak to the manager on your behalf," he said to the landlady.

"No," Les blurted out. She paused while her loud tone faded. "Don't do that. I can handle my own matters. I've been working extra hard to help with what needs to be done. I don't mind the work."

Penelope cast an eye at Rance. She knew better.

Rance took a bite of the meal to allow the tension to recede. "I'll respect your wishes, but you should consider your mother's also. Should you need my services —"

"No, Rance," she repeated with the same tone, making all in the room uncomfortable. "Please, let me be." Les took the basket filled with food and wrapped an arm around her mother. "I know you're worried. But this will pass and we'll be together. There's only a few more months left in the season." She went to the door. "Don't wait for me."

As she closed the door, Rance knew there was a lie in Les's story. The most he believed was the need to cash in during the peak of the town's business. Other than that, he suspected worse matters were yet to be discovered.

With the same aloof manner, Mrs. LaFontaine excused herself from the table, paying only minimal, if not insincere, compliments to the landlady for the meal. There was also something yet to be discovered about that woman, but Rance had greater concerns. He also paid his respects to the landlady for her cooking, but as usual, got the feeling his compliments weren't received as he might have hoped.

In a short time, the woman went to her room under the stairs, which left Rance and Penelope alone. He wanted to know more. "So where is Les working? Don't tell me in a house of ill repute."

Penelope shrugged. "I don't know. She don't tell me nothing."

Rance curled a brow. "What do you mean? You're both women."

The tall blond girl snarled her lips. "Don't mean a thing. Even if she was, it ain't something one gal brags about to another."

Rance stood, confused. He feared the prevailing demons of the town had consumed the virtue of his young friend. He looked at Penelope. "Then I intend to find out."

"I'm going with you." She grabbed a hat and went to the door as he stood, surprised. The next several seconds, he questioned his amazement. The gal had been the one to alert him to the wire for help, and had insisted on accompanying him here. She was a headstrong woman from the moment they'd met in Texas, and he never really knew how she'd acquired such a trait. Perhaps from the hardships faced without a mother and the need to assert her will over others, namely men, in order to run the ranch. Or, maybe she just had a terminal case of the curse.

Either way, he realized there in the hall, it was pointless to put up a fight and order her to stay. He, too, picked up his hat and went to the door. "I'll do all the talking," he said. He opened the door and waited for her to go first. As she passed by, a remark consistent with her attitude came out.

"For yourself."

21

Charles F. Gross swept the lobby of the Drover's Cottage. He knew there was a high standard to uphold, and he wanted to keep his job as assistant manager, even if it meant cleaning up once the day staff had left.

With the rooms nearly all full due to the height of the cattle season, more of the guests stayed longer to enjoy what Abilene had to offer. They included the cattlemen, themselves owners and sellers of the larger herds, the Eastern cattle buyers, the more notable and successful saloon owners, commission agents, and others of a higher station in life that separated them from the common drovers, who went anywhere they could to sleep off their stupors from cheap liquor.

Now, with a circus in town, even longer stays could be expected. And so, Gross wiped off the counter of the front desk and cleaned the dust from the key slots to keep up the appearance so coveted by the Gores, who'd been placed in charge by the new owners.

When the front door opened, he placed the pen for the register in its inkwell and put a smile on his face. A man and woman, who didn't appear suited to each other, entered. The man was dressed neatly in the typical garb of a gambler. She had on a riding skirt, dark blouse with wrinkles, and the floppy-brimmed, high-crowned hat worn usually by drovers. However, she did possess attractive features. This couple didn't fit in with the image of the Cottage. Whether or not they were pimp and prostitute, or just gambler and woman drover, he was not going to rent them a room.

"Good evening, sir," said the gambler. "I'd like to inquire —"

"No," Gross blurted.

The gambler blinked several times. "I didn't finish my question."

"You don't have to," Gross said, looking at the tall blonde. "We don't rent out rooms to your sort."

"And what sort is that?" she asked with a temper.

The man reached out an arm as if to hold the young woman back, then smiled. "Forgive us, sir. By the way, may I ask your name?"

"Charles Gross. And I am in charge of Drover's Cottage."

"Oh," came the reply with a nod. "Pleased to meet you, Mr. Gross. My name is Ransom Cash and the lady is Penelope Pleasant. Actually, we weren't looking for a room. We wanted to speak to one of your employees. A Miss Leslie Turnbow. I believe she may be one of the help."

Gross shook his head. "We don't have anyone here with that name."

The answer appeared to puzzle them both. "You are certain?"

"Of course," said Gross. "As I explained, I am in charge here, and I would know all the people who work here. There is no one here by that name, and besides, the staff have all left for the night."

"I see," the gambler said with several more blinks. He looked at the woman, who also seemed disappointed. "Then, I am sorry to have troubled you, Mr. Gross. I bid you a good evening." The couple turned toward the front door. Gross shook his head at the oddity of the inquiry as well as the mismatched pair.

With only a brief glance their way as they left, he looked once more at the register.

Then, from the corner of his eye, he saw another party enter from the dark. When he looked up, a man he had come to know very well over the last few years was walking into the lobby with three others.

Gross forced a greeting. "Good evening, Mr. Myers." There was no gracious reply. John Jacob Myers was a Texas cattleman of great notoriety. He was one of the first to bring his herds to Abilene and take advantage of the opportunity offered by Joseph McCoy. When the fledging rail stop needed cattle in order to convince the railroad to schedule a stop there, it was this man's considerable holdings that brought notice to Abilene.

There was also another reason Gross had to respect this man. Only a few years before, Gross had angered one of the Texans who'd gotten tipsy and brought his temper back to the Cottage. Gross had told the man that all the rooms were taken, which didn't sit well with the ill-mannered drunk. So much so that the drunk pulled his pistol and pointed it at Gross's nose with all the intention of firing at that very moment. It was Myers who called to the drunk and ordered him not only to withdraw the weapon, but to leave the premises immediately. The order seemed to sober the drunk in an instant, and was complied with to the letter. Had it not been for Myers, Charles Gross knew he might not be alive this day. He always made it known he was in the rich cattleman's debt.

Now, Myers stood at the front desk and began signing the register. "I'm going to need a room for some friends of mine."

Although the rooming house was near capacity, some of the smaller rooms were available. Gross got the key to Room Eighteen and placed it on the counter. It wasn't met with satisfaction. The broad-shouldered Texan in his fine cloth coat looked at Gross. "No. I want one on the top floor. Close to mine."

Those rooms were already spoken for, and he knew that Myers knew that also. "I believe we may be out of rooms there."

"Charles," said Myers in a fatherly tone. "These are friends of mine from Texas. They've just arrived with a herd and are tired. I want to show them a good time, and they can't get any rest with footsteps above them."

Gross knew the request was more than casual. He looked at the men behind Myers. All of them had scruffy facial hair, and did appear to have been riding a long ways. However, they didn't wear the clothes of drovers and didn't sport Stetsons as so many did who worked the range. One in particular had a long neck like that of a weasel, and appeared as fidgety as one. Gross didn't get as good a look at the others. He felt Myers's eyes upon him.

"I'll see what I can do for you." Gross turned to the key slots, and one room remained available. It was the one he himself had reserved for one of their better guests scheduled to arrive in the morning. However, he had to survive the night before he could worry about the morning. He turned back and handed the key to Myers.

"Appreciate it, Charles." Myers motioned for the trio to follow him up the stairs. The fidgety one stopped and spoke loudly.

"Hickok the marshal here? The one calling himself Wild Bill?"

The question was odd, but not completely unusual. Some of the drovers from Texas had heard of the legend of Hickok. However, the tone didn't sound the same as the other Texans Gross had heard. He nodded. "Yes, that's right."

A moment went by before more was said. All eyes went to the one who had asked the question, and appeared curious to know the reason for the inquiry. Finally, the weasel spoke. "You fetch him tomorrow. Tell him we need to talk. You hear?"

Gross nodded as subserviently as he could. Apparently satisfied that the command would be carried out, they climbed the stairs. Once they were out of sight, Gross breathed his first deep breath in more than a minute. Footsteps came back down the stairs, and he held his breath as another of the party, one with a long crooked nose, came down to the last step and pointed at Gross.

"He's the only one you tell."

22

Hickok found himself wandering about. With the burden of enforcing the new restrictions weighing heavily on his mind, he reflected on his current circumstances. The usual enticement of poker didn't hold any allure at the moment. Neither did seeking the company of some of his favorites.

Instead, he was drawn to the flow of citizens moving toward the train tracks where a show of acts, most involving animals, awaited. Though not normally attracted to carnivals, having been associated with some in the past, he had little to occupy his time, and so he strayed with the rest of the crowd to witness the exposition.

He walked past the box office and upon approaching the tent, opened his coat to display his badge as his admission. Not wanting to attract attention, he kept to the back of the tent and away from the seats, preferring to watch from the shadows.

What he saw was truly remarkable in his opinion. The little woman proprietor was quite a rider. While the white horse ran in circles, she stood on the back, then moved to the front to hang by the animal's strong neck. To his surprise, she exhibited more limber feats than could be expected from one of her age.

Once she finished, she took a bow to applause from the crowd. Despite doing his best to remain hidden, he was spotted by her, and she waved the audience to silence so she could speak.

"Ladies and gentlemen, we have a special guest in attendance." Hickok winced and shook his head at her to stop, but she continued. "It is my distinct privilege and honor to have in our midst a truly legendary figure of the frontier." More folks stood to get a look at who she might be talking about, most of them bobbing their heads past him in search of somebody else so impressive. "Your very own town marshal, Mr. Wild Bill Hickok!"

From a crowd of mostly visiting Texans came jeers mixed with scattered handclapping. He stood there, embarrassed, and stared at her bleakly. Agnes applauded loudly and encouraged the audience to join her, but not all were as enthused at his presence as she was. After several long seconds, the show moved on to another act and she came next to where he stood.

"I am so pleased you came, Marshal Hickok." She paused only a moment. "Or may I call you James?"

He didn't object to her familiarity. However, he noticed the same twinkle in her eye and didn't wish to encourage her more, although he didn't want to give a poor impression as a gentleman. "No harm in that." He wanted to steer the conversation in a different direction. "That was some pretty fancy trick riding."

"Thank you," she said with grace. "I've been riding all my life and would enjoy so very much perhaps an afternoon ride with you."

It took him a moment to determine the actual intent behind the request. Soon, he was sure he understood her genuine meaning. "That might be nice. But I have to say I don't think I'll have a chance to do so. Town matters are in more need of my attention than ever before."

Her face showed disappointment, but she bravely kept a polite grin. "There might be another time."

He nodded at the convenient excuse. "Yes. There might be."

She held out a hand just like in any business transaction. He accepted it and resisted any awkward show of more than common courtesy. "I must get back to the show. I trust you'll be here to the end?"

"Afraid not, Agnes. I just happened by, but need to return to town to watch over the rowdies." She nodded in acknowledgment. A moment or two of silence prevailed; then Hickok spoke again. "Go on. Run your show," he said in a kind manner. Agnes marched back to the center of the ring and introduced the next act. Hickok felt that it was time to creep stealthily from the shadows and out of the tent.

Rance and Penelope took a hack to Texas Street. They had been concerned they might find Les in a situation for which the young girl wouldn't be prepared. "Pray we don't find her here," said Rance.

They walked down the boardwalk through the jumble of drunks and those soon to be, attempting to get a good look at the faces of the women who peddled their wares for a quick coin. Although the demand for service never ceased through the summer, the competition usually forced the price down so that it was hard to make a living. Yet there were no fewer than fifty women to be counted just in the vicinity, all with no more talent than being of the female sex. For almost all, it was the only trade available that was easily learned, and all were qualified.

As Rance and Penelope continued west, the incident at the Bull's Head was still drawing a crowd. Rance pointed at the sign. "I think somebody is going to pay for their handiwork. I talked to Ben Thompson today. He swore revenge on whoever did it."

"Revenge," Penelope said as if it was a word she didn't expect. Rance kept looking at the faces.

"That's what I said. Thompson is bent on substituting what's missing on the sign with the real thing. Only it won't be bovine. I hope you understand, because I don't intend to explain further."

"Wait," she said, grabbing his shoulder and turning him around to face her. "You're saying he really means to do it? It's not just talk?"

He thought the interest odd, but answered her. "Ben Thompson is a man who doesn't make idle threats. He's been insulted and made a laughingstock. In New Orleans, his reputation was one that commanded respect, and he wasn't afraid to stick a knife in a man's ribs if he felt slighted. Do I believe he's serious? Oh, yes, my dear Penelope. Oh, my, yes. I wouldn't want to be that unfortunate fellow."

Her chin dropped. Rance was unsure as to why it meant anything to her.

She looked away from him several times, each time returning to face him with a confused expression. "My head feels dizzy. My gut is turning. Maybe the meal or something else. I'm going to go back to the boardinghouse and sack out."

Although she showed all the signs of the symptoms mentioned, Rance suspected another cause, but didn't know exactly what. "Very well, I'll see you back to the house."

"No," she objected. "You keep looking for Les. You can find her as easy by yourself. I can get back on my own." She didn't wait for his permission, but began the walk back to the corner of Cedar. He stood watching, concerned she would be accosted by some of the drunks who filled the boardwalk. Even though she was a woman raised in the wilds of Texas, she always seemed vulnerable and prone to take unwise chances. However, he assured himself that she would arrive unharmed.

"Taking in the night air?"

The question came from a familiar nasal

voice. Rance faced about to see Hickok standing on the boardwalk. "Why, yes," he answered. "Thought I would relieve my lungs from the constant barrage of tobacco smoke. The same for you?"

It took a moment before Hickok nodded. "You could say that." The marshal peered about the street. "Appears to be calm around here. I did give a notion to relaxing for the evening with quiet entertainment."

Rance took the inference. "I assume in surroundings more suited for privacy?"

Hickok nodded. "You could say that, too." He eyed Rance for a moment in a posture of uncertainty. "Can't say I know your likes or not, Cash. This air and the walk has put the manly spirit in my blood. What say we visit a parlor house I'm familiar with? May give us a chance to talk about your time with Thompson?"

The invitation wasn't as intriguing to Rance. Usually, he enjoyed women through seduction and not purchase. Still, he did want to learn more about Hickok, and perhaps this was as good a time as any for him to do so. "I trust your judgment, Marshal. I would assume you frequent only the finest."

Hickok grinned and he turned to walk west. "I have sampled most of what is here."

Rance followed Hickok's lead. "These ones about the street are just as likely to spread mange, the same as the stray dogs which infest the streets and alleys. I know of a particular house which holds itself to a high standard. A lady from Virginia who's been established here since the beginning. I'm sure she has some gals there that will be to your liking."

Penelope peeked around the corner of the Old Fruit Saloon. In the distance, she saw Rance and Hickok walk down the boardwalk. Once she lost sight of them through the clutter of the shirts and hats of others, she stepped back onto Texas Street. Uncertain exactly of her intention, she instinctively knew she had to find Clay. Where he might be was anyone's guess. There were no more than a thousand strangers in town and she didn't know where to start. She couldn't be sure he even was in town. But her gut told her to try and find him.

Clay, who had been the only man ever to catch her eye, seemed to be anything but attracted to her. His gruff manner only served to spark her temper, which made her revert to the only behavior she'd known since the worst incident in her life. Yet she couldn't get him out of her mind. When she first learned of what had happened to the Bull's Head sign, she knew it was he who had been responsible. All she'd witnessed had confirmed it.

Then there was the time when he had defended her from the drover. If he hadn't opened his mouth and spoiled it, denying any association with her, she would have considered giving him a peck on the cheek. She had to be careful not to be thought a floozy. She had no respect for women who used their bodies to get what they desired, and held no respect for those men who sought such women. Although she sensed Clay to be that type. Why did she care? Her mind raced with conflict.

During her pondering, she found herself across the street and heading east. The flow of men coming from and entering the numerous saloons sent her into a whirlpool of motion. She pulled her high-crowned hat tight on the brow to keep her face from showing. She didn't want trouble from the drunks who might see her as an easy way to keep from spending two dollars. She briskly evaded the cluster of cowpokes assembled on the corner, and instead of heading east straight into the dark of night and the bawling longhorns, stayed with the streets where kerosene lanterns lit the way. Peeking in saloon windows didn't show him inside. A street walker approached and mistook her for a man.

"One dollar. Right now. Be quick and step into the alley."

The whore raised her skirt to reveal the lack of any undergarment for quick access to the goods. Penelope snarled at her and kept walking. "Get to hell, slut."

"You a woman?" the street walker asked. "It's okay, I'm good for you, too." When the whore stuck out her tongue, Penelope turned her head to avoid any more offers. She increased her step. Unsure where she was, she glanced at a street sign that read FIFTH. She'd lost all sense of direction, but there were more than a few fellows outside a two-story building. She cautiously came near and in the dim light read the sign on the false front: MERCHANTS HOTEL.

Three steps led to a wide front porch where a few men gathered but remained civil. She couldn't rationalize being drawn closer. Instead of coming up the side steps to the porch, she continued along the front and peered into one of the double-framed windows.

A flash of blue whisked past her view.

She stopped and moved back, and for one second saw the blue army trousers she'd seen Clay wear. The sense of urgency along with a feeling of success took her up the main steps onto the porch. One of the men called to her.

"Where you from, cowboy?"

She ignored the friendly greeting and rushed into the lobby. A poorly built front desk was the first thing she saw. To the right was a staircase, and reflex sent her toward it. When she got to the first step, indecision set in again.

What would she do when she found him? If she found him? He'd made it plain he had no interest, and she felt like those she repelled with sharp words to keep their distance. It wasn't her duty to inform him of the threat to the vandal of the Bull's Head sign. Was she so sure it had to be him? And why?

More questions flooded her head, and indecision turned her around. Her will faced her around once more and she looked at the first step. A peek to the side showed that those sitting in the lobby were observing her with arched eyebrows. Their silent judgment of her as an idiot was enough to make her take the first step. After the first, the second came easier, and then the third. Increasing her ascent, she was on the second floor in a flurry, and she went down the hall.

The first room door was open. More indecision and fear of rejection slowed her to a creep. When she edged her face around and into the doorway, she saw an unshirted man shaving with a straight razor. Despite the lather on his face, the hair was too dark and he wasn't tall enough. When he looked at her, she moved on to the next room and saw its door open also. Once more, the same routine of caution slowed her to a snail's pace. She slid one boot on the wood planks, then scooted the other. Once she had come to the doorway, she decided to walk past and glance quickly inside.

The room was dark. She couldn't see very far inside, but it was possible someone was in there. She poked her nose in first, then garnered the courage to take another step.

"Who is that?"

The deep husky voice from the dark startled her and sent her retreating. "Beg pardon. My mistake. Wrong room." The sudden warning sent her heart pounding, and she leaned her back against the wall. She had no idea what or who was in that room, but she was confident she knew who was not. The voice was too deep and had a twang to it that she'd never heard from Clay. It was not him.

As she leaned against the wall, a vibration

came through her back. The rhythm increased and began pulsating the wood. She looked farther down the hall. The third and last room door was closed. She went to it very slowly, sensing the floor move. With every step, the tremor became more powerful. Then she heard a voice. A man's voice, only it wasn't speaking words but grunting and groaning, and soon a woman's joined it making the same sounds. As the latch rattled, Penelope fell back against the opposite wall and sank slowly to the floor.

She felt the pulse of the motion. All at once, her senses collapsed in on her. She closed her eyes and felt the tears stream down her cheeks. Chiding herself for allowing this to happen once more in her life, she suppressed the sobbing to minor squeaks.

She didn't know what could happen next. He might come from the room at any minute, but not at present. Not as long as she felt the shaking. Maybe she would be discovered?

Instead, she stayed on the floor and held her knees and ceased to care.

23

Les swept the floor in a hurry. The mud and dung tracked in by the boots of customers reflected poorly on the business. She needed to get the room ready for the next sale. Kentucky Sarah already had gone to the den to take the next one in line. When Les heard footsteps, she stopped the sweeping and left the room.

All the women had put the white powder and red rouge on their cheeks and pinned their hair to keep it off their shoulders. With as much lying down as they did, they didn't want to have the hair yanked by clumsy elbows. The exposed neck and painted face gave the appearance of fancy femininity, almost like dolls seen in store windows, and enticed the men to spend more time in anxious anticipation. Some of the eager cowpokes showed respect by removing hats and spurs, and had gleams in their eyes that were usually shown in genuine courtship.

Others with more liquor in their blood showed their urges spilling over by removing their shirts and unbuckling their belts on the way to the rooms.

One such man made his objections for all to hear when the newest gal came to take him as the next in line.

"I ain't having no Jew."

Lady Shenandoah, dressed in Sunday best for the night's business, was quick to meet the angered drunk. "She's got the same as they all do. She'll satisfy what's busting to get out of you."

"I said, I ain't sticking it in no Jew. I want a Christian woman of clean breeding, and aim to have one. That one that just went in that room was the one I want."

The lady shook her head, but put on a smile so as not to anger him anymore. "Then she'll be done soon enough. Wait until she's done with the one in there and you can be next." She motioned for Sarah the Jew to take the next in line. However, the angered drunk, with features like those of Hardin and a short temper to match, marched toward Kentucky Sarah's room.

The lady tried to get in his way, but he pushed her aside and kicked in the door. Les stood in the middle of the den where her view was clear. The angered drunk stood in the doorway.

"Get out of here, shorty," he said to the kid in the room. The kid, appearing no older than Les, had slicked hair, no doubt from a haircut that day. As he quickly stood, with only longhandles showing below the waist, he looked startled. Kentucky Sarah coiled herself on the bed at the far wall. "I'll show you how a man does this," the drunk declared.

"Wait your turn," the kid replied. "I already paid my money."

"You can have her when I'm done." The angry drunk began unbuttoning his shirt. The kid charged at him in attempt to shove the intruder from the room. The taller one grabbed that slick hair and tried to get rid of the kid. Kentucky Sarah shrieked. The two men wrestled for control. When the kid fell back against the wall and showed resolve to continue, the drunk dug in his pocket and pulled out a short-barreled pistol.

"You ain't listening to me," said the drunk. Once more, Kentucky Sarah screamed. Lady Shenandoah ran to her room. Les watched, frozen by what she saw.

"Don't shoot me," the kid shouted. Other customers yelled the same. For a few seconds, all stood motionless. Then the pistol fired. Smoke billowed into the room. As it drifted from the doorway, Les saw the kid slumped against the wall, writhing with his arms squeezing his right ribs, face contorted in agony. He groaned as he spoke. "Son of a bitch. No need to shoot."

The drunk didn't answer, standing in a trance. Les figured it was the liquor that pulled the trigger. The blast still rang in her ears, and might have put the drunk in a final stupor even if he was standing. The lady came back with a pistol of her own. Holding it in two hands, she confronted the drunk.

"Get out of my place!"

The drunk turned and pointed his pistol at her. In that instant, Les saw the muzzle aimed at herself. Every muscle tensed so much, she couldn't command her body to move.

"Drop the firearm!"

The order came from the front door. Moving her head slightly, Les saw Marshal Hickok emerge through the crowd. Right behind him came Rance Cash. When she met Rance's eyes, he showed an expression of horror. Les knew it wasn't from the shooting, but Hickok's voice drew her attention away.

"I said, drop the firearm or I'll commence with you, son."

Hickok drew both his guns and trained them on the drunk, who retreated into the room. Kentucky Sarah continued her shriek. The other gals and customers came out of their rooms. The kid kept wailing against the wall. Hickok came forward. Rance stayed right on his heels.

"I ain't going to jail," stated the drunk with a slurred tongue. In panic, he wrapped an arm around the neck of Kentucky Sarah, which turned her screams to whimpers. "I'll plug this one's head. She ain't going to be pretty no more." He heaved a breath. "I'm going back to Texas or down to hell with a fight."

"You got the hell part right," said Hickok. He entered the room. Rance did also, drawing the Walker Colt and creeping toward the other side of the room near the wounded kid. "Hang on, miss," Hickok said. "I'm going to get you out of this."

"Let me go, Wild Bill," said the drunk. "I won't cause no more trouble."

"Hardly a guarantee in that," said Rance, pointing the Colt at the drunk. The comment drew attention away from Hickok.

"Who are you? You have no badge. The marshal is a lawman, but I ain't taking nothing from a gambler. I should blast you for your sass."

Rance grinned. "You're holding a twenty-caliber. This is a .44. I'll likely survive your shot if not your impaired aim. You won't survive mine."

For a few seconds the drunk stood in place, petrified, the small pistol still cocked and ready. Rance kept his eyes on the drunk. Then the drunk's temper erupted again.

"Let's just see," shouted the drunk. He aimed the gun. Hickok swung the pistol in his right hand across the skull of the drunk with a loud thud. The offender collapsed to the wood planks.

Kentucky Sarah bolted from the room in just her shimmy. More loud voices commanded the line of customers to move aside. Two deputies with guns drawn charged forward into the den as Hickok and Rance left the room. The marshal arched a thumb at the wounded kid.

"Get that one to the doc before he bleeds to death." He angled his shoulders and again arched his thumb, only in a different direction. "Get all the gold that one has in his pockets and give it to the doc, along with any more weapons he might have, and dump him too far away to walk back." As the two deputies nodded and began their assignment, Hickok stopped one of them.

"Tom, I do mean to give all he has to the doc."

The deputy again nodded, but after a moment's pause.

Hickok looked at the lady. "You can put that away now."

"I thought I was going to have settle it myself. I thank you, J.B. You got here awful quick."

Hickok nodded his agreement. "Actually, I was planning on enjoying the evening here." He pointed at Rance. "I brought another customer and was bragging about your place."

The lady took a breath. "Jesse's not here no more."

Hickok's exasperated face showed it was the worst news he heard of the night. "Where'd she go?"

The lady spoke in a confessional tone. "She went in with Mattie Silks, the bitch. She promised Jesse part interest and they're running their own place."

The marshal cocked his head to the side. "I guess it don't matter much." He eyed the lady and spoke in a softer tone, but Les heard every word. "I'll tell you this now so you can make your plans. I'm to post notice tomorrow that all the parlors and the street walkers are to relocate just out of town. It

269

ain't my choosing, but I got to do what the council orders."

The lady's shoulders slumped. "How do they think we're to make a living?"

"Shouldn't cause too much strain. I'm thinking these horny Texans will follow you through thorn brush if need be."

The lady still shook her head. The commotion of the two deputies carrying the wounded kid stirred her attention. "I got to clean up this mess. I can't afford a stop in business." She looked a Les. "Get that blood off the floor so we can use that room." The order came in a harsh tone. Les stepped away from Rance's glare, which didn't change despite Hickok's voice.

"Sorry to disappoint," he told Rance. "Appears the mood will take a while to smooth out here. I do have a woman at my place if you're in need."

Rance looked at him. "I'm fine. Not in the mood myself. But please go ahead without me." Rance sidestepped Hickok and grabbed Les by the arm. "What are you doing here?" he asked through gritted teeth.

She pulled away from his grasp. "I'm making money. Money Jody needs. Money Miss Maggie needs. Money I need."

"By selling yourself?" The question was partly admonishment and partly disbelief.

Les stood in front of him. Only after Hickok left their presence did she speak. "I'm not humping. I'm just here to clean up and change the linen. The women pay me and I have earned over twelve dollars in two weeks." He didn't seem impressed. "I've got to do it, Rance. Lady Shenandoah gave me a chance when I needed it and I've got no other place to work." Despite the explanation, he didn't appear sympathetic.

"Les, I said now," the lady barked.

The command meant instant compliance. Les didn't have but a second to convey what needed to be said no matter how it might be received. "Leave me be." She turned and went toward the room, picking up a bucket and rag on her way.

Jody stared at the checkerboard only half interested. He'd never embraced the game, but had found himself playing nearly three times a day for the past two weeks. Across from him sat his jailer, Mike Williams. Mike jumped the last checker.

"King me."

Jody could only manage a slight grin. "I guess you're going to win again." He knew he showed a poor attitude, but didn't really care. Mike slowly removed the checkers from the board.

"That was good vittles your girl brought tonight. She must be a good cook. They're hard to find."

Jody grinned. "That's her ma's cooking. Les would be lucky not to burn water."

Mike grinned at the remark. He leaned back in his chair. "Where'd you find that little gal?"

Jody bowed his head and reflected on how it happened. "She found me. She's from here, in Abilene. Only, when I first saw her, she'd was in the duds of a kid, a boy. See, somehow she got the fool notion that there was a heaping pile of gold hidden in Texas. She wanted to find it and knew the only way was to come back with us." He shook his head. "It was some ride. I thought it was the most excitement I ever had." He thought further. "But when we got to Bexar County, there was more trouble." Another recollection entered his head. "Come to think of it, not but a few months more found us shooting it out with rustlers."

Mike slapped his knee and laughed. "Damn, son. Sounds like she's either a Jonah, or one ticket to a circus better than the one north of the tracks."

Jody had to wonder. There were many times since he'd met this girl when he'd found himself in a scrape. And if not for her, he'd not even be in Abilene in order to be arrested. Maybe she wasn't the best thing for him. However, it was his choice to promise her she'd come back home. And now, through no fault of hers, he sat jailed and unable to earn any money in a town with it dripping in the streets. Yet, she was there every day at least twice, bringing him food and making his jailer happy as well. He shook his head. "No. She's no Jonah. She's a good friend."

"Friend?" Mike's question provoked thought. "Appears to me she's more than that."

Jody shrugged. "I don't know."

Mike leaned forward in the chair. "Let me tell you, Jody. A good woman who will stand by you when trouble seems all around is something you can't get just anywhere." Mike's eyes drifted to the side. "This is a lonely ride by yourself. Ain't too many folks can spare nothing to help you when you need some. There is family, if it hasn't been torn up by sickness or politics. So, to have someone who believes that the two of you are one is something to keep close and not let pass by." He looked into Jody's eyes. "Or so says this man." He chuckled at his own remark. Jody took in all that was said.

Mike rose from his chair and took it and

the checkerboard from the cell. As he started to the front office, a thought came to Jody's mind. "How long it been with you and your wife?"

Mike stopped and closed one eye in thought. "I think maybe two years now, but I can't be sure. All told, we may not have been together one, with me scattered about with jobs like this one."

"Miss her?"

"Every day," was the quick response. The two simply looked into each other's eyes for several moments. "Get some shut-eye, Jody. I know I plan on some." He went on to the front office.

Jody lay on the bunk. The conversation stirred his thoughts about what was important to him. He needed to know what he wanted for the rest of his life, and thought it might be right in front of him.

The front office light dimmed and the outer door opened and shut.

24

The cool overcast morning was a reprieve from the summer heat. Charles Gross didn't enjoy any such relief as he walked to the other end of town.

The night's events weighed heavily on his mind, and he decided to relieve the burden of carrying a secret. While walking west toward Mud Creek, he increased his step the closer he came to his destination. After several turns, he came within sight of the small cabin. He stopped and took several deep breaths before he proceeded. His beard began to itch, a sure sign that the jittery nature he always tried to control was returning.

Nevertheless, he resumed his walk, though he went a bit slower. When he drew close to the modest single-room dwelling, with its shabbily cut wood planks masoned with mud and sand in between, he summoned the courage to rap his knuckles on the door.

"Who's there?" The question came from a woman's voice.

"Charles Gross. I need to talk to Marshal Hickok." There was no immediate reply. Unsure of the reason, he waited until it seemed an extraordinary amount of time had passed. He grew impatient due to the task he'd been assigned. "Hello?"

"Open the door," came a shout from inside in a familiar tone. "It's just Gross."

In a few seconds, the door creaked open and a woman with brunette hair grasped the latch. He'd seen her before on different occasions, but she wasn't a permanent resident. Of course, neither was Hickok, having shared numerous beds with various women in town. Gross had once shared a room with the famous frontiersman when the legend had no money of his own. It was one of the most uncomfortable nights Gross had ever spent. However, this was the home of the marshal. Gross had gotten lucky that he'd found him.

With a little hesitation, Gross entered the small cabin, removing his hat and nodding respectfully to the woman. She appeared distressed, perhaps because of his presence, or more likely due to her fiery relationship with Hickok, one most of the town knew about.

The woman wore a red dress with a white speckled pattern. It didn't appear the type of dress to do any chores in, but her hair and eyes weren't done to be viewed in public. Gross looked to the right, and saw Hickok lying in the small bed propped on an elbow and wearing a nightshirt. "Good to see you, Gross."

"Same to you," he replied in a nervous tone.

"Well, come on in. Don't stand in the doorway." Gross did as ordered, and walked to the small table where two chairs were and sat. Hickok rolled out of the bed and put his feet on the floor. The move exposed his thin white legs. "What is it I need to talk about with you?" About to answer, Gross was interrupted by a sudden command from Hickok. "Cook us up some bacon," he said to the woman. She still stood in the same place, but without any smile.

"I'm leaving, Bill." Her reply wasn't the one expected by either man. Hickok arched a brow at her.

"What's that?"

"I said, I'm leaving you. There's nothing here to keep me. I'm going back to Arkansas." The two had had many a loud vocal feud, which all the neighbors were accustomed to and some knew well enough to record in a journal. She had been Hickok's mistress for many years. At one time, this woman was the focal point of a gunfight between Hickok and a man named Dave Tutt. They both wanted her, but Hickok's habit of bedding other women made it a difficult choice to stay with him. The rumor was Dave Tutt promised her more and she chose him over Hickok.

Furthering the tension was the matter of a watch. Hickok lost it in a poker game, and Tutt paraded it around from a bob hooked to his vest. The two rivals crossed paths on a summer day five years ago in the town square of Springfield, Missouri. Without words, they both drew their revolvers and fired at each other at very same instant. Tutt, although a good shot, missed at the distance of seventy-five yards. Hickok didn't, plugging Tutt directly in the heart, killing the man instantly.

After that, this woman found herself following Hickok wherever he went and stopped long enough to hang his hat. However, his habits remained, and this woman would soon leave for what would eventually turn out to be a short term of months. Hickok confessed at one time that his affection for her was not heartfelt, but he was fond of having her with him. This time seemed to be a repeat of those in the past. Or so Gross had assumed from the rumors he'd been told.

After several seconds, Hickok nodded without a kind face. Gross expected an eruption, but the reply was calm and cold. "I have no objection." The answer didn't seem to be the one she desired. With the tension lingering heavily in the air, Gross didn't feel at ease explaining his concern in front of her as she packed clothes in a trunk. Hickok noticed his nervousness. "Let me get on my trousers."

The lawman slipped on pants and boots and waved Gross to follow him outside. Along the way, Hickok picked up the gun-belt with the pair of pistols and a leather-covered case. In front of the house, a small cross-legged table stood. They brought the two chairs outside with them. Hickok sat at the table and began dismantling one of the pistols. "Where were we?"

Gross wasn't sure how to begin. "I've come to let you know something of a secret."

The statement briefly brought Hickok's attention from the pistol. However, the next instant, he put his eyes back on the removal of the cylinder. "And what might that be?"

Gross tried to not be distracted by the

clamor coming from inside the house. The clang of metal and creak of wood being mishandled, more than likely deliberately, was hard to keep from noticing. Hickok showed no concern at all, and continued the process of cleaning the weapon. "We had some visitors last night at the Cottage."

Hickok kept cleaning. "I'd think you'd have quite a few every night. It is the biggest hotel in town."

Gross felt a fool, so he got to the point. "I think they're outlaws."

Without a pause in his routine, Hickok replied, "More than a few of those, too."

Since what he was saying didn't seem a surprise, Gross hoped the last of the information might be important. "They told me to come and 'fetch' you. Like they wanted you to know they were here." Hickok paused only a second, then began reassembling the pistol. Gross wanted to spike his interest. "I would think wanted men would want to avoid you."

"Oh, I don't know about that, Charlie. Some of my better friends are outlaws." Since Hickok appeared to dismiss his concern, Gross didn't want to waste any more of Hickok's time or his. He rose from the chair just as the door to the house opened. The woman, now wearing a floppy hat, dragged the trunk from inside, then went to a wagon beside the house.

She moved out of sight. Gross was confused at Hickok, who showed no interest in her, instead now cleaning the parts of the second pistol. Gross took a step toward the street, but Hickok's words stopped him.

"What'd they look like?"

Gross recalled the faces. "The one that told me to get you had a long thin neck and a narrow but youthful face. Looked to me like a weasel. There was another one with a longer nose who appeared older, but did show resemblance to the first. The third one I didn't get a good look at. But it's how they came in that concerned me. They arrived with a man I know, though I'd rather not give his name. But let's say I knew him from the war."

"I think I might know who you're talking about."

The woman returned with a horse, hitched it into the harness, and began walking the animal backward to reverse the wagon.

"What did they tell you exactly?"

Hickok's question didn't get Gross's attention until the marshal snapped his fingers. It was only the second time the marshal had taken his eyes away from his weapons. Gross responded. "They said to tell you that they wanted to talk to you."

The woman lugged the trunk to the wagon. Gross felt compelled, as a gentleman, to assist, but Hickok asked another, much louder question. "Did they say what about?"

With his attention pulled away, Gross shrugged. "No. Not to me. It sounded like . . . like . . ." The woman's grunts lifting the trunk drew Gross's mind from the conversation.

"Charlie!" Gross snapped his head back to Hickok. "Like what?"

He wanted to be done with this conversation and help the woman. "Like you already knew what they wanted to talk about."

The woman's shriek pulled his eyes back to her. She'd fallen into the wagon, but had managed to drag the trunk up into it.

"I think I know." The odd remark drew Gross back to the conversation. Hickok had measured a precise amount of powder poured from a flask into each chamber. Gross watched, but now was curious what it was Hickok thought he knew.

"What is it? Who are they?" Gross asked.

As Hickok loaded each chamber with a ball, the woman's voice hawed at the horse. Hickok merely glanced at her departure for a few seconds. "Good-bye, Susanna," he called to her as the wagon pulled away. He waved. "May you never darken my door again." Without pause to reflect on the woman leaving, he again looked at Gross. "Let me know if you see them around town. Any peculiar places. Anywhere near where there's money."

Gross thought the statement odd. "Every place in Abilene has money."

"Not the saloons or casinos. Anyplace there wouldn't be twenty guns surrounding them." Hickok pushed the load into each chamber, rotating the cylinder and ramming down the plunger. "If you see any one of them, tell them I got their message and will meet with them shortly." He looked up at Gross. "Appreciate you coming by, Charlie. Sorry you had to witness that ruckus."

"I am sorry for your heartbreak," Gross offered to be polite.

Hickok looked at Gross and winked. "She'll be back. She always comes back." He aimed a pistol at a distant tree and thumbed back the hammer. The action was smooth and the sound like that of a well-operated mechanism. Gross knew the one thing Hickok cared for was being sure his weapons were clean and well kept. It was a measure that had saved his life more than once. The marshal cared little for anything or anyone as much.

A woman's cackle woke Penelope. She blinked in the light to focus on a bare-chested Clay hovering above her, and the next instant saw a painted-face whore behind him. The woman looked to have brown hair pinned up and slim shoulders and arms. She continued to laugh as she walked down the hall. Clay stood in place.

"Why you here?"

Embarrassed, Penelope asked herself the same question. In an instant, she recalled the night before, and reckoned she'd fallen asleep in her depressed state. Now in a panic, she rose off the floor. He offered a hand. She swatted it away. "Keep away from me, you pig of a man."

"I find you outside my door asleep in a hall and I'm the 'pig'?"

"Damn straight you are," she replied. "Coupling with whores." She turned to leave the hall.

"What you care?" The question slowed her only slightly. "I asked what are you doing in the hall. Maybe it's you I should be wary of."

The comment stopped her. She turned to face him. "I ain't the one you should be watching for."

He crinkled his face in confusion. "How's that?"

She didn't want to tell him, she wanted to make him feel the pain she suffered, but so her following him would sound justified, she decided to say what she knew. "I'll say it this way. I ain't the one that painted over the Bull's Head sign. And from what I'm hearing, I'm glad I'm not." She turned again to leave, but his voice stopped her.

"And you think that's a matter I should be fretting?"

She turned around. "I saw you carrying the whitewash. Likely, I'm not the only one seen you neither. I heard Ben Thompson took it as a personal insult and vowed to cut the pecker off who'd ever done it and nail it to the sign. I'd think he'd be asking questions all around town."

Clay stood for a moment in a frozen stance. Then, he glanced at the open door to his room. Penelope couldn't take being there. She made up her mind in that instant to leave and find her way back home. Again, she turned to leave the hall. And again, his voice stopped her.

"Wait."

25

Although luck at monte wasn't with him, Wes Hardin was a pleased man, at peace with his accomplishments. The appreciation for his killing of Billy Cohron's murderer had come from just about all in Abilene, and had put almost a thousand dollars in his pocket. He had done his best to put the money back into the economy with his losses at cards and dice, and also his frequent visits to the brothels.

Jake Johnson stood next to him as he watched his next wager collected by the dealer. From the corner of his eye, he saw his cousins Manning and Gip Clements enter into the American House. The distraction took his attention away from the game. He went to them, and greeted each of them with a handshake and a slap to the shoulder.

"Good to see you boys," he said, noticing their dusty clothes and sweaty faces. "Y'all look like you rode all night. Did you bring in your herd today?"

Manning shook his head. "No. Another matter brought us here."

Curious, Wes wanted to know more, but the loud surroundings didn't make conversation easy. He motioned all of them, including Jake Johnson and Frank Bell, to a table where they could celebrate. In a short time, they had two bottles of spirits on the table. Wes was very gracious in the filling of glasses. "I expect you men are ready to rest and enjoy the town. I know of a heap good places for just about everything." The statement came with bobbed eyebrows, and sent all of them chuckling. However, Manning still appeared less than at ease. While loud cheers and shouts came from the crowd at the gaming tables, Wes stared at the cousin he'd known almost as closely as a brother. Finally, Manning leaned closer.

"Wes, I want to talk to you privately."

The tone wasn't good. If there was a matter bothering his kin, Wes wanted to do what he could to solve it. While the others enjoyed the spirits, he motioned for the cousins to follow him to his room upstairs. Once they were behind closed doors, Manning spoke.

"Wes, I killed Joe and Dolph Shadden last night, but I was justified."

The news surprised Wes but did not shock

him. Instantly, he thought of Billy Cohron's murder by Juan Bideno. Tempers on the cattle trails often became frayed and led to bloodshed. Usually, the one to do the killing was first to draw and often shot from behind as Bideno did to Billy. However, this must have been different. These were his kin. "Well, I am glad you are satisfied, but I would stick to you all the same even if you were not satisfied with your action."

His assurance of loyalty appeared to calm Manning. They sat in the chairs in the small room. After a few moments, Manning recounted the events.

"I was bringing up a herd from Gonzales County. I hired on the Shadden boys and all appeared good. Then not long ago, they didn't want to take their night duty. I told them they had to or pack up their leather and go back home. They didn't take to being ordered. I sensed they were spreading their foul mood amongst the other hands, and planned on doing me and Gip harm, or maybe kill us and take the herd."

Wes looked at his other cousin, who nodded in agreement with the story. Manning continued.

"When we crossed the Nations, the mood of the drive worsened. I told them to leave and take their pay for the days they worked.

They wanted a full share, and I told them I was not paying them for getting to Abilene when they only got halfway. So, I heard from a hand who told me they were talking again about taking the herd. I kept away from the camp at night to avoid trouble. The Shaddens thought me a coward."

Wes nodded, thinking he would share the opinion but would never tell Manning.

"When we crossed the Arkansas, I knew the matter would have to be settled, and told a hand who I trusted that I was not going to sleep away from the camp any longer. The Shaddens said they would kill me if I returned. When I heard that, I went to camp last night even though I was begged not to. When I got there, I told Gip to go out on night duty. Joe Shadden jumped up and pointed a pistol at me. I already had mine cocked under my slicker" — he paused — "and plugged him right in the head."

Manning wasn't a man used to gunplay. Although he and Wes had been in many scrapes, normally it was Wes who did the shooting.

"Then Dolph rushed from the dark and fired, but the ball only went through my slicker. I tried to get the gun from his hand, but never let loose of mine. I thumbed the hammer and fired. He fell back with a bullet hole in his chest." Again, Manning paused. "He said I killed him. His last words."

"I have had a heap of trouble, but I stand square in Abilene," said Wes, thinking of his now prominent stature. Since he was a hero in the community, explaining Manning's justification should be a simple manner. Wes was confident about his influence. "Wild Bill is my particular friend, and he is the one to help you here if papers come from Texas for you." He decided the next step would be to abide by the town's laws and not look like reckless gun-toting cowboys. "Now, Manning, pull off your pistols." He motioned for Gip to do the same. They left the room and went downstairs.

They needed to get word to Hickok and explain the reasons behind the killings before any outside rumors were spread. Wes looked around for someone less likely to spark a fire under the marshal than he was. When he returned to the loud lobby, he saw Columbus Carroll, a cowman with some influence among the other cattlemen. If they could get to Hickok, it was likely they could square matters that very day.

Hickok strode to the jail with troubling matters on his mind. It was a day he'd not looked forward to, and he had just learned there was more trouble he hadn't planned for but had to address. He'd put the word out he wanted all his deputies at the jail at noon. He checked his watch. He was twenty minutes late when he got to the door.

Upon entering, he saw James Gainsford, J. H. McDonald, Tom Carson, Brocky Jack Norton, and Mike Williams. All popped to attention when he closed the door, but Carson didn't immediately move from the desk. Already in a sour mood, Hickok barked, "I'll have the chair." He sat at the desk and rifled through the papers on top. He stretched some at arm's length in order to focus on them in the dim light. Once he saw the proclamation, he handed it to Tom. "It appears the council, no doubt led by Guthrie's complaints, has passed an ordinance to remove the brothels from the city limits. They are to relocate southeast of town. Take that to the *Chronicle* and have them publish it post haste. Have the necessary handbills made and posted about town for the street walkers and give every house on Texas Street a copy."

"They aren't going to like this," Carson remarked.

"It ain't up to them liking it, Tom. It's up to us to enforce it." With their orders clear,

291

Hickok waved all from the room except Mike. He knew his tone was terse and he cast an eye at his jailer, who looked like he wanted to say something. "All right. What you got to say?"

Mike took a breath that was longer than normal. "You know there ain't a one of them isn't scared of you."

It was no surprise. "If that's the way it is, then so be it. They got a job to do and it's time they started doing it. We all got worse futures without this pay."

Mike nodded. "I know that." He paused and rubbed his finger across his nose. A sure sign he wasn't done. "But there is something else." Hickok opened his palms as a gesture that he was ready to listen. "Before you came in, they were talking. Seems the story has spread there was a shooting during one of the trail drives south of here. The shooter was rumored to be Manning Clements."

The name was familiar, but Hickok couldn't place it. He tried to remember where he might have heard it. Then he recognized it just as Mike uttered, "Wes Hardin's cousin. And he and his brother Gip were seen going to the American this morning. That's where Hardin holds his court."

Hickok understood. "Killing a Mexican

makes you king among these Texans. So where are they now?"

Mike shrugged. "Haven't seen them since, but I'm sure they'll show their faces."

The matter wasn't his immediate concern. "What happens outside this town ain't worth my time. As long as they're not causing trouble, I say let them have their fun and spend their cash." He rose from the chair. "I'll be strolling about." He took a step, but stopped in front of Mike's desk. He pursed his lips. He also had something that needed to be said. "You know, I don't trust a one of them. Carson is living off his uncle's fame. McDonald is a coward. Gainsford tends to cause more fights instead of stopping them." He paused, then patted Mike's back. "You're the only one I can truly place my faith in. Appreciate you speaking up." By Mike's silence, he knew he had conveyed the sentiment. That done, he didn't want to linger.

He went to the door and opened it. Across the street, Phil Coe stood in front of the Bull's Head leaning against a pillar. Hickok peeked at the false front above the saloon. The white splatter remained unaltered. The sight pleased him. It meant he wouldn't have further trouble to solve on this day.

Another pleasing object came into view. A

well-dressed woman with attractive features walked alongside the street under a parasol. He'd not seen her before. The expensive clothes weren't the rags of a street walker, but rather showed substantial status. Why she, a woman of obvious respectful means, would be traveling along Texas Street was cause for concern, especially since she was rapidly approaching Phil Coe.

As the woman came under the awning of the Bull's Head, Coe stepped in her way and removed his hat. Hickok stepped from the jail boardwalk and marched across the street. From his view, the woman looked disturbed at Coe's attempt to obstruct her path and possibly invite her into his place. If there was one thing Hickok couldn't stand, it was a man pushing himself upon a defenseless woman.

"Stand aside, Phil. Let the lady pass."

Coe glared as his approach. "What affair is this of yours, Hickok? I was just introducing myself."

Hickok stepped up on the boardwalk. "By the look on her face, she'd rather slop hogs." He turned to her. Now closer, he saw she was a woman of beauty. Hazel eyes and dark hair, she had light powder on her face, which softened the small freckles on her cheeks and forehead. He removed his hat.

"Excuse the interruption, ma'am. Don't judge this town on the actions of this man or his rowdy place."

"Who the hell you think you are, Hickok?" Coe asked with outrage. "Get off my boardwalk."

Hickok faced him and stood nose to nose with the tall burly man before speaking in a low growl. "I am the marshal of this town. And I'll go any place that I want to." He again faced the woman. "Allow me to escort you to more pleasant surroundings." He offered his arm, and she hesitated before wrapping her arm inside his. They walked east from under the boardwalk awning. Hickok glared back at Coe, who appeared infuriated at the insult.

Once they were out of earshot of Coe, Hickok decided to make introductions of his own. "I am sorry for that, ma'am. This is actually a very nice and respectable town. I'm afraid you strayed to the evil center of our seasonal invaders from Texas. My name is J.B. Hickok and I am —"

"The marshal," she inserted. "Yes, so you told the man back there." He was caught off guard with her bold response, and found himself at a loss for words. Definitely, she appeared to be used to speaking her mind. Not a common occurrence for ladies of proper upbringing. They arrived at the corner of Cedar. "So, is this your habit with all the women you find straying onto Texas Street?"

The question amused him. "Only the ones that don't appear to belong there . . ." He stretched the last word in hopes of implying he would like to know her name instead of constantly referring to her as "ma'am," but she didn't volunteer any information. They had walked south some ways until she guided him to cross Cedar and arrived at a small two-story home. She stopped him at the gate.

"Well, it was a pleasure to make your acquaintance," he said. "However, I don't believe I got your name."

She smiled. "I am not in the habit of giving it out." She dipped her eyes for an instant. "You see, Marshal Hickok, I am just a visitor to this town. I don't plan to stay long nor begin friendships. You might be the chief peace officer, and may I say you do make a striking presence with your shirt and sash. But I have learned of your reputation. And I am a married woman." She began turning for the door. "I thank you for your escort. Good day, Marshal."

She entered the house as he stood in front of the small fence. He didn't move for several seconds, still in awe at her words and demeanor and totally intrigued. It was a feeling to which he was unaccustomed. Yet, if ever there was a woman he wished to know better and on more intimate terms, despite her marital status, it was this one whose name he didn't know.

26

Penelope kept walking. A mule team couldn't stop her. She'd almost let her heart be stolen by a man who had captured her attention. She had wanted to know more about him, but when she found out what he was, she wanted nothing else from him.

A fornicator wasn't someone to know or trust. Men who only wanted a woman to stick their prick in couldn't be counted on to accomplish a damn thing, to earn money, to build a home, to share a family.

While she was making her way from the Merchant's Hotel, her mind whirled with disgust, but it wasn't all aimed at Clay. She had allowed herself to be hurt once again. She'd not only come to Abilene to help a friend, but also to escape the trap of the man's world she'd lived in for the last four years. To exist in it, she'd adopted their ways and passed herself off as a hardworking rancher with the same knowledge and endurance as they. However, she still held the yearnings of a female and the desire to fulfill herself in that role. Hardship often got in her way, but she relied on the experience gained working a spread to get her past it so she could keep on searching for that better life yet to be discovered.

She made the turn onto Cedar. Despite her mind being in a blur, she saw Hickok walking with that city woman toward the boardinghouse. Penelope was in no mood for polite conversation, and so turned right onto Texas Street. The change put her back among the drunks stumbling about the boardwalks and lying in the shade to sleep off their liquor. As she continued, she saw the jail and thought maybe she could talk to Jody. He had always been a good ear for how she thought and the only one she told her secret.

Near the jail, she glanced across the street at the Bull's Head. She looked up at the now emasculated image. Her eyes wandered and she noticed a familiar head, although it was turned away from her. Penelope stopped. She concentrated on the head through the large plate-glass window. The hair was short, pinned up, but most of the women wore it that way, especially the ceiling inspectors. As she came slowly across the street, she noticed thin shoulders. The closer she came, the more she recognized the woman. Just as she remembered this was the whore leaving Clay's room, that whore turned about and saw Penelope standing in the middle of Texas Street. Then she pointed.

The whore must have been a spy sent to find out who painted the sign, and that horny idiot must have told her. Now, Penelope herself might be singled out as one who knew about the plot. Two men dressed like drovers came from the front door of the saloon. Penelope stepped back, at first slowly, then at a full run. She could have crossed the street and headed for the boardinghouse. Hickok would be there and would protect her. However, that would leave the men to take their revenge on Clay. When she got to the corner, her instinct took over. Instead of turning south for a certain safe haven, she went north and ran back toward the Merchant's Hotel.

Through the dense clutter of elbows and shoulders, she pushed her way back to Fifth Street. She saw the wide porch and headed straight for it, unsure exactly what she should say or even if she should say anything. Why was she running to save someone she didn't really know? Only her conscience and intuition drove her actions, and so she proceeded up the steps.

"Penelope!"

She stopped at the sound of her name. She turned and saw Clay standing in the alley saddling a Palouse. She went to him, his blue eyes wavering between confusion at seeing her and some mood less hostile than the ones she'd sensed before. "You got to leave. Now," she said. "You got to go."

"You didn't need to run here to tell me that. I didn't plan on bothering you."

She shook her head. "It ain't about me. That whore. The one you poked last night. She's working for Ben Thompson."

"Dorie?"

The fact that he knew her name squeezed Penelope's throat, but there wasn't time to complain. "Yes. Dorie," she said. "She's nothing but a spy sent to find who done painted the sign."

"What?"

"You got to get. There's two men coming, likely gunnies from the Bull's Head. I saw them and they know where you are. If you don't, they'll do what Ben said." She darted her eyes to his hips. "Shameful waste." He continued to show confusion. She felt the chance to escape slipping away. "Get on your horse and leave town or you'll not be able to poke no more whores."

Her words pushed him as hard as a shove toward the horse. Still with his head twisting in all directions, he stepped into the stirrup and pulled himself into the saddle. She stood as he reined about, not knowing if more should be said. When he appeared about to express some gratitude or disdain, she shooed him to ride. "You need to get." Her final order was what made him steer the horse down the alley. He nudged the flanks and the pony bolted between the buildings. She watched the hooves kick up dust and scamper into the distance.

She felt part of herself leave with the sight. An urge to call him back had to be swallowed. If he meant anything to her, it was only a memory based on a delusion that had grown in the back of her mind. When his figure shrank in her view, she turned her head to go back to the boardinghouse, pack what little she had, and leave this town for good.

With her head down in thought, she crossed the street, but the constant traffic forced her attention to shift back to the present. When she thought the way clear, she went to the other boardwalk.

The two gunnies rounded the corner. "There she is."

Penelope stepped back, but the two men came at her. "Get away from me. I'll smack you both down." The threat didn't stop their approach, so she turned to run, but the dense number of drovers staying in the shade kept her from evading the two men's grasp. One grabbed at her arm, the other wrapped an arm around her waist. "Sons of bitches," she yelled. "I ain't a whore. You got to help me." Her plea for help was ignored. Maybe the drover clothing had others fooled, thinking this a matter of an unpaid debt, or maybe they just didn't want to tangle in what was not their affair. The strength of the two men wasn't something she could wriggle free from.

"Where'd he go? Where is he headed?"

The questions were screamed in her ear. If she had known, she wouldn't tell. They took her into an alley and manhandled her to the dirt on her belly while barking more questions.

"Were you going to meet him? Where'd he go? Tell us and we'll let you loose."

Her reply was reflex. "Go to hell, you bastards." A knee punched her in the back. She coughed out breath.

"Don't think you're a whore? We'll make you one if you don't tell us." She fought against the grip, but only met superior force.

In an instant, it was gone.

Groans pierced her ears. She rolled to see one of them thrown against a wall. The next instant, Clay was above her. The other charged at Clay. A punch was stopped, and Clay rammed his palm into the other's nose. The first one drew a pistol, but it was slapped away. Penelope sprang to her feet. Bullets were about to fly, and she wanted to be clear of them. Clay stomped his boot into that one's gut. Both attackers lay on the ground. Clay still stood and pulled a long knife from his belt.

"No," she yelled. "There'll be more and they'll kill you."

He stood for only a moment. Then he picked up the small pistol and hurried back to the street. He jumped into the stirrup and flung his leg around the saddle. He reined about at her and held out his arm. "You coming?"

In one second, she had to decide. Safety? Les? Jody? Rance? Texas? Would she see anyone of them again? Was it worth the danger of the next few minutes?

She ran to him and reached for his arm. He grabbed her firmly and yanked her up. She straddled the top of the cantle just as he kicked the flank. The Palouse charged back through the same alley it had left before. The whirl of dirt and shadow flew by as they galloped away from Abilene.

27

Rance Cash sat facing the door. After much negotiation with the proprietors of the Elkhorn, he'd managed to get permission to run a game, only having to give the house twenty percent. It was his money, his risk, but it was their establishment. Always keeping an eye out for the next mark, he had a young drover sitting in front of him, not yet drunk enough to make rash decisions. Rance had to do some selling.

"You say you have thirty dollars in your pocket? How would you like to double that money in just a few minutes?"

The young man didn't seem to grasp the opportunity.

"How long did it take to earn that money?"

A long dopey expression followed before words came out. "Three months."

Rance smiled and nodded. "Miserable work, isn't it. You ride all day and night, herding cattle, sun on your neck, rain filling your boots. Three months and all you have left is thirty dollars. How would you like to go home with a hundred? It all starts here and now."

While the offer was being considered, Rance saw a more interesting sight enter through the front door. The Texan named Hardin came in with two other men close behind. When they looked for a table in the crowded room, Rance thought it a good chance to make some money and get information. First, he had to shoo the kid from the table. "Get out of here," he growled. The kid appeared surprised at the change in tone. Rance didn't have time to argue. "You want to lose that thirty dollars?" The kid again displayed the dopey face. "If you sit here another second, I'm going to play you for it and cheat you out of it. Now go." The threat was enough for the kid to leave the table in just enough time for Rance to wave Hardin and his friends to have a chair. "You gentlemen like to parlay at cards?" The invitation wasn't immediately accepted, but in a short time the open table in the crowded room lured all of them to sit. Once all were seated, some having to steal chairs from evicted occupants, Rance held out his hand to Hardin. "Ransom Cash."

"Wes Hardin," was the reply. A finger pointed out the others. "Gip and Manning Clements."

"Pleased to meet you all. What kind of game interests you boys?"

"I'm particular to monte," said Hardin.

Although not his specialty, Rance knew the game well. It was simple to understand, which was likely the reason Wes chose it. Rance shuffled the cards and decided to make conversation. "What part of Texas do you call home?"

All three appeared alarmed at the question. "Why you think we're from Texas?"

Unsure why they were worried, Rance shrugged. "Isn't everyone in this town?" When a few moments passed with no answer, he decided to ally himself with them while dealing the four cards faceup. "I have been through most of that great state. From Fort Worth to San Antonio to parts west. I can see why Texans have great pride in their heritage. I do admire that," he lied. With the exception of his friends and a few acquaintances, he shared the same opinion as Hickok about the state. However, this was not the place, time, or company to debate the issue.

Hardin pointed at the king of diamonds. The wager of five dollars was placed on it.

The bet was another diamond would be drawn before a matching suit of the other three cards. Rance flipped over the three of diamonds. The bet went to Hardin. The game continued, but with little conversation. Each time Rance tried to bring up a topic, all three were tight-lipped and seemed annoyed by his attempts to talk. Then Hardin motioned at Rance's coat.

"How is it you carry a weapon?" The inquiry was odd since Hardin himself sported two pistols in a belt. Rance voiced his observation, and Hardin responded, "I carry these with special permission from the marshal himself. My cousins here are law biding and don't offend the public by toting iron."

Rance wasn't sure if he was being threatened or if it was just a polite observation that was being made. Hardin, with every word accented in a tone that twisted between belligerence and benevolence, kept a smirk on his lips that Rance couldn't read. And so, Rance replied with the same ominous fervor.

"I, too, sir, am licensed by the marshal to be armed. We have an agreement which will remain between him and me. However, rest assured one reason for our agreement is my assurance not to recklessly brandish it nor provoke an engagement of gunplay" — he paused to let the words sink into their thick skulls — "despite my skill as a marksman."

The bluff was one of his better ones to judge from the looks on all three faces. From the corner of his eye, Rance saw real reason to worry. Without drawing attention to the latest patron to enter, Rance kept his focus on the cards, not knowing if gunfire might erupt at any moment. As confrontation surely approached, he wiggled his fingers to ready the derringer wrapped around his right forearm in case he needed it to save his life.

"Hello, Little Arkansas."

Hardin turned his head at Hickok in surprise. "Hello yourself," was the terse reply. "How would you like to be called 'Hello'."

Rance didn't understand the angered response but decided once Hickok grinned, that little attention was to be paid to the remark.

Upon finding a chair, Hickok looked at Rance. "How'd you find Cash? Been looking for him all day."

"Didn't take no finding," said Hardin. "He booted a trail bum from this table and called us to sit down."

Rance continued the game, knowing there

was another purpose for Hickok's presence than to find him.

"Deal me in, Cash," said Hickok. Rance cast an eye at one of the owners behind the bar. A nod was given and the marker was approved backed by the house. It was good business to keep the chief peace officer happy. Rance slid twenty chips in front of the marshal. "Don't believe I've met your friends," Hickok said to Hardin.

The Texans all looked apprehensive. Finally, after several silent seconds, Hardin introduced them proudly. "These are my cousins, Gip and Manning Clements. Boys, this here is the famous Wild Bill Hickok, marshal of Abilene."

During the next few hands, Hickok's inspection of the Clements brothers was hard to ignore. Rance sat confused. It had always been his impression that Hardin was the one to be watched. Besides, both of the cousins were unarmed. Wine was brought to the table and glasses were filled. In little time, Hickok had lost the chips, and another approval from the bar provided forty more. The same streak of bad luck continued, and Hickok shook his head.

"This is like when I was surrounded by savages in a narrow canyon."

Rance couldn't resist. "Tell us all about it,

Marshal."

Hickok imbibed another glass, but his nasal voice remained clear. "I had crossed into the territory of the Cheyenne. They didn't take to me being in their hunting grounds. I didn't take to them not taking to me," Hickok said, losing another hand. "They commenced their attack. I was holed up in the only spot where I didn't have to shoot but in one direction. I shot six times and killed six. Once I exhausted my bullets, I drew my bowie knife and proceeded to slashing at them as they came one by one."

Rance drew another card, which didn't meet Hickok's wager. The one named Gip noticed the story had paused and had to ask, "What happened next?"

Hickok looked up at the younger man and guffawed. "By God. They killed me, boys." The three of them joined the laughter. Even Rance thought the story amusing, taking into account the marshal's legend. Hickok tapped Rance on the shoulder, and once more Rance looked to the bar for guidance. With another nod, Rance slid over one hundred dollars in chips.

The Palouse tired. Clay eased up on the horse and allowed it to walk. For the past hour, they had passed two herds heading north. With a price on his head, he didn't want to be spreading his name or whereabouts among the Texans, knowing it would be told to those at the Bull's Head. He saw a ridge that rose from the flat prairie, and steered for it.

When they reached the plateau, they dismounted and looked out over the plain. "Damn," was the only word from him upon observation of a stream of cattle stretching to the horizon.

"There's three thousand head down there," said Penelope, drawing his surprised face to her. "And there's another herd just like it a week behind them."

He couldn't argue. Even if she was a woman, she was right, and seemed awfully clear about her judgment about cattle. He shook his head. "We can't get past that many without being seen." He looked at the ground. "We'll make some sort of camp here until dark, then try to pass by them."

"Camp?" she asked. "From what?"

He didn't like her tone. "I don't know. I have a bedroll is all." When she scoffed and shook her head and walked away, it touched a nerve. "I didn't have time to pack, you know."

She stopped her walk and faced him. "What's that mean?"

He didn't want to say it, but had to settle the air. "You led them right to me. To take some revenge would be my guess. Can't say I know how you think."

Her nostrils flared as she gritted her teeth. "That whore Dorie, the one you stuck it in last night, told them. I told you she was spying for them." She huffed breath and her chin quivered. "That's what those men were trying to get me to tell them, where you went. I risked my life to come and tell you." She faced away from him.

He watched her shoulders sag. In the brief time he'd seen this gal, it seemed they were always having angry words with each other, yet here they were together, running from the same threat. "Why did you?"

She turned around.

"Why did you?" he asked, looking into her moist eyes. "Why did you come and warn me? You owe me nothing. You could of watched them drag me from a rope and had nothing to do with where we are now. So, why did you?"

Her eyes darted around looking everywhere but at him. Finally, her breath calmed and she peeked up at the sky. "I'll get some wood for a fire."

Hickok spun more yarns while losing more

of the money Rance, through the Elkhorn, had staked him. By the third bottle of wine. Hardin began scratching his side. "Feeling a mite hungry." He looked at his cousins. "We'll eat and come back." He rose from the table and proceeded to the door. Before he left the Elkhorn, he turned and nodded at Hickok. "Good to see you again, Wild Bill."

Once the Texans were gone, Hickok's mood changed. "How long they been here?"

Rance shrugged. "Not long before you got here. May I ask why you care?"

Hickok cracked a smile. "No. You can't." Although his tone held authority, he did speak with some friendliness. "Official town business. Not for all to know." After a few moments, he curled a brow at Rance. "Didn't you say once you were staying at a boardinghouse on Cedar?"

Rance, while shuffling the cards, didn't know how this question was meant to satisfy official town business. "I believe I may have. Are there more secrets I'm not to know?"

Hickok's grin broadened. "I saw a woman today. A real lady of refinement. She walked along Texas Street where she didn't belong. Real fancy dress and cool manners, that one. She wouldn't tell me her name. But I walked her to —"

315

"Wearing ear bobs and a chip hat?" Rance's description hit the mark, as evidenced by the enthused widening of Hickok's usually squinted eyes. "I believe I may be aware of the lady in question."

"Who is she?" Hickok asked with childish eagerness.

It was a chance to play a different hand. "I'm sorry, Marshal. That's official boardinghouse business. On a need-to-know basis." The reply soured Hickok's face. No doubt perturbed at the game Rance now played, the marshal was about to invoke his powers as a peace officer, and perhaps even arrest Rance for concealing needed evidence. However, before such a tirade could begin, a deputy came through the front door and directly to the table.

"I need to talk to you."

Hickok glanced at the deputy. "Not now, McDonald. I'm interrogating a witness." Hickok resumed his glare at Rance, which did seem somewhat wine-influenced.

"You're going to want to know about this," said McDonald. "You'll ask me why I didn't tell when a fight breaks out."

Reluctantly, the marshal looked at his deputy, then back at Rance. The choice of following duty or personal curiosity weighed heavily on his mind. After several seconds,

316

Hickok rose from the table. As he waved McDonald to leave the saloon with him, he cast one last eye at Rance.

"We're not done here!"

28

J.H. McDonald led Hickok out of the Elkhorn and down the street. Whatever the news, it couldn't be good, which increased the marshal's irritation. Once McDonald stopped, Hickok was anxious to get the matter resolved, get back to Cash, and extract the information he really wanted.

"Spit it out."

McDonald darted his eyes around before looking directly at him. "There's going to be a fight. There's some cowboys getting liquored up to face Manning Clements. Seems the story that's he's been telling around town ain't what happened, according to these men. They say Manning came into camp in the middle of the night and shot the Shadden brothers in their bedrolls."

Hickok appreciated the news. It was important enough to drag him from the Elkhorn. "Seems to go along with the family trait. Any witnesses?"

McDonald shrugged. "None but the usual talk. They seen it their way. Of course, most of them are so drunk, can't decipher what exactly happened from what they want to do to Clements."

Vengeful cowboys with enough alcohol in their blood was a burning fuse that likely would send lead all about the town. The longer it burned, the bigger the blast. The last few days had remained relatively peaceful by Abilene standards, and Hickok wanted to keep it that way. Another matter also had to be seen to, but this one needed to be squashed at the present moment.

He peeked at the setting sun. "Let's go and take them in. We'll say we got a wire to arrest them. If we get them in the jail, maybe we can keep this from getting bloody." He motioned McDonald to follow, and they headed toward the American House.

Although it was a short walk, the neighborhood changed dramatically. As Hickok made his way, he felt eyes on his back. The neighborhood wasn't filled with the rowdies looking for a good time on Texas Street, nor was it the more sedate east side of the town where the affluent locals made their homes and where the Drover's Cottage was located. The American House was a hastily

319

built barn of a hotel that attracted the least sophisticated among the Texans. The ones Hickok and McDonald sought were typical of that type of men who liked to flock together.

When they reached the steps, Hickok readied the twin fifty-ones just in case things turned against them. When they entered, the crowd saw him and McDonald and the jabber turned to low muttering. Hickok saw Hardin and his cousins at a table eating. He slowly approached, and their eyes told him they knew why he was there. Hardin, his plate finished, leaned back, showing the pistols in his belt, while the other two had yet to clean their plates.

"Are you through eating?" Hickok asked in a direct but tempered tone. "I have a telegram here to arrest Manning Clements, so consider yourself under arrest." He paused, noticing the yet-uneaten portion in front of Manning. There wasn't a reason to make the situation brutal. "I can wait until you finish your supper."

Manning looked at his cousin, then his brother. "That's not necessary, Marshal. It ain't the best I ever tasted anyhow." Manning rose. The chair legs scooting across the wood floor sent an eerie sound, triggering Hickok's hand to palm the right pistol butt.

He looked at Hardin to watch for any attempt to resist. None of them appeared ready to put up a fight. In fact, Hickok sensed Hardin was regretful at the arrest.

McDonald followed Manning as they left the room. Hardin rose from his chair, but his hands were in clear sight, yet Hickok never released his grip on the butt. They walked outside together with Hardin holding an anxious expression. "Didn't Columbus Carroll talk to you?"

Hickok shook his head. "No. He's drunk. I saw him earlier."

The tall Texas kid snarled, "He was supposed to post it with you."

The idea of squaring a murder wasn't in Hickok's nature, but he didn't want to anger the kid and so decided to turn Hardin's guilt to his advantage. "Why didn't *you* post it with me?"

Hardin took a deep breath. "I thought it better coming from a man like Carroll. I guess I was wrong." They continued into the dusk heading back toward Cedar.

As all around were seeing the arrest take place, it wouldn't be a simple matter to allow Hardin and his cousin to leave town and then try to enforce laws that affected Abilene. Hickok's sole concern was to maintain order among the drovers and enjoy his steady pay. The problem would be keeping the peace when so many drovers were drinking their courage up in order to take vengeance against Manning. A plan needed to be agreed on. "Let's have a drink and settle this matter."

They went to a less crowded gambling hall where few cared to enter. Hickok didn't want to make a show with Hardin for it might hurt his reputation as a peace officer. A faro table allowed the two to talk and play at the same time. Hickok placed a bet. "I think it wise to put your cousin behind bars at this time. There's words running about the street that the affair which took place, which neither of us saw, might not have been as your cousin described."

Hardin also placed a wager on the green table. "Manning said he was satisfied with his action. If he is satisfied, then so am I. But I do understand how this makes you look with your citizens."

They both won and placed another wager at the same time, adding the winnings to the wager. "I have no willful intent on holding your cousin. The action which took place was outside Abilene, and for that I'm thankful. The fact remains, all of you are in Abilene, which makes it my affair now." Hickok and Hardin won their bets and again placed a wager on the same suit on the table, again adding the winnings to the wager. The stacks gradually grew.

"I think I know of an answer," Hardin said while continuing to play. "You put Manning in the jail for all to see."

Hickok listened, but was distracted by another presence in the small room. A man dressed in a fine tweed coat and bowler sat at a table alone with a bottle. The coat was buttoned and there was no firearm in sight. However, his look and manner were odd. The clothes weren't those of someone who worked the plains for his living and certainly they didn't suggest a planned ride back to Texas. This man looked like someone accustomed to visiting the more established cities. Hickok stared into the man's eyes, but the dim light didn't allow him to see clearly. However, the posture of the man, along with the fact that he wasn't engaging in the games, made Hickok wary.

"What be your thinking of that?"

Hardin's voice returned and pierced Hickok's consciousness. He hadn't concentrated on the proposal, but already had planned out what to do. They continued their betting and ordered a bottle of wine. "If I let Manning go, he's got to leave Abilene and never return."

"I said he would agree to that," Hardin answered with a bit of irritation. "I think it should be late. Perhaps an hour before dawn."

"More like midnight. I don't want to have to keep my jailer up through the night." Hickok kept his eye on the suspicious man on the far side of the room. Hickok and Hardin kept betting, and to Hickok's surprise, they kept winning. Once his stack had split into two, he decided to keep the bet riding on his winning streak while trying to keep an eye on the one with the tweed coat.

The wine soon ran out and another bottle took its place. Hickok became less distracted by the man's continual presence, and more attention was paid to the amounts won at this faro table. The game called for the wagering on a card painted on a green table. Then two actual cards were drawn from a caged deck, with the first discarded and the second one in play. It was an easy game to understand, but not as challenging as draw poker. Yet, it appeared to keep Hardin's temper under control, and also didn't require Hickok to gauge opposing players' cards by subtle ticks in the hands or the face. He often glanced at the fellow in the corner.

■ ■ ■ ■

Les looked about the parlor. A midweek night didn't bring in as many customers as did the afternoon. Most of the customers came later, if they came at all. However, she'd been too busy in the late afternoon to hurry home, as was her routine, in order to be at supper and bring some food back for Jody and the jailer. Once she saw that the rooms were quiet, and the lady was away on some errand, she decided to steal away from the parlor and try to keep her schedule although it was late.

She quietly left through the front door and ran down the dirt path toward town. The darkness made it easy for her not to be noticed, but it also made it difficult to see very far in front of her. She recalled the nights on the trail in Texas, when all there was to see was the glow of campfire in the distance. She used the experience to guide her toward Texas Street.

She turned the corner onto what the locals called A Street. The crowd standing on the dimly lit boardwalks stopped her pace. Not wanting to have to pass through them and suffer their drunken attempts to charm her, she decided to take a detour to the next street and cross through the alleys to the boardinghouse.

The lamps that lit the street weren't as numerous, and so she hurried past them in apprehension of what she couldn't see. One more turn would put her back on course, but when she made that turn, she saw two silhouettes in the dark. Instant by instant, she came to recognize the two figures. They weren't tall. They were women. One was Lady Shenandoah and the other was the raven-haired Jesse Hazel. They saw her approach, and the next instant she heard the question from the dark.

"What are you doing here?" asked the lady.

A lie was too hard to think of so quickly, so the truth had to do. "I thought I could run out and get a meal. The parlor isn't crowded right now." She heard Jesse giggle.

"Sure that's all? Not something else on your mind?"

Shenandoah was quick to defend Les. "No. She's not of the calling. She's going to keep herself pure for some man." They both giggled. "Until she finds out there's only so much they'll give her and she can get more on her own."

Les didn't take to the suggestion and turned the tables on them, although with respect. "What are you two doing? I thought you were working another house, Jesse."

"We're talking about that very matter," the lady answered. "We've settled our differences."

"Not quite yet," Jesse replied. "But I am agreeable to what's being offered." She looked at Les, who could now focus on their faces. "When you get your regular tricks following you, you don't have to hump every night."

It wasn't an idea she wanted to consider. She'd seen the dirty, smelly men file one by one into the parlor to be alone in the rooms with the girls. She'd heard the sounds and listened to the tales told about the pain. In front of her stood two women not much more than five years older than she. However, she knew they'd spent as much time with men as a woman married for ten years. They had no man to call their own, only a list of regulars who provided them with coins.

Les kept her thoughts to herself. "I'll be back soon to sweep. I won't be gone longer than a half hour." As she slipped past them both, another deeper voice pierced the night.

"Evening, ladies," said a man. Footsteps brought the voice closer. "I suppose you have reason for being here."

Les saw the tin gleam in the dark. The next few seconds, she recognized the man as one of the deputies.

"We're just talking, Tom," said Jesse. "We ain't working the street. My business isn't that bad."

"Still and all, you are in violation of the ordinance keeping whores away from the church, which you are just feet from."

"Who is in church at this time?" the lady complained.

"Not a matter for judgment. The law is the law. Now, I have to take you gals to the jail." Les saw him point at her. "Even you, little one. I see they have recruited you into their line."

"You can't take me to jail, Tom. I wasn't doing nothing. You see any men around here?"

He chuckled. "As a matter of fact," he said, grabbing Jesse's arm and pulling her closer. He shoved her arm down. In the shadows Les couldn't see, but heard the rustle of leather, cloth, and metal. "I do." He paused and took a deep breath. "The fine is seventy-five dollars for being where you shouldn't. But we can barter the amount."

Jesse ripped away from his grasp. "Go to

hell. I ain't a little girl you can force your way on, badge or no."

"So be it," said the deputy. The same rustle of noise came and went and he stepped around them all. "We're going to the jail, you bunch of whores."

Les thought to explain, but he nudged everyone's back and made them all march away from her intended path to the boardinghouse and toward the numerous street lamps and the jail. She hadn't wanted to be there this soon, and thoughts of what others would think entered her head. She didn't know what to say, or how to make it sound right.

They came through the light, and the drovers lining the boardwalks and the street watched with sly grins on their faces.

"Round up your own harem?" came a call from across the street. Les glanced at the Bull's Head, with its normal crowd spilling out into the street. When one of the more liquored cowboys tried to steal a pinch of hip from Shenandoah, she slapped his hand, then his face, to the guffaws of the others.

As they neared the jail's front door, Les's heart was in her throat. She couldn't hold back or even try to escape. Before any plan could enter her mind, the door was opened. In his usual chair sat Mike the jailer. His eyes lit up when he saw her in the company of the other women. She felt a chill go through her as the deputy marched them to the hall while another deputy sat at the marshal's desk. Les lagged behind the other two, and for an instant saw Jody smile when he saw Jesse and the lady put in the other cell.

With each heartbeat, she watched him turn his head toward her, the smile on his face sinking like a rock in water, his eyes spread as wide as a river. With the deputy's call, she went to the cell with the other women. Another man was in Jody's cell sitting on the bunk, but it was that cold disbelief coming from her man that squeezed her ribs hard enough to make her gasp for breath.

"I caught these whores strolling by the church," said the deputy.

Jody stepped back from her until the far side's bars stopped him. His mouth agape, he faced away from her. Her throat choked tears to her eyes. Mike closed the cell door. He, too, was looking into her eyes with disappointment. "I guess you had to do what it took."

She shook her head. "It ain't how it is."

She felt the lady's hands on her shoulders. "Don't fret it. We won't be here long."

Les knew what it sounded like. She faced the lady who had befriended her years before, and given her a means to earn money without having to sell herself. Now, that association had cost her what she treasured most, and she had only a moment to rescue it. She backed away. "I ain't one of you." She looked at Jody, hoping he'd turn around, but he didn't. "I swear, I ain't one of you." She went to clutch the bars. "Please, Jody. Believe me."

He stood with his back to her. She glanced at Mike, who nodded his head. "He will," he said quietly to her. "But it's not the time. Not here."

With the wine and winnings flowing in, Hickok lost interest in the man in the corner. Although he was still present, the man in the fine duds hadn't moved in the two hours they'd all spent there. Even Hardin showed all the signs of a man at ease with the moment. Probably that mood was due to the anticipation of Manning's release.

About the time all seemed well, Hickok noticed McDonald enter the place with another concern written on his face. The marshal didn't want to hear any more bad news.

"The prisoner secure?" he asked.

McDonald nodded. "Yeah. All of them."

The reference sounded odd. There was only one other prisoner Hickok was aware of. "All? How many you got locked up?"

"There's the kid from San Antonio, and Manning in one cell." McDonald paused to allow the dealer to draw the second card. The bet was lost. McDonald went on. "Carson locked up three whores. Two of them you know." Hickok stopped his hand from placing a bet. Instead, he turned his attention to the standing deputy, who answered the silent question. "The one that runs the dogwood house" — he paused — "and Jesse Hazel."

Hickok slammed down his stack. "Son of a bitch," he lamented. "Damn him. What did he do that for?"

McDonald explained. "Claims they were over by the church."

"Those women don't work the street. He should be thrashed with a whip." Hardin appeared amused at his distress. About the time the thought hit Hickok that he would have to see to the matter, he glanced at the far side of the room. The table was now empty and the lone bottle mostly full. It was an extravagance to leave paid-for liquor behind, even if it was cheaply distilled and tasted like grass. He rose from the table,

332

tucking his stacks in both pockets. He didn't have the time nor the patience to count them.

Hickok marched out with McDonald and Hardin close behind. The wine had affected him, but not to the point where he stumbled. During the trek, his anger grew. It was common knowledge among those who worked for him that there were private acquaintances not to be harassed without his knowledge and permission. It was unspoken, unofficial, and understood. If he ever again enjoyed the complimentary delight of those women's favors, it would take the expression of a wagon load of remorse to salvage the relationship.

He turned onto Texas Street and ignored the jeers from the crowd outside the Bull's Head. He opened the front door of the jail, and Carson and Mike Williams snapped to attention. They'd seen his glare before. He slowed his step to the full jail cells. The two women had smug grins, but the chambermaid looked scared. He looked to Carson in disbelief. He'd arrested two of his favorites and their cleanup girl.

Carson handed Hickok the key. Without a word, he went to the cell door and opened it. First out was the Virginia woman, then Jesse, who stopped at the cell door opening.

She looked directly at Carson. "He tried to force me to suck him, Bill."

Carson tried to deny the charge with a shake of the head. Hickok wasn't believing him. He shooed the women out, although the little chambermaid didn't appear to want to leave. He signaled for Mike to get her out of the office. Once only men were left, he turned again to Carson.

"Why'd you do that?" asked the arresting deputy.

Hickok fired a fist into Carson's jaw, dropping the man to the floor. Anger filled him. He knelt and punched again four more times. The lips bled, the eyes swelled before he stopped himself. When he stood, he heaved breath while staring at the writhing man.

He looked around. McDonald and Williams stood in awe and fear. Hardin held a smirk. A glance at the two men in the cell showed their indifference to the event. Hickok felt a bit embarrassed for losing his temper, but the insult had been answered. He considered firing Carson and sending him out of town, but didn't act on the thought.

He waved at the cell. "Let them out."

Mike went to the cell with a key and opened the door. Manning was first to leave, and shook the hand of his cousin. The kid from San Antonio stood in place with the door open. Hardin took notice at the delay and went to the cell.

"Ain't you going to leave, boy?"

The kid took a breath. "My name ain't boy. It's Jody Barnes." Hardin appeared eager for the kid to walk the streets. Hickok thought again about his order, but he didn't have time to nanny anymore. The kid looked defiant. "I got a heap on my mind. But I ain't fearing you," he said to Hardin. "If it's between staying locked up or being about with you in town, I take to walking free. And if it's a fight you're looking for, I'll oblige you."

"No, you won't," Hickok boomed. "I'm ordering you out of town. Tonight." He looked at Mike. "Get him his gear and get his horse from the livery. Send him on his way." He looked at Hardin. "And you're going to let him go unharmed."

Hardin shrugged. "I lost interest in him."

"No reason for the order," said Barnes, who looked at Mike. "I'm going back to Texas. Nothing here to keep me. Not now."

The anguished wails of Carson disturbed the room. Hickok motioned at McDonald. "Get him over to the doc. Have him put it on my bill." He took a deep breath and wanted to cleanse the event from his mind. He waved at Hardin. "Let's get back there and finish what we started." Reaching into his pocket, he drew the handful of chips. "Seems we left some of these behind." They both chuckled and left the jail.

McDonald helped Carson off the floor and out the door.

Jody looked at Mike. His anger at Les put him in an unfriendly mood, but he didn't want to take any of it out on the jailer. Mike was first to speak.

"Well, you got what you want. I think you should take the marshal's advice and get back to your family."

"Don't need no advice for that," said Jody in a low mutter. His heart still beat from his chest and thoughts of Les seized his breath. As Mike handed him the hat, he stood in front of Jody to prevent him from acting rashly.

"Am going to miss them vittles. Now, I'll have to cook my own grub and be pained for it."

It took a moment, but Jody couldn't crack a grin. "Sorry."

"Oh, don't feel sorry for me," said Mike. "You know, it might take a piece of time to ponder it all out. But I have a feeling that little gal does care for you. Whatever she done, you got to remember that. Ain't often a fellow has that waiting on him. You should take a spell, think things out. But don't feel you have to close off something or someone due to what might be. Without you truly knowing." He took a deep breath and looked into Jody's eyes. "You take care of yourself, young buck. I don't want to be going to your funeral."

Jody nodded. It was sage advice despite the fact that he was not in a mood to hear it. "Let's get my horse."

29

Robert Clayton Cole II looked upon the plain below. Dawn broke none too soon. A night of dodging drovers riding nighthawk had put Clay and Penelope miles from where they wanted to be. With the sun's help, they could mark their whereabouts.

They came to a ridge allowing for a view of the plain below. Not a steer was in sight, which meant they were likely due east and far from food and water. "Any ideas?" he asked.

"Can't be near any cattle trail. The ground looks too good." He had noticed that also, as the prairie grass hadn't been trampled by thousands of hooves. Without much certainty, Clay nudged the horse down the slope and rode toward the south. If there was to be shelter found, it would have to be near where the trail drives were, spawning towns eager to soak up some of the money.

Another hour put them beyond anywhere

in sight, until they came upon a house in the distance and a change of color in the grass. Clay knew what it was. "Wheat farmers."

He steered the horse toward the house, but not at a quick pace. Unsure of the owner's attitude to those riding up, he wanted to have distance should any unwelcome warning come their way. When they neared the rickety structure with sod surrounding the back and sides, a silence he wasn't used to had him rein in the horse.

"What's wrong?" she asked.

"It's mid-morning and nobody is moving." He stood in the stirrups. "Hello in the house," he called. Scanning in all directions, he saw not a soul. "This ain't right." He slid off the saddle and offered help to her. She didn't take it, preferring to jump to the ground. Ignoring her act of independence, he took the reins and walked slowly toward the house.

Once they were within ten feet of the house, he saw the door ajar. Not sure who or what was inside, he turned to her. "Stay here."

"I want to go."

"Damn you, woman. Can't nobody tell you something without you having to fuss about it?" He pointed at the house. "Might

not be something in there you want to see."
He handed her the reins and went to the
front. With each step taken, he peered
about, ready to take cover should something
spring his way. He pushed the door open,
but stayed on the dirt outside. "Anybody
here?"

There was no answer. He took a step
inside. The single room showed a dirt floor,
a fire-pit center, and a few wood-hammered
furnishings. The typical home on the prairie
of those making their way by plowing the
soil and making do with what could be
found. He was raised in such a place.
However, this house appeared abandoned,
which made little sense. Satisfied no one
was inside, since there didn't appear anyplace to hide in, he went back outside.

"What'd you see?"

He shook his head. "Ain't nobody in
there." He looked at the wheat field. The
crop was nearly at full stalk. In a month or
two, it would be ready for harvest. Someone
had done some hard work, but had left it
behind. The mystery pushed him out into
the field. Penelope followed.

With the two of them twenty feet apart,
they marched through the field swatting the
stalks from their path. Clay had walked deep
into the crop when he saw a space among

the top of the stalks in the distance. That alone wasn't much to fear, but it meant something weighed the stalks down. He went to it and within ten feet, a stench filled his nose. From his years as a trooper, he knew the smell.

Cautiously, he went closer. It was possible some carcass had been dragged by a predator, but when he saw different colors, the colors of cloth through the blur of stalks, he knew he'd solved the mystery.

"What'd you find?"

"Stay back," he called. The order served only to encourage the woman to approach. "Ain't nothing you want to see." He pushed the rest of the stalks from his way as she came near.

"Oh, Lord," she said, stopping when the stench got to her nose. "Who was it?"

Clay bent down to try to see better. He saw a face rotted from days in the sun. A slash below the chin had turned black. "Likely, the one that owned the place. The throat's been cut. May have been here a few days, maybe a week."

He stood and stepped back. There was nothing he could do about it now. He looked around for any other signs.

"Indians do this?"

He shook his head. "The Ponca Sioux

haven't been around here for years, those that didn't go to reservations. There's been peace for a long while now." The longer he looked, the more he saw what happened. "This is white man's work."

"Why would they do such a thing?"

The answer surrounded them. "You're standing in it." He pointed south. "Likely some kind of wire fence a ways from here blocked the trail north. Some drovers didn't take to the extra days on the trail and come and did this." He looked again at the body. "Probably from the East, coming out here to grow a crop, make a living. Could have had a wife and some kids from where he came. Might not have. Explains why no one else is here now. Could have been told to leave and put up a fight, or he was just killed to make a point. They might have been drunk or just plain mean." He looked around at the crop. "But there's more like him a-coming, and there'll be more like him dying as long as there is cattle heading to the rails." He gave her a look. She showed her distress at the killing. "You're the one wanted to come over here."

He walked back toward the house, but she stayed in place. "Aren't you going to put him in the ground? Give him a Christian burial."

He stopped and looked back at the body. "How you know he's Christian? Been with the army a few years and know of quite a number of fellows from other parts of the world that ain't."

When he resumed his walk, she answered. "Because we are." Her words didn't stop him. A few moments passed as he trudged through the wheat. "Ain't you got no decency?"

He'd already made up his mind and had an answer for her with a smart tone to his voice. "Likely, there's a shovel in the house."

Rance came down the stairs of the boardinghouse. He knew he'd missed breakfast, and was prepared to make apologies. When he reached the bottom, he peeked at the stove and saw Les washing dishes. Considering the time of day, that was unusual. He walked over carefully and peeked over her shoulder. She looked up at him with bloodshot eyes. There were only two reasons for that, and Les didn't drink. "Here, here, little one. Why are you crying?" She shook her head so she'd not have to explain. He wasn't accepting her refusal. "What's got you so upset?"

After a few moments, she faced him. "Jody left town."

The news surprised him on two accounts. "He's out of jail?"

She pursed her lips, about to burst into tears, but then choked out the story. "He saw me with the women last night. The parlor women. We got took to jail for being near the church. I was trying to come home and get him supper, but a deputy hauled us to jail." She heaved a breath. "He called us all whores right in front of Jody. Jody thought I was one of them."

Rance couldn't believe it. "Impossible. How could he think that?"

"I guess when you keep company with those of that reputation, it can't help but be thought the same of me." Her chin quivered. "He wouldn't even talk to me. I went back there today, but Mike Williams said he was let go and left last night."

Rance opened his arms, and she buried her teary face in his chest. He'd known the girl for two years, and knew she wouldn't give away something so precious just for money. At a loss for words, he was hardly the guardian of piety. Yet, he owed to it her to comfort her in some way. They'd been through many an ordeal since they'd met on the trail to Texas. He was the one she'd sent for, and it wasn't to gamble and drink. He gently held her shoulders and met her eyes when he spoke.

"He will come back. Sooner than you think, he will realize what he left behind and return to take you."

The speech didn't change her mood. "He thinks I'm a parlor woman. Maybe I am. Maybe I am a whore."

"Don't say that, Les. You know better. I know better."

She shook her head. "I quit last night. I said some things to the lady I'm sure made her think I was betraying her. But I can't go back there. Not with knowing what it's cost me."

Once more, Rance hugged his young female friend. He didn't know how, nor what means it would take, but he silently vowed to make things right with these two sweethearts. An idea struck him about how he might solve that dilemma. "I'll get Penelope to go after him. She said they could talk, and maybe she might be able to talk some sense into him." His confidence in the idea waned slightly as he thought about the challenge of sending the hard-as-nails woman after Jody on his way to Texas. But if he could trust any woman to make it, it was that tall blonde.

Les shook her head. "She's not here. Miss Maggie said she didn't come back last night.

Her bed wasn't slept in."

The news wasn't entirely surprising. The reckless soul of a woman after a man might have taken her into one of the flophouses around town. However, he sighed at the discovery. Now, he had two women to shepherd back into the fold of happiness.

30

Wes Hardin awoke in his room at the American House. It was well into the afternoon. He was not surprised nor disappointed. He'd had a busy and purposeful night. The previous evening had started in the afternoon with his play at the Elkhorn with Hickok. With a killing hanging over the head of his cousin Manning, he'd feared the worst, but had managed to get all he wanted. After the release of his cousin from jail, he had won nearly one thousand dollars. With his winnings and his cash rewards for his courageous killing of Juan Bideno, he had a small fortune. After more gambling with Wild Bill, he'd ridden south with Manning and handed over a sizable amount so his kin could make it back to Texas.

However, he had taken to the town of Abilene and as long as he remained prosperous, he saw no reason to leave it. And so he'd ridden back, and hadn't arrived until what the clock on the wall in the lobby said was three in the morning.

As he shook off slumber, he felt like satisfying manly urges and then getting something to eat. He had plenty of money for both. He threw a pillow at his cousin Gip, and they soon both dressed and went out into the hot afternoon.

They headed to the first place up the path. He'd been in the mood since before he awoke, and wanted to get it done and past him so he could enjoy some bacon and maybe two or three eggs. He came up the dirt path and saw the front door of the place wide open and the gals hauling their belongings into a cart.

"Howdy," he called. He didn't get a bright reply. "What's going on here? Don't tell me you're going out of business."

"Might as well be, if it were up to the town council," said the tall gal whose rump likely still showed the imprint of his palm from days before. Still confused, he looked at Gip and shrugged. The woman who ran the place came from the front hauling linen herself.

"We're closed right now, boys. But we'll be opening in a new part of town. I think we can be open by tomorrow night."

"Tomorrow night?" Hardin repeated,

dismayed at the postponement of his plans. "How come?"

She tossed the linen in the cart and faced him. "The council is moving all of us to the southeast of town. Won't be any of us to take care of your needs around here." She walked back to the house, but stopped on the front porch. "Tell all your friends if they're wanting women, they'll have to come a little farther." She smiled. "But tell them we'll make their coming worthwhile." She went back into the house.

The promise didn't change the present. He stood there ready to relieve his carnal passion, then get on with his day. But the women didn't appear as accommodating as when he'd visited before. As he and Gip stood in the afternoon sun watching women enter and leave the house carrying their wares, the boss lady once more came from the front and saw him standing there.

She sighed. "If it's a quick one you're needing, Carolina will take your money. But you'll have to do it on the floor."

The offer was insulting. Who did they think he was? Without a reply, he turned back to town, his urges subsided in the despondency of being made to feel like some varmint. Just because they had no pride didn't mean she had to imply that he had none either. He waved Gip to follow. If he found something he liked along the way, he might be obliged to make a play, but for now, all he wanted to do was get out of the heat and relax with a drink in his hand.

With money to spare, he walked into town and stopped in the first place he saw. The faro table was showing a crowd, and the success the previous night put him at the table. He placed a bet of five dollars, which brought attention from the others. He took some pride in their notice, but it quickly vanished along with his wager. Continual tries to recapture the luck enjoyed the previous night only led to further losses.

"Can't buck this tiger," said a voice from behind him. Hardin turned and saw the source of the advice. The face was familiar, but only in the sense that he'd seen it recently before and not in a social way. "Been here all day seems like." The man shook his head. "Haven't won enough for spit." Hardin felt the same way, and the impulse pushed him away from the table.

"I'm leaving." He waved at Gip, then cast an eye at the fellow with the advice. "We'll find us a place with more respect for us." The man followed, and they proceeded to walk across the street. No particular establishment appeared to offer a cool place to sit and gamble where they could end their losing streaks and be spared the heat of the late afternoon.

Ideas came and went. The Bull's Head was a place full of Texans where Hardin knew he was always welcome, but there were always men eager for a loan to offset their losses. The more places he ran through his mind, the less interested he became. The Alamo was a fine establishment for a man of stature, which he considered himself to be. However, that was Hickok's place, and Hardin was in no mood to meet the lawman and hear another lecture. The Pearl never proved profitable for him. The Elkhorn was a good place, but a mite far to walk in the heat. The Old Fruit also only served as a place to stay out of the sun, since their games of chance were only a risk to the player. As he strolled about, hunger forced him to seek those eggs he'd promised himself.

While searching for suitable restaurants, he did take notice of the frequent sightings of deputies patrolling the street. Even the swollen face of Tom Carson was seen, and at the same time Hardin noticed that there were no street-walking whores anywhere. The observation further depressed him. Not that he would lower himself to a back-alley

351

interlude, but the signals were there that the delights offered by Abilene were not as available as they had been.

The smell of lard took away his depression, and he followed the smell to a narrow building where a stove could be seen through the window. The three of them went inside and enjoyed a meal of eggs and bacon. He paid for himself and Gip, then eyed their newest compadre, who dug into his pockets for a few coins. "Just who are you?" asked Hardin. The friend offered his hand.

"Charlie Couger."

Hardin accepted the handshake. "Wes Hardin. This my cousin Gip. Where do I know you from?"

Couger shook his head. "You don't. But I have seen you at the American House."

The reply hit Hardin like a revelation. He'd seen that face among the crowd in the lobby. Relieved this man wasn't after him in the name of the law, Hardin treated the table, to the grateful nod of his new friend. The bill was considerable for such common food. Hardin would have been better off playing faro. Nevertheless, the meal and the knowledge of Couger's identity soothed his concern. At least he'd satisfied one of his urges.

Along about dusk, they found another of the small gambling halls that wasn't too crowded and provided them with an easy way to gamble and drink. Hardin did both without caution in celebration of his time in Abilene. An hour into their play, he felt himself become bleary-eyed. The effects of the previous late night hadn't yet left him. He nudged Gip, who appeared just as tired. With a bob of the head, he made his intention clear. They rose and took a step toward the door. Couger looked at them and rose, too.

"I'm going to turn in for the night," said Hardin.

"Was thinking the same," said Couger. "Been up most of last night."

The admission surprised and slightly alarmed Hardin. Yet he proceeded out the front door, leading the way back to the American House with Gip and Couger following. As they walked through the darker streets, the town sounded calm. A good sign for Hardin, who sought a quiet night's sleep. When they arrived in the lobby, he marched up the steps toward his room and Gip came by his side. Couger did also. Hardin felt a cold tingle. When Couger stopped at the next door down, the tingle lessened but wasn't gone. Fatigue pushed Hardin's thoughts toward the interior of his own room and the cousins went inside, shed their clothes quickly, and fell onto the mattress.

Although his body was tired, his mind wasn't. The stuffy air didn't allow for much relaxation. Hardin changed positions frequently, forcing Gip to do the same, in an effort to become comfortable. The cloth nightshirt was scratchy, and soon became wet with sweat. Rolling on his side or staying on his back didn't allow for slumber. The longer he lay still, the more he found his mind at ease, releasing the tension in his muscles. Even Gip didn't move as much. He closed his eyes, and didn't find a need to open them.

A loud strained eruption echoed through the wall. Then came another. It was a growling snore coming from the next room like there was no wall at all. Hardin took a deep breath in hopes it would pass, but found after several more eruptions that that outlook was unrealistic.

He sat up in the bed. "Roll over, Couger!"

He repeated the call twice before noticing the snoring ceased. Thankful, he resumed lying prone and tried to recapture his lost sleep. He closed his eyes. Not five minutes passed.

Long, nasal gasps pierced the silence.

Hardin opened his eyes, disturbed to the point that his mind wandered. Who was this Charles Couger? Might it be no accident that he was staying in the next room? Why would he have been up so late the previous night as Wes had been? Had he had a late-night ride, and why? Of course, Abilene was a town where a man could find reason to be up at any hour, and there were a few saloons that encouraged the practice.

Another choking growl crashed into his ears.

Hardin didn't have any more patience. He sat up in the bed and felt into the dark for one of his .44-caliber pistols. Even if it were just an irritating habit, and most men had at least one, he could no longer stand the torture. If yelling through the wall wasn't enough, then maybe a warning shot might get the message across to either roll over or find another room.

Hardin cocked the hammer.

"What are you doing?" asked Gip from the dark.

"I'm fixing to let him know I mean to be sleeping."

"Well," Gip said with the same determination, "give me mine." Pleased his kin had the same gumption as he, Hardin found his other pistol and handed it to Gip. When he heard the hammer cocked, he stretched his arm in aim to send lead high above the bed in the next room. They both fired.

Flame lit up the dark room. The small interior filled with smoke, sulphur stinging the inside of their nostrils. As they coughed, the loud snort in the next room boomed again. Their discomfort while Couger slept sent Hardin into a rage. He cocked the hammer quickly in the dark and sent another shot where he thought he'd aimed before. Once again, the room was alight for an instant and more smoke clouded any vision in the room.

He waited before he pulled the hammer again to see if any more snoring was going to disturb his rest. For over one minute, he heard nothing. Satisfied, he started to lie back down. Then booming footsteps sounded on the wood boards outside. He rose from the bed to see if the place was on fire. He stuck his head out into the hall to see others running for the stairs. All the other rooms were quickly vacated, but the door to the room next door never opened.

His shoulders slumped. A premonition forced him to go to that room. He sensed Gip right behind him. Taking a deep breath, he opened the door. He found the lamp in the dark room with one hand while still holding the pistol with the other. He lit the lamp and saw Charlie Couger in the bed, blood flowing from the back of his head. Hardin sighed. The previous night's fortune had turned sour. Now, he was on a run of bad luck.

He thought about the circumstances of the act. He ran through his mind ways of justifying the shooting. As he went back to his room, he stumbled over his pants, which lay near the doorway. He didn't recall where he'd dropped them, but he didn't think they would be so near the door. Perhaps a thief in the night had attempted to steal his money. No one could blame him for defending himself and his property. As he thought about how he could make that explanation seem plausible, the sound of hurried horses clomping through the streets interrupted him.

He went to the window and saw a hack pulling up in front of the hotel. Out of the cab came two men with badges clearly visible, but the third man didn't need a badge. Hickok straightened his curled-brim hat and went directly into the hotel. There would be no explanation accepted. After all the lectures about gunplay in the town, he was sure Hickok and his deputies would gun him down just to set an example and further the lawman's reputation. He had to escape.

He motioned for Gip to follow as he opened the window and squeezed through the opening. A portico over the porch provided a landing. They hit with a thud and without resting for even an instant, leapt to the ground in front of the horses. The hack driver reined down the shocked team.

With only a moment to think, Hardin pointed at Gip. "Go to the Bull's Head and have them hide you." He knew he himself would never find safe haven for he was too well known about the town. They left in opposite directions. Hardin took off down an alley.

Hickok marched into the lobby. The guests all pointed in the same direction. He knew this to be Wes Hardin's hotel, and since the Texas kid wasn't among those in the crowd, it confirmed in his mind what had been rumored since the shots rang out from this part of town. Moments before, he was enjoying a quiet game of draw poker when he heard the pops. Then they stopped. When he heard the second volley, he thought a fight had broken out away from Texas Street, and talk of Hardin returning to his murderous ways broke out among players in the game.

As he went to the stairs, he drew both pistols, ready for any attempt to shoot a path to escape. As he neared the top of the steps, he slowed his gait in case anyone from the shadows bolted at him. He motioned for Carson to provide a lamp to illuminate the hall. One of the two doors at the end of the hall he knew to be Hardin's.

With caution, he took one step then another, ready to shoot at the first figure he saw. He didn't even want to call out for fear it would allow any shooter in the shadows to get a bead on him. He approached the first door slowly but once at the threshold, charged in with Carson holding the lamp over his shoulder. A body lay in the bed. Blood dripped from the side. Further inspection showed three holes in the wall. Two were higher than the one which had mortal aim.

He went to the other room with the same caution, and took a deep breath. He gave himself to the silent count of three, but charged in at two. The light showed an empty room. Clothes lay on the floor, but he didn't spot any firearms. Then he saw the open window, and he went to see the portico below leading to the street. The hack was still there.

"Goddamn him." He faced around and saw three of his deputies with dumbfounded expressions. "You go after him." He marched with the same determination out of the room and toward the stairs. "Find him wherever he went and bring him in. I can't have it on our record." Three murders by this one man, even if one was away from town, were too much to overcome in the council's eyes and still let Hickok keep his job. He came down the stairs. "I want him found before he shoots another Mexican to become a hero again."

Once in the lobby, he walked toward the front and out to the waiting hack. He didn't stop until Carson asked a question. "You coming with us?"

He turned around slowly. The encounter he'd put off too long had to be faced before something worse occurred. Despite his displeasure at the thought, and despite the encounter's possible fatal outcome, he knew he had waited long enough. A moment passed before he shook his head.

31

Charles Gross swept the wide veranda of the daily dust that littered it. He glanced behind at the dark prairie where the rich cattlemen watched from the shade as their vast herds were driven into the market, filling their pockets with more money.

He wondered what it must be like to be so rich that all one had to do was watch the thousands of dollars multiply. However, that was not his position in life, and he understood what he had to do to keep his job. With the way inside clear of dirt, he stopping sweeping, satisfied he'd done what he could in the dark.

He went back to the desk and wiped the dust that had settled there from his sweeping. There was little else to do. The night didn't bring the rowdies from town. This wasn't their place. Only the wealthy could stay here. Which brought to mind the matter that had troubled him for the last two days. Who were those men upstairs?

John Jacob Myers had vouched for them as cowboys, but they showed none of the clothes or mannerisms of men from the plains punching cattle. Although Gross had trust in Myers, he was a man to be both respected and feared. His ties to the guerrillas in Missouri during the war gave the rich cattle baron the reputation of not completely adhering to the law of the land. During these thoughts, as luck would have it, Myers himself came down the stairs. Gross wished at that moment that he'd never been thinking about him, for it seemed to have summoned the very man he feared the most.

"Evening, Charlie," Myers said as he approached.

"Good evening to you, Mr. Myers."

"Jacob will do. You know that." The large man came up to the desk. "I would appreciate some steaks and potatoes sent up to the room for my friends. Seems they've gotten an appetite late."

Gross did as he was ordered. Serving food in the rooms wasn't policy, but exceptions were made, especially for those of status. As he wrote the order down, he couldn't help broaching the subject recently on his mind. "I'll have them cooked and sent up to your friends as fast as possible. What name should I put on the order?"

The question was odd since the room was registered to Myers and both men knew it. The large Texan leaned onto the desk. "You can put it on my bill." Gross looked into the man's eyes, and they each immediately understood what the other was thinking. Myers was first to address the matter. "Why do you ask that, Charlie?"

Trapped by his own curiosity, Gross had two choices. He could lie and say it was the procedure at the best hotel in town to write the guest's name on any order so it could be delivered to the proper room, or he could rely on the relationship the two men had. Charles Gross took that chance.

"How well do you know those men? They don't appear to be cowboys. I would hate to know that the Cottage might be in jeopardy."

Myers grinned at the remark. "I'll tell you what you should do." His tone was foreboding, shaking Gross's confidence in their relationship and the wisdom of his choice. "If you can keep quiet about my friends, then I'll satisfy what you're needing to know. After they've ate and settled, why don't you visit. You'll be under my protection. Then you'll know what you need to know for the good of the Cottage."

Gross nodded in agreement, unsure exactly what he'd agreed to. He put in the order at the kitchen. Dinner service had ended hours before, but after threatening to report the cooks' insubordination to Mrs. Gore, who was in charge of the place, they complied with his order and fried the steaks and boiled the potatoes. He had one cook bring the food to the room door and simply knock and go.

An hour and a half passed by very slowly, and Gross wondered whether he should ignore on the invitation. He had an idea of what type of men were in the room, and wasn't excited about putting himself in jeopardy. However, after waiting so long, he couldn't resist climbing the stairs to the second floor and going to the room door. Only after several breaths did he knock, then stand there waiting until the door opened.

Myers himself greeted him, and invited him inside.

The three men all sat in chairs relaxing after their meal. The one with the weasel neck didn't appear too interested in Gross, and the one whom he'd never had a good look at tended to his firearm. It was the oldest one with the odd nose who took notice of him as Myers introduced them.

"I want you to meet my friends. The one in the corner there is Jesse James, and the one next to him is his brother Frank. And that one fiddling with his piece is Cole Younger."

Gross's eyes bulged. He hadn't expected so notorious a gang staying under the Cottage roof. Petrified at the company in the same room with him, he stood rigid, not knowing if he should expect a bullet any second.

Frank James, the one who took notice of him, spoke. "Our friend has told us all about you, and we are not afraid to have you know. In fact, it's best, because he says you are getting very suspicious and are liable to attract attention. We prefer not to have that happen." Gross could only nod at the reasoning as Younger continued.

"We are not here to pull off anything out of the way. Rather, we are trying to stay clear of that for the present."

Frank James added, "Your money and everything else is safe as far as we are concerned." He grinned at the other two. "We are not going to do a thing in this town that is wrong. We cannot do any jobs here because we promised Wild Bill." His grin widened with the mention of the marshal.

Then Younger shrugged. "Also, if we did,

it would be blamed on the cowboys, and we don't want to cast any bad reflection on them. They already have enough troubles." Jesse James, the one with the weasel neck, nodded in agreement.

Frank finished with a friendly voice. "So, as long as our secret remains only with you, consider yourself among friends."

There remained a question Gross couldn't keep from asking. "How is it you know the marshal?"

Younger looked to the others, then Myers, before he spoke. "Our paths have crossed several times. During the war, your marshal was a Union spy. While delivering supplies, he was divulging locations of Confederate troops and their strength to the generals while pretending to give our generals the same about Federal troops. If he had been discovered, he'd not be your marshal today. For that he owes us a certain debt." Gross shook his head, which triggered a response from Younger. "Well, it's a smart thing for him to do. No doubt he would like to capture us and add to his legend, but our people watch every move he makes. If he tries for us by himself, it's three to one. If he tries through the help of others" — he paused and spoke in an eerie, threatening tone — "we will get him first, even if we die for it, and he knows it." He pointed at Myers. "And he has been promised through our friend here that nothing bad will occur in Abilene. We will not molest anyone or in any way make trouble. All we want is to come here to relax without anyone's notice. All we'll take is fresh horses, ammunition, clothes, food" — he paused, casting an eye at the others — "and a little entertainment. All of which will be properly bought and paid for."

With all appearing calm, the men acted casually with Gross in the room. Even Myers showed no fear of the famous outlaws. It was that behavior that eased Gross's concern. As Younger picked up a bottle and pulled the cork, expecting to relax into the calm of night, a knock came at the door.

All three of them instantly drew pistols and aimed at the door. Gross's heart jumped in his chest with the clack of gun metal. Only after a moment passed did Myers go to the door and open it. Without a word, Marshal Hickok entered the room dressed in a fine silk scarf of purple shade, with a light gray hat and matching neatly pressed coat, a white silk shirt, and the shiny badge pinned to his lapel. His dual pistols remained in his belt as the other men trained theirs on him.

"You're late," said Jesse.

Hickok spoke in his calm nasal voice. "Evening to you as well, Jesse." He nodded at the other two. "Frank. Cole. Trust all is well with our deal."

Jesse stared at him, then eased his pistol hammer to rest. "What took so long?" he said with impatience. "Been waiting here a long time."

Hickok looked away. "Unexpected business had to be seen to."

A grin grew on Jesse's face as he glanced at Myers. "Sounds like that kid Hardin."

Gross thought the remark odd, since Jesse didn't appear much older or any more responsible. A moment passed before Hickok acknowledged Gross, then removed his hat and took the last remaining chair. Gross stood in awe at the two men with the most infamous reputations sitting in the same room. Hickok, the frontiersman turned lawman, and Jesse James, the Quantrill guerrilla turned bandit, both regarding each other with alert attention, yet not acting as adversaries but rather as respectful rivals. The story told by Younger still didn't sound believable to Gross, but he couldn't deny what he was seeing.

"It's just as well," said Hickok. "At least he's out of town, probably on his way to

Texas. I say good riddance. If he comes back, then I'll arrest him. That is, if he doesn't murder another Mexican to impress his friends."

"Since when is that a crime?" Jesse chimed in. The others laughed.

Hickok didn't join in. "Let's get down to our agreement. You are welcome to stay here as long as you do not conduct any of your normal business. In plain words . . ." He paused, then spoke with authority. "Lay off Abilene. Pass it down the line to your associates."

The others, who'd just expressed the very same sentiment, appeared distressed at Hickok's tone of voice. However, none of them responded to the contrary. "We have an agreement," said Frank.

"As long as you keep your side," Younger said, taking a swig from the bottle. He passed it to Frank, who did the same and then passed it to Jesse, who followed suit. Then, Jesse James passed the bottle to Wild Bill Hickok, who showed his fellowship with the outlaws with a gulp of rye whiskey.

During that the brief spell, there were spoken recollections of days past during the war when Hickok was a driver for Union supply trains. The observations of the James brothers didn't reflect the reverence the marshal had gained since the war.

After a good laugh at Hickok's expense, Jesse peered at the famed marshal. "Didn't you turn out to be a dandy. Haven't seen that much silky duds on a Southern belle. Makes me think about you, Hickok. And look at that hair. Don't they have barbers in this town?" Again the three laughed, along with Myers. Neither Hickok nor Gross joined in.

"It lures the ladies. Just like Samson," Hickok responded, then took a long look at Jesse. "At least I have the hair where it counts in order to grow a proper beard," he said, pointing toward Jesse's scruffy chin hair. The outlaw didn't take the good-natured ribbing with the same humility.

"Watch your mouth, yankee," Jesse said with a firm tone.

Frank quickly settled everyone down. "Take it easy, Dingus." He looked around. "Remember what we all agreed to. We are all friends." Chuckling pierced the tension, and even Hickok and Jesse seemed to let their slights to each other be forgotten.

Gross didn't breathe normally for another half hour. It was then Hickok rose from the chair and put on his hat. "Then we have an agreement. As long as I know that, you will not be harassed while you are here. I have given instructions to all under my authority that the guests in this room are untouchable. Enjoy your stay in Abilene." He started for the door.

"If you break your word," Jesse said, stopping Hickok, "and try to shoot or detain us, you know damned well that one of my men will be watching you and get you."

Hickok didn't appear shaken at the threat. "Despite what you might think of me, I am a smart fellow. I've seen your men around town and hold no desire to start a war between yours and mine, nor to be planning my own funeral." He paused and cast an eye at each man in the room. "We have a deal. I am sure we are all smart enough to keep to it."

The clack of a hammer broke the silence. Cole Younger pointed his cocked revolver at Gross's head. "And that goes for you, too, our little friend. You hear?"

Gross nodded emphatically. When Hickok opened the door and exited the room, Gross was close on his heels. As the door shut, laughter could be heard inside the room. It did not stop the marshal from walking down the stairs. When he got to the lobby, he went directly to the front door.

Gross was full of questions, but knew just to ask one might make Hickok suspicious of him. Instead, he held his tongue as the marshal stepped off the veranda. Gross was unsure exactly what he'd witnessed, and also unsure, if he ever told another soul as long as he lived, whether he would be believed.

32

Wes Hardin bit his tongue to stay still and not scratch the itch from the dry straw rubbing against his bare skin. For the last three hours, he'd hidden in a haystack just behind the buildings of Abilene trying to shake his pursuers. Only minutes at a time had he been able to rest his eyes, but not long enough to get real sleep. Now the posse after him had returned as daylight broke over the east. If he stayed, it was only a matter of time before he was found, then surely shot without a fair trial.

He emerged from the stack, careful not to be seen. There were calls out for him and threats to burn the hay. He'd been worried about that, but the proximity of the stack to the wood buildings, with only dry grass in between, would make the tactic a disaster.

Slowly, he crept away from the hay, using it as a shield between himself and those riding all around. A cornfield was just a short sprint from the stack. Once there, he crept as silently as he could in the humid dawn to the other side of the field, all the while listening to his pursuers' calls to each other and their shouted threats to do him harm.

The urge to stand and fight had to be resisted. It had been a long time since he relieved himself, and he feared if he were to do so, it might attract attention with either the noise or the odor. However, he kept on his course to the far side of the cornfield, ever watchful of the riders circling about.

Each move past a stalk might bring unwanted attention to him. Carefully, he slid past every green stem on his hands and knees, one hand on the pistol trying to keep it free from dirt so it would not misfire when needed. He saw the sun between the stalks, and knew he was close to the road leading to and from town. After only a few more steps, he would be at the end of the cornfield.

A horse approaching stopped him.

He readied his thumb around the hammer of his pistol. Delicately, he raised his head as high as the silks to view who was coming so close. Between the seed pods, he saw a single rider approaching. Unsure where the posse might be, Hardin had about a second to decide whether to take this chance or not.

The rider came parallel to him and Hardin stood, exposed for all to see. The next instant might determine if he died or not. "You know who I am?" Hardin demanded.

The rider reined to a stop, then nodded. "Yes," he answered in panic.

Hardin hid his right arm behind his back. "Slide off down on the other side." In quick compliance, the man did so. Hardin wasted no time waiting for him to dismount, climbing up on the left side, but a shout from behind meant he'd been discovered.

"There! There he is!"

Hardin didn't look back, smacking the dun mare's rump and sending it bolting down the road. A whir passed by his ear and the crackle of a shot was quickly heard. He crouched in the stirrups with his bare feet, his hands full with the reins and the mane, pumping against the horse's neck to go faster. With the horse's lighter load, he gained confidence he would spread distance between him and his pursuers.

During the chase, he thought of a place he'd seen two nights before. It was on the far side of the Cottonwood River and quite a dash for the mare, but if he didn't head there, he had nowhere else to go. He steered the horse off the road and onto the prairie grass.

With a small distance gained, he kicked at the horse's flanks to increase the distance for what lay ahead. Mud Creek had to be crossed first, and any delay could cost him his life. Without pants, he stood in the stirrups to ready himself for the splash. At the water's edge, he leaned against the mare's neck and the animal lunged into the stream, hitting the waves in stride, drenching him in his nightshirt. To his surprise, the horse had no fear of the water, and the gentle current allowed it to swim across without any real loss of time.

When hooves met solid ground, the mare charged up the bank. Gunshots rippled through the air, but none came close. Hardin spanked the rump to keep the horse at a steady pace. The terrain was rolling hills, with Abilene in a valley. He knew if he could get the horse past the high hill, it would be mostly downhill until he found what he wanted.

Doing just that, he thought about what he had to do. Likely, Hickok had sent out word to bring him back across a saddle so as to not embarrass the lawman in front of the citizens of Abilene. He recognized the necessity. A few times in Texas, he'd had to decide whether to kill someone, or let him live and take the chance that he might cause Hardin harm later on. Often, he'd chosen the first option just to be sure. He was certain Wild Bill would do the same. He kicked the horse harder.

With the incline taking its toll on the mare's strength, he gave it its own rein. Its pace still kept Hardin far in front of his pursuers, and he was sure they were at least a half hour behind him. Finally, he got to the crest of the hill and rode downhill for the next half hour.

Soon, he was able to see what he'd anticipated. A herd driving north had reached the Cottonwood River. He swatted the mare to charge forward toward the chuck wagon, which was set up for the midday meal along the river bank. He rode in before any of the drovers had come in for food.

He knew he was a sorry sight when he approached and that he had no means of forcing his intentions upon the cook. "Howdy," he said, out of breath. He slid off the saddle. "I'm from Bonham and I'm needing your help. A posse are following me not a half hour behind and mean to do me harm unjustly. Can you help me with some food and weapons?"

The cook took only a single glance at the

way north, then handed Hardin a biscuit with some bacon inside. He'd gulped it down by the time cookie handed him a plate of beans. Since he hadn't eaten since the night before, the beans tasted as sweet as buttermilk. He gulped them down, then went to the water barrel and ladled himself three helpings to quench his thirst from the summer heat. Following the cook to the back of the wagon, he saw the cache of weapons stored there in case of run-ins with rustlers or renegades. He took two loaded pistols and a Winchester rifle, along with another plate of beans. He hid at the back of the wagon until he saw a better spot. Then he went to hide under the bank of the shallow river.

There, he waited until he heard the clomping of hooves approach. Silently, he put down the plate, pulled back the hammer of the rifle, and listened.

"We're after a killer," shouted the familiar voice of Tom Carson. "Shot a man while he was sleeping in a hotel. Goes by the name of Wes Hardin. Some know him just as Little Arkansas."

Hardin raised his head over the top of the bank. Through the underside of the wagon, he could see the boots of three men plus the cook.

"I think I may know who you're talking about. A young fellow in nightclothes with no shirt, pants, or hat?" said the cook. The admission sent a shiver through Hardin, and he readied himself for a gun battle. Then the cook spoke again. "He rode off into the herd. He may be a mile away by now."

"You sure?" asked Carson in skeptical voice.

"Sure as I am standing here. Said he was going back home. I think he mentioned he was from Bonham." Moments passed before those boots moved about. They came close to the far side of the wagon. After another moment, he heard the wood top to the water barrel come loose. The cook spoke again. "You fellows look rode out. Got plenty of food to spare if you're hungry."

Hardin smiled. That cook was a smart man.

"Can't say we mind," answered Carson. As the deputies neared the fire, they came into full view. There was Carson, McDonald, and Brocky Jack Norton all huddled about the pot of beans. Each took a plate and they gave themselves healthy helpings. It was time to take advantage of the ruse.

Hardin climbed up from the side of the bank, careful to keep himself hidden from sight on the back side of the wagon. Only when he was sure the deputies were fully engaged with their meal did he come around the front of the teamless wagon, stepping over the harness and in front of the boot. He peeked around the corner. He had only one chance to make this right, and he didn't want to find himself in a gunfight with three men.

With all their backs to him, he came out from cover, rifle stock at the shoulder. "All hands up or I'll shoot." He trained the barrel on the surprised puffy-faced Carson. "Mister," he called to the cook. "I'm obliged for your help. Now, I ask you one more favor. Take these men's arms from them and be sure they have nothing in their boots." Carson moved his shoulders about as the cook complied with the order. "Easy, Tom. Any resistance will surely mean your certain and untimely death. Same for you other two."

The cook collected all three pistols and patted the boots for any hidden weapons. Only Carson had a derringer hidden there. Once he was sure they had no weapons, Hardin eased his rifle's aim only slightly.

"I must say I know what it's like to not have eaten for such a long time. Wouldn't be Christian to send you on your way without a good meal, and this man's cooking is very tasty." The cook winked at him for the compliment. "So, I'll just sit here in this box while you men get your fill. I've got nowhere to go."

Hardin watched while sitting on the wooden box, and the deputies ate their food while ill at ease. He knew them from his time in Abilene, and didn't care for any of them. Hired killers was what they were, and to shoot them all at that spot wouldn't really be a crime. However, there was the cook, without whose help this escape could not have happened. It wouldn't be right to cause this man the harm that would come from gunning down three lawmen no matter how much they deserved it. Instead, he honored his word as the trustworthy fellow he considered himself to be until they cleaned all the plates.

"Good so far, men. Now, I'll have you shed your clothes."

"The hell you say," Carson protested.

"I'm not a man doesn't mean what I say, Tom. I don't want to see nothing on you but what you came into this world with." Hardin bobbed the rifle muzzle to enhance the seriousness of his words. One by one, they complied, removing hats, pants, shirts, and socks. Finally, they all stood in only hair and white skin. Hardin couldn't resist humiliating them further. "No wonder, Tom, you've got to force yourself on the ladies with that puny tool. Not much to offer."

The deputy bit his lip at Hardin, but did turn to eye the cook. "I better not see you in Abilene."

Hardin considered the threat offensive to him. "Hold on, Tom. If not for this man, you and your friends would be dead. I better not hear or read of any harm coming to this man." He paused and looked the deputy in the eye. "Or I'll come back. And I'll kill you. And you know I'll do it." He motioned for them to start their march of shame back to Abilene in the heat of the afternoon. It would take them until beyond nightfall to walk the some thirty-five miles, plenty of time for Hardin to be long gone.

"Hickok is going to be glad to be rid of you. You come to Abilene and he'll shoot you dead. And if not him, then I'll have the pleasure," shouted Carson as he kept walking.

"Don't you worry about that none, Tom. I'm glad to be clean of you and your lady-dressing marshal. You tell Wild Bill." As he watched them march on, with the pile of clothes and weapons strewn on the ground,

Hardin shook the hand of the cook who might have saved his life, and planned his path back to Texas.

33

After a day of casual searching, Rance hadn't found either of his friends. He could understand Jody. His restless soul had been locked up for near three weeks and after the accusation against Les, raw emotion might have sent him on his way back to Texas. Penelope was a bigger concern.

The tall blond gal didn't have enough money to supply herself for the trip, but she nevertheless was full of enough spite to attempt the journey. Rance had no means of finding either of them if they'd left the town, which he concluded after a second day of searching they must have.

His steps brought him back to the center of Abilene. While crossing Texas Street, he approached the jail with the hope of gaining some information from the helpful jailer. Instead, someone calling him stopped his progress.

"Hey, Cash!"

He turned to see Ben Thompson in the front of the Bull's Head, sitting in a chair as if on the front porch of a country home. His greeting was unusual since the gambler gunfighter had showed little patience with Thompson before. Rance couldn't resist his curiosity, and strolled over to the saloon. Once he was at the steps, he noted that Thompson looked friendly.

"Join me," said Thompson. Rance accepted the invitation. A bottle of rye sat on the table with some empty glasses. Thompson quickly filled one each for himself and Rance. "Have a shot of spirit on this hot afternoon."

Rance did exactly that. The taste was genuine, unlike the whiskey offered by most of the saloons. With cordiality out of the way, the two men settled down into a more businesslike atmosphere.

"What have you been doing to bide your time here?" asked Thompson.

The question sounded more like an offer. Rance shrugged. "I've been playing for the house at the Elkhorn. Mostly monte and some poker with a twenty-percent take. Other than that" — he looked about, attempting to be coy — "I've been taking in your lovely little hamlet."

The tactic didn't work as hoped. Thompson stared at him directly. "Not exactly what I've heard."

Unsure what the comment referred to, Rance played dumb. "Oh? And how is that?"

Thompson continued with the same vigor. "I've learned that you've been gathering information for Hickok. In fact, it would appear you're in conspiracy with those that are trying to run me out of business and are associates with the ones that defaced my property."

The accusation was accurate. How, when, and where Thompson had learned such information befuddled Rance. Had Rance been so clumsy as to show his true intent during his many questions around town? Did Thompson have so many spies that Rance must have talked to more than one? In disbelief, Rance sat with a smug smile, not having a notion how to answer, except with the obvious. "I don't know what you are talking about, Ben."

"Oh, I think you do," Thompson stated. "Two of my men were beaten by a man bragging about the town that he was the one that vandalized my sign, and all they wanted was to ask him some questions. And the tall gal that squealed to him had been seen around the streets with you."

Rance imagined well what type of questions those men wanted to ask and under what circumstances. A moment later, when he realized Penelope could have been subjected to the same brutality, he gulped, and Thompson saw it. An immediate response was needed if Rance didn't want to suffer the same fate. "I haven't seen that gal in some time. Where is she? She owes me money."

"Why? Are you her pimp?"

The inference was insulting, but understandable. He shook his head. "That type of commerce in this town has never interested me. No, I loaned her the funds needed to come here," he said, recalling how he'd truly gotten the money in the first place.

Thompson sighed. "Well, that side of commerce, as you say, is what built this town. Look around you. Without us and our type, this would still be a dusty rail stop. The Kansas Pacific didn't do this. We did. These folks here don't realize that without the money brought in by vice and sin, they wouldn't have been able to bring in or buy a single board to build these houses you see around you. Now they've taken that away from us and banished the trade in women to the south of town. But I'm tired of this life, Mr. Cash. Soon, I'll be joining my wife and family in Kansas City, and I'll have time to think over if I wish to continue my operation here. In the meantime, I do have a sizable investment. An investment for which I'll need men who know how to turn a dime into a dollar. My partner, although he is a friend, lacks those qualities. I see them in you. So, I'm offering you a job here at the Bull's Head, to run the games and measure the liquor. What is your answer?"

Rance leaned back in the chair and took a long breath. When the conversation started, he'd thought he was being interrogated about the painted sign. Now, he was being offered a job. A steady job with more promise than the one he held. There was the issue with Penelope, but he had to think of himself. A minor thought was his commitment to Hickok, but perhaps he could turn this opportunity to his advantage.

Although he might later chastise himself for a hasty decision, he offered his hand in agreement. "I accept."

Thompson nodded without celebration. "I'll put you on today. Go tell Phil I said to let you handle —"

"Go tell Phil what?"

The interruption came from the tall wavy-haired man with a goatee. Thompson looked up at his partner. "I was telling Cash here that I was putting him on to help you with

388

matters while I'm gone."

"Since when do I need help with running my own place?" The jealous tone laced every word.

"Our place," Thompson asserted. "You're still the co-owner. But Cash here is good at what he does. I've been watching." Rance was flattered by the comment, then wondered when Thompson would have seen him play. Thompson continued. "Besides, he's a Southerner." Thompson looked directly into Rance's eyes. "Southerners know that we have to band together against those that wish to oppress us." He glanced across the street at the jail.

As the moments went by, Thompson awoke from his private thoughts. "If you gentlemen will excuse me, I have some other matters to see to before I leave." He once more offered his hand across the table. "Glad to have you on our side, Cash."

Rance received the handshake with a smile, not certain what he'd gotten himself into. "Couldn't be more pleased." Thompson rose from his chair, and after only a momentary match of eyes between himself and Coe, he went back into the saloon. Phil Coe quickly filled the chair. After a long stare, gauging Rance as either friend or foe, he spoke in his husky voice.

"Ben didn't tell me nothing about this, so you'll have to get used to me looking you over. I didn't expect any help nor ask for any. But if he says that you are a man to be trusted, then I'll go along with what he decides. Ben is a good man despite what some people have to say about him. That's because they don't know better. But I do." Coe raised his brow. "I know him likely better than any man." He raised his brow again. "And he knows me." He snorted a breath. "So, you do what I tell you, and we'll get along just the same."

Rance was cold in the afternoon heat. Minutes before, he was talking to a rational man who made sense when he spoke. Now, he'd agreed to be left with a maniac whose attempts to intimidate him were obvious and admittedly effective. "I'll do what I can to help in any way." His eyes wandered to the jail across the street. It seemed like a distant shore, and he felt like he was adrift at sea. And it had taken less than a minute. The longer his eyes remained on that front door, the more he realized he had to make the best of things.

With Jody released from jail, Rance's original purpose for coming to town had been achieved. In a way. And as far as his deal with Hickok was concerned, he really held no allegiance to the lawman, who had treated him as an informant and not embraced him as any kind of friend.

Phil Coe stood and went toward the saloon interior. "Come on and I'll show you the setup."

About to rise, Rance caught sight of a familiar shape among those on the sunny boardwalk on the other side of the street. An instant later, he recognized it as Les carrying a basket. With Jody gone, he wondered why she'd put herself in such dangerous surroundings unneccessarily.

"Cash. Let's go."

Coe's beckoning brought him out of his thoughts. He followed his new boss into the saloon.

With a only a small chance to learn any information, Les came to a stop at the jail door. She knocked instead of immediately entering. When the door opened, a surprised Mike Williams stood in the doorway.

"No reason for you to stop eating," she said. He smiled and waved her inside, shutting the door behind them. She went to his desk and set out the plate of hash, which was covered with bacon-grease gravy. Mike stuck his nose over it and inhaled the appetizing aroma.

"Can't say I didn't miss this," he told her, taking the fork she provided. Les had brought nothing for herself, but did take a chair across the desk. Her intent was made plain. He took a bite, then looked at her. "I can't be sure where he went."

"What did he say?" she asked quickly. More than anything, she needed to know what had been on Jody's mind when he left.

Mike shrugged. "Not much. Can't say what a man's thinking when he thinks something is true" — he paused, looking at her — "when it's not."

His words surprised and touched her so, she had to hold back the tears. "Then you know."

He smiled and nodded, then took another bite. "When you've seen the gals that sell themselves as long as I have, you get to noticing certain signs. I never saw those in you."

Confused and curious, Les sat intrigued by the man's observations, and couldn't resist asking, "What signs?"

Mike swallowed and nodded as if he'd known she would ask. "Their ways of walking are different. Get a heap of aches when you letting ten or more fellows . . ." He paused, not wanting to be vulgar. "Well, you know. Takes something from them. I seen a bit from you, but not enough to make me think that. Reckoned it was the hard work you were doing." He filled his fork. "But that ain't what cinched it in my mind." He ate the food.

Now she really wanted to know and gestured for him to finish. "What *did* cinch it?"

He leaned back in his chair as he chewed, looking at her with those fond eyes. A grin cracked his face. When he swallowed, he blurted out the answer. "Your eyes."

Unaware of what he saw, she leaned closer to hear every word from the soft-spoken man. He continued without encouragement.

"Ain't something a fellow or gal can control. Just happens natural. Sometimes you can't even see it so much, but when you're a step back from it, you do." He shook his head. "I know you didn't take to the trade, not to come here every day and look at him. Just wouldn't be something I think a woman could do." He paused in thought. "Of course, I ain't one." They both chuckled. "But a man, he can't neither. Not when he has true feelings for a woman. He has needs to fulfill, that is true. But if he's going to get a chance to have it mean something rather than be done in a minute, most men I know will wait. I saw that in

Jody. He was going to wait. And I see that in you, too."

She pursed her lips, and thought about the man they spoke of, now on his way back to Texas. "I guess he didn't see what you saw."

"He will." Mike slid his fork into the hash.

Les thought the same, but didn't know how long it might take. "When?"

Mike shrugged and took the bite, chewed a short while, then swallowed. "Can't say. Every man is different." He looked to her. "He was hurting bad when he left here. A few things were on his mind. He didn't take to being behind bars, and wanted to get away from here quick and far. Add that with what he saw with you and Jesse and the Virginia woman, it was all a mite too much at one time." He grinned slightly. "I 'spect he just needs a little more time to ponder matters. Don't think he would quit what he thought so much of. Not so quick. But it may take some time for him to settle his mind."

Mike scooped with the fork again. Les thought about what he'd said. In her mind, she felt the same way as Mike had described. Half of her was determined to go after Jody, not knowing which trail he took and how far he'd gotten. The other half tried to remain confident that Mike was right. That Jody might realize she would never sell away what she had saved so long to give.

34

He hadn't gotten very far. Jody kept reminding himself of that fact. Why he hadn't ridden through the night and day since he'd
walked from jail confused him.

After as long a delay as he could justify,
he set back on the trail south, uncertain of
the answer. He'd left something behind him
that he wasn't ready to leave. However, he
didn't miss Abilene itself.

Two years before, he'd regretted leaving
behind the frolic he'd enjoyed in the free-
wheeling town. Anything a man wanted cost
just a few dollars, and with more than
ninety to spend, he'd put most of it into
Abilene's cash drawers. Now, though, was
not the same. Now, the spirit that made the
cattle town so appealing had paled next to
something he hadn't expected. Something
he thought he'd earned and owned that was
more important than money.

He viewed the trail ahead with less anticipation than he had at first. Still, when he set out in one direction, he seldom turned around. He kept the sorrel at a slow but steady walk.

As he peered into the distance with his mind focused on anything but what lay in front, he saw an unusual amount of movement from the tall grass. The wind wasn't blowing that hard. Fearing robbers, he reached for the Yellow Boy rifle and levered the action.

"Who's ever in there better show themselves or face a shot through them weeds."

"Hold your fire. We're deputies with the Abilene marshal's office."

The voice sounded familiar, but the circumstances were more than odd. "What are you doing hiding in the brush if you're deputies?"

Seconds went by before a reply. " 'Cause we're naked."

The reply stunned Jody, but amused him at the same time. He remembered when the tactic had been used on him. "Who took your clothes?"

"The outlaw Hardin. He murdered a man last night and we went after him. He ambushed us with help from his drover friends, and probably is in Newton by now. Soon, he's going to be Texas's problem. But we're

397

needing to get back to our jobs. I'm coming out. Don't shoot me." Slowly, a head popped up from the tall grass. It was Tom Carson, still showing the effects of the beating Hickok gave him two nights before. "You're the kid from San Antonio. I'm ordering you in the name of the law to assist us to get back to Abilene."

Jody still held the rifle firm in hand. The way he figured it, they probably weren't armed, and the more he thought about what he was being ordered to do and by whom, the less his desire to comply.

"Seems like you fellows are doing just fine. Probably have another twenty miles to go and you'll be there." He nudged the sorrel to a walk.

"Wait," Carson called. Jody kept the animal moving. "I'll be after you when the time comes, boy." The empty threat from a man who never seemed to make good on any of his promises was of no concern. Besides, the only place Carson could try to make good on his threat would be in Abilene, a place Jody had no plans to return to.

Clay and Penelope packed what they could on the Palouse. Out of frustration and worry, she made plain what had bothered her for the last day and a half. "Where is it we're going?"

He didn't stop or look her way. "A place south of here. Called Newton. There be a town there that will have some supplies." He looked her way, but didn't stop packing. "Supplies to get you back to where you're from."

The idea struck her dumb. Although she yearned to be back in Texas among her own folk, she hadn't thought it a notion he shared, and the way he'd said it meant he wasn't coming. Not wanting to spark a worse fight than the several they'd already had, she thought of a different way of finding out what she wanted to know. "When do we get there?"

His attention was on stuffing the saddlebag and nothing else. "A day. Maybe two at the most."

Something she felt she could no longer be silent about came to mind, and she dared bring it up. "I seen a rider. A single rider behind us. Might be miles, but I seen him on the some of the high spots we crossed. I think he'll catch us before two days."

He stopped his packing. "How long ago you seen him?"

"Maybe midday. Maybe longer. It's been a few hours. But I know he's getting closer."

His shoulders slumped, but he didn't stop his routine. "If he's that far back, it ain't going to matter."

Although the words sounded like he'd lost his spirit, his tone didn't show it and she was confused. "What are you talking about? We can't outrun him. We barely make two hours before we got to rest the horse."

"It's doing the best we can expect with two riders," he barked.

The words stung her. It was the first time he'd said anything about riding double, and he'd said it in a tone that made her the problem. "Are you saying I'm slowing you down?" she asked.

He stopped his routine and looked at her. A moment passed before he spoke. "That what you think?"

She wanted to reply sharply. She did think that but it might cost her life if she admitted it. Whoever was riding behind might threaten *her* as much as Clay. Despite her pride, she didn't want to be alone on the prairie without a horse. Instead, she steered the conversation back to something else Clay had said. "What'd you mean it ain't going to matter?"

He didn't answer immediately. Penelope knew to ask again would only be met with another thorny reaction and she was tired of fighting. Only after she came to that realization did he respond. "The rain will wash out our tracks."

She scanned in all directions, and could only see small puffy clouds. "What rain? I can't see no clouds."

He stopped his packing, took a deep breath, and looked straight at her. "Believe me. I know the smell. I know when it's going to rain." He went back to his packing. "And it'll be here in less than an hour. We got that much time to get to shelter."

Hickok sat in The Alamo Saloon watching the game and the rest of the patrons. Satisfied from his conversation with the James gang that peace would be kept, and with the knowledge John Wesley Hardin was well out of his jurisdiction, he relaxed into the poker game. Even the move of all the women to the south of town was going well. They had set up tents and were quickly back in business without the expected protests by them and their customers.

With all but the play of cards going in his favor, he threw in the third consecutive hand with less irritation than usual. A glance through the window outside showed the normal daily traffic proceeding without disturbance. Since his mood was good, he thought about calling on the society woman who had caught his eye but wouldn't give her name. While he was looking out the window, another woman who'd shown interest in him strolled by. Immediately, his gut tightened as she smiled at him through the glass.

"Excuse me, boys," he said, leaving the table. "I'll be back. This shouldn't take long." He left the saloon and stopped just feet from the door under the shaded awning. She met him there. The small woman extended her hand and he took it.

"James, our final show is tonight. I would like you to be my guest for the performance," said Agnes Thatcher.

He was caught without a quick reply to her bold request. No excuse came to mind. He decided to tell the truth. "Little lady, I regret to have to decline. Matters I've committed to recently will keep me from accepting your invitation. Although I am sure the show you and your troupe will put on will be the best to date."

The disappointment could be seen on her face, which he'd expected. However, despite the inclination to take back what he'd just said and attend the show so as not hurt the woman's feelings, he knew that if he did, he'd kick himself for not standing stronger.

Instead, he endured the next few minutes.

With her expression unchanged, he sought a compromise. "Perhaps I could share with you a nice dinner before your show?" he asked.

She shook her head. "No, thank you," she said with a polite but not beaming smile. "I've got to return and oversee the last preparations. We must finish, as you said, with our best show to date." She tucked her lower lip inside her mouth. "You know, should you ever tire of your duties as a law-man, or even wish to take a sabbatical, I'm sure you would sell out the shows with an exhibition of your skills as a marksman. Could I at least hope that you will consider it someday?"

Hickok was vulnerable to flattery. He cocked his head to the side. "The idea does sound appealing." He gave it a second thought and still found no objection. He wasn't much for performing, but it sounded like easy money. "By God, yes, Agnes. Should I need a job or a rest, I'd much enjoy that."

The acceptance changed her face dramatically. That kind smile returned. "Then I'll take it as an agreement. May I correspond with you from time to time just to maintain your status?"

He shrugged and shook his head. "Can't say as to why not."

"Good," she said, again offering her hand, which again he took gently. "I must return, James. But please, should the duties you refer to somehow be finished, I hope you'll attend tonight."

"Agnes," he said in a soft tone. "I'll do all in my power." She nodded at the statement and stepped away.

"Good-bye, James B. Hickok. I do hope to see you sooner than later."

He waved his hat at her. "And farewell to you, Agnes." He watched her walk down the street toward the tracks. He was unsure exactly what it was about the gal. Each time he crossed paths with her, he wanted either to evade her like a band of renegades, or to find a reason to stay in her company. Although her features brought little stimulation to his loins, it was her kind and polite manner he somehow enjoyed beyond explanation.

Concluding that he wasn't going to discover any answers, he returned to The Alamo Saloon.

Clay reined in on the Palouse. Penelope had felt the uneven step for miles, but feared any word to the man would set off another tirade. One that she didn't want. However, he'd apparently noticed, and he slid off the saddle. She did the same off the rump. Clay lifted a front hoof. Dusk settled in, making the operation to clean the shoe of whatever was stuck in it all the more difficult.

As she watched, her senses observed her surroundings. So focused was she on the trail ahead to the south that she hadn't bothered looking around, instead preferring to lean her head against his shoulder from exhaustion and hunger. Now, the constant heat, which fatigued them both, was absent. She slowly faced about and saw the black clouds creeping closer from the north. At the same time, the fresh smell of moist air shot into her nose. The cooler air gushed against her face, refreshing her lungs and sending a shiver through her spine. "You were right," she muttered.

"What's that?"

She faced him just to repeat her words. "You were right." She resumed her view of the oncoming rain. "You do know when it's going to rain."

She felt him come near. With the sun setting and the clouds spreading over the remaining light, the land began to darken. Clay stepped around her and walked in front, his hand raised into the wind. Lightning bolted down onto the prairie miles away. Penelope stood in amazement. His stance in the wind reminded her of stories in the Bible.

He pointed farther to the northwest. A curtain of water falling could be seen against the lighter sky behind. "It's ten miles away," he said. "Everything we left behind is washed away." He turned and approached her. He grinned. "I told you we'd be safe. But we still need shelter. Can you ride another five miles?"

It wasn't a question she could answer any other way. She nodded. "I'll make it." He motioned his head to the horse. Before, she had always stepped into the stirrup and edged back onto the cantle. Instead, this time, he helped her into the saddle, then mounted behind her, securing her in place. A nudge to the flanks and they continued across the plain.

35

The storm overtook them sooner than expected. For the last two hours, they'd ridden through the wind and rain. The Palouse pony struggled with the weight and thick mud left from the grass trampled by longhorns moving north. The cool wind relieved the heat, but now sent chills through Clay's skin. He felt her shiver against his arms. Just a short distance away, he knew they would find some shelter. This was his Kansas and he knew it in his soul. Newton couldn't be but just over the next hill.

While rain pelted them, Clay steered the horse over the hill. Through the blur of drops, a single dim light shone in the darkness. He kicked the Palouse, which went to a trot, sloshing through the puddles not yet soaked into the hard ground. When they got to the structure with the light, he saw it was a farmhouse with an oil lamp sitting on a table inside. With this their best chance, he gambled they would find friendly folks living there. He dismounted, went to the door, and knocked.

A few minutes passed before another light slowly threaded its way through the dark interior. When the door opened, a short but stout man with a mustache stood with his coat and hat on. In one hand he held a lantern, and in the other was a double-barreled shotgun. Clay took a step back as the farmer emerged from the house.

Clay nodded at him. "Evening. Sorry to wake you, friend. But we're on our way to Newton and saw your light. Was wondering if you might have a place we can sit out this storm."

The man eyed Clay carefully, then raised the lantern to view Penelope on the horse. He looked again at Clay and the shotgun came more in line toward him. "What's your business?"

Clay opened his palm for caution. "Mean no harm. I am working for the army hunting buffalo."

The farmer bobbed his head at Penelope. "And her?"

Clay shrugged. "We ran into trouble with some Texans in Abilene. She's going with me for now. Likely going back to Texas where she belongs."

The explanation didn't ease the stern jaw of the farmer. An instant later, he pointed the twin barrels at Clay and called to Penelope. "You there. You traveling with this man on your own free will? Speak the truth."

Clay froze. Just a twitch from the chilled air might send lead balls to tear away his flesh. He didn't know if he feared the farmer's attitude or the blond gal's answer. What seemed like minutes came in a second. "Yes, sir. I am."

Clay exhaled. The farmer lowered the shotgun only slightly. "I'll have no sin going on in my house. If you ain't belonging to each other in a Christian marriage, I'd as soon you pass on. But Newton is another five miles. And it looks like she could take fever. So, there's space above the barn I'll let you stay until morning. Then, I want you both gone. And don't approach the house. I'll give no warning."

Clay nodded. "Understood. And I'm beholding to you for the kindness." The farmer slipped back inside, never easing his finger far from the trigger. When the door shut, Clay went to the horse. "We're staying in the barn." He took the reins and walked the animal far from the house to the tall structure barely visible in the rain. When he got to the double door, he slipped the bolt free and opened the door. Penelope nudged the horse inside, and Clay shut the door behind them.

Manure odor filled the air. In the pitch black, he heard her dismount and felt her close to him. "He said there was a space cleared in the loft," said Clay as he loosened the cinch and pulled the saddle and bit from the Palouse.

"I found the ladder," Penelope said. As his eyes adjusted to the dark, he saw her near a post. His fingers found the rungs and he followed her to the loft. A single small window allowed the frequent lightning flashes outside to provide enough guidance for them to spot full grain sacks stacked along the wall.

Clay saw what was needed, and laid the canvas sacks along the wood planks to form a type of mattress, although it was anything but soft. He recognized the girl needed to rest, and once there were enough sacks to allow a body to lie down, he stood back and pointed. "See if that don't help the ache in your bones."

She looked at him with an arched brow. "Where are you going?"

"I'll be down with the stock." A moment passed by without a question asked, but he knew there was one coming and decided to answer it unasked. "I'll be shedding these wet clothes. You need to do the same or we'll be both catch fever. Ain't something we need right now." A thought occurred to him. "If we're getting killed, let's not have it be that way." He thought the remark amusing. However, when he heard no reply, he thought again. "Didn't mean to scare you none."

He heard her reply in the dark. "You think they will chase us all the way here?"

The prospect had been one he didn't want to consider. With her bringing it up, he had a decision to make. If he answered honestly, it might send her into tears or even some crazed fits. If he lied, then she likely would sense it since he wasn't a convincing liar. "I can't say someone might not be coming."

"Like the one I saw riding behind us?"

Her tone held some panic, and he didn't want to have raised voices wake the family and have that farmer visit with the scattergun. He approached her in the dark. "Don't fret. Ain't no way anyone's going to find us here."

He saw her glistening face in the dark. "How are you sure?"

The past was his assurance. "Been through times like this before. Ain't nothing you can do but wait and trust in yourself. If someone is coming for us, we'll do what we have to." He reached in the dark and touched her hand. Her fingers wrapped around his. "You had no business warning me about them. I had none telling you to come."

"I ain't no whore. But I ain't no flower neither." With the distant flashes, he saw fresh tears on her face. "There's things a female tells herself. One of them is when to go and when not to." He sensed her come near. "Clay, the reason I come to warn you is because I didn't want nothing bad to come your way." She sniffed. "You see, I don't have much to go to Texas with or for." She paused as if the words were heavy weights to carry. "I don't have much to offer a man. I lost it a long time ago. Not for a man who wanted to call a woman his only."

He didn't understand fully, but knew what she was trying to say was shameful to her. "I don't know for sure what you're saying, but if it's a past you ain't proud of, don't let that be bigger than a hair on your head. Pretty gal like you ain't ripening every day everywhere. And a brave one at that? Can't think what man wouldn't be camping at your door."

She giggled slightly, then stopped. "When you held me on the horse, I felt for the first time what I was supposed to feel."

He took the signal to pull her closer, and she willingly slipped between his arms. "I been through many a time when I thought I wasn't going to be seeing another day. Can't say this might not be one of them." He nudged her chin up with a finger. "But if this be that time, I can't think of a prettier woman to spend it with."

A moment passed, then another. As they felt each other's warmth, Penelope put her lips on his. Embarrassed, she faced away from him. Clay turned her back with a grip on her arm. Penelope's breath quickened. He mashed his lips to hers. At first, she didn't resist. Seconds later, he felt her lips recede and her hands push against his chest. He continued to force his lips onto hers until she shoved him on his back on the canvas sacks. She fell on top of him. Between heaves of breath, she stared from the dark into his eyes. "I made myself a promise that no man would have me on my back again."

She straddled over him as they shed their wet clothing. The sensation of each other's bare flesh showed in their frenzy for more. Laces slipping loose and buttons undone led to merger of two lonesome souls. Straps fell away. Breasts rubbed together, until

Clay succumbed to the urge to suckle while she hiked her hem to her waist. The shred of cotton heightened their mutual desire.

She found the object of her deep feminine yearning. Within her grasp, she guided it between her legs, eased down, and enveloped his erection. Her breath shortened. Penelope forced herself down upon him vigorously. She panted with each thrust, each quicker than the one before. Clay couldn't suspend the primal demands to be male any longer. He gripped her hair, which fell from the bun within his fingers to her shoulders, and brought her around and down so he could assume the man's position. She accepted his entry without complaint in the woman's position.

Daylight brought refreshed air. Clay rose and slipped on his pants. The night had brought a better sense to his plans. He wanted to saddle the Palouse and get to Newton. As he stood, Penelope called to him. "Clay." Her blond strands dangled in front of her brow. "Don't leave without me."

He smiled. The thought had never entered his head, but he bent down and gave her a reassuring peck on the lips. He put on his boots and went down the ladder. In a few minutes, he had the horse saddled and ready to be watered and fed for the five-mile ride. As he walked it from the barn toward the well, he looked up. Penelope stood in the window, her bosom naked for only him to see, perhaps as an incentive for him to make good on his kiss.

In a short time, the horse was ready for the ride, and he met her dressed for the journey at the barn door. With some gentle guidance, he helped her into the saddle although it was unnecessary. He hadn't felt so spirited in years.

They rode southwest to Newton. The streets were lined with saloons and bawdy houses just like Abilene, but not nearly as many. Train tracks skirted the town, giving hope that it might become another cattle boomtown. They came to a restaurant. With the cash earned from Hickok, he bought their breakfast despite the fact that according to the sun it was nearly noon.

As he looked for a hotel to sleep off the meal and resume what they'd started the night before, they walked on the boardwalk until she grabbed his arm. "If they're looking for someone like you, maybe you ought not look like they think." She pointed to a wagon where a sutler peddled goods from the back to some of the drovers.

Clay went to it and pulled out a pair of

trousers the shade of the dust in the street. It was far different from the army issue all had seen him wearing. A white shirt appeared his size as Penelope stretched it across his wide chest. She looked at his head and snatched off the cavalry cap he'd been given when he'd first joined the troopers.

"A hat you're needing, son," said the sutler. "I have a whole supply of milliner wares." He opened a locker full of derbies and bowlers. A stray Stetson caught his eye, until Penelope tapped the sutler's shoulder and asked a question.

"What about the hat you're wearing?"

Clay had first noticed the black wide-brimmed hat with a flat crown. The brim had a wave dipped in front that provided shade to cover the eyes and nose.

"Got that from a fellow far out west," said the sutler. "Says they make them in Australia. Don't know if I can part with it, though. Don't have another like it and wouldn't know where to get one."

Clay looked at Penelope. Her eyes told him she thought the hat the best choice despite the peddler's objection. Clay didn't have time or patience to dicker. "What say we find a bonnet for the lady." He paused, unsure if he should spend so much on himself. However, her approval was difficult to disregard. "And twenty dollars for the hat."

The peddler's eyes widened. "Twenty dollars? Just for the hat?" Clay drew a double-eagle gold piece to show he meant it. The peddler removed the hat and tossed it to him. Clay flipped the coin at the same time.

When he put the hat on, she arranged it at an angle that shaded his eyes from the midday sun. She took a step back and studied him. Finally, with an approving nod, she spoke. "It fits you."

36

Bright sunlight illuminated the prairie for miles. Jody rode the sorrel at ease. He was in no hurry. A farmhouse not far ahead brought to mind thoughts of home. Perhaps simple folks like himself might live there and might provide some fresh water. He approached with some caution, knowing he was a stranger and that the passing of cattle herds nearby might make the people in the farmhouse leery of strangers. As he came closer, he saw a stocky man of strong build come from a barn not far from the house. The man was rolling a wheelbarrow when he noticed Jody.

"Howdy," Jody called to show he had no harmful intent. The man didn't looked pleased at him. "Don't mean to bother. Just passing through and thought I might fill a canteen at your well."

The man stood with a dumbfounded expression. Only after a few moments did he nod. "Take it and go."

The terse reply was all Jody needed to hear. At first, he thought to forget the well and leave this one in his tracks. Thirst changed his mind. He dismounted and took the canteen over to the round wood enclosure with a roof where a bucket had a rope tied to the handle. Jody threw the bucket down and then wiped his brow from the sweat. "Don't remember a summer this hot."

The man wheeled over to a pile where he dumped the contents of the wheelbarrow. "Same as last year." He eyed Jody with a wary expression. "You ain't from around here?"

Jody shook his head. "No, sir. I'm from Texas. Bexar County. My folks have a place near San Antonio. Does get hot there, too, but there's a few more trees for shade than here."

The man looked back at the barn. "Had two from Texas here in the middle of the night. Man and woman. You know them?"

Jody smiled and shook his head. "Can't say that. Texas is an awful big place. Great many folks from there. Especially with the Chisholm leading from there." He reeled up the bucket and began filling it.

"Wasn't sure about them. The girl, she

was young and appeared scared. The man, he struck me as someone who might try to treat her mean."

Jody responded to keep the conversation going to be polite. "What did she look like?"

"Tall, at least looked like it, but she was on a horse. Blond hair from what I could see in the dark."

Jody stopped filling the bucket. "You say tall blond girl? Would you say she might be my age? I'm twenty-one."

The man swayed his head. "Not much more or less than that. I asked if she were with him by free will and she said yes." He looked at the barn. "I hope that was the truth." The tone was laced with regret.

"Why do you say that?"

With a deep breath, he continued. "It's only my concern because I let them stay in my barn. I had a mind to run them off, but I thought they could at least stay the night and out of the rain." He looked long at Jody. "I'll tell you since you're a man of twenty-one. There are signs that a grown man can recognize. I think sin was committed last night. I can't think that a girl that age would do such a thing by free will. But I have to hope so, even though I don't think it true."

Jody's eyes bulged. The thought of Penelope in trouble made his heart race. He'd not seen her in weeks, and hadn't given her much reason to return to the jail to see *him*. Now, she may have taken up with one of the drovers or some thief, robber, or murderer who might be keeping her from returning to her pa. It was Jody who'd let her come along on the drive to Colorado. If now she was in trouble, it was really his fault. "What did he look like?"

The man nodded once. "Big. Had the body and arms of a man who'd done work in his life. I held a gun on him last night and thought I was going to have to use it. Had a look about him which made him seem like he'd been in trouble with the law. Had soldier britches on. Said he was killing buffalo for them. He did say she was from Texas. Probably shouldn't have asked you." The man took hold of the wheelbarrow. "I can't even say I know anything as a fact. Didn't mean to make it none of your trouble, son. She could have been just some harlot bought and paid for."

Jody stood in shock. The more the man said, the more he thought that the woman described had to be Penelope Pleasant. "I'm thankful for the water. If I come across them, I will check that the woman is all right." He mounted the sorrel and rode at a trot south.

The day passed too fast and the horse traveled too slow. Even at a trot, he didn't arrive in Newton until mid-afternoon. Jody had been there only once, two years before. The small stop along the Chisholm had since grown into a hastily built den for the depraved in order to gather all the money possible from lonely drovers.

He rode through the center of town, and the few locals there all stayed under the shaded boardwalks. Jody was thirsty, and hunger from two days on the trail had set him on a path to find the nearest eatery. There were more saloons than any other businesses, but he finally saw a place where he smelled fried bacon in the smoke billowing out of a stove stack.

He tethered the sorrel to the hitch, and noticed a pair of blue trousers with a yellow stripe down the leg draped over the rail. He recalled the farmer's description, and his breath quickened at the thought of what he might find. Standing in the street, Jody saw a tall man come out of the eatery. He was wearing a new white shirt and light brown dungarees. He placed a wide black-brimmed hat on his head. Jody couldn't think of but one question.

"These belong to you?" he asked pointing at the army trousers.

The man looked puzzled at the inquiry. "And if they be?"

The casual reply spurred Jody to charge at him. He marched directly at the man in the hat, reared back, and threw a punch into his jaw, knocking the man onto the dirt street with hat flying. "You son of a bitch. What did you do with her?"

Dazed from the blow, the man furrowed his brow. He swung a leg and raked Jody off his feet. With cat quickness, he jumped on top of Jody, who rolled and threw him to the side. They both got to their feet. When they were standing in front of each other, Jody again charged forward to force the man to the ground, but a kick to the chest sent Jody backward, landing on the seat of his pants. The force took his breath for a second, but he couldn't stay down. He got to his feet, but stopped upon hearing the click of a pistol hammer being cocked. Jody stared at the muzzle, frozen, expecting to be shot.

"Clay! No!" Penelope's voice turned both their heads to the boardwalk. "He's a friend of mine," she said, looking at Jody with the scorn of a mother. "What are you doing?"

Catching his wind, Jody wondered what to explain first. He pointed at the pants, but the kick had stolen all his air and he couldn't speak. After a few seconds, he was able to say, "I heard from a man who said a pretty blond gal stayed in his barn with a man who didn't look like . . ." He trailed off, not knowing exactly how to say it with someone holding a pistol aimed at him.

"Like what?" asked the man with the gun.

There was no word except the one on his mind. "Didn't look like he could be trusted. Not with a woman." Jody looked at Penelope. "And I guess maybe he was right."

She looked at the man, then back at him. "I don't know what you think you're right about, Jody Barnes. But whatever it is, it ain't your concern to be worrying about me," she said loudly, eyeing him up and down. "They let you out of jail just to come find me?"

The question made him take a deep breath. "No." He didn't want to say any more, but she had struck a nerve.

"Then why did they?"

The real reason he was here with her and her new friend wasn't a matter for her neither. "I ain't saying nothing. Not in front of him," he said, bobbing his head at the man. "Sorry for the fight. But you do appear as that sodbuster described."

The man she called Clay rested the hammer and tucked the pistol in his belt. "Ain't

424

the first time." He looked at Penelope. "Are we leaving or not?" His tone held disrespect for Penelope, and Jody took offense.

"Don't be talking to her like that."

"I see no chevrons on your sleeve. I ain't taking orders from the likes of you."

Jody took a step toward him. "Put the gun aside and we'll finish this."

Clay huffed a laugh. "You didn't get enough the first time, junior?" As they came closer, Jody clenched a fist and Clay put up his arms.

"Stop it!" Penelope screamed for the whole street to hear. She heaved a breath, then repeated the plea in a gasped tone. "Just leave each other be." She inhaled deeply. Then her head spun to the side while her eyes rolled up. She collapsed, but her man caught her before she hit the street.

"She's sick," Jody said. He looked at her man, and their desire to fight had vanished from both of their faces. Jody wiped the sweat from her brow. "Get her inside."

37

August 1871

Les wiped the table for the next customer. She hadn't minded slinging hash since leaving Shenandoah's brothel a month ago. It didn't pay as much as she got from the gals to clean up, but it was steady and helped Miss Maggie pay her bills, along with the extended stay of Beatrice LaFontaine.

When she prepared the table, the next customer quickly sat in front of her. She asked the usual before looking at him. "What'll it be?"

"How 'bout them home-cooked vittles."

She looked down at Mike Williams. "Sorry," she said, smiling. "Don't get that here."

He shook his head. "And I do miss it. But I understand. I'll take the house special."

Les took the order, and dished the stew into a bowl and returned quickly, ignoring the other customers. He sniffed the food and picked up a spoon, but she couldn't leave the table for the moment. She missed him, too. "So, things steady at the jail?"

He spoke with his mouth full. "Not so bad. With Fisher's Addition" — he paused — "or Texas Village, or whatever they call the place south of town, Texas Street has been fairly quiet. With no street walkers, there's fewer fights and less men to jail." He took another bite. "How 'bout you?"

She took the chance to take the seat next to him, hoping the owner wouldn't notice. "Much the same. Just trying to make some money."

"For going back to Texas?" She nodded, knowing Mike knew the reason why. He shook his head. "Can't say I thought he would be gone this long. Thought he would come to his senses by now."

"I think it was his time in jail that turned him sour for this town. We have Wild Bill to thank for that."

"Oh, he ain't as bad a fellow as you think. I think he kind of liked Jody. Is why he kept him locked so long to keep him safe, is all." Mike took another bite, but took time to finish chewing and swallow before talking. "He is a stickler for getting things done when he sets his mind to it. Some months ago, he had to throw Councilman Burroughs over his shoulder in order to have enough folks to vote in license fees. J.B. wasn't going to take no for an answer when the councilman refused. Even though he does rile some folks, he did settle this town down when it came time."

Les couldn't share that opinion, but she didn't have the heart to say otherwise. Mike Williams was an honest and decent man, unlike the rest of the deputies, and she didn't want to offend him.

When he dug in his pocket for the money to pay for his meal, Les held up her hand. "On the house," she said, although she had no authority to give food away. He took her hand and stuck the two coins in her hand.

"Then you keep it." He rose from his chair and picked up his hat to put it on once he got outside. Before he left through the door, he glanced back at her and winked.

Jody sat by Penelope. She'd been sick nearly three weeks, and the cough was said by the doctor to be a sign of pneumonia. It was also said that few survived such an illness in the Kansas heat. Nevertheless, Jody and Clay had taken turns sitting next to her bed in the shanty of a hotel. The two of them had no extra money, and had found work as laborers in the different expansion projects that sprang up around town. The railroad brought needed visitors to sample the local casinos, and even some of the Texas cattlemen were selling their herds in Newton rather than drive them farther north to Abilene.

As Jody sat wiping Penelope's brow, he thought about when the two of them were kids. This girl had been the sparkle of her father's eye, and it was thought she would grow up to be a teacher or something even more respected. It wasn't until just a year ago that he'd learned the truth about what had changed her into such a rowdy person. Her virtue had been stolen by a slick-talking man, and she'd never come to deal with being soiled. It was why, despite Clay's gruff manner, Jody was beginning to take to him. Usually, a man with no ties wouldn't spend his time caring for a woman who didn't belong to him. However, the former trooper went to work every day in order to pay for the room and the doctor's fee to treat Penelope. It made Jody think about how he'd come to be there, and what he would do if Les had taken ill.

His thoughts were interrupted as Clay entered the room looking concerned. "How is she?"

Jody looked at the weak, sleeping body.

"No change. The doc said she'd have to get all the rest she could and to keep her warm and dry." Clay appeared distracted. "What's happening in town?" asked Jody.

Clay glanced at him, then spoke while looking at Penelope. "McCluskie is back."

The news stunned Jody. "After murdering Bill Bailey a week ago?"

Clay shrugged. "Some say he was told there wouldn't be no charges 'cause he fired in self-defense. Even though Bailey had no gun." Clay took the cloth from Jody and wiped the girl's brow. "How long she been asleep?"

"A few hours. I tried to get her to drink water, but she wouldn't take it." A knock on the door took them both by surprise. Clay pulled the pistol from his belt as Jody went to open the door, then stepped aside in case visitors from the Bull's Head had come to visit. Instead, it was the doctor with a tray, which Jody quickly took. Clay put the pistol away.

"As I thought," said the doctor. "You two being here at the same time don't do her any good. You foul her air with dirt and sweat. We need to open some windows and let in some night air."

Clay looked at Jody. "I'll stay with her," said Clay.

"No," the doctor replied. "You both need to go. She's going to need to be bled." He turned his attention from her to them. "I don't think she would want either of you in the room at a time like this." He returned his attention to Penelope. "After that, I've got some warm broth I'm going to get down her. Go get a drink with the money you're paying me. It'll be better spent than on her."

The two men looked at each other. The order sounded strange. But if it was what the man wanted, they wouldn't argue. They left the room to the doctor and went into the twilight toward the center of town. As night fell, they came to Tuttle's Dance Hall in the Hyde Park section of the small town.

They sat in a corner of the smoky room and ordered a bottle of rye whiskey. Clay was quick to uncork the bottle and fill both glasses. He held up his glass as a toast. "Here's to Pen."

Jody hadn't heard her called that, and since he'd known her had never dared called her anything else except for her rightful name. However, this man wasn't him. People with affection for each other had different rules. Jody clinked the glass.

"To Pen," he responded. They both threw down the liquor, which was the first for Jody in some while. He grunted his down while

Clay didn't seem affected at all. While the glasses were refilled, Jody felt obligated to speak. "I owe you an apology."

Clay belched wind from the shot. "Why you say that? For sucker punching me?" He smiled and took a swig. "You do owe me for that."

Jody grinned at the remark. "That, too. But not all." He took a deep breath. Admissions of fault weren't easy. "I didn't think you were the man that you've showed to be."

Clay looked at him, then refilled the two glasses. "Here's to giving men a second impression." They both threw down the whiskey. Clay poured more into their glasses. Jody wasn't anxious to drink it down. He'd been drunk before, and knew they'd not be in a condition to tend to Penelope if they drank too much.

"That girl has been through a heap of hell in her life. She needed someone to match her strong will. Maybe that might be you," said Jody. "I thank you for that. As a long-time friend of hers, I thank you for that."

"She is a mule with a kick, that gal is," remarked Clay. "She does have some spirit in her. I must say, I've been in plenty of spots on the frontier and have seen a better share of trouble, some I caused, and others

I settled when I got there." He swigged the shot. "I can't say I mind someone along for the ride." He looked at Jody. "So why were you in Hickok's jail?"

Jody drank his liquor, thinking about his ordeal. "A bastard name of Wes Hardin damned near shot me in cold blood. Hickok put me in there so he couldn't."

"I saw him. That Hardin fellow," said Clay. "A mean one he was. Made more sense to put *him* in the cell."

"What I thought," said Jody. "Can't say it was bad. The jailer, name of Mike Williams, he was good to me."

"Mike?" Clay asked. "I know Mike from the trooper days. He was at Fort Laramie when Hickok was scouting." They refilled their shots. "So, you served your time."

Jody shook his head. He felt the bubbling in his blood from the alcohol, but it was settling his nerves. "I had enough and Hickok had enough of me. He told me to leave town." He paused a long time. "And I had nothing to keep me there."

"No pretty gals to take your money?" asked Clay. "At least something to send you back home?"

Jody understood the reference. He took a deep breath. "No," he answered, wanting to get if off his chest. "I thought I had one," he hesitated. "But she took to whoring." He shook his head. "I still can't believe it. She did it for the money."

"They all do it for the money," remarked Clay, filling his glass, then Jody's.

"No," Jody asserted. "She did it to get money for me. She came and brought me meals every day." He took the shot. "I would have eaten mud had I known she was having to do that. For me."

"Damn," Clay said loudly. "Sorry to learn the news if it hurts you. I'm sure she was the prettiest gal in town, too, was she not?"

Jody thought about the question. After half a minute, he shook his head. "I wouldn't say that. Les is kind of plain, short, not quite a full woman yet." He thought long and hard about what he would say next. "But she is a fighter, too. We've been through a few scrapes together." He recalled fonder moments. "I first met her and thought she was a boy. She was dressed as one to get me and another old drover to take her back to Texas."

"The hell you say," Clay declared. They chuckled at the notion. He refilled their glasses. Jody continued. "She told me later it was some whores she knew that had cut her hair and stole a friend of ours' clothes in order to fool us." He blew out a breath, thinking of a more recent time. "I guess she went to whoring with that same lady. A Virginia woman calling herself Shenandoah."

Clay filled the glasses. He put down the bottle and slumped back in the chair. "Have a flower painted on the door?"

Jody shrugged. "Ain't never been there." He chuckled, feeling the liquor. "Didn't have a chance to go whoring. I was in jail."

Clay laughed, too, at the remark. Then he stopped. "Short girl?" Jody looked to Clay. "Brown, partly red hair?"

The description was fueling Jody's rage. The very thought of what was likely to be said next would make him fight to the death.

Clay smiled and shook his head. "She ain't no whore." Jody's chest tightened. The idea that this man had seen Les in the brothel increased his rage. Clay showed no concern for Jody's angry expression. Instead, he kept grinning. "I was there. She was there. It's a place Hickok told me about. That girl you're telling about let me in, but she wasn't dressed for humping. She was sweeping floors."

Jody felt a tingle in his chest. He wanted so much to believe. "Clay," he slurred. "I was just beginning to like you. But don't be telling me no lies to make me feel better."

Clay nodded. "I think the same of you." He raised a finger. "So far. And I can say that the gal we're talking about was no whore."

A wave came over Jody. The memory of the jail came to mind. "But they brought her in with the other whores for walking the street. Near a church."

Clay poured himself another shot, then shrugged. "Where'd she live?" The reference hit Jody like a hammer. Two blocks away from the boardinghouse stood the church. If Les was retrieving meals from home, she had to pass by there. Clay began laughing. "They bring the stray dogs, too?"

The notion sent them both into laughter. Never was Jody so relieved. For the first time in a month, he took a deep, clean breath. As he did, three men in drover duds entered into the saloon. Jody looked over at them. In the same group, he saw Mike Mc-Cluskie. The story was known by all in town. A week earlier, he'd gunned down a fellow railroad agent over local politics. Jody sensed trouble, but the liquor dulled his movements and sapped his energy. Clay was in even worse condition.

One of the drovers came to the table with a full bottle. "Mind if I sit?" Jody looked at Clay and they both had no objection.

"Names is Jim. Jim Wilkerson."

"Mine's Jody Barnes and this is Clay . . ." Jody looked at his friend, not knowing his last name. Jim continued.

"Y'all live here?" asked Jim.

Jody shook his head. "I'm from Bexar County, Texas. Yonder 'bouts San Antone." Jim looked at Clay. From Jody's angle, Clay showed that he didn't like the question.

"I'm with him," Clay answered.

Jim nodded. "It's good to have some Texas in the room." He uncorked his bottle and filled all three glasses, then pointed over at the faro table. "See that Yankee over there?" Jody followed the finger to McCluskie. "We're fixing to kill him for what he done to Billy Bailey." He threw the shot down. Clay did also, and Jody joined them not to seem odd. Jim refilled the glasses. "Then we're going to kill that Yankee marshal in Abilene."

Jody turned his head to Clay, who only gave him a quick look. It was better not to show concern at this time.

Another man entered the saloon. Clay nudged Jody. "I've seen him. Scuffled with him. Hardin's friend."

Jim saw Clay's notice. "That's Hugh Anderson. Just watch, fellows." Jody knew the name as belonging to a prominent

437

rancher's son from Bell County. He saw Anderson march straight to the faro table, drawing a pistol from his holster.

"You are a cowardly son of a bitch. I will blow your head off." Another man at the table jumped to his feet and pleaded for calm, but Anderson pulled back the hammer and squeezed the trigger. Gun smoke plumed from the muzzle. McCluskie fell back with a wound in the neck, drew his weapon, and pulled the trigger, but the hammer fell on a dead hole. Anderson stood over McCluskie, cocking and firing into him three more times.

Jody felt his collar pulled back and he hit the floor. Clay yanked him farther from the line of fire. Jim Wilkerson stood and drew his pistols and fired wildly, as did another of the Texans. One bullet splintered the floor. Both Jody and Clay crawled under the table. Clay pulled the revolver from his belt.

"Stay out of this," Jody yelled.

Clay replied in the same tone. "Just in case they think we're in it."

A man at the faro table stood, drew a pair of a pistols, cocked, and fired as fast as could be done. Bullets whirred by; agony and moans were heard through the blasts and pops of the guns.

The man that had pleaded for calm went stumbling through the haze out the front of the saloon with blood dripping from his throat. Another cry came from the first shooter, who dropped from a wound in the leg. When he fell, a bullet found Jim standing above them. He dropped to the floor, blood covering his face, his jaws open in agony. Seconds later, another slug slammed into Jim's leg and he writhed, rolling on the floor.

More shots sounded and bodies fell. Once the blasts ceased, the room was filled with smoke. Only Clay and Jody could see the carnage below the smoke. Loud footsteps came their way. They saw the legs of the last shooter headed in their direction. Clay rolled to the side. Jody followed. He didn't want to be trapped under the table with shots coming through the top. When he stood, the double-fisted shooter walked by, with Clay aiming the revolver at arm's length at him. The shooter paid Clay no mind, but just continued out the front door.

The heavy sulphur in the air made it hard for them to breathe. With anguished screams for help piercing their ears, Jody and Clay ran from the front, with Clay holding the pistol poised to shoot at whatever came their way. Instead, the rest of the town stood in horror surrounding Tuttle's Dance Hall. Several of the onlookers gathered around a body across the street on the boardwalk of another dance hall. Jody saw it was the one who had tried to stop the bloodshed at the beginning.

It was then that Jody felt a twinge on his right leg. When he went to rub it, he felt warmth. He brought his hand to the light and saw his own blood. The instant he saw it, pain shot through his nerves, and he lost his balance. Clay grabbed his arm and kept him from falling.

"I'm hit in the leg," said Jody. The gun battle had sobered the both of them. "We got to get back." His thoughts were of Penelope, and Clay appeared to agree.

"The doc is going to be mending night and day for the next week," Clay said, wrapping Jody's arm around his neck. "Let's get to him first."

38

Hickok played poker in The Alamo Saloon. The day had been as hot as the day before. However, the night had cooled both the air and the tempers. He'd watched his hand and the other players, expecting to enjoy a good game and maybe win some money. However, his luck hadn't gone as planned. With his chip count slowly falling, he decided the light wasn't sufficient to continue and feigned disinterest.

"Night, fellows," he said. "I need to see to a few matters." He rose from the chair, and the rest of the players stacked the cards and ended their game as well, or moved to another table. No one sat in the marshal's chair.

As he went through the open glass doors, he stood on the boardwalk and looked at Cedar Street in front of him. A few more weeks of the cattle season remained, and he was satisfied he'd done a good job. With self-congratulations in mind, he went toward the jail to pick up a few things before heading to his house and calling it a night.

When he got to the jail, he saw the usual crowd standing outside the Bull's Head. He glared at the bunch of Texans, then went inside. McDonald and Carson were laughing. Mike Williams wasn't. "He doesn't want to know," said Mike.

Hickok shut the door. "Don't want to know what?"

The trio kept silent for a second as the marshal stood by the door and waited.

"He's got her over there now, Boss," said Carson.

The who and the where weren't obvious. "Speak plain, Tom."

Carson took a deep breath, then pointed through the window across the street. "Jesse Hazel. She's over there with Phil Coe."

The news was alarming and insulting. The notion of her serving other men wasn't as bad as the thought that the fat Texan Coe was the one she'd taken up with. "How do you know this?"

Fearful at being the messenger, Carson spoke after a moment. "I saw her out under the awning" — he paused — "with her arm around him and his around her."

It was worse than he imagined. Behind

closed doors was one matter. To show it in public was another. Hickok faced about and threw the door open. He marched across the street with the crowd of Texans standing there in wonder. When they didn't move, he palmed the Colts and shouted. "Stand aside!" The men parted, making a path inside. Hickok threw the doors open into the smoky interior. When he didn't see who he was after, he glanced at the gambler Cash. "Which way?"

Cash took the cigar from his mouth and arched a thumb to the back room. Hickok needed no further guidance. He found the door and threw it open. Coe and Jesse sat at the table like lovebirds giggling. Then Coe stood and shouted.

"Get out of my place, you son of a bitch."

Hickok stood his ground. He looked at the whore he'd spent good money on in the past. "Taking up with him, are you?"

"With you running my business out of town," she sassed, "Phil made me an offer. I'm a part owner. I ain't humping no more, Bill. You should of thought of that before."

Hickok turned his anger toward Coe. "Cheating cowboys out of their money, now you're going to cheat whores, too?"

The tall burly Coe came around the table and met the shorter Hickok nose to nose.

"I'll snap you like a twig if you don't leave here now."

Hickok palmed the pistols. "Go ahead and try."

Coe opened his coat. "I ain't heeled, Hickok. You want to settle this like men, take off them pistols and that badge and I'll oblige you."

Hickok stood, snorting his anger. With Jesse Hazel sneering at him the same way, he had a mind to shoot them both. The witnesses outside changed his mind. Cash came around from behind him.

"This isn't your domain, Marshal. I suggest you cool off your temper back across the street." With Hickok and Coe nose to nose, the question was whether to kill him or not. Hickok stepped back.

"Someday, Coe."

"I'll be waiting," was the answer.

Hickok stormed out of the room, and marched through the saloon to the jeers and insults of the patrons. When he saw a kid no older than fifteen threaten to take a swing at him, he couldn't take it any longer.

He spun around at the crowd of Texans, drawing both Navy Colts, spinning them upright. He squeezed both triggers while thumbing the hammers back and let them slip free. The twin blasts sent percussions through the small saloon and silenced all those insults. "I am Wild Bill Hickok! Marshal of Abilene! And you will respect me!" With all eyes locked on him, he shook with rage. He lowered the pistols in line with the crowd. "Or I'll kill every one of you."

Late September 1871
Penelope's cough brought Jody from his sleep. She sounded pained, and that had Jody struggle to get to his feet. The sting from the wound brought a sharp pain to his leg. He hobbled around to the right side of the bed. Sweat beaded on her forehead, and her body shivered despite being covered by blankets. He knelt beside her and blotted the sweat with a cloth. Her eyes fluttered open and she focused on him. "How you feeling?" he whispered.

Her smile tugged at his heart. To see this strong healthy girl whom he'd known since childhood so weak for so long had been hard to accept. Her smile vanished, replaced by more hacking. Once she'd regained control, he gave her water from a cup. The pitcher on the floor was nearly dry. She swallowed, then again looked at him. "How long?" she asked.

The question confused him. "How long

you been here? More than a month."

She shook her head, then meekly pointed at him. "How long you been here?"

Again, he was confused. Surely, she remembered when he'd seen her in the street when he'd found her with Clay. Then he realized she'd forgotten all that, likely due to the sickness. "I been here the whole time."

Brief coughs choked her, but she managed to get her question understood. "How long you staying?"

There was no choice about the answer. "I ain't leaving you."

Penelope shook her head. "Clay told me about you and Les. You need find her. Tell her why you left and go back to her."

He'd thought many times about doing just that. However, with his friend sick and with the need for money, which he hadn't been able to work for, it wouldn't have been right. Besides, he wasn't sure if he had the courage to go back and see Les. She might have moved on with her life. Almost two months had passed, and people changed. She might not want him anymore. From the look on Penelope's face, she could see his indecision.

"You can't be here. You should be with her." Penelope coughed, saliva and small drops of blood seeping over her lips. Yet she strained to get her meaning across to him. She reached for his hand, and he took hers gently and softly squeezed it. She smiled once more at him. Jody battled back tears.

Penelope's eyelids drooped. Once more, she was falling back into her long slumber, but before she fell asleep, she murmured, "Go and get Les back, Jody." When her eyelids didn't open again, he checked her breath, fearing the worst. His heart beat again upon feeling a warm push of air from her nose.

Jody thought about what his friend wished him to do. As he considered it, he sensed the presence of someone behind him, and turned to see Clay standing near the door. Their eyes met for only a second. Then the big man left. Jody looked at Penelope once last time, then rose with the stabbing ache in his leg. He hobbled outside and walked around to the south side of the shack. There, he saw Clay with a shovel.

"What are you doing?"

Clay sunk the spade into the soil without looking back. "I seen this before. It won't be long now."

Despite his own experience with this illness, Jody wasn't going to admit it. "She ain't dead. And she ain't dying. I know this gal. She's strong as an ox and worser in stubbornness."

Clay threw a spadeful of dirt to the side and nodded. "She was. That's why she's lasted this long. But it ain't going to let go of her." He stood, ready to pick up the shovel again, but stopped. "You know her better," he said, then paused. "She means something to me, too. She'd want a Christian burial."

The notion wasn't wrong, but Jody couldn't come to terms with it. Thinking about the impending loss of someone beloved, he couldn't help remembering Les. He looked at Clay. "Did you hear what she told me to do?"

Clay nodded. "Yeah." He stopped digging. "And if you go, I should dig two of these." He pointed at Jody's leg. "The doc told you to stay off it, but you ain't been. To ride to Abilene will tear open that patch he sewed and you'll bleed to death."

"It was her last wish. That should mean something." Jody thought about the truth. "I have to say, it means something to me. More than I was willing or ready to say. I miss that girl."

Again, Clay stopped digging. "Hugh Anderson left on a train some days ago, headed north. With what was said by his friend and the talk of a high price on

Hickok's head, I did give thought to going to warn him. He *is* a friend of mine," Clay stated. After a few seconds, he let the shovel fall and faced away. "I can't stay, Jody. I feel bad about Pen. I can't bring myself to leave her. She did in a way save my skin, and I'm ain't one not to be grateful. But I don't know what I'd think if J.B. gets shot and I could have done something about it."

The idea surprised Jody. "So, you're going to go?"

Clay faced him. He hesitated, his eyes darting to the side toward the shack. "I was going to wait. As long as I could."

Phillip Houston Coe walked through the Bull's Head with a purpose. He needed something done to insure his business continued with all the success of the previous months. As he threaded his way through the tables, he locked eyes with Ben's choice to manage the profits. A decision he didn't agree with, but now things had changed and they needed to be dealt with.

When Rance nodded, Phil signaled for the two to meet in the back room. He marched through the hall to the room and opened the door. Jesse Hazel was counting the stack of coins, and he indicated she should leave.

"What for?" she complained.

"I need the room. For just a few minutes," he said sweetly, although the sweetness had now gone out of their partnership. When she huffed her disapproval, he stated his needs louder. "Get out, Jesse. Take your twat out into the saloon." Rance arrived. "We have business to discuss," Phil said. The forceful statement made plain she was little more than a money counter. She stood scornfully. As she passed by, she once more showed the only power women had over men with money.

"Yours is the littlest I ever seen," she remarked while leaving.

Phil hesitated, talking himself out of slapping her across the room and out the front door. Instead, he only shook his head to Cash as they entered the room. "Splits. Why can't we do without them?"

Cash smiled and cocked his head to the side. "Seems that's what made you and Ben such prosperous men."

The comment brought to mind the business at hand. "Ben ain't coming back here. At least, no time soon." Cash looked dismayed. "He and his family had an accident in Kansas City. They all got thrown from a buggy. Ben broke his arm and leg. The wife had hers so mangled, they had to amputate. The boy was hurt, too, but not as bad."

Cash shook his head at the bad news. "That's awful. Terrible to learn. Are you going to Kansas City to see them?"

The suggestion amused Phil. "I don't think Ben would approve of me leaving the business here alone. No. The reason I'm telling you this is because there's going to be changes. Starting with Ben Thompson ain't no owner anymore. At least, not until he comes back, and that's *if* he comes back."

Cash looked alarmed, which was exactly what Phil wanted. Fear had a way of getting the point across. "How about the money Ben has tied up in this place?" Cash asked.

Phil nodded. "I'll look after his interests. But I'm not going to hear any more about how Ben would have wanted affairs to go." He motioned for Cash to sit, which the gambler did. "I've known for a long time that you and Ben had an agreement. And I know you and Hickok have been spying on us for some time. Ben told me so." Cash opened his mouth in denial. Phil shook his head. "Don't lie. I've known it for a while now. But I've decided to turn it my way." He reached into the drawer and set out a small strongbox. Taking a key from his vest, he opened the lock and removed the stacks of bills he'd collected over the long summer. He took a single stack and slapped it

451

down on the desk. "That's five thousand dollars, Cash," he said, pointing to it.

The gambler looked the money over carefully, but didn't touch it. After a few seconds, he peered up at Phil. "What's this for?"

Phil couldn't help but grin. "You strike me as a man ready to seize opportunity, Cash. Here's the biggest one you'll ever get." He jabbed his finger at the stack. "That's just to whet your appetite. There's twenty thousand more for you" — he paused, the grin fading from his lips — "when Hickok is dead."

Cash recoiled from the stack as if it were a snake.

Phil needed to explain his intentions. "Ben went soft on things the last few weeks he was here. At first, he felt the same as me, but later he thought to get along with the yankee bastard. I see it different." He eyed the walls of the room. "We've got to get this town back to what it was intended to be. The council means to run us out of it if we don't do something to stop them. Without their marshal, they'll have no way to enforce their ordinances."

Cash leaned back in the chair with a worried face. "And you expect me to kill him?"

The point had been made clear enough.

However, with his plan put into words, he couldn't afford for it to be known outside that room. Phil nodded. "I do." Again, he pointed at the stack. "You're going to take that money," he said, reaching into the other drawer and removing the .45 Smith and Wesson. "And you're going to get close to your friend and blow the back of his head off." He cocked the hammer and pointed the pistol at Cash. "Or I'll claim you stole the money and have you hung." He eased the hammer to rest and waved at Cash. "Now, get back out there and run your game. Make us some money."

39

October 5, 1871

It was a mild autumn day. Marshal J. B. Hickok walked the streets of Abilene in full view of the townspeople, not because he wished to, but because he had no choice. The slack in the trades of sin due to the ever-decreasing amount of drovers put the pinch on the town council's purse. The result was a mandatory reduction in payroll that forced him to dismiss Carson, McDonald, Norton, and Gainsford, leaving only Mike Williams and Hickok himself to patrol the streets. Hickok regretted the move, but not from remorse over cutting those men loose. He didn't concern himself with their plight of being out of work. The last few weeks, walking the town had put on a strain on his poker playing.

As he ambled about, he spotted a pleasant distraction. The society lady he'd seen only a few times walked north on Cedar near the intersection. He changed his direction so he would politely cross paths with the lady. However, she surprised him by directly approaching him.

"Good day," he said, removing his hat. She wore an orange dress with matching hat, and had a much more appealing smile than the one she'd previously shown him.

"Good day to you, Marshal Hickok." She came to stand in front of him. "I saw you from Mrs. Turnbow's house and felt I needed to speak to you." She paused and dipped her head for an instant. "I haven't been very friendly to those who have shown me only courtesy." She darted her eyes away a moment, then stared at him in a defiant posture. "I was not in sound mind for the last several weeks. I've come to the realization my husband has abandoned me here for reasons I do not know. However, I've received no wire as to his whereabouts, and concluded he has no concern for me." She softened her face. "And now, I have none for him."

Hickok suddenly felt hopeful, and his heart beat a bit quicker. However, he had to express the gentlemanly point of view. "I am saddened by your troubles, madam."

She smiled briefly. "My name is —"

"Mrs. LaFontaine?" She appeared surprised. He smiled. "I am the chief peace officer. I have my private sources of information."

"Nonetheless," she began. Then her voice suddenly lost its defiant courage and resembled that of a shy girl. "I wish to express my regrets for my demeanor. I would very much enjoy your company for the evening meal at Mrs. Turnbow's tonight. She is a very good cook."

The boardinghouse wasn't his first choice for a meeting place. He shook his head. "Not necessary."

"Please," she said, her powdered-over freckles reminding him of his youth. "I insist." Once more, she dipped her head for a moment. "It would give me a chance to perhaps to get to know the chief peace officer of Abilene a little better and . . . perhaps learn more about you . . . and you about me?"

The invitation suddenly was far more appealing. "In that case, how can I not accept?"

Her smile broadened. "Very well, then. Thank you, Marshal Hickok, for your understanding of my dilemma over these past weeks. I look forward to seeing you at four thirty? I'll tell Mrs. Turnbow to set another plate, which I will be responsible for."

"I very much thank you, Mrs. LaFontaine. And I look forward to a pleasant experience." They stood for only an instant before she turned to leave.

"You may call me Beatrice," she said at the very last as she began her short walk back to the boardinghouse. As he watched her from that perspective, he again had thoughts of his youth and remembered memories he'd since forgotten.

Les walked toward home as the sun shone its last hour of the day. Exhausted from her work, she just wanted to go home and have the meal from her mother and rest her weary bones. As she threaded through the men moving about the boardwalk, a presence had her raise her head.

She saw a tall broad-shouldered man with a black hat. His face reminded her of something not too long ago, but she couldn't place exactly where she'd seen him. However, he had a mean look about him and it stopped her cold in her tracks.

Her heart beat quick when he didn't move from her way. Unsure of his intent, she thought to cross the street, but when she took a single step, she saw him move in the same direction from corner of her eye. The other side of the street held no promise of safety, and instantly she decided to turn around and walk back in the opposite direction. She heard a single boot step when she increased her retreat. As she took another step, it was matched by another thud on the planks.

This man frightened her and she wanted to escape him. If he did mean her harm for some reason, she'd as soon not be on this side of town where she'd get no help. Texas Street was two more streets over, and she didn't know if she could get to the safety of the jail. As she turned the corner, more men of ill appearance forced her to continue farther away from her home. She came to a stop where an alley with a fence blocked the way.

"Les Turnbow," said a gruff-sounding voice that resounded with evil. She panicked, and ran to the other side of the street, glancing behind to see if he gave chase. With the blur of bodies mixing into the twilight, she couldn't see clearly, but kept her fast pace back down the only clear path she could find. It would take her farther north and toward the trains, where there were fewer lights to see by.

40

James B. Hickok gazed at the society woman across the table. He had an appetite for more than just food. Mrs. LaFontaine graciously held her fork, slowly wrapping her fingers around the rigid instrument, tempting him to lay her prone on the white cloth and take her there. Her discreet glances at him showed her desire for a risky adventure, and he was busting inside his clothes to take her to regions he was sure she'd never remotely dreamed of.

"Marshal?"

The hostess's voice pierced his consciousness. He looked at her and smiled. "Beg pardon?"

"I was asking if you thought the town would be quiet soon, now that the most of the Texans are leaving." The lady who owned the house kept slicing her food in a proper manner as she waited for an answer.

"I certainly expect so, ma'am. There'll be

a few days to go before they all head south." He looked at Mrs. LaFontaine. "Then we can count on the peace and quiet to return for the rest of the year until late next spring."

He continued his gaze as he heard the landlady again speak. "I certainly hope so. I believe this has been the worst year in memory. I hope it's not as bad next year."

Her criticism brought him back to reality. Slowly, he turned to her, reminding himself to be polite. However, since her remark was a reflection on him as a peace officer, he felt compelled to address it. "I can say in no uncertain terms that next year will be an even better season than the one we just enjoyed." His positive replay brought the expected reaction from the landlady, but also from the society woman. "We have had more cattle come here than any year before. The town has collected more license fees and fines than any such city, and that includes Chicago," he said with emphasis. "Not another town in Kansas, not Wichita, not Topeka, not even Kansas City, can make that boast. I was advised recently that over seven hundred thousand steers have shipped to market from our small but growing city. And next year, we will beat that." He took a bite of food to put an emphasis on that statement.

Mrs. LaFontaine smiled, no doubt because of his confidence, but she stylishly kept her display for his eyes only.

"But what about the Texans, Marshal? They tear up more of our city every year." The landlady had a point.

"It's to be expected, good lady, when you have men of that trade who have been without family or pleasure letting their exuberance explode all at once. And we have the means to contain that. Next year, we will have double the peace officers we had this year. I give you my word, there won't be the recklessness shown on so few occasions in recent months."

A fist pounded on the front door. All eyes went in that direction, and the landlady rose to answer. She opened the door, and no less than five men barged into the house. "The marshal here?"

Hickok sighed at being proven wrong so quickly, but just as fast, put on a smile to show that he could handle the intrusion. He didn't want the society woman to lose her mood. "Yes, I am," he said from the table. The five drunken men came forward without invitation. "What are you boys doing here?" he asked with a mild tone of inquiry.

"We're collecting some of our fines back, Marshal. We come to have you to treat us on our last days here. Reckoned only fair."

He'd seen this before. These were among the few stragglers left in town whose money had long been taken by the commerce of Abilene. Now they were out on the streets to beg, borrow, or steal enough to buy whiskey before they left. Rather than try to arrest them all, it was less stressful to sponsor a round of drinks. He didn't want to send these rowdies to The Alamo, and so thought of a place where he wasn't held in high esteem. Hickok looked at the shocked landlady, and winked to instill confidence that all was under control.

"Listen, fellows," he said. "We've enjoyed the evening supper here and it'd be rude of me to leave on your account. But go to the Novelty and tell them I said to buy each one of you a shot. They'll know I'm good for it."

The tactic worked as all five nearly stampeded over each other to leave the boarding-house and head to the Novelty Theater nearly a quarter mile away. The landlady shut the door and threw the latch. As she returned to the table, Hickok once more tried to reassure her, not so much for either of the ladies' sake, but more for his own and to further his plans for later. He finished the meal. The women did also, with more polite conversation. He stood, embarrassed after the invasion of drunks.

Hickok felt a need for a drink to ease into the evening. He paid his respects to the landlady. "I am most appreciative, good lady, for the fine meal. It is no wonder that so many people seek out this home for lodging." He cast an eye at the society woman. He stood there five seconds, then felt awkward and made his way to the door. "Once again, I am in your debt for the kind evening," he said in hopes of making amends for the earlier intrusion. To his surprise, Mrs. LaFontaine also stood and made a startling statement.

"I'll show the marshal out, Mrs. Turnbow."

She followed him to the door, and he acted ever the gentleman when he opened it and she stood in the doorway for a mere second. When he saw the door closing behind her with her enticing smile sent his way, he instinctively reached for her arm.

Once he held it, he didn't have to tug. She came willingly into his arms, embracing him and kissing his lips with the same carnal desire. He matched her fervor, wrapping his arms around her back and pulling her to him. Her breath sent a twitch to his loins, and he wanted to take her there on the porch. She broke the kiss and spoke in heated whispers.

"Come back after midnight. Signal me and I'll let you in. The old woman will be long asleep."

He wanted to kiss her again, but she put a finger to his lips, then eased from his embrace and slid away from him, smoothing the wrinkles in her dress. With the same enticing smile, she disappeared behind the closing door.

Hickok took a long breath. He checked his watch. It was half past five. He had a long wait.

He strolled up Cedar and looked for ways to bide his time. Poker was always appealing. With little need for his services, he stepped across A Street and continued north to his favorite place. The Alamo Saloon's doors were always open to him. He stepped into the establishment and the smaller-than-usual crowd greeted him with respect. The table in the corner, his table, was ready and vacant in expectation of his arrival. He'd grown accustomed to the accommodation. He took the chair with the wall to his back.

He sat and shuffled cards, and a few of

the patrons asked for permission to sit and play with Abilene's biggest celebrity. All the while, he thought of the rendezvous that awaited him several hours from now.

The gambler Cash arrived after the first deal, but since he was a player who could be tolerated, Hickok allowed him to fill the one remaining seat. The man's manner had changed. The face looked like it hadn't seen a razor in days. The eyes drooped and the clothes had been worn before. This wasn't normal for the gambler. "Can't say I expected you here," said Hickok, throwing him the first card from the deck.

"I much agree." Cash took the card with some indifference, again not a normal act for him.

"You all right, Cash?" The question was meant as more of a ribbing than a true inquiry. Cash darted his eyes around to the other gentlemen players.

"I've come to a crossroads in the last few days, Marshal." Once more, he scanned the table. "I think it best we leave the subject for another time."

The statement stuck in Hickok's mind as a warning. If there was town news to be discussed, usually it wouldn't involve a private matter that would be concealed from the other players. However, if there were more personal concerns involved, it might be of interest to take them up prior to the end of the game. For the time being, Hickok chose to continue play.

He soon lost the deal, which didn't disappoint him. He squinted across the room to take note of the unfamiliar faces there. Most of the customers he knew. The ones with money enough to lose and enjoy it. A few straggling cowhands wagered their last wages at the monte table, and would soon be too drunk to complain, and would fall asleep and be thrown out to sleep it off in the street. The billiard tables were empty.

Nothing seemed out of place. Perhaps, it was the gambler's new way of influencing play. However, he hadn't used the tactic before. He was a skilled player, and often took Hickok's money. But three hands into the play, it became noticeable that Cash wasn't raising with the usual flair. Hickok, on the other hand, had actually won more hands than normal, and enjoyed the play. He'd been biding his time well until he could mosey down Cedar to cap off his evening. He'd even sneaked an occasional glimpse at the nudes displayed on the walls. He couldn't help substituting the society woman's features for those painted in prone positions with longings to be satisfied drawn on their lips.

"Marshal Hickok," came the reminder from one player. "The play is with you."

Caught with his mind not on the game, he placed his cards facedown. "Gentlemen, I fold. I have need of the privy. Watch my stakes." He rose from the table and walked toward the door. Only seconds later did he see a movement from the corner of his eye. He whirled, only to see the gambler Cash rise from his chair.

"I'll join you, Marshal. Don't seem to be having much luck tonight."

They both went to the door and out. The nearest relief was at the side of the building, which was where Hickok went. "Don't seem to be in the game, Cash. Like something else is on your mind."

"I noticed the same in you."

Both men stood in the alley a foot away from the painted boards and relieved themselves into the dirt. "I have good reason," said Hickok. "Mrs. LaFontaine had me over for supper." He glanced at Rance Cash as they both finished. "Since you are a gentleman of similar tastes, I'll share with you my intent to spend time with her this very evening."

Cash shook his head. "I hope you make it

there. With all due respect meant to the lady."

The comment was peculiar in words and delivery. "What was that meaning?"

Cash heaved a breath. "Marshal, there are men about that mean you harm. I can't say more because I don't know who or where they are. But I do have reliable knowledge that they are coming from Texas and may be here now. Tonight."

The warning stopped all thoughts about plans with Beatrice LaFontaine. Hickok chided himself silently for letting his guard down and not being aware of newcomers. "How do you know this?"

Again, Cash appeared ill at ease. "You know how I know this."

A loud hoot pierced the night. The party of Texans seeking another treat, most likely. It wouldn't be long before they caused harm with their fun. Despite the warning, he was still the town marshal and had a job to do. He straightened his hat and stepped around Cash to return to Cedar Street.

As he passed, he patted the gambler on the shoulder. "When you get inside, deal me out. Tell them I had to see to some affairs."

Les came from the tracks. She wanted to

get home and lock the door behind her. As she crossed the street, she came to the corner near the Novelty. Loud shouts of drunken cowboys filled the air. As she approached, she saw a figure shrouded in the dark, crouching. Her single footstep on the walk was enough to turn his head. As he did, she saw he held a long shiny tube, a rifle. Whatever his intent, she knew it to be bad.

She turned and took first a casual step, then ran, hearing the loud pounding of boots and the jangle of spurs behind her. The night had closed many of the day businesses and she looked for an escape. But doors were locked and she could only continue running, grabbing at her skirt to lift it high enough to stretch her stride. The boot steps became louder.

An opening to the right brought an enclosed alley. More fenced alleys awaited in her path. A hand snatched her shoulder. She shrugged it off, then turned to the sole route she had left. She turned for the train cars.

Once off the boardwalk, she no longer heard the boot steps. When she got to the track, her foot was clipped by a hand sending her to the dirt and gravel. She spit the dust from her lips and rose to begin again. Heavy breathing was close behind her. In the dark, she saw the gap underneath a car and slid beneath it. Her attacker followed.

Les emerged from the other side and ran for the distant depot, hoping a flagman would be waiting. She sought the protection of anyone. With two cars separated to the left, she crossed the track and looked for the depot. A dim light broke the dark. She ran straight for it.

A hand grabbed at her arm. She shook it free and picked up her hem once more to run. Her side pounded with agony. If she could just get to the light, she'd be safe. The thought repeated through her mind with each stride.

From between the cars in front of her a figure emerged. A tall silhouette. Les stopped. Someone else was after her. In panic, she turned once more and went under the cars to the opposite side. Disoriented in the dark, she ran in the other direction, seeking any safe spot to hide. As she ran, the attacker who chased her came out of the dark from under a car and tripped her. In an instant, he had her pinned on the dirt.

"I know you," he said. "You're the little one that's with the whore lady." His breath stank. His weight on her body kept her from moving. "You caused me trouble tonight, little one. I'm going to have to teach you a lesson." He pawed at her shoulder, pulling the top of her blouse from her skin. Les squirmed to free herself but with him lying on her, she couldn't move. His hands skimmed along her knee and thigh. She tried to scream, but she had no breath. His mouth wiped across her lips. "This is what I do to teach —"

A hand covered his mouth and swiped his lips, mouth, head away. His weight disappeared.

Les was too weak to run, but she sat up to see the two silhouettes of men fighting. One behind the other. Gasping and gurgling was all she heard. The attacker kicked his feet as his body left the ground. She saw the arms of the other lifting the attacker up by what she thought was his neck. As the attacker fought, his feet kicking, his body movements slowed gradually. A loud pop stopped the gasping. The feet drooped. The body collapsed on the ground.

Not knowing if she'd been saved or just had a different man after her, she sat petrified. The lone silhouette faced away from her. If she'd been saved, there was only one man she knew who could and would have risked life for her.

"Jody?"

The figure paused only a moment. The dim light allowed her to see only the outline of the head turn to her. A second passed. Then, the figure continued on for a few more steps, turning left and stepping between the cars.

Les lay back on the dirt. The frantic minutes before raced through her mind. Should she leave? Where should she go and what path should she take? Was the man still waiting for her? The questions only confused and upset her mind. Instead, she chose to lay on the dirt and pray that all would be right. Tears welled in her eyes, and she rolled face-first into the dirt to muffle her sobbing.

Hickok walked north on Cedar until he got to the Novelty Theater. He intended to pay off the treat he'd sponsored and enjoy the complaints of the owners. He heard movement and palmed a revolver, but didn't draw it. He poked his head around and saw Mike standing on the north side of the theater. "What you doing here?"

The deputy turned to him and came closer. "Thought I heard some commotion going on out here. But I can't see nothing."

"Pay no attention over there," Hickok said. "We got Texans about hurrahing folks for treats. We need to keep them under control." Mike came back to stand next to him. A moment or two passed before Hickok looked at him. "Little like old times. Just me and you. With them others gone, we're going to have to be watching just a few more days. Then this season will be over." He paused to look ahead at the railroad tracks. "Nobody I could think to count on more." Mike stood on the boardwalk. He said not a word, but even in the silence Hickok knew that his deputy and friend realized the sentiment was heartfelt.

Loud yells came from around the corner. An instant later, a gunshot rang through the air. Hickok turned to Mike on his right while taking a step to the left. "Stay here."

Michael A. Williams watched the marshal turn the corner onto Cedar Street. The voices grew louder as he listened from around the edge of the Novelty Theater, but they soon became faint. Then footsteps from behind turned him back to the right. Instinct had him draw his revolver. A short figure approached him, but with no visible intent to attack nor any effort to hide its presence. Through the dark, he gradually recognized the shape of the young girl he'd befriended.

"Les? That you? What are you doing out here?" She didn't appear scared or jovial, just walked as if in a trance. "You should take better caution, young lady. There's trouble on the streets tonight and you never know what might be waiting for you in the dark. There are dangerous people about."

She came to him and when he focused on her face, she seemed unable to speak. When he was able to get her close, he touched her shoulder to see if she'd been hurt. Other than dirt and a few pebbles, her clothes showed no sign of a wound. "What's the trouble, child?"

She looked at him with glistening eyes. Between gulps for breath, she murmured, "There was . . . a man . . . here. He . . . chased . . . me. He . . . had . . . a gun. A rifle. I think . . . he . . . was going to . . . kill me."

She strained just to talk, which forced him to pull her closer to him. "Where is he now?" Mike asked.

She pointed to the tracks, and Mike gave thought to trying to search for this man in the dark. As he considered it, he suddenly realized why a man would have a rifle, and why this man with a rifle would be at that very spot. "Was he looking for you?"

She shook her head. "No. I . . . surprised

him. He was . . . looking . . ." Her pause made him want to shake her, but he restrained himself and waited precious seconds. "Up Cedar . . . Street."

Mike realized at that moment why the man would be waiting. To kill Wild Bill Hickok. And now the marshal stood alone in the street surrounded by Texans that wanted him dead.

J.B. Hickok walked south on Cedar and came upon a crowd of jubilant Texans. He didn't share their mood. He swung the frock coat away from his hips. "Who fired that shot?"

"I did," said a voice from the west boardwalk near the Pearl. Phil Coe stood there with a glazed look about him. "I was shooting a stray dog." His voice didn't have its usual argumentative tone, but rather one of challenging contempt.

It was not a matter nor the man to back away from. "You know there are no firearms allowed in town. Hand over that piece and pay the fine of fifty dollars."

Coe stood for several moments. Hickok knew it as the stance of a man ready to settle all past affairs.

Coe grinned smugly. "Go to hell, Yankee. If you want this gun, you come get it."

Hickok bent his elbows and readied for the draw of iron. The move twitched Coe's right arm. He raised the pistol. Hickok instinctively reached for the pair of Navy Colts. Coe extended his arm and fired. Hickok snatched the revolvers and drew them in line with Coe, thumbing the hammers and squeezing the triggers at the very same instant. Two shots rang from his pistols.

One instant later, Coe crouched, knees buckling, then slumped atop the boardwalk. The crowd of Texans encircled the two and closed in. Hickok sensed that another attacker would come from the crowd of agitators. He stepped back at an angle to view what or who might come from behind him. He swung his head left and right, attempting to spot anyone threatening harm. Continuing back and to the right, he heard loud steps on the wood planks coming at a fast pace from the left. A blur of white pierced the crowd and charged at him. Hickok aimed the pistol in his left hand in reflex and thumbed the hammer with the trigger back. The shot crackled through the night air. The white blur fell to the dirt. Ready for another attacker, he called to the crowd in a heated spirit. "Come get the rest of these pills!"

The crowd receded and screams of shock came from all about. Expecting another shot to come his way, Hickok continued his backward step, and came to face the people on the east side of Cedar. The crowd huddled around the fallen figure. A single word muttered from the crowd caught his ear.

"Deputy."

His nerves ceased all movement in his arms, legs, and body. He looked at the figure lying on the dark street. He saw no details from a distance, so he came closer, to within ten feet. The hat appeared familiar. He took another step, and disbelief filled his mind.

"Mike?" He walked closer, the revolvers now heavy in his hands. Another step brought more clarity. The shirt he'd seen before. "Mike?" His heart beat faster and faster in denial. It couldn't have happened. Hickok slipped the pistols into holsters and hurried closer. "MIKE!" He knelt next to the body of his friend. It could not have actually happened. He had to remedy the situation. He had to save his friend.

Hickok picked up the body of Mike Williams and carried it directly into the light of The Alamo Saloon. A billiard table stood empty, and he laid his friend prone on the cloth. In the clear light, he saw the bloody hole in the chest that his accurate aim, poor vision, and errant judgment had caused. He bent to hear a breath, a huff of wind, a sign of life. He heard nothing.

The realization hit his face like a cold gale. Every nerve went dead. Flames washed through his gut. It had not happened. He repeated the demand over and over in his head, willing it to be true. The repetitions seized his own breath as he viewed the body. Tears dripped from his eyes onto the bloody shirt. He couldn't breathe, and choked sobs loudly. Fluid dripped from his nose. He stared until, finally, his mind overcame the denial. It had happened. It was real. He did shoot his best friend. Mike Williams lay dead on the billiard table.

A moment later, J. B. Hickok regained his breath and his senses. He spoke his mind aloud. "You tell them to clear the streets. If I see any of them when I come out, I'll kill every last one of those sons of bitches."

He stood straight and stepped backward to sit in a chair. He stared at the body. Heaving breaths, he rationalized who and what had caused this to happen. It was his own tolerance of the Texans and their rowdy ways that had put him in a state of mind to fire wild. It was their doing. They had caused this. If he had enforced the laws as written, this would not have happened. He had caused this. He had to exorcise the rage building in his soul. He had to shut down the town.

Hickok rose from the chair and marched to the front door. With a determined charge, he went to the other side of the street. The first place to meet his wrath was the Pearl. He passed by the slumped and moaning Phil Coe. His first urge, to plug the Texan in the head, was restrained. Instead, he had to make amends for his own acts, which had stirred this trouble. "Call the doc. Then get him a preacher."

He went into the Pearl Saloon and drew both pistols. "Get out of Abilene. Ride to the camps and stay out of my town!" He aimed the revolvers at the stunned drovers, waiting for any complaints. None came. They scrambled out of the Pearl, and he went to the next place selling drink and debauchery to do the same. He wasn't going to have any more of them in his town. It was time to make things right. He couldn't bring Mike back from the dead, but he could and would put a stop to what had killed his friend.

41

The service was too brief, but Les had heard all the talk from the preacher that she could stand. That man didn't know Mike Williams. Not like she did. She thought of who else might think the same. She looked at the marshal. He sat quietly in the first pew with his black coat and pants. Maybe Marshal Hickok had known Mike longer, but she'd known the kind, gentlemanly deputy in a different way.

With the service concluded, it was time to put Mike back with his own. Out of respect, Les watched as the pallbearers carried the fine polished casket outside. It had been mentioned about Abilene that Hickok had paid all the expenses, including paying for the final trip back to Kansas City.

The pretty hearse that Abilene had seen too much of paraded the casket east on A Street. As she walked along, she took notice of the other mourners. She recognized

Mayor McCoy and Councilman Henry, each with black armbands. The same respect was shown by Mr. Case and Mr. Karatofsky and other respectable townspeople. Even the Hersheys made a rare appearance in public. Miss Maggie was too shaken to attend the funeral. As they passed along Texas Street, some of the parlor women lined the boardwalk, most with tears in their eyes. Les even caught a glimpse of Lady Shenandoah shrouded in the shade of the awning, but saw no tears in her eyes. There was no sight of Jesse Hazel.

In silence, they all marched behind the hearse. As she walked, Les sensed a different mood about the town since Mike Williams's death three nights before. The sinful ways that had brought the money to build a town had cost them a fine man. Although he'd been here but a few months, it was a loss felt by all who called Abilene home.

When the hearse arrived at the depot, the pallbearers took the casket from the pretty glass wagon. It would soon be seen again. The whispers about town told of Phil Coe's final passing.

Les watched as the casket was carried into a train car. Marshal Hickok's face was drawn, the mustache drooping beside the mouth, the eyes moist and glassy. Behind

481

him stood Rance Cash. He, too, appeared saddened, although she didn't know if he had ever met the friendly jailer. Rance's presence made her wonder about the other friends she had. She'd not seen Penelope for near two months, and reckoned the strong-willed blond girl had made it to Texas by now. And then she thought of Jody.

He, too, likely had made the trip back to his home. It was a feeling that left her cold. So often she'd dreamed of coming back to the home she knew, and hadn't paid much thought at first to whether he'd stay here. It was during their journey to and from Colorado that she'd formed a bond with Jody Barnes, and when they'd arrived, she'd allowed herself to dream that maybe she'd found herself the man needed for a family she'd never had. Now, she was again alone in Abilene with only Miss Maggie.

As the massive locomotive exhaled steam, Les caught sight of Beatrice LaFontaine boarding one of the passenger cars. Les hadn't had the time to get to know the fancy woman in the long weeks of her stay at the boardinghouse. Perhaps it was time to say something polite. "Are you leaving for home?" she asked.

The fancy city woman merely glared at her. "I'm leaving to anywhere this train takes me as long as it is away from this lawless town." She took steps up the landing with grace and care for her fine dress. Before she went into the car, she gave Les one last look and snapped a final remark. "The whole city of Chicago burned to the ground last night." The woman went into the passenger car. Les had no real understanding what was meant.

With the hearse steered away from the train car, she gave one last look at Marshal Hickok. His face was washed with sorrow, and he slowly walked back toward town with his hat in hand. Rance, too, had his hat in hand, and he stood in place looking back at Les, then over her shoulder. It was just a feeling, but she felt there was a surprise behind at which Rance was staring. She twisted around in hopes of seeing Jody.

Instead, a tall man in a white shirt now was in front of her. His face she knew. The clear afternoon lit his sharp features — the high cheekbones, the blue eyes, the broad shoulders. He was the one who'd stormed into the parlor that morning nearly three months ago. Les, at first, was alarmed at his presence, but as she focused on the outline of his frame, she recalled a more recent memory of where she'd seen him. "It was you," she murmured.

He put on his broad-brimmed black hat, which shaded his eyes from clear view, and reached out his hand to her. "I know where he is."

EPITAPH

Although Texas Cowboys is a work of fiction, it is inspired, in part, by actual figures in the Old West. Below is an account of what actually happened to those living and breathing men and women such as Wild Bill Hickok, Jesse James, and John Wesley Hardin who people the pages of this novel and continue to haunt the American imagination.

James B. Hickok remained in a reserved state of melancholy following that summer in Abilene. Another attempt on his life occurred in Wichita in November 1871. He warded off the assassins on a train. It didn't save his job. Failing eyesight from syphilis rendered him near blind by his late thirties, perhaps explaining that tragic shot on that night in Abilene. The town council dismissed him in December 1871, officially finding no reason to retain a city marshal during the winter. In truth, they found Hickok attracted more trouble than he prevented. He cashed in on his fame by joining the Western show of William Frederick (Buffalo Bill) Cody, but soon left the show due to his dislike for falsely portraying his exaggerated exploits and frontier life. Hickok had no skills other than being himself. He languished from town to town, benefiting from his larger-than-life persona as depicted in the dime novels of the era. Usually short of money, he sought to strike it rich in the ever-expanding American West. Through the years, he kept up a correspondence with Agnes Lake Thatcher. They married in March 1876. Five months later, Hickok traveled to a mining camp called Deadwood in the Black Hills of the Dakota Territory to win some of the money that was gambled away by the miners. He lost his life just days after arrival, murdered by Jack McCall on August 2, 1876. The poker hand Hickok held was aces over eights, forever known as "the dead man's hand." Mike Williams was the last man killed by Hickok.

John Wesley Hardin continued his murderous ways, becoming involved in the infamous Sutton-Taylor Feud in southeast

Texas. He married Jane Bowen in February 1872, and immediately began a family. Hardin became embroiled in many gunfights for various reasons, in all of which he claimed justification. When he was wounded badly in a gunfight, he surrendered to "clear the slate," but when he learned how many murders were charged against him, he escaped once again and fled to Florida. He was captured in Pensacola and sent to the Texas prison in 1878. He earned a law degree, and upon his early release became a lawyer. He continued a reckless life while trying to pass himself off as a reformed man. In August 1895, he was killed by John Selman, who claimed Hardin had threatened his life.

Jesse James furthered his criminal career after Abilene. He represented a noble bandit to those in the South, despite killing in cold blood. Jesse married his first cousin Zerelda (named for his own mother), and settled in St. Joseph, Missouri, under the name Thomas Howard. In 1876, the James-Younger gang attempted a robbery in Northfield, Minnesota. The robbery failed and only Jesse and Frank James escaped being killed or captured. The years following saw few such risky robberies. With a bounty for his apprehension, Jesse feared those around him, and is said to have slain any suspected turncoat. He was killed by Robert (Bob) Ford, a James gang member, on April 3, 1882.

Wild Bill Hickok, John Wesley Hardin, and Jesse James were all killed by gunshots to the back of the head at point-blank range.

Jack McCall, John Selman, and Bob Ford were all killed in retribution. McCall was at first acquitted of the crime, but later retried and hanged. John Selman was shot in an El Paso alley in an argument over a poker game by a Hardin sympathizer. Bob Ford was killed by a shotgun blast in Colorado by a follower of Jesse James.

In 1872, the town council of Abilene formally made it known to the Texas cattle trade that they were no longer welcome. The town outlawed all liquor and prostitution soon after, and quietly became part of the wheat belt over the years. Abilene later became the fondly recalled boyhood home of President Dwight D. Eisenhower, although he was born in Denison, Texas. In its heyday, Abilene was a rich oasis on the barren prairie. During that time it never suffered a single robbery of a bank, saloon, or casino.

Ben Thompson returned to Abilene and professed no desire for vengeance against Hickok. He pronounced the killing of Phil Coe "a fair act of self-defense," despite Coe's mother placing a $25,000 bounty on Hickok's head. Thompson moved his business to Ellsworth, Kansas, where he joined with his brother Billy in running another saloon. There, too, he ran into conflict with Hickok, although not over the law, but a woman. He gave up his business there, and eventually wound up as the city marshal of Austin, Texas. Thompson had many enemies from his frequent gunfights. In one, he killed a theater owner. Although he was acquitted of the crime, hard feelings continued for years, and he was shot to death by ambush inside a San Antonio theater in 1884.

Luke Short bounced around the West, attaining a reputation as a gambling gunslinger. Later in his life, he owned the White Elephant Saloon in Fort Worth, which is still in business to this day. He had a well-known dispute with Jim Courtright, a former marshal used to collecting protection money. Short never paid and a feud began. Short and Courtright traded bullets in a street shoot-out in front of his establishment in 1887, the exchange killing Courtright. Luke Short died of natural causes in 1893.

Mattie Silks in Abilene is at best a rumor. She did move West at age sixteen, and ran one of the most successful brothels in Denver. She had a street gunfight with a rival madam over Cort Thomson, whom she loved. Neither woman was hit, but two bystanders were wounded. She bought the famous House of Mirrors brothel in Denver, and ran it until her death in 1929.

Jesse Hazel and Susanna Moore were lost to history after 1871. The Great Chicago Fire occurred on October 8–10, 1871, burning through the center of the city and eventually leading to the rebuilding of Chicago as the largest incorporated city in the nation until the end of the 19th century.

Henry Morgan Stanley interviewed Hickok in 1867 for the *New York Herald*. Stanley would later become immortalized with the line "Dr. Livingstone, I presume," when he found explorer Dr. David Livingstone in Africa on November 10, 1871.

The Texas cattle trade migrated to other

Kansas towns such as Ellsworth and Dodge City. The same raucous events emerged, making legends of such lawmen as Wyatt Earp and Bat Masterson. Although those towns never shunned the trade as did Abilene, the eventual coming of the railroad to Texas in the 1880s brought an end to the long Texas-to-Kansas cattle drives. Today, Fort Worth, Texas, is nicknamed "Cowtown" for its stockyards and its role in the meatpacking industry of the late-19th to mid-20th centuries.

ABOUT THE AUTHOR

Tim McGuire's vivid imagination and fascination with history formed an early ambition to be a writer. He lives in Grand Prairie, Texas. Learn more about the author at www.timmcguire.com.